John Bainbridge is the author of over thi
historical fiction, as well as non-fiction an
has also written widely for newspapers a
history at the University of East Anglia l
countryside.

By the same author

Fiction
The Shadow of William Quest
Deadly Quest
Dark Shadow
Gibbet Hill
The Newgate Shadow
Balmoral Kill
Dangerous Game
Loxley
Wolfshead
Villain
Legend

Non-Fiction
The Compleat Trespasser
Wayfarer's Dole
Footloose with George Borrow
Rambling – Some Thoughts on Country Walking
Footloose in Devon

The Newgate Shadow was first published in Great Britain in 2024 by Gaslight Crime.

Copyright © J and A Bainbridge
The right of John Bainbridge to be identified as the author of this work has been asserted by him in accordance with the Copyright, Designs and Patent Act 1988. All rights reserved. No part of this publication may be reproduced, stored in or introduced into a retrieval system, or transmitted, in any form, or by any means (electronic, mechanical, photocopying, recording or otherwise) without the prior written permission of the author. Any person who does any unauthorised act in relation to this publication may be liable to criminal prosecution and civil claims for damages. This publication must not be circulated in any form of binding or cover other than that in which it is now published and without a similar condition including this condition being imposed on the subsequent purchaser. All characters and places in this novel are fictitious and the creation of the author's imagination, and any resemblance to places or real persons, living or dead, firms and institutions, is purely coincidental.

THE NEWGATE SHADOW

John Bainbridge

One

October 1854

A dark evening in the Cremorne Gardens.

'Not the kind of place you'd choose to die', Quest remarked later. 'Not the place it used to be, the Cremorne. Another of those London pleasure grounds that's become disreputable – the haunt of the thief and the *demi-monde*. Not the place to die at all.'

'Poor Colley Johnson would almost certainly agree with you,' said Wren Angier. 'Colley was born to die in bed, with his graveyard cough and his endless ailments. And he never liked to make a show of himself in public... what pickpocket does?'

Quest smiled.

'A harmless old dip, Wren. One of the first thieves I knew in town, when I came here as a boy. You know, he always said we'd end up swinging side by side outside Newgate. Now he's gone and I'm still here.'

'Wouldn't have wanted to die there,' said Jasper Feedle, adding another log to the fire.

'He had little choice,' said Quest. 'Not with a throwing knife in the back. Hurled by an expert as well – among all those people! Nobody saw anything, that's what puzzles me? It was crowded in the Cremorne, dark certainly, but there was light from the fires burning in the braziers. So many people.'

'It might have been very difficult for you, William,' said Josef Critzman, who was toasting muffins over the fire. 'Given that he died in your arms and you were seen touching the knife.'

'Ah, but fortunately, I had two of the best witnesses for the defence with me. If a murdered man's going to die in your grasp, who better to have at your side than Inspector Anders and Sergeant Berry of Scotland Yard?'

Isaac Critzman, as plump as his brother was thin, warmed his hands by the fire. 'I think it would be helpful if you described the events of yesterday evening to us again. We know that Colley was seeking you out, William. He'd searched the Seven Dials for you – even called at your house in Bloomsbury, even though our associates were specifically asked never to go there. He had an urgent message for you.'

'But there was nothing in his pockets?' said Wren Angier.

'Nothing at all,' said Quest. 'Sergeant Berry searched him most diligently.'

'But he said something before he died?' said Josef.

'A couple of words, Josef. Words that made no sense. He was breathing his last, so what he said might not be at all relevant.'

'I think it best if you start at the beginning,' Isaac said.

~

The previous evening...

'I hear you've been to Dartmoor, Quest?'

'A week or two ago, Bram. To visit an old friend.'

Inspector Abraham Anders turned to face him in the dying light of the autumn evening. Quest thought the detective was looking very old, with his long grey hair and side-whiskers, though Anders had always looked more ancient than his years.

'That friend being Jonas Lyddon, sometime radical Member of Parliament?'

'You're very well informed, Bram.'

'A meeting between rebels is usually noted by the spies of Queen Victoria's Secret Service. A paper on your visit came down to Scotland Yard from the home secretary.'

'I'm pleased I'm keeping Wissilcraft and his agents so well amused. Have you seen Wissilcraft lately?'

'Only in passing on the streets of Westminster. But in a way, that's why I asked for this meeting with you.'

'You could have come to my home...'

'Your home is much too well watched, William. Though as a policeman I shouldn't be telling you that.'

Quest sighed. 'I know I'm continually watched, and not just by Wissilcraft and his spies. They really are such an inconvenience, Bram.'

'You are surprised? You've killed members of the Establishment, blackmailed the powers that be, preached discontent and sedition... it's a miracle to me that Lord Palmerston's let you live at all? Not many people can cross the home secretary and get away with it.'

'That old mongoose knows what the consequences would be if he tried to end my life...'

'You still have the notebook?'

'The notebook that would bring the Establishment crashing down? It's in a safe place. If I have to, well, I'll use it. Not even some members of the Queen's family would be safe if I did. You know that?'

'What I don't understand, given your revolutionary ambitions, is why you *don't* use it?'

'Interestingly enough, I had a similar discussion with Mr Lyddon on Dartmoor. About whether the notebook should be used or not? Jonas Lyddon favours reform. Better education, legislation to protect workers in fields and manufactories. Winning the vote for working people.'

'Dreams then?'

'We can all dream, Bram... and there are still the lower level of villains and those who exploit the poor. While I'm free, I may deal with them.'

Anders grimaced.

'And that... out of my, no doubt, misguided friendship for you, William, is why we're here tonight. Ah, here's Sergeant Berry. Anyone about, sergeant?'

'Pickpockets and whores and gentry seeking a poke – and worse. Nobody to concern us. Certainly none of Wissilcraft's spies, well, none that are known to me, anyway. Though the Cremorne's a bit crowded for my liking. Hardly room to breathe in this press of people...'

'We may be safe enough then...'

The three men were lost in the middle of the vast, whirling crowd. They kept their hands close to their pockets as they watched out for dips. Watched as slightly drunken gents led servant girls into the bushes. Heard the complaints as some of those same gentry emerged with heads bruised and all their possessions gone.

They heard people on the edge of the crowd laugh, as one misguided youth emerged from the undergrowth minus all his clothes as well as his money, having been lured there by a pretty face - before being beaten and robbed by her bludging ponce.

'A lawless place this,' Berry muttered. 'Time to put its shutters up...'

'There'll always be places like this in a city of desperate millions,' said Anders. 'But there might not always be a place for you, Quest. That's why I've arranged our meeting. Have you heard of Inspector Bright?'

Quest considered for a moment.

'You mean Inspector Charles Savage Bright?'

'*Honour* Bright the beat constables call him. Usually works south of the river, when he's not running errands for Police Commissioner Mayne and Lord Palmerston. That's the man, William.'

'What's he to do with me?'

'Well, he's my replacement, Sergeant Berry and I are being sent off on other duties. Honour Bright is to take over from me with one particular brief. And *you* are it, William. Bright has been brought out as Palmerston's ratcatcher.'

'And I'm the rat?'

'Don't flatter yourself, William. Not even you qualify for the undivided attentions of a Scotland Yard inspector. No, Bright is not just seeking you, but every radical, every reformer, everyone who protests against the way our society is run. But you are near the top of the list.'

'Only near?'

'Well, second on that list.'

'And the first?'

'I'm not at liberty to tell you that, well not the name anyway. All I'll say is that the home secretary and my Commissioner took a great interest in your journey to Dartmoor – and the man you met there.'

'You mean Jonas Lyddon?'

'I didn't say that name...'

'But Jonas is very well connected, a former member of Parliament. Even many of his opponents respect him. It'd be a brave police inspector who took on the likes of Jonas Lyddon.'

Anders waved a hand.

'Honour Bright isn't lacking in courage.'

Quest watched the crowds for a moment, deep in thought.

'Well, thank you for the warning, Bram. But tell me what does Commissioner Mayne intend you to do?'

'Berry and I have been detailed to suppress vice in London. Houses of ill repute, disgusting literature... that kind of thing. Mayne's view is that vice so often leads to much worse crimes.'

'There is unhappily some truth in that,' Quest said.

'There are a great many Christian campaigners in this town who believe that London is a new City of the Plain. They've a lot of influence with my Commissioner. Our dear Queen has books sent up to Balmoral for her to read... she favours Mr Dickens. Unfortunately, amid the latest batch was a scrappy novel penned by one of the pornographers who base themselves in Holywell Street.'

'Shocking for her!'

Anders chuckled, 'I doubt the Queen was very much shocked... she's more familiar with the ways of the world than people imagine. She probably wouldn't even have mentioned it to anyone. Unfortunately, the publication was noticed by an interfering courtier with a strong sense of morality. He penned a furious epistle to Scotland Yard. Hence my new task!'

'You have my sympathy, Bram. I shall miss our little encounters. In the meantime I...'

Quest was interrupted by shouts in the crowd. They turned to see what was happening, watched as the hordes parted to make way for a man who was pushing his way through towards them. In the half-light, Quest recognised Colley Johnson, that elderly pickpocket who'd taught him a few lessons in dipping, when he'd arrived on the streets of London as a fugitive boy.

'Colley Johnson,' Berry muttered. 'Collared him a few times.'

Quest's first thought was that Colley must have tried and failed to pick a pocket, and that a hue and cry was in full motion. But, although a gap had opened up in the crowd behind the dip, nobody seemed to be in pursuit of him.

Johnson almost collided with Quest and looked up into his face.

'Young Willy? Thank Gawd! Trailed you all over the place. Thought I'd never... never...'

A look of puzzlement came over Johnson's face. His eyes met Quest's own and his mouth opened. Then he was falling forward into Quest's arms. Only a little man, Colley Johnson. A man who didn't take a lot of holding. But he was falling to the ground, half-twisting as he went.

It was then that Quest saw the throwing knife in Colley Johnson's back. He touched it briefly, as the pickpocket fell to the ground. Knelt down as the victim of that knife touched the filthy path. Anders had caught Johnson's arm and was there alongside the dying man.

'Who did this, Johnson?' asked the detective.

Colley Johnson gasped and spluttered blood.

Quest put his head close to Colley Johnson's mouth.

'Tin... tinny brer... tinny brer...' Johnson said the words with his dying breath.

The pickpocket's eyes rolled upwards as he died.

Quest looked across at Anders, then they both looked up to see Berry pushing his way back through the gawping crowd.

'Whoever it was, I couldn't see them,' Berry said. 'Too many people here and they'll all have gone by the time we're hunting witnesses. Nobody'll want their families and employers to know they spent the evening in the Cremorne Gardens.'

'Get some constables here, Sergeant,' said Anders.

~

'And that was all Colley said?' asked Isaac Critzman.

'His last mutterings on this earth,' said Quest. 'Tinny brer... it makes no sense at all. Perhaps just the ravings of a dying brain. Tinny brer...'

'But is that what he meant to say?' asked Wren Angier. 'He was a cockney and there are some words he might never have encountered before.'

Quest looked across the room.

'Wren, you think you know what Colley meant?'

'I'd hazard a guess...'

'What then?'

'*Tenebrae.*'

'What the 'ells tenebrae mean?' asked Jasper Feedle.

'Is it Latin?' asked Quest. 'You had a better education than mine, Wren. What does tenebrae mean? It sounds familiar now you've mentioned it. A word I've heard before. What does it mean?'

'Darkness,' said Wren Angier.

Two

A breeze starting up from the river became a wilder wind.

The young man walked past St Mary's church in the Strand and up into Holywell Street, popularly known as Bookseller's Row. He paused for a moment and regarded the glass windows, some shaded, of the many shops lining the road.

An elderly gentleman, coming out of a bookshop doorway, caught his eye, looked down with an expression of guilt, and tucked a leather-bound volume inside his cloak before hurrying away.

'Mr Daniel, sir?'

The young man turned to find Dugdale standing close by, his very wide eyes regarding him with curiosity and a broad smile.

'I've been looking out for you, Mr Daniel, sir,' the little man continued. 'About the matters we discussed the other day. Would you care to come into my shop?'

Daniel nodded and followed in the man's steps.

It was a bookshop no different from most of the others, a display of classics on one side of the window and bound volumes of the works of Mr Dickens on the other. On the shelf furthest back from the glass were a great many books by authors few had ever heard of, with strange and mysterious titles.

In the middle of the shop stood a table piled with many more volumes, all by writers unknown to wider society. Daniel paused for a moment and picked one out of the pile. Mr Dugdale held out his arms in an approving manner.

'Now that one's fresh in,' he beamed at Daniel. 'And already taking wing from my shelves. It's called *The Yokel's Preceptor*, and very cleverly composed. See for yourself...'

Daniel thumbed a few pages.

'Some kind of tract against sodomites?' he remarked.

'That's what it purports to be,' Dugdale replied. 'Cleverly composed! But if you read through the rant, you'll see it's a fine guide to the molly houses, and where gents of a certain inclination might find a margery when they want one.'

Daniel hurriedly put it down.

'Not my inclination!' he declared.

'Mine neither, but we booksellers have to stock our shelves for all sorts. I do have a great many volumes for more straightforward gentlemen – and ladies too.' He smiled again. 'And how are you settling into our little street? I take it the room's satisfactory?'

'Comfortable enough, Mr Dugdale, comfortable enough.'

'I don't normally let a room to writing gentlemen, despite my calling as a bookseller. They tend not to have any money.' He gave a humourless little laugh. 'But I could see how you're a man of some talent. And I do like to encourage literary endeavour. And not many who stays are prepared to pay three months in advance.'

'I'm sure the room will do very well.'

'And how is your writing going, Mr Daniel? Verse is it, or perhaps a novel?'

'Perhaps a novel,' Daniel replied.

'A budding Mr Dickens? Or Thack'ray maybe?'

'I would never dream of aiming so high.'

Dugdale gave a knowing wink.

'Very wise, Mr Daniel, very wise.' He stepped closer. 'Between you and me, there's little blunt to be made out of such writings. The day of the novel's coming to an end. Well, that's my opinion. Gents and ladies want more than the authors are allowed to give them.'

'I'm saddened to hear that...'

'But take heart, Mr Daniel. I never want to discourage genius. And I might be able to come to your assistance.'

'My assistance, Mr Dugdale?'

'You've come up to London from the country, I b'lieve?'

Daniel nodded.

'This is a very expensive town, Mr Daniel. Money flows through the fingers like water. Especially for young gents unproven in the writing trade. I knows of many a young author come to town with considerable expectations. But where are they now? In the debtors' gaols or the workhouse. The books they *tried* to write but a distant memory. And all because they took the wrong path...'

He waved Daniel into a chair and drew a stool up close by.

'There is, of course, my dear Mr Daniel, a wiser path. A more profitable course. Not all writing gents has to starve. Many an author who works for me has a fine life.'

He winked.

'Blunt in their pockets and rooms in Bloomsbury or Chelsea. Even St John's Wood. And all because they catered for the market, so to speak. Something all wise authors has to do, Mr Daniel, in these hard times. Learn as how to cater for the market, don't you see?'

Daniel thought for a moment.

'I suppose that's true,' he conceded, 'but can't it get you into a lot of trouble? I understand that your premises have been raided by the Vice Society and the police. I've been told you're not long out of gaol?'

'Two years! And for just publishing something a trifle *recherché*. Outrageous that free spirits mayn't be catered for in this supposed land of liberty. And the Vice Society are a bunch of hypocrites, persecuting honest businessmen in the name of morality, and half of them expending their energies in the night houses when nobody's looking.'

Daniel glanced around the shop.

'I see you've had your doors reinforced?'

Dugdale tapped the side of his nose.

'Better than the last time,' he said. 'The old doors gave me just a few minutes to burn certain volumes. I calculate these new doors will give me a half hour.'

'But is it worth it, Mr Dugdale? There are other booksellers on the Row that simply sell more... mainstream literature. They seem to thrive without the gaol or the house of correction hanging over their heads?'

Dugdale reached into his pocket and brought out an ornate snuffbox. He held it out to Daniel, who took a pinch, and then he indulged himself.

'Don't be fooled, Mr Daniel,' the bookseller said at last. 'Most of the sellers in this street sell exactly what I do, though they keeps it better hidden. If you wants legitimate you has to go up to Paternoster Row and St. Paul's Churchyard. You'll find it there, though most offer nothing more enticing than the latest novel of Newgate.'

'I'm not sure I could write what you desire...'

'A good writer can write anything, Mr Daniel. And I can tell as how you're a young man of rare talent.' Dugdale looked thoughtful. 'I might be prepared to go to twenty guineas for a novel of doings in a convent, or about the amorous ambitions of a young girl come up from the country.'

'I've little experience of such matters...'

Dugdale sat back on his stool and regarded him for a few moments.

'I see how it is,' he smiled. 'You've led a sheltered existence. And things are done different in some of those country towns, no doubt. I might be able to help you there. I know a number of young ladies of the town, girls of an instructive nature...'

Daniel stood up and looked again around the shop.

'I did come to London with the intention of penning my own novel, Mr Dugdale.'

'And how far have you got?'

'I'm several chapters in ...'

Dugdale shrugged his shoulders and gave a despairing look at the ceiling.

'But it could be years before that brings in the blunt ...'

'And I went to see the publisher of the *New Review*. He said that he might commission me to write some appraisals of recent publications. And eventually let me write more considered literary pieces.'

Dugdale laughed.

'And how much would he pay you?' he asked.

'A shilling a thousand words, and I might sell on any volumes I've reviewed.'

Dugdale took in a deep breath and shook his head again.

'It's a sad thing that literature's so poorly rewarded,' he said 'You're very like to starve.'

He reached across and took Daniel by the hand.

'I like you, young man. You're polite and I can see that you're a promising candidate for my patronage. You come and work for me. Write what I ask and I'll put plenty of tin in your pocket. You can still write your novel in your spare time, and I'm confident you'll find fame with it. But there's no sense in knocking on the gates of the workhouse in the meantime, is there?'

'But wouldn't penning what you ask blight my literary reputation?'

Dugdale wagged a finger, before reaching over to the table and picking up a volume bound in green cloth, placing it into Daniel's hands.

Daniel looked at the title: *The Exotic Adventures of a Dairyman's Daughter*.

'By one of my regular writers,' said Dugdale. 'Written under a *nom de plume*. Anton Febrizzi. In reality he's a most learned gentleman, a Fellow of the Royal Society, no less. And the author of some brilliant and much applauded works on the history of England. But his regular publications don't pay the bills. And so he writes for me as well.'

'Doesn't he fear discovery?' asked Daniel, thumbing through the book. 'Surely if his connection with *this* was discovered, it could be the ruin of him?'

'Why should he ever fear discovery? Discretion is the motto I'll put on my coat of arms one day, Mr Daniel. It's the core requirement of my whole business.'

Daniel held out the volume.

'No, you keep it and read it, Mr Daniel. See how it's put together. Let me know if you could do something of the like. And then we'd have to think up a name for you to write under...'

'A name...'

Dugdale wandered around the shop for several moments.

'I likes the Daniel in your own name. It has a strength about it, like the man in the Bible. But your surname, well, you'll want that for your own novel. And for the sake of your character, we needs to avoid it... We wants something mysterious. Something of the night...'

'Of the night?'

'Of the night, Mr Daniel. Something romantic for the women readers, but with a touch of menace and the dark. Daniel... Daniel...'

He slapped a hand down on to the table.

'Daniel Moonlight! That'll do.... Daniel Moonlight.'

~

'Colley Johnson was no Latin scholar,' Josef Critzman remarked. 'Why then should he know a word like tenebrae? Assuming that Wren's theory is correct. And it's not just the question of him having that word on his lips as he died, but the fact he was so desperate to find you, William. So desperate that he trailed you from Bloomsbury to Chelsea?'

'I suppose we'll never know,' said his brother. 'How could we possibly ever find out?'

William Quest stared into the fire, seeing a picture of the last moments of Colley Johnson's life played out in the flames. He'd liked Colley, a man who'd put food in his mouth when he'd first arrived in London, who'd taught him the way to survive in the rookeries of St Giles and Seven Dials.

'Well, I'm going to try and find out. Apart from anything else, Colley was a member of Monkshood. I tried to offer him a better life and lodgings, but he always said he'd never be happy too far from St Giles.'

'Don't see how you can start?' said Wren Angier.

'There's always Pokey Nibbs...' said Jasper Feedle.

'My God! Haven't they hanged old Pokey yet?' said Isaac.

'You know perfectly well they haven't!' Quest smiled. 'I'm aware that Pokey's been the bane of your life, coming begging every week at your charity for the poor, Isaac. But he's one of the best dips in London and he was Colley's partner in crime for the past year. They even lodged in the same ken in the Dials. If anyone knows what Colley had been doing, it'll be Pokey.'

'I suppose it's a start,' said Wren. 'William, if you're minded to have a wander over to Seven Dials, I'd like to come with you. Would we go as ourselves?'

Quest shook his head.

'Wren, you wouldn't last a minute dressed as smartly as that. No, better that we go back to my home in Bloomsbury and change into something more appropriate.

A couple of bludgers, that's what we need to be... and it might be as well to go armed too.'

'Mayn't I come with yer?' said Jasper, pulling himself up on his crutch.

'I'd thought of something else for you to do, Jasper,' said Quest. 'Might be an idea if you spent the evening at Rat's Castle. See what gossip you can pick up. You're known and trusted there, folk will talk to you. And if we don't find Pokey Nibbs at the lodging ken, he's just as likely to be there.'

Josef Critzman stood up and tapped the table.

'Gentlemen... gentlemen... I admire your lust for adventure, but surely there are more important matters to attend to right now. There is the question of our old friend Jonas Lyddon. Did not Inspector Anders warn William that this policeman, Bright, intended to bring him down? Should we not warn Jonas that his liberty... perhaps even his life might be in jeopardy?'

'Ah, I thought of that,' said Quest. 'But Jonas is making a speech in Manchester later today. We can do little before he returns to London in a few days' time, though I've sent a coded message by the telegraph system and followed that up with a letter. I've also used the same methods to instruct the northern members of Monkshood to put a ring of steel around our friend.'

'That's good, but not a permanent solution,' said Isaac. 'We need to discover what this Inspector *Honour* Bright intends to do to bring down the rebels in our land – it would be too much to expect Anders to put his police career on the line by telling us more than he has. But no, we must await Jonas Lyddon's return to London and then put him out of reach of this ambitious detective.'

'Very well, but there is the other plan we had,' said Josef. 'We told our friends in Saffron Hill that we'd attend to the depredations of the Cooper gang. There's scarce a tavern keeper or shop proprietor not being threatened by them. There'll be more deaths and premises burned down unless that evil man Cooper and his henchmen are brought to account. Old Barry at the *Merry Parson* fears for his life. And he's not a man easily scared.'

Jasper sat down again.

'Known Barry a good long time. Needs our help.'

'And he shall have it,' said Quest. 'And the others who've been threatened into paying out a weekly sum to be left alone. But we could hang around Saffron Hill for days and not get a glimpse of the Cooper gang. We need word of when they're going to be about. Perhaps Sticks could...'

He looked across at the retired prizefighter sitting on the old wooden rocking chair in the corner of the room, chomping muffins.

'I was hoping you was going to find me somethin' to do? Well, I knows Saffron Hill mighty well and I'm always happy to see Barry – as long as he appreciates I won't taste a drop of his foul liquor. I'll soon get word if Cooper and his ruffians are going to make an appearance.'

~

Police Commissioner Sir Richard Mayne was not in the best of moods, glaring up at Anders and taking sideways glances at a thin man who was hovering close to the door.

'Inspector Anders... are you seriously telling me that it was pure coincidence that you happened to be standing next to this villain Quest when a murder took place? I find that hard to believe?'

'Pure coincidence,' Anders lied.

'Only a few weeks ago, Inspector, you were working alongside Quest in York. Working with a murderous rebel that I recall sending you after, in the hope that you might secure a conviction. A murderous rebel who should have been turned off on the Newgate gallows a long while ago.'

'You will recall, sir, that I was sent to York to work alongside the city police. They were using William Quest a while before I got there. I'm sure you are aware that Her Majesty's Secret Service will not let the police touch Quest for the time being. And he has been of use to us in the past.'

'He's a villain!' roared Mayne.

'There's very little we can do about that,' said Anders.

The man near the door stepped closer to them both.

'You seem to have an extraordinary relationship with this Quest, Anders?'

Anders looked the man up and down. Inspector Honour Bright had a face as eager as a hungry rat, and a wide mouth that smirked every time he spoke.

'Must say, Anders, like Sir Richard, I do find it odd that you happened to be alongside this rogue at the very moment this wretched pickpocket was done to death. Coincidence, Anders? I find it very hard to believe in such coincidences. Why were you in the Cremorne Gardens at all in the dark hours?'

'Yes, why were you there, Anders?' asked Sir Richard.

Anders shrugged.

'My new duties, Sir Richard... to seek out and suppress vice in the metropolis. Where better place to start than at Cremorne – there's a great deal of vice to be found in those few acres.'

'There's some truth in that, I suppose,' Sir Richard conceded.

'But I still find it hard to accept that Quest should be there at the same moment...' said Bright.

'Strange things happen in London,' Anders replied.

Inspector Bright studied him for a long moment.

'Indeed they do, Anders. Indeed they do...'

Sir Richard tapped his desk, breaking the spell.

'Well, dealing with Quest is your responsibility now, Bright. Within the remit of the instructions we've received from on high. Be mindful, how you go, Inspector. Quest has caused Scotland Yard more pother than every other criminal in London put together. If you can bring him and his associates down, well, so much the better. But you know the hold he has over our masters? Go wary, Inspector Bright. Go wary.'

Mayne dismissed Bright with a wave of his hand.

When Bright had gone, he looked up again at Anders.

'Don't take me for a fool, Anders. I don't believe for a moment that you and Quest met by accident in the dark in the Cremorne Gardens. Your career hangs by a thread, Anders. Men like Bright are the future... detectives without a grain of compassion or sentimentality. If you want to survive, go and do your job. Get out there and collar some villains... bring in those pedlars of vice and depravity. And stay away from William Quest.'

Three

Daniel Moonlight shut the door, turned the key in the lock and drew across the heavy bolt.

It was a small room and barely furnished. Apart from the bed, with his own trunk at its foot, there was a writing table and a chair, a washstand and ewer. A tiny bookshelf, bearing a few volumes, was affixed to the wall next to the mirror. The ashes of last evening's fire were still in the tiny grate and a couple of dirty dishes were piled on the table.

He rested the green-bound copy of *The Exotic Adventures of a Dairyman's Daughter* between the dishes and a large pile of manuscript paper and the inkwell.

The solitary and narrow window above the table offered a long view down Holywell Street. Daniel paused there for a while and watched the pedestrians come and go. He smiled at the furtive gents who looked all around before entering the bookshops.

A dolly-mop hovered on the edge of the nearest alley, a suggestive smile playing on her face, in the hope that some of the passing customers might wish to bring fictive lusts to reality.

Daniel had never talked to the girl, but he felt that he knew her quite well. She worked as a maid for an old lady who kept a house at the further end of the Strand. The girl's mistress was a valetudinarian and slept for much of the day, giving her maid ample opportunity to supplement her meagre wages by occasionally working the streets.

All of this Daniel had learned from the loquacious Mr Dugdale, who knew everything that happened in the district and the background of all of the regular passers-by.

'Have to know it all,' said Dugdale, tapping his nose. 'In my best interests to have knowledge of everyone in the Row. Half the costermongers work for me, pushing their barrows up and down. They keeps the money from what they sells, but are always maintaining a beady-eye on who comes and goes. Always ready to upset their barrows to obstruct the crushers and the puritans, should they come rushing along to enter any of my premises.'

A fat, very bald gent left one of the bookshops, a brown-papered parcel of volumes under one arm. He put on his tall hat and strode along the pavement, for all his bulk cutting a dash, silver-topped cane working the air.

He walked past the girl, but turned as she said something to him. He glanced around before approaching her. They talked for a moment or two. She smiled and gave a little curtsy. And then took him by the arm and led him into the darkness of the alley.

Daniel had watched the same manoeuvre a dozen times since he had taken on the room. The girl was not only pretty, but very proficient. He had never talked to her because he had never known what he might say. But he had put the girl into the early pages of his novel.

Not of course as a dolly-mop, but as the honest daughter of a tradesman in a country town. One of the heroes of his story. Daniel felt he had captured her looks very well in his prose, not to mention that bewitching smile. He often used real people from the streets as models. It made it easier that he knew nothing of their personalities, or the way they spoke. The sound of a voice, or any revealing snatch of conversation could wreck the creation of his imagination.

He came away from the window and looked at himself in the tiny mirror, wondering what a novelist might make of him.

He was just twenty, dark-haired, with a nose that was ever so slightly too large. His eyes were dark and expressive – any novelist would say that – revealing, perhaps, too much of what he was thinking. The mouth was good. He smiled a lot, very often when he wasn't feeling particularly in good humour. It was a disarming smile. He would very often grin at the people he hated the most. Beguiling your opponent at the most crucial moment was a particularly useful tactic.

He sighed and sat down in the chair.

It wasn't going to be as simple as he'd imagined. He'd never thought that London could be so huge a place. He had been in town for a fortnight now and still hadn't really started with his search. Finding the room had taken a lot of time, somewhere convenient but not too expensive. His funds were limited and he was going through them at a rapid rate.

Perhaps Mr Dugdale was right. He should think of writing much more commercially. Catering for the market, rather than trying to emulate the grander work of his literary idols. He picked up the green-backed volume he'd been given and thumbed its pages.

The text conjured up some bewildering images in his mind. He had often thought of such matters, but the reality was beyond his experience of life. And perhaps that was the problem. Hadn't a beginning author once asked one of the masters, "how shall I write?" and received the reply, 'well, first you must live!"

There had to be some truth in that wise advice.

How could you create people and situations if you'd never experienced them? Daniel considered this for a few moments. Perhaps he should actually talk to the dolly-mop. Her own story might be well worth telling. More valid than the one-dimensional characters in his own emerging novel.

The real London, as opposed to the one he had visualised from his room in a far-away country vicarage.

He thumbed through his own writing for a while. How flat it seemed when compared to those works of Mr Dickens, which adorned his own little bookshelf. The characters seemed lifeless on the page, the turn of events contrived, the language clumsy...

A piece of notepaper fell out of the manuscript and reminded him of the other reason he had come to London. His search, so long envisaged, had not even been properly begun. And that was far more important than dreams of literary greatness.

He swung round on the chair and threw open the lid of his trunk, pulling to one side his spare clothing and a few more books, scattering them on to the floor. He pressed down on the panel on the bottom and eased it upwards. In this secret compartment were a small bag of golden sovereigns and a beautifully polished wooden box.

He lifted this up on to the table and opened the lid. His proudest possession. It contained a pair of fine little pistols and a powder flask engraved with country scenes. It was a gift from his uncle, a kind of legacy, though it had been given to Daniel when that old soldier was still alive. With the strict instruction that Daniel's father must never know that it had been given to him.

'You know what your father's like!' His uncle, the brother of Daniel's dead mother, had grinned. 'Parsons don't approve of such things!'

Daniel ran his fingers along the beautifully polished wood of one of the pistols. A work of art in itself – but quite deadly. And London could be a dangerous place. Sometimes a walking cane was not enough protection in its more perilous corners. He really should carry a pistol more often.

Or perhaps find a less noticeable weapon.

He put the gun down and picked up the sheet of notepaper. It bore one word, the solitary clue in his search. A word that had puzzled him since the letter had arrived at the parsonage, containing this one hint that might solve a family puzzle.

The word on the notepaper was "Quest".

~

'Mrs Bendig would like to cut your throat, Wren,' said Quest, as they walked away from the Critzman's walking stick and umbrella shop in Cheapside, on the way to Tavistock Place.

'What have I done to offend that old haybag?'

'Well, word's reached me that you stole the best girl in her wretched night house. And you never go there any more to spend your sovereigns. My informant said that she was ranting and raving about it as she chaired her gentlemen's party, only the other night.'

Wren smiled at the thought of Mrs Bendig, groaning and moaning at her loss. The old witch ran the most popular gentlemen's haunt in London, an imposing building on the corner of Leicester Square. A brothel where only the wealthiest might pass the hours, first sitting at a long table in the hall, at a party controlled by Molly Bendig, before going upstairs with the prettiest girls in London.

'I don't need such entertainment,' said Wren. 'I took Phoebe away from there because she didn't need to be in such a place. And as I recall, the odious Mrs Bendig said I might steal that particular girl away, if we sorted out the threats that were being made against that licentious enterprise.'

'That was the agreement,' Quest said. 'How is Phoebe?'

'Glad to be away from Bendig's. And very grateful to you for rescuing her from her original ponce, Bluff Todd. I've taken a new property up in Highgate village. Phoebe is there at the moment as my housekeeper – though I fully intend to make her my wife.'

Quest stopped dead and faced him.

'Your wife!'

'Why not? She's a good and loving girl and we are very happy together. What better than we should be married?'

'I admire her virtues too. It's just a surprise to me. Forgive me, Wren, but you've always cut such a dash in society. You're a baronet and a member of Parliament. You're one of the wealthiest men in London. Can you imagine what your friends in society will say when they meet Phoebe?'

'You think I care? Many of them only keep my company because of my title and my wealth. I'd happily cut them all loose. After all, it was *their* company that led me into the bad old ways that you rescued me from. What better than I should break from them all? I've new friends now, the folk we've just left – and you...'

Quest shook his hand.

'Then I'm very happy for you both.'

Quest was smiling, but Wren Angier couldn't help noticing the sadness in his eyes. He'd avoided mentioning the possible reason for that misery for so long. Thought how lonely Quest had looked, the time he'd seen him off on the railway train to York.

'I know you miss your Rosa, Quest.'

'Not my Rosa... not at all. Miss Stanton chose the theatrical life over me, by joining the company of Miss Vestris. I've not heard from her since. I understand that the production was not a success, though Miss Stanton apparently was.'

'A woman of much talent. I've not mentioned it to you, but I went to see her play Polly Peachum, in *The Beggar's Opera* at Drury Lane. A revival to fill in a sennight's gap between other productions, that was all. As I understand it, the lady hasn't worked since. She really was a most enchanting Polly, with a singing voice that could melt hearts.'

'I know. I went to see her too! I'm aware of her many talents!'

'But she's not working now, William. I met Miss Vestris at a dinner the other night – the poor lady's not in good health. She told me that it was the fault of the proprietor of the theatre that the production failed. She regretted that it led to misfortune for Miss Stanton.'

'Did she know where Rosa is?'

'She did not... why, have you sought her out?'

'I've not sought her out. That chapter of my life is finished. But I do care for Rosa's welfare, so I asked some of the members of Monkshood to report on her well-being. But nobody seems to know where she's gone? It's a puzzle to me. I'm trying to put her out of my mind.'

Quest walked on, so swiftly that Angier had difficulty keeping up with him.

~

'How's the good work, young Daniel?' asked Dugdale.

Daniel Moonlight closed the heavy door of the bookshop, noticing that three more bolts had been installed since his last visit and bars put across the window.

'My novel seems to have stalled,' he replied. 'I see you've taken fresh precautions, Mr Dugdale? Have the Vice Society been threatening you again?'

'Not just those puritanical bastards! I've a few crushers... policemen... on my payroll. They've told me that Scotland Yard's launched a new campaign against the freedoms of my writers and illustrators. Put a noted detective on the case, they seem so determined to shut down the freedom of the press and the liberties of the individual.'

'What will you do?'

'Do what gentlemen of the arts have always done, fight on and publish! Half the respectable gents of the town come here, to Holywell Street, to buy my sort of literature. Why should they be denied their harmless pleasures? Just because of a few puritans. And believe me, those God-plaguers have just as many secret vices, if truth be told. Now, have you read that volume I gave you and had any thoughts as to whether you might pen something similar?'

'I'm not sure as to whether I can recount such experiences... I mean between men and women. You see... I've never... never...'

Dugdale opened his mouth wide, winked an eye and nodded his head.

'You mean you've never... *been* with a woman?' he sucked in a breath. 'Well, that's nothing to be ashamed of, me lad! Many a country gent has no experience of the fairer sex until he comes to this place. That's why so many gents come to London in the first place!'

'I read your book... it seemed so explicit.... do men and women really do such things? It seems so strange...'

'Here, lad, have some porter,' Dugdale said, pouring out two glasses. 'There ain't no shame in it. How d'ye think you came here? By your father and mother crossing over each other in just the ways that book mentions.'

'But my father's a parson,' said Daniel.

'Even vicars have to sow their seeds. Don't it say so in the Bible? Aren't we all born into a world of sin? Yes, that's what the Bible says. And gaining experience - all in the causes of literature - well, it ain't that difficult... haven't you seen the trollops parading up and down this very street?'

'I've seen one taking men into the alley yonder.'

'Well, there you are!'

'It seems so sordid...'

'Only the first time, lad. Only the first time...'

'I'm not sure I could... in an alley.'

'If you were a man of means, you could patronise one of the night houses in Piccadilly or Leicester Square. I expend much of my profits and strength at Mrs Bendig's establishment, though I fear such a place would be beyond your pocket - unless you have some sovereigns hidden away? No? Ah well, then you must seek the lowlier places around the Seven Dials. D'ye know the Dials? No, well, if you hang around the drinking dens thither, you'll soon find a lady to accommodate you, I'm sure.'

'It's not just that - the novel you gave me to read was full of low life. Thieves and pickpockets. I've no knowledge of such persons. Where would I meet them, so that I might portray them in my work?'

Dugdale smiled and sipped the porter.

'Well, there's Rat's Castle. Few places worse'n that. But I wouldn't advise it. Even the crushers go in there armed and mob-handed. I know what you literary gents are like. Wonderful place for a writer seeking to put some colour into his work. Not that far from Seven Dials, neither.'

'You suggest I shouldn't go there, though?'

'Not really - but then! I can see you're a lad who likes a challenge. I did hear that Mr Dickens has took quite an interest in the place.'

'I'll take your advice then. Mr Dugdale?'

'Yes, lad?'

'Do you know of a man called Quest?'

'Can't say nothing comes to mind... Why?'

'Oh, nothing.'

As he was leaving the shop, Mr Dugdale called him back.

'Take my advice, boy. Get up the Dials and see a bit of life. Nothing like the Dials for a touch of inspiration - soon get the juices flowing!'

Four

Inspector Honour Bright thought that the watcher looked too obviously a policeman. Just as though the man was still in uniform and pounding the beat. Constables in the detective force needed to do a lot better than that. He'd have to give Constable Wells some instruction when he was back at the Yard. The damn fool even half-saluted as Bright approached.

'Anything happening, Wells?'

'Nothing for a long time, sir. But, about an hour ago, the man Quest and his friend Angier came up from the direction of the city and went into the house. Constable Parkin tailed them from Cheapside.'

Bright looked across at the property, so similar to the houses on either side of Tavistock Place. The home of William Quest, that murdering criminal and political renegade.

'See anything else?'

'There was some movement near a window at the top.'

'Anyone else about?'

'People passing through the street, of course. Oh, and him.'

Wells nodded in the direction of a youth leaning against the railing at the corner of the street. A slim lad in fustian, with a canvas cap. Bright regarded the youth for a while, his mind travelling through a long catalogue of possibilities. An errand boy, maybe? Or one of those Londoners from the lower orders, who were always hanging around in the hope of some casual work? After a moment, his mind came to a conclusion.

'He's a dip, looking to pick a pocket. Why else would he be lingering so long on such a respectable street?'

'Would you like us to take him in charge, sir?'

'Don't be a fool, Wells. Do you think Quest might not hear the noise, if you laid that little villain by the heels? No, leave him alone. The beat constable can move him along when the time comes. We must keep watching Quest. Who's guarding the back of the property?'

'Parkin's stationed himself there. To the best of our knowledge, Quest owns the house at the back as well, with just a yard between them.'

'Owns two houses? Quest does very well for himself, for a champion of the poor.'

'As you know, sir, I worked with Inspector Anders when the man first came to our attention. Quest has a lease on the house. The whole area belongs to the duke of Bedford, including that property. Nice houses though. Scarce fifty years old, and Quest has some very respectable neighbours.'

'Let's hope they'll all come and see him at Newgate, when he's turned off by the hangman,' Bright said drily. 'Anyway, I'll go down that street to the side and see if Parkin has anything to report. If Quest should leave, I want you to follow him – and try and be discreet, Wells...'

'And Angier? Should I follow him if he leaves?'

'Only if he's with Quest.'

Bright walked along, crossing the street as he headed towards the road leading down past the end of the terrace. As he went he passed the youth, who gave him such a dirty-faced and insolent glance that the inspector fought hard to resist the temptation to nab him by the collar there and then.

He found Parkin on the far side of the street, gazing into a shop window, watching the passage that came into the other side of Marchmont Street, running between some commercial properties, and then to the rear of Tavistock Place. Now here was a lad that knew how to keep watch and not stand out from the crowd. Honour Bright made a mental note that Parkin could be sergeant material.

'Anything happening, Parkin?'

'Not yet, sir. But if the man Quest comes out the back way, he's got to emerge from that passage. It's a dead-end the other way, unless Quest is inclined to clamber up a high wall. Inspector Anders and Sergeant Berry once watched him come out of that very passage.'

'Very good.'

'Am I to tail him if he should come out this way?'

Bright looked back at the reflection of the passage in the shop window.

'No, Parkin, you followed him from Cheapside. He might recognise you if you tailed him further. No... you get round there and take over from Wells. He can go off duty until tonight. If Quest comes out through his front door, you may tail him – and send the first beat constable you encounter to warn me. But I suspect, if he goes out on some nefarious business, he'll come this way. In which case, I'll follow him myself.'

Bright watched as Parkin walked back up to the junction with Tavistock Place, moving as casually as any street loafer, not even glancing at the insolent, pickpocketing youth as he walked within a yard of him.

Promising lad, Parkin, Bright thought.

Most police officers hated keeping a watch in the street like this, trying to look inconspicuous, but never leaving the spot. Boredom soon set in and that's when mistakes were made. But Bright never minded a task he'd always excelled in, from his own days as a constable on the beat. He had the ability of losing himself in his thoughts and memories, without once relaxing his guard.

In most cases, keeping a dodge on suspects was thoroughly pointless. They seldom did anything suspicious in those moments when they were being watched. That was the curse of the thing. Villains were only villainous in brief intervals of their existence, and those intervals tended not to be when they were being tailed by policemen from Scotland Yard.

Bright wandered some yards down the street, always glancing back at the passage, seemingly without moving his head. Marchmont Street was busy with pedestrians, errand boys, local servants acquiring goods for their masters. Nobody paid any attention to the watching policeman – and yet...

The inspector couldn't get over the feeling that somebody was taking an interest in him. Inspector Bright had but one hobby in the rare hours that he was off duty. He took a great interest in the prehistoric past, liking to consider himself very much an antiquarian.

As a boy near Peterborough, he'd often collected old flint axes and arrowheads, lost all those centuries ago by the men of the Stone Age. He kept his collection in a *bijouterie* in his little house in Acton – not that he was there often, Acton being too far out from Scotland Yard to make for an easy daily journey. No, he journeyed home only on the rare occasions when he had some time to himself, spending much of the week in respectable lodgings just the other side of Westminster Bridge.

But his interest in the distant past subscribed him to one theory – that the instincts, necessary for survival, of prehistoric hunter-gatherers remained in the feelings of modern man. An essential warning of potential peril. A remarkable and very useful remnant that civilisation had not cast away.

Bright could see nobody obviously watching him from any of the high windows above the shops. He took the measure of all the pedestrians he passed, but not a single one seemed interested in him. He glanced into the passage once more – there was nobody there.

He looked back up towards Tavistock Place.

The youthful pickpocket was still there, indolently leaning back against a house railing. And Bright knew who the watcher was. The lad was not even making any pretence of *not* glaring at him in that insolent manner. In Bright's experience, pickpockets had a talent for summing up the folk who walked down any street – it was a necessity of their trade to quickly decide who was worth robbing and who should be left alone.

I've marked you well, my lad...

Bright muttered the words to himself, making a promise to arrest the thief on charges of suspicious behaviour, if he ever saw him again on the streets of London. *He knows I'm a crusher.* Of course he does... the youth had watched him for long enough, watched the discreet conversation with Parkin, probably noticed his earlier talk with the incompetent Wells. Dips were often the canniest members of the underworld. Their very safety from arrest depended on their constant vigilance.

So wrapped up was Bright with these considerations, that he almost missed the two men who emerged, very suddenly, from the passage on the far side of the street. Two villainous individuals, dressed as labouring men in ragged clothing, each carrying blackthorn clubs that doubled as walking sticks.

Bright smiled – others might be fooled, but he'd secretly watched both Quest and Angier a great many times over the past weeks, in more respectable garb. *You can't fool Honour Bright, gentlemen.*

He turned away from them, glancing into the shop window, noticing their speedy progress down Marchmont Street. *Dressed like that, they must be going somewhere very interesting.*

Bright gave them fifty yards start and wandered down the street after them, staying on the opposite pavement, keeping close to the shop fronts so that the pedestrians might shield him from their gaze.

Halfway down the street, the pavement was obstructed by a barrow crammed with fruit and vegetables. A clear blockage of the thoroughfare, which might have led to a summons in the magistrates' court if he'd had more time in hand – the barrow boy gave him a similar impudent look to the pickpocket.

Bright started to step around this impediment, watching as Quest and Angier reached the end of the street, when he was suddenly pushed very hard in the back, sending him flying through the air. He crashed with some force into the barrow, knocking it on to its side, the fruit and vegetables flying everywhere. He hit the pavement very heavily, noting – as he gasped for breath – the pickpocket running back up the street, vanishing into the crowds as he reached the junction with Tavistock Place.

The barrow boy knelt on the pavement, trying to stop his wares rolling into the road, cursing and muttering threats. The usual gawping mob had assembled, expressing sympathy with the barrow boy's plight. The inspector reached inside his jacket and brought out the cudgel he always carried for just such situations, only to find his arm being grasped by a beat constable.

'Now then. None of that!'

Then the constable recognised the detective.

'Beg pardon, sir.'

'Never mind, constable. I want you to take this man in charge for obstructing the highway with his barrow. And get this crowd cleared away.'

Bright walked out into the road, but there was no sign of Quest and Angier - and not a glimpse of the pickpocket. The inspector brushed the dust off his jacket and retrieved his hat, which one of the crowd had picked up, looking as if he intended to make away with it.

'I'll know that pickpocketing bastard when I see him again.'

'Beg pardon, sir?' said the constable, who was busy shooing away the spectators.

'Never mind, constable. Never mind.'

~

Quest and Angier were halfway to Seven Dials before they paused for breath.

'You saw that?' Quest asked.

'Very nice of that dip to divert the attention of Inspector Bright.'

'That was Bright? I've never set eyes on the man until today.'

'He came to the House of Commons a while ago, for a meeting with the home secretary. I was there. Well, perhaps he doesn't deserve his reputation - he was easily spotted. Is that dip a member of Monkshood?'

'No, he isn't. But he seems to be tailing me too. I've noticed him a couple of times hanging around my home. More than that, I think I spotted him at the Cremorne Gardens the night Colley Johnson was topped. Can't swear to it, but I'm sure that lad was there on the edge of the crowd.'

'You think he had something to do with Colley's death?'

'I can't see why he would. No, if anything he's on our side. That collision with Bright wasn't accidental.'

Quest looked back along the street.

'Can't see him now. Let's hunt down Pokey Nibbs.'

Five

'Not sure as how I can bring meself ter talk of it, Mr Quest. Not sure it's wise. Not sure it's healthy. Yer saw what happened to poor Colley? Oh, Mr Quest, yer should have seen the state Colley was in the day he died. Looked everywhere for yer, he did... searched high and low.'

It was a grubby little room, not far from the gaff Quest, himself sometimes used in Neals Yard. A narrow little space, with a table and chair and a mattress on the floor, one floor up from the similar room where Colley Johnson had spent his last days.

'Not sure it's wise ter talk of it at all.'

Pokey Nibbs had been in the dipping trade for so many years that his hands were never still. Every now and then, he'd stretch out his calloused fingers as though he was reaching into a pocket, depriving someone of their shillings or their wipes. Then he'd stretch out his arms, gazing at them, as though he was making sure they were still there.

'We need to know, Pokey,' Quest said. 'For Colley's sake...'

Nibbs leaned forward.

'What if I should end up with a chiv in me back, Mr Quest? There ain't no locks on these doors, like yer have in that big house yer lodge in. I could have me throat cut in a second. I got nowhere else ter go, Mr Quest...'

Quest felt he'd been too long in this game. Every rogue in the Dials seemed to know him now by his real name, even when he came into the rookeries in disguise. For years he'd been Bill, the bludging and dangerous villain who kept a room in Neals Yard and a similar gaff in Whitechapel. It felt as though the whole world could now see through the masquerade.

'Pokey, I can get you away from here, somewhere nobody would ever find you. Well away from Seven Dials. Miles away from London. You know I have a house in the country? I could get you somewhere to lodge out there.'

Nibbs gave him a pitiful look.

'And what would I do, Mr Quest? Me father was an ostler at a tavern in Southwark, but I could never abide horses. That's why I took ter the dippin' trade. And if Colley had stuck ter just dippin' he might have breath in his lungs now. But he was getting rheumaticky in his digits. Told me that his days as a dip were numbered. That's why he decided to crack a crib. Up near Piccadilly where the flash gentry lives. And that cost him, Mr Quest. That cost him dear, poor blighter. He cracked that crib and they topped him for it...'

'What crib?'

'All he told me was that it was one of them places in Piccadilly. A huge house with bow windows, one that'd been empty all the years he'd known of it. A flight o' steps leadin' up from the street. It had a name, Colley said... now what did he call it...Tinny somethin' like that.'

'Tenebrae?' Angier suggested.

'Not sure that's what he said, but somethin' like it. Had a brass plate on the railings outside with the name. But don't yer go there, Mr Quest. Don't yer dare. Colley come back here in a terrible state. Told me what he'd seen in that flash crib. The thought of it gives me nightmares, I'll tell yer that...'

'What did he see?' Quest asked.

Pokey Nibbs stretched out his hands, waved the fingers, clutched his head for a moment and began the tale...

'Yer been at the drink again, Colley?'

Colley Johnson flung himself down on the filthy mattress and looked up at Nibbs.

'Yer don't want to know, me old pal, truth and no lie yer don't. I seen summat today what'd make yer heart wrench and yer belly turn. Up in the 'dilly. A house that's been empty all me time in this town. Yer might know it. Big place with bow windows.'

'It got a name or a number?'

'Hundred and thirty somethin' and a brass on the railings what gives it a name. tinny bree. Something like that. Anyways, the street was quiet for once and I sees this flash gent come out, pulling the door after him. He walks away at a real lick, so fast he don't realise he hadn't shut the door proper.'

'So yer was tempted?'

'Well, I knows the house to be empty, but I thinks as how there might be somethin' to make it worth me while. So I gives the street a cavey look and nobody bein' about, I goes in...'

'It were empty?'

'It was that, Pokey. Bare boards and no carpets. Not a stick of furniture. And dust, my gawd, yer should a see'd the dust! Yet the flash gent or some other must go in from time to time, cos there was a clear path right across the hall to the staircase. It was dark, but the windows bein' big and bowed, well, there was a lot of light comin' in from the 'dilly.'

'But if there was nothin' there, why stick around? Yer says the rooms was empty?'

'So they were, Pokey, so they were. I was in and out of them as quick as a ferret. But nothin'. Absolutely nothin'. As empty as me pocket on a bad day on the dip.'

Pokey Nibbs poured out two mugs of small beer from a jug he'd gone off with earlier in the day, from a tavern on the fringes of St Giles' rookery.

'Here, Colley... have a sup o' this to settle yer nerves.'

Johnson swallowed the foul liquid in one sup.

'Nothin'll ever settle me nerves, Pokey. I see'd a sight that'll haunt me all me days. Somethin' more. I think the creature's after me, on account of what I took. Come the dawn, I've got to seek out Quest. This concerns him... what I took concerns him... what I took...'

'Thought you said the gaff was empty?'

'Wish to gawd it had been, Pokey. Oh, how I wish...'

Nibbs poured out the last of the small beer.

'Not findin' anythin' below, I went up the stairs. It was the same on the next landin' and around about. But there was still tracks on the dusty carpets, where someone had walked, goin' up the next stairs to the third floor. Old house that... hundred years old or more. Empty as it was, it was as though I could hear talk and laughter. I've heard tell that house used ter be a gamblin' hell – when old George, and then William, were on the throne. Evil places, Pokey, evil places, that drawed in the worst types o' the gentry.'

Pokey Nibbs nodded.

'I've heard talk of such places,' he said. 'Those who welshed on their bets havin' their throats slit. Cheatin' too! Cheatin' that led to many a duel in Green Park across the road – there's a wicked place too! Haunted by the ghosts of all the lepers they buried there.'

Johnson reached out and grasped one of Nibbs' roaming hands.

'Yer don't need to go to the park ter see a haunt o' the devil, Pokey. The devil was waitin' for me in that house. I saw his...'

'What did yer see?'

'Told yer, I could hear laughter and voices. Thought the noise might be comin' in from the 'dilly. But no... Pokey... the house was empty and dark, but it was as though those sounds was all around me. Comin' from somewhere beyond the last landin'. Like a fool I went on... like a fool I went from room to room. But all empty apart from the stinkin' carpets an' the dust. But there were still the tracks, crossing the landin', then into one room, larger than the others.

'It was dark now, oh, gawd, so dark, for there was just one narrow window in the ceilin' lettin' in the moonlight. But as I watched, I noticed somethin' on the far side of the room. A small window of stained glass, like yer might get in a church, but just colours, no pictures of Bible scenes. And through it came a light, a soft light like candles burning. The tracks in the dust led ter a wall nearby, a wall of wooden panels.'

'Yer went over?'

'I went over, though I wish ter gawd I hadn't. Yer see, Pokey, one of them panels was like a secret door. The gent what I'd seen leavin' the gaff must have not shut it proper. Just a gap, no more than an inch...'

'Yer didn't go through?'

'Not then... not then. But I looked through that window of coloured glass. At first I couldn't see anythin', but then – as my eyes got used to the light – I could see into another room. Just a small room, but the one that secret door led into...'

Pokey Nibbs' hands were very still, as he leaned forward.

'What did yer see?'

'There was a table... with candles... four men sittin' round it, three I could see so clearly, shufflin' a paper around between them. But the other... the other... had his back to me... he was the one in charge though. Yer could just tell...'

Colley Johnson's breath came in great gasps.

'All of a sudden, Pokey... all of a sudden the man stood... took a pace towards the coloured window. Like he was lookin' into my soul. Only he couldn't have been. He couldn't have been...'

Colley shook his head quite viciously.

'He couldn't have been...'

'Couldn't have been?'

'*Yer see... he had no eyes. He had no face.*'

Six

'Well, that explains the Tenebrae,' said Wren Angier, 'but a man without a face? Surely just someone wearing a mask?'

Pokey Nibbs gave him a foul look.

'Yer sayin' Colley was a liar?'

'Not saying that at all, but it stands to reason. Everyone has a face, even if it's damaged in some way. Therefore it's obvious that it must have been a man in a mask. Remember, Colley was seeing him through stained glass. That must have distorted what Colley saw. Smoothed out the details of the mask, where the eye-slits would be. It stands to reason.'

Nibbs gave a nervous laugh.

'Educated gents thinks that they knows it all. Yer say it was the stained glass makin' this devil look that way. Well, ye're wrong, Mr Clever, though I confess I did say the same thing to Colley. And I'll tell yer why, shall I? I'll tell yer why...'

Colley Johnson wiped the sweat from his brow with a dirty rag

'No, it weren't a mask, Pokey. And if yer gives me a moment to draw breath, I'll tell yer why. Don't think the thought didn't cross me mind, lookin' as I was through that thick glass. But I knows for certain it was no mask. I knows an' I'll tell yer why, gawd help me...'

Nibbs leaned forward, his hands and arms circling like windmills.

'Go on then, go on...'

'I watched 'em for a time through the window, as they sat around that table in the candlelight. It dawned on me that cos there was no light on my side o' the glass, well, they couldn't glimpse me. The man without a face paced up and down, up and down, then went back to his chair. They was all lookin' at this paper, and I could hear harsh words, harsh words...'

'Yer heard what they was sayin'?' said Nibbs.

'Just the tone of it... then all of a sudden, they all got up and left that room through a door on the far side. Well, I was fer getting' out of there, I can tell yer, but I noticed they'd left the paper on the table. Bein' lettered, I thought as how I might have a glimpse of that. So I went through the door in the panel, crossed over to the table and picked it up. And that's why I got ter find Mr Quest...'

'What's it got ter do with him?'

'Only glanced at the paper, just a glimpse, Pokey, for the whole page was covered with details. Most of 'em about William Quest. There it was, his name in big, bold writing.'

'What did it say?'

'I was readin' it through when all hell broke loose.'

Nibbs was dry with the excitement of the tale. He wished he'd saved some of the small beer to wet his gums.

'Go on...'

'I turned... the devil had come back into the room. I didn't hear him come through the door, Pokey. Me, what's got such sharp hearin' and can hear a crusher's footsteps in the next street, even if my sight's not what it was. But somethin' made me turn and there he was, not a yard away, his arms raised in the air to clutch me. When I say he had no eyes... no face... I means it... nothin' just nothin' – and there was no coloured glass in the way then! He gives a horrible screech... that creature... and would have seized me if I'd been slower on me feet. But I was out o' there... through the panel and down them three flights of stairs.'

'Did they give chase?'

'I could hear 'em, Pokey... clumberin' down the stairs behind me. But I'd got a start, and was out on the pavement of the 'dilly afore they could nab me. There were folk about... I was never so glad as to see crowds, like I saw that night in the 'dilly. I've never knowed such fear in all me born days. I ran and ran all the way back here. I was comin' in to the ken here, when I realised I was still clutchin' that piece o' paper in me hand.'

'Yer got it now?'

'Not here, somethin' told me that I should cache it away, far from the gaff I lived in. So I took it somewhere, gave it to a pal to mind. But I got to go and find Mr Quest. Tell him all about that paper what has his moniker on it. I b'lives Mr Quest's in peril, Pokey... real peril. Yer know what? I think I'm in peril too. I was comin' through the Dials on the way back here, and I saw a man takin' a great interest in me... a burly bludger with a great round head. I knowed him, Pokey. I knowed him. He was one of the crew in that room. Sittin' next to the demon with no face.'

'Then he went out lookin' for yer, Mr Quest,' Pokey said. 'Desperate he was to find yer. Never knowed him in such a state. There was truth in what he said, no doubt of that.'

'Did you see him again?'

'Just fer a minute. Late in the day, I met him again in the Dials. Colley told me he'd been everywhere in search of yer. But he'd just met Old Sparky, the fence. Sparky told him he'd seen yer walking by the river. Must have been when you was goin' to the Cremorne. Anyroad up, Colley went off in chase of yer at a mad dash. An' that was the last I saw of me old pal...'

'And you don't know where he put the paper?'

Pokey Nibbs gave him a broad smile.

'Oh, I knows where he put the paper all right, Mr Quest. There's one place old Colley would always take things, yer know, stolen things from the dippin' that was too hot to hold before Colley might get to a fence. He'd always cache them overnight with Hawky Dewer, yer knows old Hawky? Runs a slop shop in that alley runnin' down ter the river from the Strand?'

'I know him.'

'Well, that's the place to go then.'

Quest nodded.

'And what about you, Pokey? This ken isn't safe... you can't even lock the door. Better that you come with us. If you won't take to the country, then we've got other rooms around London where we can hide you away.'

Nibbs looked him in the eye.

'No, Mr Quest. I ain't goin' ter be driven from me home by a bunch of Piccadilly toffs and a demon with no face. I got a livin' ter make. If things get wild I'll nip up to the St Giles rookery. They wouldn't dare follow me there. An' I got a chiv of me own. I'll slit all their bleedin' throats before they lay me down.'

~

Daniel Moonlight hid the change from the money he'd spent, in the secret compartment in the trunk at the foot of the bed. The old clothes from the slop shop hadn't cost much, just a couple of tanners, but the other purchase had taken up several of the sovereigns he'd brought with him from the country.

It was only a small percussion-cap pistol, but he'd wanted something that could be secreted in the inside pocket of the rough fustian jacket he'd acquired as part of his disguise.

Daniel had only fired such a weapon once before. His parson father owned such a gun, purchased at a period when there was much lawlessness in the countryside. It had never been used by either of them, though his sister had proved to be a crack shot, on the occasions when she managed to sneak it out of the parsonage. She had a cool and deadly aim, which quite surprised Daniel – who was wont to jump every time the gun went off.

He looked at himself in the mirror, a regular rascal in the ragged clothes, pistol in hand. Much like a character in the wilder novels he'd so often read, back in his shady room at the parsonage. In his heart, he hoped he would never have to use the pistol against the rogues of London town.

Daniel Moonlight only wished one man dead, and hoped to save the pistol and shot for that one foul individual he'd come to London to kill.

~

They were on the street just outside Pokey Nibbs' ken when they saw Sticks coming up the road, waving an arm. The old prizefighter had clearly come at a run, for he was out of breath.

'Come at a dash all the way from Saffron Hill. Blimey, I'm getting too old for this lark. Wouldn't be much good at the bare-knuckle fights now, for all my wind's gone. Think I'll retire from your service soon and stick to reading my books.'

'You've got some news on the Coopers?'

'Old Barry at the *Merry Parson* has got word he's to be paid a visit tomorrow night. I says as how we'd be there to give those villains a little surprise. How did you get on with Pokey?'

Quest gave him an account of everything Nibbs had said.

'A man with no face? Well, makes a change from the two-faced variety down the road there at Westminster. You think they'll come after Pokey?'

'They'll know their piece of paper wasn't found on Colley, so they're bound to believe Pokey might have it. There's no doubt they tailed Colley back here on the night he cracked the crib in Piccadilly.'

Sticks looked up and down the road.

'You wants me to put a friendly dodge on Nibbs?'

Quest thought for a moment.

'No,' he opined. 'We'll need your fists if we're to deal with the Coopers. Best get a few of our Monkshood toughs to tail Pokey wherever he goes. If they catch someone on his tail, it might be helpful if they cosh the follower and bring him to me. I'd like to know what this is all about. You arrange that, Sticks. We're off to see Hawky Dewer right now.'

'What about this house in Piccadilly,' said Wren, 'shouldn't we go and have a look at it for ourselves?'

'Perhaps not,' Quest replied. 'Well, not just yet, anyway. Whoever lives there'll be jumpy after Colley's visit. From what Sticks says, we'll be occupied tomorrow night in Saffron Hill. Perhaps the night after that – that's when we'll have a poke around that crib. When whoever lives there has settled down a bit.'

~

Daniel Moonlight walked along the Strand, feeling very odd in the worn and rather baggy fustian jacket, a canvas cap upon his head and trousers as grimy as the dirt on the street. He could feel the bulge of the pistol in his inside pocket. It all felt so strange, this disguise, and he began to regret ever setting out on this perilous journey to Rat's Castle, in the heart of one of the most notorious of London rookeries.

It all seemed so *artificial* – he felt like an actor in one of those performances at the playhouse, the kind of low entertainments his sister used to drag him to see in the neighbouring town. Those little expeditions that his father was never told anything about.

Daniel looked around at the passers-by, almost amazed that nobody was taking much notice of him. After a moment he relaxed, convinced that everyone was taken in by the disguise. But somehow, he had a sinking feeling that something was wrong. He glanced at others of his kind, then discovered *what* the something was, remembering all those players upon the stage.

Oh, he was dressed for the part all right, but he wasn't giving the right performance. He tried to picture himself walking along that pavement of the Strand, and then he grasped what was wrong. Just a glimpse of those other pedestrians, of the class he purported to be, told him what the error was.

He might be dressed like a rough labourer, but he was walking like a gentleman. Far too upright, much too sure of himself and his position in society. Those others of a similar class, the workers from the docks, the barrow boys, even the beggars – didn't stroll with that air of confidence – they shuffled, mostly looking down at the ground and not even glancing at anyone else.

Daniel tried to do an impression of just such a walk, but the more he tried the more he thought he was becoming noticeable. He rested for a moment and studied himself in a shop window. Looked fine for the part in his costume, but there was something else wrong and he couldn't quite work out what it was.

Two men were walking towards him, obviously of the same class as he was purporting to be, but with a sureness that was missing from most of the working folk of London.

They each carried blackthorn sticks, which could easily be used as clubs. He'd seen such villains passing through Holywell Street – bludgers, Mr Dugdale had called them. Men who'd cast respectable work aside in favour of a life of crime. They seemed to be in a hurry. Daniel wondered just what their mission was. Something nefarious, no doubt.

When they drew near to him, they crossed the Strand and vanished down one of those narrow alleys leading to the river. He felt an incredible temptation to follow them, to discover what they intended to do down there. It would be lovely to find some excuse to abandon his journey to Rat's Castle, any old excuse, for his nerve was failing every step of the way.

But he took a deep breath and walked on...

Had he lingered a moment longer, he would have seen another of those characters of the London streets – a pickpocket on the opposite side of the Strand, who stationed himself on a corner, looking down the alley where the two bludgers were entering a small shop with very dirty windows.

~

'An unprepossessing alley,' Wren Angier said, glancing down the vile little slope that led to the river.

Just a couple of shops on one side of the alley and the high walls of a blacking manufactory on the other. The kind of place where footpads might lurk and whores bring customers, picked up on the Strand on dark nights.

Quest nodded, but said nothing, recalling the times he'd come down the alley to Hawky Dewer's shop when he worked the streets as a dip, during a distant boyhood. Mr Dewer wasn't a fence in the strictest sense of the word.

His slop shop, selling much-used old clothes, was a legitimate trade, and Hawky would frown at the sudden arrival of stolen goods. He might secrete such hot materials for a friend for a day or two, but that was as far as his involvement with the criminal underworld went. Not that he didn't have many friends on the shadier side of illegality – he did. But he made a reasonable living from trading old clothes and never favoured the prospect of getting lagged.

'My golly, Billy! it's been an age since you've been down to see me.'

Quest thought that Hawky was looking much older these days, though his hair was still long and curly and his short beard remained dyed a vivid red. Dewar was sat at his counter reading an old book with a greasy leather cover.

'*Moll Flanders*, by Mr Defoe,' Dewer said. 'I've your friend Sticks to thank for introducing me to such a giddy read. Never read such literary pieces since I was a lad in Hockley-in-the-Hole. Oh, a rough place that was when I was a lad, though we could read and write. Oh, yes, my old dad had me taught letters and gave me a *Robinson Crusoe* he stole from outside a shop on Clerkenwell Green. But in recent times, I've been distracted by crime pamphlets from a little printer in Newgate Street. And particularly *The Newgate Shadow* – and I hear Mr Feedle has something to do with that?'

'Sticks never mentioned he'd been to see you.'

Hawky smiled. 'Not what you might call social visits, though he's wont to drop in when he's passing this way. Calls in to hear the gossip, you know? Good lad,

Sticks. I mind the days of his prizefighting. Many a bout I watched in the times I followed the fancy. Hardly leave the shop now... shame... shame...'

Quest had a sudden thought.

'Something I've never asked you. Is Hawky Dewer your real name? You see, I was on Dartmoor recently, and a rascal there, an old man called Weasel, told me that the moorland folk always call the devil Hawky Dewer...'

The shopkeeper gave him a broad smile.

'You're the first to see through my alias, Billy, why, the very first. My old mother came from Dartmoor, a place called Poundsgate. Come to London she did to make her fortune. Not that that happened! She was on the verge of falling into bad ways, when she met my old father. A Jew, he was... come all the way from Russia, so he said, though he could speak English better than most. My old ma could never pronounce his name and she was reluctant to use her own, so we settled on Dewer. Now that explains why. I was Emmanuel as a lad, but she called me Hawky - perhaps because I was full of mischief?'

He studied Wren Angier for a moment.

'And I know you too, don't I, sir. For all your disguise. Aren't you Angier, the landlord and money lender?' He glanced at Quest. 'You're keeping strange company, Billy?'

'Those were the bad old days, Mr Dewer,' Wren said. 'Before William Quest found me and saved my soul. I have a lot of evil ways to make up for, and now I am saved.'

Hawky Dewer reached across the counter and shook Wren's hand.

'There's more joy, etcetera... and any friend of Billy's is a friend of mine. As a matter of fact, Billy, I was minded to come and see you, but I couldn't leave the shop. I heard about poor Colley... you know I saw him only hours before he perished. Stood where you are now, he did.'

'And gave you a piece of paper.'

Dewer smiled and tapped the counter.

'I read it, of course. Colley insisted on that. That's why I was anxious to bring it to you. And he told me what happened, up in the 'dilly. A nightmare, Colley said, and what he told me, and his death in such a horrible way, has fair haunted my dreams.'

He turned away to the bare wall of London Brick that made up the back of the shop. He removed one of the bricks to reveal a cavity, reached in and pulled out a folded piece of paper, spreading it out on the counter.

'Read what it says, Billy. Not a nice message. Not nice at all. It fair frazzled poor Colley. Read what it says, Billy, for most of it's all about you.'

'Are you feeling tired, sir?'

Jonas Lyddon had been nodding away into an afternoon sleep, starting awake as James Brendon, his secretary, spoke. For a moment, he wondered just where he was and what time of the day it might be? These afternoon naps had become a habit since he'd given up his seat in Parliament. A bad habit for a man who felt that he had so much still to do.

He tapped the pile of papers in front of him on the desk.

'I've completed this, James. I want you to make a fair copy for my friend, William Quest. The original I intend to place in the public domain...'

Brendon glanced down at the title page, written in smart copperplate writing.

GIBBET HILL - AN ACCOUNT OF THE REBELLIOUS EVENTS WHICH TOOK PLACE ON DARTMOOR IN THE YEAR 1817

by

Mr Jonas Lyddon, formerly Member of Parliament for South Manchester

'Is it much altered from the draft you let me read, sir?'

'The chapters relating to Dartmoor, hardly at all. Though I've added a prefatory section relating to my time as a Blanketeer here in Manchester, before I arrived on the Moor. And an epilogue giving an account of my involvement in the massacre here in St Peter's Fields. It is important, James, that people never forget the massacre of Peterloo.'

Brendon sank down into a chair.

'The Peterloo Massacre is a matter of historical note, and your part in it is well known, sir. But the Dartmoor events - nobody is aware that you were the ringleader of the rebels there. Members of the militia died in that revolt - and not just the militia... by putting your account in to the public domain... well...'

Jonas Lyddon brushed away the annoying lock of grey hair that had taken to falling down over his eyes. He must get to a barber before he left Manchester. Must do several things...

'You believe that they might still put the hangman's noose around my throat, James? Well, I suppose they could. Happily, there's no danger of my corpse swinging on a gibbet any more. That was one of the better reforms I managed to get through Parliament.'

'They still hang people outside Newgate Prison, sir. The Class would argue that what you did on Dartmoor amounted to treason as well as murder. Your distinguished career in Parliament and your contribution to the Chartist movement, not to mention all the other reforms you championed, wouldn't save you. Your good works would be cast away from memory if your enemies close in on you. This is a very dangerous document.'

'I believe I am past caring, James. Ah, you are young, you grew up in a better age. There is at least now some hope of social reform, though there is much still to do. These events on Dartmoor were nearly forty years ago. I was young then, and we were living under a dictatorship. We *had* to fight the way we did. Do you not see that?'

'The law gives no time limit for the prosecution of such offences, Mr Lyddon. They would hang you as readily today as they would have done then. Your reforms have made you many enemies.'

'Every man in politics has enemies.'

'Have you thought, sir, of your associates?'

'Associates? Comrades in arms, you mean? Mostly dead...'

Lyddon's mind drifted through a procession of long gone faces. Captain Tremaine gone. Aunt Ford sleeping in Manaton churchyard. Cock Lorel? Well, the Gypsy would be ancient if he were still alive and hard to find. Billy Links had died of a consumption only last year...

'You are right, of course,' he said at last. 'I saw that rogue Weasel, but a few weeks ago, hale and hearty and still supping the moorland cider. Harry Blizzard and his wife... true. The most dangerously placed would be Jasper Feedle – a young curly-haired rascal he was then... yes, but he's still involved in rebellious activities alongside William Quest.'

Brendon rubbed his chin in thought.

'You could excise their names – if you intend to go on with this.'

'I could, James, but you see in a century from now, perhaps men will want to write the history of those times. Those who fought will deserve the credit for what they did. Oh, don't look at me like that, my lad! You think it vanity that I need to record what I did on Dartmoor? No... no... not vanity, more a regard for historical truth. Or call it the foolishness of an old man.'

'Then what is to be done?'

'Your fair copy will be safe enough in the hands of William Quest. As for mine, well, I intend to put it into the safe keeping of another friend from my political days. You've heard me talk of Joshua Blount. I intend to give the original to him.

As you know, he is on the governing board of the British Museum, a remarkable attainment given his disability.'

'You intend to deposit your account in the library *there?*'

'That is my thought – but with the proviso that the document be sealed for thirty years, before it can be read at all. They made such arrangements for others when I was on the governing board. It seems the best solution. So please take it and start work on your copy. One more thing, James. Now I'm no longer a member of Parliament, I intend to give up this Manchester house. I shall only reside in London, now. I think – if you'll excuse me – I'll have a little sleep...'

When his secretary had left, Jonas Lyddon lay back on the *chaise longue*, and sank into a proper sleep. At first his dreams were restful, walking across the heathery slopes of Hameldon and Easdon. But then his memories carried him back to the ambush at Holne Bridge and the rattle of musketry. That woke him, briefly.

But, after a moment or two, he drifted into unbroken rest.

Seven

It was a much worse place than Daniel Moonlight had imagined, a foul little tavern of low ceilings and smoke-blackened walls, sunk beneath the ground down a flight of steep steps.

The stench of unwashed human bodies had been overwhelming from the moment he'd wandered away from the Strand and into the winding alleys leading towards St Giles Church.

The dark of evening had fallen and only the occasional gas lamp lit his way.

He had scarce left the more reputable highway before some ancient crone approached him, toothless and with wild grey hair, offering to sell herself for tuppence. He'd brushed her aside and strode swiftly on into an alley that was scarcely broader than his shoulders.

At one point he stumbled over something lying on the cobbles. A drunken child? A fair-haired boy of about twelve, the face filthy with grime, naked except for a few rags. Ribs poking through bruised and sallow skin. The lad's eyes reflected the glow of the distant gaslight.

As he stood there, Daniel came to the terrible realisation that the boy was dead. A rat was nibbling at the decaying remnants of the left foot.

Daniel hurried on, aware that there were figures in nearby doorways looking in his direction. He felt a trembling in his spine, an instinctive notion of danger. He yearned for the light again. A hundred yards further on he found it, pouring up from a hole in the ground, through the open doorway of the tavern.

He nearly turned back as he gazed down the grimy steps and smelt the foul air coming up from below. But he steeled himself. He'd come so far, after all.

Daniel almost stumbled down the steps and found himself in the long but narrow room - with walls so filthy that they seemed to absorb the light from the candles that ill-lit the dreadful place.

The room was heaving with unwashed sweaty bodies, most dressed in rags. Threatening faces all seemed to be looking at him. Rat's Castle indeed. He ordered a measure of small beer, noticing the silence as he approached the serving table and the suspicious glance of the one-eyed landlord who served him.

He thanked God he had dressed in old clothes to make this expedition, silently cursing Dugdale, who'd first mentioned the horrors of Rat's Castle to him. It had been a stupid idea to come.

He recalled Dugdale's words...

Well, there's Rat's Castle. Few places worse'n that. But I wouldn't advise it. Even the crushers go in there armed and mob-handed. But I know what you literary gents are like...

Daniel Moonlight had sought out descriptions of the place by other writers. Ghastly, but he knew how much those slumming brothers of the pen were given to exaggeration.

Nowhere in Victoria's realm could really be as bad as all that, surely?

But within minutes of journeying into the slums, Daniel could quite believe that those other chroniclers of the underworld had moderated their account of Rat's Castle, not wishing to give too much of a shock to a genteel readership.

A girl in a tatty dress, her breasts completely exposed, had begun to sing, swaying from side to side as she delivered the tuneless melody. Once or twice between verses she stared at Daniel and drew a tongue over her lips. Then she resumed the ballad, making obscene gestures in accompaniment to the words. At the conclusion of the entertainment, the landlord strode over to her and forced his tongue into her mouth and a hand up her dress. The girl groaned and laughed.

'Got summat to sell?'

A man with bulging eyes and foul breath had eased his way on to the bench next to Daniel.

'Not seen yer here afore,' the man continued. 'I knows everyone about here. I don't know yer...'

'New here... new to London,' Daniel muttered. 'First time in this place.'

'Where yer from?'

'The country...' said Daniel, easing his way further down the bench. 'A long way away.'

The man gave a burst of drunken laughter.

'He's from the country!' he yelled at the top of his voice. 'From green-land! We knows his type, don't we my lads!'

A deathly hush fell over the tavern. Everyone stood stock still and stared at Daniel Moonlight.

'And don't he talk proper...' the man went on. 'A proper little gent come among us.' A look of mock-concern crossed his face. 'He looks frightened, my lads. Poor little chap.' He put his face close to Daniel. 'No need to be frightened of us, is there boys?'

There was a raucous cry of denial.

Daniel stood.

'Oh, not thinking of leaving, were we? Yer've only just got here and yer beer's only half drunk.'

The man took in the room with a sweep of his hand. 'I don't think 'as how he likes our company, my lads! And here we are, just trying' to be friendly.'

'I really do have to go,' Daniel said firmly.

'D'yer really? Oh, I don't think so. Yer ain't paid yer dues yet.'

'I paid for the beer...'

'Those ain't the dues I mean. Yer come to our Castle and yer ain't paid the entrance fee.' The man laughed uproariously for a few seconds. And then the laughter died. His grimy hand reached out and seized Daniel's shoulder. 'Or the fee to leave...'

'What do you want?'

'Oh, not much! Just what's in yer pocket. And the clothes off yer back. Yer too well dressed to come to our Castle. And those what comes slummin' ain't allowed to leave without payin' us a tribute.'

'I'll see you in hell!'

The man looked around the room.

'I think as how we're goin' to have to take 'em, my boys. Who wants to help me strip him naked?'

He reached out and grabbed Daniel's other shoulder.

'Then we'll send him home to his mama...'

He began to ease back the old coat that Daniel was wearing.

He laughed again.

'He's reachin' into his pocket, boys! What's he a-reachin' for? Let me see...'

The man's hand followed the path of Daniel's own. But before it was halfway down Daniel's chest, the man suddenly reeled back with a cry of pain. Daniel had seen something crash down on the exploring hand. A piece of wood. A cudgel? No, a crutch. He became aware of a little man, in a green jacket, standing on one side of him.

'Damn yer, Feedle!' the man shouted, 'this ain't none of yer business!'

'Well, as I just happen to be passin' I decided to make it me business. The lad's one of mine and I won't stand by an' see him robbed by someone like yerself.'

The cripple whispered into Daniel's ear. 'Keep your pistol in your jacket, you bloody fool. They'll top the both of us to get a weapon like that. Just do as I tells you and follow me out of here.'

Daniel Moonlight took his hand away from the inside of his coat.

'We're leavin' now,' said Jasper. 'An' if you fancies followin' you'll have the Bludger to deal with. He's outside an' in a bad mood. And he hates you at the best o' times.'

Jasper Feedle backed away to the door, dragging Daniel with him. The town seemed to whirl by as they ran at great speed through the alleys, past the entries of sinister blind closes, until emerging on to a better-lit place that Daniel recognised as Oxford Street.

'You travel fast for a man with one leg?'

'In my line of work I have to,' said Feedle.

Some distant church bells struck eight of the clock.

Jasper Feedle led Daniel a few hundred yards further on, before he stopped and faced the young man.

'You knows where you've just bin, don't yer?'

'Rat's Castle...' Daniel replied.

'You're not entirely stupid then?'

'I'm not stupid at all. I wanted to see the place.'

'No, you ain't stupid, you're stirrin' mad. You goes in there, in the worse disguise I ever saw. You talks like a toff and your face is far too clean for a rookery rat. Not a bit of grime on it. And then you almost brandishes a barker...'

'A what?'

'That!'

Jasper tapped the concealed pistol.

'I carry it for protection,' said Daniel. 'I wasn't intending to use it. I was just going to threaten them with it.'

'They'd strip the skin off your bones to get hold of a pistol. Someone'd make a fortune sellin' that to a fence. And you'd have ended up floating in the sewers.'

'The man who threatened me then... he's dangerous?'

'You're mad! You oughter be in Bedlam! Jabez Mostin's topped more blokes wots been slummin' than you've been to prayer meetings.'

Daniel straightened himself up.

'Then I'm grateful to you, mister...?'

'Just call me Jasper, given that we're not likely to meet again.'

'Who's this Bludger you mentioned? The one you said was outside? I thought a bludger was a footpad?'

'And so it is, but this Bludger's somethin' special. And he ain't within miles of the Castle tonight. It was only the threat of him that got you out of there alive.'

'I'd like to meet this Bludger,' said Daniel. 'I'm a writer of books and reviews for the press. It would be interesting to interview such a man.'

Jasper gave a despairing look up at the sky.

'I don't thinks as how he'd appreciate the honour!'

'What a pity!'

'Pity? You'd know no pity if you met the Bludger. Where d'you live?'

'I'm up from the country. I've taken rooms in Holywell Street.'

'Oh,' said Jasper, 'you writes *them* sort of books?'

'I've come to London to write literature. And to seek someone. Is it hard to find someone in London?'

Jasper gave a little laugh.

'Depends if they wants to be found. If they've gone into hidin,' then you've got no chance. If they're anywhere like the Castle, the chances are they're already dead. As you'll be if you goes back in there. Just remember, I won't be there the next time. What's yer name, boy?'

'Daniel. Daniel... Moonlight.'

'Then take some advice from one as knows, Daniel. Stick to the main roads and keep away from the alleys. And leave that barker at home. That way you might just avoid having your throat cut. If you must carry a weapon, get yourself a good stout blackthorn, or even a discreet swordstick. There's a shop in Cheapside... Critzman's. You go in there and tell 'em Jasper sent you...'

And without another word, Jasper walked away at terrific speed along Oxford Street, his stout wooden crutch tapping the paving with a regular and menacing beat.

~

'This means trouble,' said Josef Critzman, as he studied the piece of paper that Quest had spread on the table. 'Why should someone compose such a threatening list? A paper that cost poor Colley his life?'

Quest read the paper again.

Nota Bene

Item One: *the destruction of the man who calls himself William Quest, and the recovery of the notebook that once belonged to the head of the Secret Service.*

Item Two: *The removal of the dangerous radical, Jonas Lyddon, as his removal might be used to achieve the ambitions stated in the above Item.*

Item Three: *Joshua Blount is a most dangerous man, on that we all agree. He too must be made to vanish from the face of the world.*

Tenebrae

'I wouldn't take it so seriously, but for the fact that they killed Colley Johnson,' Quest said. 'Few people know about the existence of the notebook we have hidden away – fewer still its contents. We've used the notebook to protect ourselves, given that the information in it could bring about the destruction of much of the establishment, from royalty and politicians down. They haven't dared touch us, because of it. Yet the men in that house in Piccadilly know all about it. So we assume that they are all well connected.'

'But who are they?' asked Isaac Critzman. 'And supposing you go into this house, Tenebrae, Will? Colley told Pikey Nibbs that it stood empty apart from a table and chairs. What would you hope to find there?'

'If the faceless man and his friends are there, we could force the truth from them,' suggested Wren Angier. 'Or we could just wipe them out and settle the matter that way.'

'Might be the simplest solution,' said Sticks.

Quest sat back in his chair and stared into the fire.

'There's no doubt in my mind that we must at least go and look inside the house,' he said. 'I suspect we'll find it empty, but who's to say? It's not just me being threatened here, but Jonas Lyddon and his friend Joshua Blount. I don't know the latter, except by reputation.'

'Blount's a most remarkable man,' said Isaac. 'I've known him for a great many years. Perhaps it's time you met, Will. I think you'd be most impressed. He can be found at the new British Museum – indeed he's been much involved in planning the museum's expansion and the new buildings. Blount is currently working on the proposals for the splendid new library there. A remarkable man, as you'll find out. I'll give you a letter of introduction.'

'It might be as well,' said Quest. 'I'll explain the circumstances to him and we must increase the protection we're giving to Mr Lyddon as well. I'll visit Blount as soon as possible.'

'We mustn't forget we have to deal with the Cooper gang,' said Sticks. 'We need to be in Saffron Hill tomorrow night. Ready for an affray. But I'm game to come into the 'dilly house the night after that.'

Josef Critzman looked across to his brother.

'Isaac, we should postpone our cathedral trip on the morrow. There is too much happening for us to be journeying to Canterbury and Rochester at the moment, do you not think?'

'Perhaps...'

'No', said Quest. 'You go and enjoy the expedition. There's little you can do here, but give me a note of introduction to Blount. Better that you take this opportunity for an interval away from London. Sticks will mind the walking stick shop...'

Josef glanced in the direction of the old prizefighter.

'You are sure you will be able to cope?'

'Done it before...'

'Or there's always Jasper,' Quest said mischievously.

'I think not,' said Josef, 'better Sticks here. Figures were never dear Jasper's strong point, ah here he is...'

Jasper Feedle stood in the doorway leading from the shop.

'Did you get any gossip at Rat's Castle?' asked Quest.

'Nothin'. Well, a little adventure, but not pertainin' to Colley Johnson.'

'A pity,' said Quest. 'But we've a few things to tell you.'

Eight

'I believe it would be as well to return to London very soon,' said Jonas Lyddon. 'There's nothing more I can do here in Manchester. Three more days – then I'll take the railway down. Ah, so much easier now. Though I confess I used to rather enjoy the journey on foot.'

'I have the fair copy of your Dartmoor account ready, sir,' said Brendon. 'Though I feel that just being in possession of it is a positive danger. I appreciate your motives in producing the document, but I believe we must be very wary. Spies working for the home secretary are all around us. And despite your retirement from Parliament, the Class still have a great interest in you.'

Lyddon chuckled.

'I'm honoured to have spent much of this present century causing them trouble!'

'Sir... if they arrest you on some capital charge, your age and your considerable reputation will not save you. Is it your wish that I should accompany you on the railway to London?'

'I think not, James. I'm mindful of the fact that you're only just back from there. Besides, much better that we travel separately. We must keep our two manuscripts apart. I want you to go to Liverpool. In three days' time, there's a steam packet sailing for London. You are to take the original to Mr Blount, with a note I shall write. Then you are to go to see William Quest at his home in Tavistock Place. I shall already be there and will have handed over your copy. You may leave for Liverpool tonight. Book a passage on the steamer and stay at some discreet hotel until the time comes to make your voyage.'

'But, sir... you haven't been well... would it not make more sense for us to travel together?'

Lyddon shook his head.

'Better this way, James. Two simple journeys. One on the train and one on a ship. Safe enough, I think – and every precaution taken. Neither as dangerous as the perilous travels of my past.' He took Brendon and shook his hand. 'My friend, I will see you in London!'

~

A fine London morning, Inspector Honour Bright thought as he looked through his window at Scotland Yard, though he did wonder whether it might be a false brightness, the kind that preceded a showery day. London mornings were often like that, bright starts descending into darkness, much like life itself.

There was a tap at the door.

'Come!'

Bright turned to find Parkin hesitating in the doorway.

'You may come in, Parkin. Indeed, you may sit in that chair, for I have some excellent news for you.'

'Inspector?'

Bright sat down opposite the fair-haired young man, noting the intelligence in that narrow face and the smartness in his appearance. Rare qualities in some of the constables of these times.

'How long have you been a constable, Parkin?'

'Four years, sir, but I've only been in the detective division for three months.'

'Have you not sought promotion?'

'I've sought it, sir, but promotions are hard to come by. There are a great many constables and few opportunities to move on and upwards. It has always been my wish to be in the detective force. But achieving that took a great deal of effort and lobbying.'

'Lobbying?'

'It is hard to rise through the ranks of the Metropolitan Police, sir. Especially if you have few friends and no inside influence. Might I speak frankly?'

'You may.'

'Sir, I've spent all my days on the streets of London. I know the city well. My father is a druggist and has his own shop, but that provides employment only for himself and my elder brother. I cast around for a situation I could feel passionate about, trying several trades before joining the police. I feel at home in the work I'm doing now, almost as though I was born to it.'

Bright could see the passion in the young man's face. He remembered his own struggles to get on in the police. He'd spent three years in the army, before being invalided out. It had taken a great effort to even become a constable, given that he had a weakness of the lungs. Everything he had achieved since had been down to hard work and determination, and the sort of passion he saw in the face of this young man.

'Well, I'm pleased to tell you, Parkin, that you are to move at least one rung up the ladder. When I saw Commissioner Mayne yesterday, I expressed my admiration for your work in this present case. Following my recommendation, Parkin, Sir Richard has agreed to promote you to sergeant in the detective force.'

Parkin stood and then sat back down on the edge of the seat.

'I'm very honoured, sir. Thank you for your recommendation. I don't...'

Bright waved a hand.

'It is nothing. Now let us get back to work...'

'Well... as instructed, I kept a watch in Cheapside last night. At the walking stick and umbrella shop belonging to the Critzman brothers. Quest was there, and his friend Angier. Feedle, the cripple, joined them much later on. There was another individual, but I only saw him briefly through the shop glass. My surmise is that that person was Albert Sticks, who poses as Quest's valet but is, in reality, a partner in this criminal conspiracy.'

'I know of Sticks - a notorious bare-knuckle prizefighter in his day. Did this meeting last long?'

'About two hours before the meeting broke up. I tailed Quest and Sticks back to the house in Tavistock Place. Constable Thessaly followed Angier back to his set of rooms at Albany. The Critzman brothers and Feedle clearly spent the night in their quarters above the shop.'

'Two hours...' Bright considered. 'Clearly an important meeting. Something going on, Parkin. Something going on. We must arrange a roster of constables, so that these dangerous characters are watched all the time. Your first task as sergeant will be to arrange that.'

'Very good, sir.'

Parkin stood and was at the door when Bright called out to him.

'Do you know Sergeant Berry, Parkin?'

'Not well, sir. To talk to sometimes. He's usually very busy with Inspector Anders. I believe they are both now detailed to bringing an end to the vice that plagues this town.'

Bright rubbed his chin.

'What I'm going to say next is... well... it's a delicate situation, Parkin. Both Inspector Anders and Berry have struck up a most unwise relationship with this villain Quest. I know why and... to be fair to them, there are matters concerning Quest I can't confide in you just yet. But in view of this, it is most important that neither Anders or Berry gets to hear of the mission we are undertaking. Or any news of our endeavours - whatsoever...'

'I understand, sir.'

A clever lad, Bright considered after Parkin had left the room.

A clever lad indeed.

~

Daniel Moonlight, on one of his long walks of exploration of London, found himself walking for the first time along Cheapside. He knew it to be one of the most ancient trading streets in London.

His new author hero, Mr George Borrow, had described it so well in his recent and very strange book *Lavengro*. Daniel wished he could emulate such vivid and colourful descriptions of the urban scene. How thrilling to have the adventures with Gypsies, rogues and bruisers that Mr Borrow had enjoyed.

How it would all be grist to the writer's mill...

And then he remembered his encounter with the man with the crutch, in the low tavern in St Giles. Surely that was an adventure that might feature in a novel?

He thought again of the villainous and threatening landlord, the young and nearly naked girl who had mouthed the vulgar song, how he had nearly been robbed or worse. How the cripple had prevented him producing his pistol?

Surely that adventure could be written up? albeit, toned down for a genteel audience?

It was quite a thought.

Dare he go back and visit the rookery again?

Mr Dickens or Mr Borrow surely would.

And then Daniel recalled the very real fear he had felt when he was pinned against the wall of the tavern. How he thought that death, or at least robbery and humiliation, were very near. Perhaps carrying a pistol into such a place was too much of a risk, as the man with the crutch had suggested?

He stepped away from an approaching throng of pedestrians, raising his hat as some ladies went by. On turning, he found himself looking into the window of a most peculiar shop. The display was filled with racks of walking sticks for the countryside and more ornamental canes for town use. A notice to the rear of the window advertised "Mr Samuel Fox's Patent Steel-Ribbed Umbrellas" – with some examples of that novelty standing in a wooden box, just under the lowest lettering of the board.

Now *there* was a thought!

He had noticed how most of the gentlemen of the place seemed to carry a cane. Something light and decorated around the wealthiest districts of the town, stouter sticks in the rougher areas. After his recent alarm, he could understand why. A stick was not just a support for walking, but could be a formidable weapon.

Daniel Moonlight had half-forgotten the recommendation the man called Jasper had made the night before. Of how a stout stick – or even a swordstick – might be of far more use in the more dangerous areas of the town than a pistol. Cheapside, of course! That's what the man had said – a shop called Critzman's...

And there was that name over the door.

Messrs Critzman – Canes, Sticks and Umbrellas for All Occasions

He had scarcely read the words before he found himself inside the shop. The sight that greeted him made him almost believe he was back in the rookery.

A stout and very muscular giant of a man stood to one side of the counter, a challenging look coming from his deep-set eyes. He was over fifty but still very clearly fit and active. His bulbous nose seemed to have only just survived numerous breakings, and the ears sprawled outwards like fleshy cauliflowers.

Daniel was lost for words at the sight of the creature, and all the more amazed when it gave a low bow of the head.

Its voice when it came was almost a growl.

'Good day to you, sir. Nice to see the rain's gone away. But not for long being London. We do a fine line in these damn-fangled umbrellas if that's your desire?'

'You are the proprietor?'

The man scratched his red nose.

'Well, not exactly in the way of being the owner as such, though I do have a few shares in the enterprise. The Messrs Critzman are on their travels at this present instant, so I'm minding the shop. I just seen Mr Josef and Mr Isaac off at the railway station. Was it a walking cane you was after?'

Daniel looked around at the hundreds of sticks in their racks all around the walls of the shop. A huge display of umbrellas covered much of the floor.

'Yes, a good stout stick...'

'Nothing like one for aiding the feet and seeing off the rascals what plagues our streets.'

'Exactly my desire,' said Daniel. 'But I've never really used one before and am in need of guidance. I met a man last night who gave me a recommendation of your products. A man with a crutch, his name was Jasper...'

The prizefighter looked Daniel up and down.

'Oh, yes?...'

'He was an aid to me when I was in something of a dangerous situation.'

The man gave a smile.

'Was he indeed? You're perhaps a stranger in town?' he asked.

'I am indeed. I've not been in London for very long. I've spent most of my life in the countryside.'

The man nodded.

'Well, there's good folks here and bad. It's wise to be prepared for both. But there's mostly good 'uns here in Cheapside. Have you been to our street before?'

Daniel shook his head.

'I've heard of it, of course. Most recently in the writings of Mr Borrow?'

'Mr Borrow!'

The man's voice filled the shop.

'You know of Mr Borrow?'

'Knows of him? I should say I knows of him. He was at a fight I was once in and wagered upon me. I think he'd a liked to put out his fists and try a bout with me himself. I read his books all the time. He's up there with the greats like Mr Dickens and Mr Defoe.'

'I like all of them too,' said Daniel, excitedly. 'It was partly the reading of them that brought me to London.' He suddenly felt shy. 'You see... I'm trying to write books myself.'

The man's eyes widened.

'You're a literary gent? Then let me shake you by the hand. I'd be privileged to learn your name so that I might read your own books...'

The man almost crushed Daniel's hand as he gave it a most vigorous shaking.

'It's Daniel. Daniel Moonlight. Though that's really just a *nom de plume*, Mister...'

'And mine's Sticks. Properly Albert Sticks, though I can't abide the Mister or the Albert. So just Sticks...'

Daniel felt the look of embarrassment on his own face.

'To be honest, Mister...er, Sticks, I haven't yet published any books... though I'm trying to write one at the moment. I have had some reviews and essays printed in some of the journals...'

'Only a matter of time, I'm sure,' said Sticks. 'It's rare I get the chance to talk to a lover of books. Though a gent I knows is a great reader and has a fine collection of books in his library. Who knows? Perhaps if you was to drop in later in the week he might be here, so I can introduce you.'

'That would be quite splendid!'

'Then I'll mention you to him... and in the meantime, let's find you a good stick to wield about the place. And there'll be a special price for a literary gent such as your good self. Do you want a cane just for walking, or for protection as well? We has them all here. Heavy ash walking sticks, and blackthorns that'd open the head of any unfortunate bludger who happens to accost you. We've got sword sticks that'll see off the most vicious of characters. Though they needs a little instruction as to use. Come and look along the wall over here...'

Sticks took him to the rear wall of the shop and reached up for a cane of dark rattan wood. He twisted the handle and drew out a slender and deadly blade.

'One of our best-selling lines of merchandise,' he said. 'The blade might look a trifle thin, but it's of the finest steel. Some of the inferior stick shops sell sword sticks of very bad quality. The kind that'd get snagged going in through the flesh or against the ribs. But ours? See how flexible that blade is?' He drew two fingers along the metal until they reached the point. 'That's so it bends round any obstruction. And the ends as sharp as a knife at Surgeons' Hall...'

'I hadn't thought of a sword stick,' said Daniel.

The old bruiser regarded him for a moment or two.

'Have you been in many fights?' he inquired.

'Not since I was a boy at school,' said Daniel, 'and even then I usually lost the bout.'

'Mmm, what you need, my lad, is instruction. Now, I was a scrapper from the moment I was born. Always in trouble, always in a brawl. If I hadn't gone into the prize ring, I'd a probably been topped by now. But it earned me a living and I won more than I lost.'

He reached out and seized Daniel's hands.

'Too soft for brawling,' he said after a brief study. 'And fighting with a sword stick takes a bit of skill. And the other disadvantage is you might kill someone who don't deserve it and find yourself on a rope's end outside Newgate.'

'A stick then?'

'Something heavy, but not too heavy as to manoeuvrin'. Something like this one.'

He looked around and produced a stick of stout ash, still bearing the original bark and with a knob at the end for a fist to grasp.

He passed it to Daniel.

'And just the right length too, as though it was cut for you,' he said. 'Such a stick's a good friend. It'll take the weight off your feet as you walk, and makes an admirable neddy stick if you runs into bother.'

Daniel held the ash-stick up to the light and admired the colour of the bark. He waved it to and fro and raised it above his head, as though rehearsing a downward blow at some assailant's head.

Mr Sticks took in a loud breath.

'No, no, not like that! Such a blow looks powerful but it's easily countered. I can see you needs some instruction in the noble arts.' He thought for a moment, head slightly to one side as he regarded Daniel. 'Would you be free at dawn tomorrow morning?'

Daniel wondered at the purpose of the question.

'I could be,' he said at last. 'What for?'

'Well, it seems to me that I might give you some instruction on just how to use that fine stick. But when I says dawn I means dawn. First light. Can you be about then?'

'Well, yes...'

'Then be in Hyde Park at that time. On Rotten Row, just up from the Corner. I knows a quiet spot in the trees, where I can show you just how to win a match with such a stick. It'll take but an hour. And you can pay for the stick when you sees how you gets on with it.'

'I appreciate the offer, but I have very limited funds. I can afford the ash, but probably not a course of instruction.'

Sticks glowered.

'Now did I say anything about money?'

'But you can't be unrewarded?'

Sticks thought for a moment.

'I'll tell you the deal,' he said. 'You're in the way of becoming a literary gent. And I likes my books. When your volumes are published, you can give me copies to read. That'd be a richer reward than any. And with that I takes your hand. But dawn, mind! I waits not a minute longer!'

He grasped Daniel's hand so tightly that it brought tears to the young man's eyes.

Sticks watched Daniel as he left the shop, remembering Jasper's account of the incident at Rat's Castle. Nice lad, he thought, though not really built to be a scrapper. But something could be done to help him. And there was something familiar about his face? Sticks wondered why he seemed to recognise him. No, no good, he couldn't place meeting him in the past.

And yet?...

~

'You worry me, Sir Richard.'

Sir Richard Mayne looked across his desk at the man now in charge of Her Majesty's Secret Service. Benjamin Wissilcraft had put on at least two stone in weight since the last time he'd been seen within the precincts of Scotland Yard. Perhaps due to his recent family tragedy, the police Commissioner considered. Wissilcraft's great bulk entirely hid the chair he was sitting in.

'You worry me a very great deal, Commissioner.'

'In what way?'

Wissilcraft's words came between the gasps of his breathing, as though his weight was pushing inwards on his lungs. He paused, now and again, to take in a full breath as he delivered his opinion.

'Quest... William Quest... what else?'

Sir Richard tapped the desk.

'Is it not my task to bring this man to justice? He's a villain, a cold-blooded killer. Worse than that – a traitor, seeking the overthrow of our Class. Surely it is my duty to get this man on to the Newgate gallows?'

'But have you considered the consequences?'

'Ah, the infamous notebook! Tell me, Wissilcraft, are we all supposed to tremble with fear because Quest has information that might be damaging to our masters? No, rest assured, I never tremble. I intend to get Quest arrested and to bring him before me on some capital charge. Once I have him in a cell, you won't find him quite as bold, my friend. What if his associates should then use the notebook to expose the doings of a few fools in our politics and royalty? Scandals soon pass. None of them could be so threatening as the politics of this revolutionary, who wants a world where the many prosper rather than just the select few.'

Wissilcraft took in a breath.

'I do believe... Sir Richard... that you underestimate the dangers to the Class in the notebook. Very well, we may not be... living in the revolutionary times we saw in the last decade... but the spirit of rebellion is still there... a red volcano bubbling away under the surface... waiting for just a chance to erupt. And your bold actions might just be the spark that triggers an uprising.'

'I don't see that at all! It's individuals that promote revolution. Not scandals and notebooks. It's those individuals we have to destroy – not scraps of paper. Remove rebels like Quest from the equation and the revelations in some notebook become irrelevant.'

'If you believe that... Sir Richard... you are a fool!'

Mayne jumped to his feet.

'How dare you insult me in my own office!'

Wissilcraft waved a hand.

'Forgive me, Sir Richard. I was simply passing on what would be the thoughts of my masters – who all consider that Quest should be left alone. They also recognise that... in the past... Quest has actually been of some use to our country.'

Mayne sat down and glared at the spymaster.

'Are you suggesting that we should tolerate this brigand?'

'Not at all, but why rock the boat unnecessarily? Especially now?'

'Because he is a criminal!'

Wissilcraft sighed. 'There are a great many criminals in our society. Some of them in the highest positions of power. Our country rubs along with them all quite well, really... better to let sleeping dogs lie.'

'I do not agree.'

'And that's why you now have Inspector Anders... the best detective at the Yard... chasing down the purveyors of naughty publications?'

'Anders was much too close to this man Quest. Almost culpable in some of Quest's criminal activities. Anders needed to be removed. He made mistakes when he investigated Quest. Far too many errors. That is why I've put matters into the capable hands of Inspector Bright. A detective officer less likely to fall under the spell of this rascal.'

Wissilcraft leaned forward into a position that made his breathing even more difficult. Mayne thought that the man might actually be dying, in the sanctity of the Commissioner's office, and that would be a great embarrassment. The face of his visitor had turned a bright red. Wissilcraft raised his head, taking in a great breath, then his words came out in stutters.

'Very well... for now... but there is to be no actual arrest... without my personal approval... is that clearly understood?... no arrest at all... and do remember... Sir Richard... you are not liked... not liked by some of my masters... not liked at all... and if you put them in the way of a scandal... they might... very well have your head.'

Nine

'Is Jasper in place?'

Sticks was leaning against the wall, holding his blackthorn cosh.

'He's there. And Mr Angier. To be honest, we could do with a few more. There's six of 'em. And they're all a damn sight younger than us.'

'Feeling your age?'

'Aren't we all?'

'Let's get on with it.'

'I'll be watching your back then,' Sticks said.

'Nice to know!'

The gas lights fluttered as Quest walked down the street in Saffron Hill. It all seemed so familiar. The times that members of Monkshood, the secret society that fought for justice, had done this. Fighting for the poor and oppressed. Taking the battle to an enemy that the law didn't want to touch.

Just the four of them. Sticks was right, they were outnumbered. The old fighter was still handy with his cosh and his fists. And despite being one-legged and over sixty, Jasper Feedle was a bonny warrior. But Wren Angier hadn't been brought up to brawling in the streets. He still fought like the gent he was, though Sticks had taught him a few dirty tricks.

They hadn't had time to rope in any more street fighters. Word had come late that these Field Lane louts intended to trash the *Merry Parson* tavern. Old Barry, the landlord, could no longer afford to pay them protection money. Barry was a friend of Jasper. They'd served together in the 95th Rifles all those years ago, when Wellington had battled them through Spain.

These villains might not have guns, but they'd certainly know how to fight in the filthiest of ways. Not just with knuckle-duster fists, but life-preservers as well. A violent encounter then, but the lesson had to be taught.

If the poor spent all their time attacking each other, they'd never take on the rich.

Out of the corner of his eye, Quest detected a movement. An alley ran parallel to the street, connected by a few narrow passages. Someone was walking in the same direction. You had to be careful. You never knew who it might be? Quest glanced again. Just a stevedore making his way home from his work on the river.

He breathed again, but it could so easily have been a crusher.

Quest reached into his inside pocket and checked that the little percussion pistol was in its place. Not that he wanted to use it. He only wanted to hand out a good leathering.

Apart from the sound of water dripping down the walls after the afternoon rain, the street was quiet. The gaslights hardly lit it, but Quest had a great ability to see in the dark.

He glanced over his shoulder.

There was no sign of Sticks, but he knew he was there. For a big fellow, Albert Sticks made no more sound than a falling feather. Sticks was one of the very best people in London for putting on the dodge.

Then, in the distance, was a brighter light. Coming from the place where the street ended in another vile thoroughfare of slums reaching up from Saffron Hill.

Where the *Merry Parson* was to be found.

Apart from the gaslights, the residents often kept fires in braziers going all night. To light up the street and keep the rats at bay. Despite their poverty, the residents of this street off Saffron Hill were honest folk. They didn't deserve to be persecuted by rogues who wanted to take from them the little they had.

There were a thousand streets like this in London. Places where people dreamed. Streets where most folk were disillusioned. The streets of the poor outnumbered the places where the rich lived. The wealth of the nation was clutched in just a few hands.

Quest wondered just how much it would take to get the poor to rise up against their exploiters?

Then he started as he collided with a boy. The young lad had moved out of one of the doorways, so silently that had he been an enemy, Quest might be dead. He looked down at the lad in the dim light. The usual pinched face, the starved body, the pleading eyes. A tiny hand held out expecting, well, something...

For William Quest it was like seeing his own young ghost. He remembered his first months in London, after he'd fled Norfolk as a child. Begging in just such a way, before turning to petty crime so that he might survive.

Quest had been one of the fortunate, taken up by a wealthy protector, persuaded to become the leader of Monkshood.

The child's lips trembled. Quest knew the symptoms. The boy was too hungry even to utter the words. Begging was hard to do on an empty stomach.

Quest felt into his pocket. He carried little coin on these expeditions, just a sovereign and a sixpence. He wanted to give the boy the sovereign, but that would be stupidity. If the youngster was caught with it by the crushers, they'd take him up for dipping into a rich man's pocket.

Better to give him the tanner.

He slipped the little coin into the boy's palm. The child studied it for a moment and managed a smile. The most he'd ever had before in his entire life of begging was a penny. He gave Quest another smile and walked slowly away.

'You can't forget, can you?'

Sticks was beside him.

'Let's get on with it,' Quest said.

From somewhere up ahead there was a wild neighing and a bunch of horses crossed the end of the street, led by a struggling ostler.

Suddenly, there was a burst of shouting ahead of him. Up where the braziers threw out their heat and light. Quest knew they were too late as he saw a huddle of men pushing someone against the tavern wall.

In the light of the braziers and gas lamps, he could see that it was Old Barry.

Someone was yelling in the landlord's face.

'Told yer we'd be back, old man. Told yer so. If yer'd paid up, we wouldn't be here. How stupid can yer be?'

The lout who was talking held the old man by the throat. He was pulling his fist back when Quest ran forward and grabbed his arm.

'Not as stupid as you,' Quest said.

The lout swung round. Quest recognised him. Silas Cooper. A footpad with ambition. Like Quest, he'd started working these streets as a pickpocket and moved on to more vicious crimes. Cooper had gathered a gang; the five villains assembled around him. They'd all been lagged at one time or another. Served sentences in the nearby gaol at Clerkenwell.

Never gone so far as might get them transported or hanged.

But prison had taught them a lesson. Rob the rich and there are consequences. Rob the poor instead and you can get away with murder. The law didn't care much for the downtrodden.

Cooper gazed at Quest in the poor light. Knew him vaguely as a bludger and footpad who worked out of Seven Dials. A man with a scar on his cheek and dark stubble, a belcher handkerchief around his throat and a canvas cap on his head.

'This ain't yer territory!'

'It is now,' said Quest. 'You see, Old Barry here's a pal of mine. And I don't like little bastards like you leaning on my friends. So if you're here again, I intend to top you.'

'Yer what?'

'You heard.'

Cooper looked Quest up and down. Saw the worn fustian jacket and scuffed boots. No obvious cosh or life-preserver, just a walking stick. A slim cove. Not young, but not ancient either. Not too hard to do over. He caught a glimpse of the hand that was clutching his arm. It was covered in ghastly scars. And he talked like a flash cove from up west.

'I think as how yer should get out of me face.'

'I don't think so,' said Quest.

'Yer want to get buried?'

Quest smiled as Cooper's gang clustered around him. Cooper was puzzled. Perhaps this bludger was a loon, for all his reputation? That might explain it. No one in their right mind would come here on a dark night and threaten the Cooper gang.

'Yer too stupid to live,' Cooper said.

Quest shook his head.

'I'm not stupid. But you are. Get out of this street now and there need be no trouble. Stay away from my friend here and his tavern. All I'm asking.'

Cooper gave a raucous laugh.

'Yer gonna make me?'

'If I have to.'

'All on yer own?'

'He's not on his own.'

A figure detached himself from a dark shadow on the far side of the street. A well-dressed flash cove. A toff out slumming was Cooper's first thought. The kind you get in the poorer parts of Saffron Hill from time to time. Perhaps looking for a moll to grope. The footpad considered this new arrival. You had to be a bit wary of his kind. Gentry like him often came slumming with a pistol in their pocket.

Best to get in first...

Cooper took a pace away from Quest, lowering his arm away from that restraining hand.

Even as he moved, his fist came up towards the chin of the newcomer.

What happened next took even Quest by surprise.

The flash gent deflected the uppercut with his left hand even as he pushed a right fist into Cooper's face. The blow had hardly struck home before Cooper found himself flying through the air and crashing down on the cobbles.

'My God, Wren! Where did you learn that one?' Quest asked.

Wren Angier waved an arm in the direction of Albert Sticks.

'A little instruction from our friend there.'

'He'll have to teach me,' Quest said.

'I have,' said Sticks. 'You've obviously forgot.'

There was a cry and a curse from further along the street. One of the horses had broken free from the ostler and was kicking and bucking, the one animal's wildness spreading to the others. The ostler laid into the rebellious horse with his crop, sending it to greater heights of fury.

Quest wanted to go over there and beat the cruel little man to the ground, but he still had this other matter to deal with. Best to end this business with Cooper and his mob now.

He looked down to where Cooper was sprawled on the ground, wiping blood from his lips. His gang had edged away from the door of the tavern. Quest had seen this before, how men were easily frightened away once a loudmouthed leader had been vanquished.

But this time he was wrong...

Even as they gave the appearance of turning, one of them came charging towards him, raising a great blackthorn cosh above his head. If it struck home it would crush any man's skull. Quest saw Sticks move forward to intercept the attacker but knew he couldn't reach the man in time.

Quest had wanted this matter to be bloodless.

It was not to be.

He pulled the long and slender blade from his walking cane, stepped aside and thrust forward into the body of the charging villain. Saw the familiar look of puzzlement on his victim's face, as the steel tore into his lungs. Watched as the cosh fell to the cobbles. Saw the attacker crumple to the ground, gasping out a breath against the rain-soaked stones.

The man's fall was enough, as it persuaded the other members of the gang to flee down towards Saffron Hill.

But not quite enough...

The noise of the horses made Quest look in their direction, then down to where Cooper was stretched out on the ground. Cooper still seemed dazed by Wren Angier's blow, but even so was reaching into his jacket.

At first, Quest thought that the thug was clutching his chest in an attempt to regain his breath. But then he saw the hand slowly withdrawing, saw him pulling out a pistol and levelling it in Angier's direction. Watched as Cooper used the palm of his hand to cock the weapon.

Without thinking, Quest had his own percussion pistol out. He was just a yard away from Cooper as he discharged the gun, drilling a neat red hole into the villain's forehead. As Cooper fell backwards, his contracting finger pulled back the trigger of his own pistol sending a shot up into the cloudy sky.

There was a great cry from somewhere behind Quest. He swung round and saw the ostler being dragged to the ground by the terrified horses.

The bolting animals tore down the street, forcing Quest into the doorway of the tavern, dragging the landlord with him. Wren Angier was there too.

But in what seemed a crazed dream, he saw Jasper Feedle run out of the dangerous path of the terrified creatures. Sticks was not so fortunate. He almost made it to safety but a glancing blow, from the furthermost horse, sent the prizefighter sprawling into the gutter.

As Quest watched, a figure came running up the street, arms waving above his head, vainly trying to halt the stampede of screaming horses. Yelling out some words that Quest couldn't understand.

It was the beggar boy.

For a moment, Quest thought the boy's words had done the trick. All the horses, but one, seemed to skeer away from the lad. But the horse beaten by the ostler was in no mood to stop. It was heading straight towards the boy, who seemed unable to move out of its careering path.

But as the boy put out his arms, the horse stopped dead, rearing upwards, its front hooves coming down towards the beggar's head. The boy was inches from death...

Where the boy's saviour came from was always a puzzle to Quest. Out of the shadows of a long wall, a figure seemed to roll forward, grabbing the boy and pushing him clear across the street.

The rescuer placed the lad beside a gaslamp and gave a facetious bow in Quest's direction, before dodging away into the narrowest of alleys. But not before Quest recognised him as the pickpocketing youth, who'd been trailing him for the past days.

Its anger assuaged, the horse looked back the way it had come and calmly trotted along to the other animals. Quest saw Sticks clamber to his feet and cross to the beggar boy.

'My God, that took some courage,' said Angier, who was at his side. 'Did you see who it was?'

'Yes, I saw!'

Sticks came along the street, carrying the boy over one shoulder.

'You topped Cooper?'

'He gave me no choice,' said Quest. 'Nor the other one. I doubt who's left will bother anyone in Saffron Hill again.'

'Just like old times!' Jasper Feedle muttered.

'The noise of your shot'll bring along every crusher for miles,' Sticks said.

'Better that we weren't here then.'

'What about the lad?' asked Sticks, lowering the beggar on to the cobbles.

Quest looked down at the boy. He was in a state of shock, for he sat down on the wet ground the moment Sticks let go of him, his face pale and his eyes half-closed.

'Best bring him with us,' Quest said. 'At the very least he needs new clothes and a warm meal. And the fewer witnesses around here when the police come... well, the better.'

Ten

'I'm pleased you came, lad!'

It was a cool but bright morning as Sticks and Daniel Moonlight wandered along Rotten Row and then off into a quiet tree-lined corner of Hyde Park.

'It's very kind of you to give me instruction, Mr...er...Sticks. I see you brought the ash-stick with you.'

Sticks looked admiringly at the stout piece of wood.

'Ideal for a young gent like yourself. Not too heavy to handle, but hard enough for defence. There's lots of folk who feel you need a great heavy branch to fight off opponents, but it ain't true.' He swirled the ash above his head. 'What's the good of a great log, if its weight robs you of speed and being flexible?'

There was nobody about as the old bruiser led Daniel into a long glade out of sight of the rest of the park.

'You see, that's what it's all about,' Sticks continued. 'It's not the heaviest fighter in the square what wins the bout. The victor's the man what delivers the blows fastest and can get out of harm's way, before the opponent can retaliate.'

He reached deep inside his jacket and brought out a lead-weighted cosh, some two feet long. Daniel Moonlight thought it seemed quite deadly.

'That looks like it's had some wear,' he commented.

Sticks gave him a broad broken-toothed grin.

'A good old neddy stick this. A friend indeed! I could tell you a dozen yarns of how this cosh has saved me. It's seen off many a bludger in its time. In the alleys of London you can't always fight fair with fists. It's not like the prize ring. There are folk who don't respect bare knuckles. They might come at you with a dagger at least. That's when old neddy comes into his own.'

Daniel looked down at the cosh with some trepidation.

'You're going to fight me with that?'

'You're safe enough lad! I'll not bruise ye! But if you wants to learn to fight for yourself, you have to learn to take the sight of such instruments for granted. In a real mix, you'll face worse. And with my instruction, that ash stick of your'n will see off most that the lowest in the town'll bring up against you.'

He turned to face Daniel and held out the ash stick. The young man took it by its natural handle and pointed the narrow end at Sticks. He looked up to see a grin on the old boxer's face.

Sticks shook his head.

'Not the way, son. Not the way at all. Though I've seen many a gent try to defend himself with a stick in just such a manner. You don't hold it as though you was out for a country ramble! There's no weight in that end. Nothing that'll do much damage. Turn it round, lad. Turn it round. That knob on the top's where all the weight is. That's the bit to clobber 'em with! Now attack me with it. Don't hold back. Try to slay me with that stick!'

Daniel raised the ash high above his head and brought it downwards at an angle towards Sticks. Before it got anywhere near, Sticks brought the blow to a jarring halt with his cosh. Then, with a sudden twist and a grasp of his hand, tore the ash away.

'And if I was a bludger in some rookery close, you'd be dead a second from now,' Sticks said. 'I told you back in Cheapside not to try that move. Too easy to see off.'

'But then how?'

'Nine out of ten will expect you to do just that. It's a natural reaction when a gent what carries a stick's threatened. And nine out of ten of 'em will immediately expect it. Doesn't mean there's not a time for waving it above your head. But mostly as a feint, boy. Mostly as a feint. Here, swap weapons.'

He passed Daniel the cosh and took the ash into his own great hand, holding it about a foot up from its narrowest end.

'Now defend yourself, Daniel lad!'

Sticks pulled the ash high. A moment later it started down at great speed towards Daniel's head. Daniel raised the cosh to ward off the blow in the way that Sticks had. But even before his mind could comprehend what was happening, Sticks had pulled the ash back in a great circle.

The bulbous knob was no longer above Daniel's head but was coming in fast towards the pit of his stomach. Sticks stopped the thrust just as the ash made contact.

Instinctively, Daniel reached down, the cosh falling on to the grass. He tried to seize the ash but even as his hands went down, Sticks swirled the ash back and upwards in a tight circle. As Daniel raised his head to see what was happening, he became aware of the ash coming sideways at great speed towards his right temple. Sticks brought it to a sudden halt, a hairs-breadth away from Daniel's skin.

'And there's how you get 'em, Daniel, old son. A blow of force on the side of the head just like that and they'll not bother you for a time – if at all!'

'It was so quick... so unexpected...'

'Like I says, the weight of it counts for nothing if you ain't got the speed and the flexibility. And that's just the first trick I intends to teach you. We'll practice again and again until you gets it to heart. But first, we'll have a break.'

He reached inside his jacket and brought out a brandy flask. He took a swig and then offered it to Daniel.

'It's just water...'

'Indeed it is,' said Sticks. 'I haven't touched drink for years now. For it's the ruination of the best of men. Killed some of those dearest to me. Try not to touch it boy. It's been the wrecking of many a fighter.'

'My father preached against it,' said Daniel. 'He's a parson...'

'You bear in mind those preachings. So did you come to London just to write books?'

Daniel thought for a moment and decided to take Sticks into his confidence.

'Not altogether. I came to the town to find somebody. A man who did my family a very great wrong.'

'And what do you intend to do when you find this man?'

Daniel reached down and picked up the ash and the cosh.

'I intend to kill him.'

Sticks considered his words for a while before replying. He took Daniel by the shoulders and stared him in the face.

'I've seen a lot of evil things in this town, Daniel. A lot of misery and despair. I had the fortune to fall in with some good men over the years, when my fighting days were done. If I hadn't, I'd probably have been lagged and taken across to Botany Bay. Or maybe found myself dancing a jig on the Newgate scaffold. I've seen too much violence...'

'I hate violence too,' said Daniel. 'But there are some matters...'

'And I've seen young men like you bent on vengeance. I knew... I know one very well. A good man who suffered a very great wrong. Saw him eaten up with the desire to get revenge. I didn't blame him. If I'd suffered as how he did, I'd probably have been just the same. But it almost destroyed him. Nearly killed him. A good man... a son to me.'

'Did he get his vengeance?'

'He did,' said Sticks. 'After a lifetime of hate, he got his revenge. But he ain't been the same since. And getting that revenge almost finished him.' He gave a little laugh. 'And that man's a bonny fighter. Skilled in all the arts you need to know to fight back.'

'And I don't know how to fight!' Daniel said bitterly.

'I'd hate to think that anything I taught you helped put a rope round your neck.'

'It won't...'

'Take my advice, lad. Go back home and leave vengeance to the Almighty. Or if you must stay in London, then put it all out of your mind and write them novels instead. You're a good lad. I can see that. Don't go down the path to destruction.'

'You'll not teach me to fight then?'

Sticks looked up at the trees and the blue sky beyond before replying.

'Oh I'll teach you all right,' he said at last. 'I can see in your eyes that you'll not heed my words. At least I can give you a chance of living to see old age. But it'll take more than what I can show you today. We'd best meet here a few mornings a week. I'll show you all I can. But I'll still try to talk you out of what you have in mind.'

'That's all I ask,' said Daniel.

'Anyhow, you did well. Not at my best for this fighting lark. Got run down by a horse last night. But you did well.'

Sticks gave Daniel a big grin. The youth couldn't tell whether the old prizefighter was jesting or not.

~

'Quest!'

Inspector Honour Bright and Parkin looked down at the bodies lying on the cobbles of Field Lane, saw how the now-dried blood had flooded down towards the gutter. The dawn had come and - it seemed to Bright - a tragedy that these men had not lived to see such a beautiful morning.

'It's William Quest. Do you know these men, Parkin?'

'No, sir, but the beat constable said that one's Silas Cooper. A well-known local bludger and villain. The other one's his cousin Mordecai. No great loss to the world by all accounts. There'll be a lot less crime around Saffron Hill with them gone. But surely... we can't be sure Quest and his gang are responsible?'

Bright was silent for a long while, as he looked again at the bodies and studied the grim buildings of Field Lane. He'd seen a lot of corpses in his time; the slaying of villains never bothered him, but deaths on beautiful mornings diminished the joys of the world.

'It's Quest,' he said again.

'But I seem to recall that when Quest killed, he left a string nearby... a string knotted like a hangman's noose?'

Bright nodded. 'When he began his murderous regime he certainly did. But – as I understand it – he dropped that practice when his personal vengeances were accounted for. But taking into account all the other circumstances of these murders, I have no doubt that our killer is William Quest.'

'But sir, we had constables watching all the premises associated with Quest... how could he have slipped out without coming to our notice?'

Bright took in a breath.

'Never underestimate your opponent, Parkin. He's a cunning villain. You hear of people securing their property against rats. But even when they believe every gap is filled, the vermin manage to assault their defences.'

'Do you intend to arrest him, sir?'

Bright shrugged.

'On what evidence? Oh, we could go trooping over to Bloomsbury with warrants in our pockets. But we'd find that this rogue had been playing cards all night with some notable figures of London society. Or helping at a kitchen dispensing food to the poor. Quest has too many friends for us to bring him down that easily. No, we'll keep a watch on him. See where he goes and who he meets. He won't bother to evade us on his more lawful journeys around the capital. But one day, Parkin... one day, we'll bring this villain to his heels – with the blood of a victim still on his swordstick.'

~

'How's the boy?' Wren Angier asked.

He'd joined Quest on the steps of his home in Tavistock Place and they were strolling down Gower Street, heading towards the British Museum. A beautiful morning, and such a beautiful row of houses, so different from the awfulness of Field Lane just those few hours before. Parts of London seemed to be in different worlds, a thought that often occurred to him as he dashed between the worlds of the poor and the very rich.

'The boy? Still sleeping when I left the house. Sticks is looking after him – and *he* only arrived home a couple of hours ago. Apparently he'd been to Hyde Park, teaching some customer of the walking stick shop just how to defend himself. Young lad from the country. Whoever he is, he must have made an impression on Sticks. Not often he goes to the trouble of giving instruction these days.'

'He taught you well, Will. And I appreciate the tricks he's taught me. What will you do with the boy? Feed him up and send him back to Saffron Hill?'

'I don't know, Wren. I really don't. You know, I was looking at that boy last night and kept seeing myself as a young beggar and dip on the streets of London. If I'd stayed in that life, well, I'd probably be dead now. Dead with some foul disease, or starved or hanged at Newgate. And that's the only future for that boy if he goes back there.'

'You can't save them all, Will. There are thousands of children in a similar position all over town. Too many to help, at least our way.'

Quest was silent, as they swung off towards the museum, looking up to where so many labourers were beginning work on the new library. A library that would be a great addition to learning and the improvement of society. He made a mental note that it would be a kind gesture to donate some books from his father's collection at Hope Down...

And perhaps to send someone back to his country home...

'When the boy is well... I might give him the opportunity to go and live at Hope Down? Do you think he might consider that? Oh, I know, there's as much poverty and wretchedness in the country as there is in the town. But better than a rookery... anything is better than that...'

'A long way to go with the library building,' said Wren, looking across at the workmen. 'Still, worth it in the end. Does Joshua Blount know we are coming?'

'I sent a note round earlier this morning. Have you met the man?'

'Never met him, though I've seen him at gatherings in Parliament.'

'A good man by all accounts,' Quest said. 'This library alone will be his monument. And I believe he has a great reputation for charitable endeavours. Apart from that I know little about him, except that he's a friend of Jonas Lyddon.'

'Not popular in some quarters, for his radicalism. And his love of reform's surprising considering his background.'

They were approaching the door of the museum offices.

'His background?'

'My dear William! You really don't know?'

'What is there to know?'

'I thought you kept abreast of all the London scandals.'

'Evidently not. I've heard of no scandal.'

'Well, it may not be true, of course. Though I'm inclined to believe it is.'

'Wren... what are you talking about?'

'Well, in a nutshell... Joshua Blount is a by-blow. His father was the late king.'

'King William?'

'No, King George... Blount is the result of a little romantic adventure that Fat George had when he was Prince Regent, with a lady of the court. Blount's mother went on to marry respectably a year or two later, hence the other Blount brother, Magnus. Interesting thought, isn't it? But for the fact that George couldn't marry Blount's mother, the man we're about to meet would be king. Of course the other thing you should know about Joshua Blount is...'

But before Wren could continue, they were hailed by a man coming down the museum steps. A slim man of a similar age to themselves, pale in complexion with hair so fair it was almost white.

'Mr Quest is it?' the man said, shaking both their hands. 'And you are Sir Wren Angier – I've seen you at Westminster. I'm Magnus Blount. I understand you wish to see my brother? Joshua knows of you both by reputation. Our friend Mr Lyddon speaks so highly of you. Is he still in Manchester?'

'I believe so,' said Quest. 'You are working with your brother here?'

Magnus Blount smiled.

'I try to help Joshua in any way I can. He's a remarkable man, Mr Quest. It's a privilege to devote my life to his service, to help him fulfil his many dreams. I serve as his secretary among other duties.'

He led them into the building.

'Joshua maintains an office here and spends an increasing amount of time at the museum. Getting the library built is his most important project at the moment. "Knowledge is all" – that's my brother's belief. Did you wish to see him about the library?'

'I would wish to donate some books,' said Quest. 'But there is another urgent matter...'

'Then come this way...'

He led them down a wide corridor and opened a great oak door.

'Brother... here is Mr Quest and Sir Wren Angier.'

Quest looked at the man sitting in the window seat. He seemed to be contemplating the book-lined far wall of the room, as he leaned forward on his walking cane. Where the younger brother was fair, Joshua Blount had chestnut hair and was fuller in the face. A good-looking man, but try as he might, Quest couldn't see much resemblance to the late king.

'It's very good of you to come to see me, Mr Quest,' said Joshua Blount. 'My dear friend Mr Lyddon always speaks so highly of you, and I was privileged to meet your late father when I was barely in my youth. You'll forgive me if I do not stand? Seats are an anchor to me. I navigate all rooms, knowing where they are.'

He gave a sad laugh and held out a hand, though not in Quest's direction.

Quest stepped nearer.

Only as he took the hand, did he realise that Joshua Blount was blind.

'It's an honour to meet you, Mr Blount. What you are doing here – this library – a wonderful achievement. I would wish to donate some books to the collection, but perhaps more of that later. But I've come on a most important mission...'

Quest told the brothers about the death of Colley Johnson and the house in Piccadilly, before taking out the paper that Colley Johnson had stolen and reading out its contents. Joshua Blount stood and then sat down again, tapping his walking cane on the ground.

'This is outrageous!' said Magnus Blount. 'Whoever is behind this... how can they possibly believe my brother to be a dangerous man? Someone so renowned for his good works?'

Joshua Blount held up his hand.

'It is inevitable that one makes some enemies as we go through life. It's true I've been outspoken on social matters – as has my good friend Jonas Lyddon. But I've mostly stood to one side with those great campaigns. My... circumstances... have always meant that I could only give moral support. And in recent years, I've devoted my time to this museum.'

'Surely this threatening paper is just the product of a deranged mind?' said Magnus Blount. 'We should not take it seriously, surely?'

'I think we must,' said Quest. 'This note has cost the life of the man who obtained it. We can only assume that there is a very real danger to the three of us mentioned in it.'

Quest told them more about how Colley Johnson had come into the paper's possession, and how he'd been murdered in the Cremorne Gardens.

'The poor devil!' said Magnus Blount.

'I'm at a loss to know what to say,' said his brother. 'This house in Piccadilly? Do we know who owns it?'

'I've made some inquiries,' said Quest, 'there is a law firm in Westminster who seem to hold the lease. But they were not forthcoming about who holds the lease now – I had my own lawyer inquire.'

Joshua Blount stood and walked towards the open window. To Quest's puzzlement, he seemed to be looking out towards where the builders were at work. Joshua turned back and faced them, laughing.

'No, sadly I can't see out, Mr Quest. I come over here guided by the fresh air, one of the reasons I always have it opened a trifle. My dear brother has described the scene so well that I can picture it in my mind. I know what objects look like. I was seventeen when I lost my sight. I fell from the family carriage and the rear wheel went over my head. So I still have memories... now my disability seldom bothers me.'

'What can be done to protect my brother, Mr Quest?' asked Magnus.

Quest thought for a while.

'I do have associates who work with me, in Monkshood. They could guard your brother wherever he goes.'

Joshua Blount walked back to his chair.

'I think not,' he said at last. 'If someone is that determined to silence me, then they will. But I'll not have the way I live my life curtailed. I live with my blindness

– do you know, Mr Quest, I can walk many of the streets of London all on my own, finding my way about. Sometimes I need to be by myself. I'll not give up my freedom to do that.'

'But there is a danger to you,' said Angier.

'There may well be, but I'll not bow down to this threat.'

'You're a remarkable man,' said Quest.

'Mr Quest – I am a very ordinary man. I live a privileged life compared to the poor of this city. I'll take my chances. But what of Jonas Lyddon? He's lived much of his life with such perils. Does he know about this?'

'He's in Manchester, but I sent him a telegraphic message and followed that with a letter. I had a reply this morning. He's coming to London in a day or two and his secretary, James Brendon, is travelling by a different route. Mr Lyddon says in his note that he has a document – he desires that you and I should both have copies.'

'May I ask what you intend to do about this house in Piccadilly – Tenebrae? There's a sinister name!' asked Magnus Blount. 'Isn't it likely that that is where the answer to all this will be found?'

'I agree with you, Mr Blount. I intend to look inside the house this very night. I might find nothing at all. Indeed, it's likely that the house will have been abandoned following Colley Johnson's intrusion and his taking of this paper.'

Joshua Blount smiled.

'My friend Jonas has told me a great deal about your background, Mr Quest – might I call you William as he does? But I do urge you not to put your life in danger on my account.'

'My name is on the paper as well.'

'Indeed!'

Joshua Blount held out a hand.

'All I can do is wish you well, my friend.'

Magnus Blount saw them back out on to the street.

'You'll keep us informed, William? I must say, it's a pleasure to meet you at last. You're a legend in our circles. I could tell that Joshua was thrilled to meet you. I hope you will consider us both to be good friends?'

'I've met many remarkable men – but it's been a privilege to get to know your brother.'

~

'You lied to Quest,' said Sergeant Berry. 'That night at the Cremorne...'

They were sitting in Anders' office at Scotland Yard.

Inspector Anders looked peeved.

'Not altogether lied. And I'm not obliged to share confidences with one of the worst criminals in London, am I? There was substance in what I said. Inspector Honour Bright has been tasked with Quest's capture. We are on other duties, are we not. Well, two sets of other duties, Sergeant. One a cover for the other?'

'I thought Quest had become your friend?'

Anders swung his chair round and looked out of the window.

'He's a strange man, this Quest,' he said at last. 'I would like to pretend that I don't like him, but I do. I admire his mission in life, even if I do deplore his methods. But if I have to arrest him, I will. Even if that means the gallows. I have my own duty, and I will carry it out. Quest has been most fortunate so far – and the secret service are keen that he should be left alone, provided that he doesn't cross the line from his practice of slaughtering the foulest representatives of our society. Providing that he doesn't succumb to more rebellious activities.'

'You heard about the killings in Field Lane?'

'I heard. Inspector Bright is convinced that those murders must be blamed on William Quest. Inspector Bright is quite correct. I've not the slightest doubt that William... Quest is responsible.'

'Bright will want to bring him to book...'

'I suspect Bright will have a hard job doing that. If he gets too close, Wissilcraft will intervene. As long as Quest possesses that notebook, well, he's safe enough. The best Bright can hope for is that by dogging Quest's footsteps, he'll curtail some of the rogue's activities.'

Berry grinned.

'You don't believe Bright will achieve that, any more than I do! Quest is too fly a villain to be inconvenienced by Honour Bright...'

'Bright is a damned fine detective, Berry! He shouldn't be underestimated. He's like a crack shot fired from a pistol. You only have to look at his fine catalogue of arrests.'

They were silent for a long time.

'So we are to keep up the pretence?' said Berry.

'We have our orders. Wissilcraft has decreed what we must do. Palmerston has no choice but to obey Wissilcraft, if it comes to it.'

'Which leaves us with two tasks – our real mission and the one we must do to cover our backs. And we are doing very little so far on wiping out vice in this city.'

Anders rocked back in his chair.

'Yes, I've been thinking about that, Berry. Time we paid a more forceful visit to Holywell Street. Perhaps the notorious Mr Dugdale?'

'Dugdale's been prosecuted before for selling his filthy books. He's still at it! He's turned his bookshop into something of a fortress. He keeps the door locked between customers. Likely he'll burn anything incriminating, before we can even crash down the door.'

'Books take a while to burn,' said Anders.

Eleven

'How long should we wait?' Wren Angier asked.

The street in Piccadilly was quieter than usual, the evening crowds had moved on and the lights from the houses were extinguished one after another. But there had been no lights in the house called Tenebrae. No shutters closed or drapes drawn. Its dark windows looked out upon the street like sightless eyes.

'An hour,' Quest said. 'I'll need that for a good look around. If I'm not out in an hour, you can assume something's gone wrong.'

'I really do think I should come in with you,' said Sticks.

He looked anxiously at Quest, noting the tired look in his eyes.

Quest tapped him on the shoulder.

'No, old friend. I shall need you and Wren out here, ready to come rushing in if something goes wrong.'

'Are you carrying?' Sticks asked.

'A short cosh, a dagger, and my little pistol.'

'Don't you hesitate to use them then!'

Quest left them, crossing the road and wandering along the street like any late pedestrian. He walked past the steps of Tenebrae, looked around and then stepped backwards and up to the door. Reaching into his pocket, he brought out the little case of bettys, the picklocks Sticks had presented to him when he was no more than a boy.

An easy lock, he considered, far too simple for a house of secrets. Had it been his house, he would have made it much more difficult for intruders.

He stepped into an abandoned hall, looking across at the dusty staircase. It was just as Colley Johnson had described it to Pokey Nibbs. He'd contemplated bringing a dark lantern to light his way, but recalled that Johnson had managed without. The gas-lamps in the street and the full moon lit up the uncarpeted hall. And Quest had always had a great ability to see his way in dark places.

If the house held any secrets, it wouldn't be on this ground floor, or the two landings of rooms above. Colley Johnson had climbed three flights of stairs before entering the big room with the stained glass window in the partition.

Three floors before encountering the man with no face...

As he climbed the stairs, Quest noticed that the dust was not thick everywhere. There was a clearer passage closer to the banister, just as Colley Johnson had described. Looking at it, Quest could see that someone had been this way very recently, for there were the marks of steps which hadn't gathered any fresh dust.

He reached inside his pocket and gripped the neddy, the good stout cosh that he always used in preference to his swordstick or pistol. A good friend that had broken many heads in its long career. Sticks had taught him how to use it most effectively, just as he was teaching his new pupil out in the park. As he crossed the next landing, Quest wondered whether he'd made a mistake not letting the old bruiser come with him on this adventure?

There was a door, half-open, on the last landing and Quest halted for a moment, waiting for the moon to come from behind a cloud to illuminate the way he had to go. At last he moved forward, easing his way past the door, to find himself in a partitioned room.

And there was the stained glass window, just as Colley had said it would be, such an odd addition in the interior of a London house.

He couldn't see the point of it?

He walked across to it and examined the setting and the thick glass. It was obviously very old, perhaps a relic from a church or great house. But only of interest to an enthusiast of stained glass. He could see no point in it being set in the partition, rather than some outside wall?

He ran his fingers down the glass, noting that it was kept not only free from dust but clean.

What was the purpose of that...

Then Quest looked up.

His heart missed a beat, for beyond the glass was the figure of a man.

A man wearing a black cloak...

A man who had no face...

Quest began to reach into his inside pocket, seeking his percussion-cap pistol. But even as his fingers grasped the stock, his head exploded.

He fell into darkness.

~

'Did you see that?'

Wren Angier was looking up towards the top of the house.

'Didn't see anything,' Sticks replied. 'What was it?'

'Up at the highest window – a flash of light.'

'Must have been looking the other way.'

'Did Quest have a lantern with him?'

'No. He said the outside gas-lamps and the moonlight would be enough.'

Angier considered.

'Perhaps it was just the moonlight on the window glass. Mind, the moon's out now and I don't see it. Do you think we should go in?'

Sticks, a practised burglar, gave the matter some thought.

'No... not just now. We'll let the lad have his hour. Now what's this coming along?'

A youth was sidling along the opposite pavement, glancing up at each house as he went past, sometimes walking swiftly, occasionally lingering by the steps of the houses.

They watched as he walked past Tenebrae, then pulled even further back into the shadows, as the youth turned sharply and scampered up the steps of the house. They saw him push on the door and, finding it open, enter the house.

'Trouble there!' Wren Angier said. 'That's the pickpocketing youth who's been following us around for days. The one we told you about. I really think we should go in now! Grab that youth and discover his business.'

'Oh, I don't think so!' said Sticks.

'You think Quest can handle that youth?'

Angier couldn't understand why Sticks was grinning.

Sticks sucked in a breath.

'Oh, I doubt he can handle *that* youth at all. Never could and probably never will...'

~

As he lay there, Quest couldn't believe he'd been so stupid!

The times in the past he'd avoided being so distracted, managing to never fall victim to so obvious a trap. So he'd been as stunned at the sight of the man with no face as Colley Johnson had been. But Colley had said that the grim figure hadn't been alone in that dark house.

Quest wondered how long he'd been unconscious. He tried to reach up and feel the wound on his head, where he'd been struck. But he couldn't move an inch; his hands were secured behind his back, his feet were tied together, and there was clearly a rope between the two - hog-tied an American friend of his had once described such a shackling.

He could hear a hissing noise and felt nauseous. Managing to half-turn, he was able to see across the room, the partition and - the stained glass had gone! Someone had lifted the glass and its tracery holding clear away. And the door was open.

He felt relieved - there was nobody there.

Quest thought the hissing noise must be inside his head, a result of the blow that had knocked him out. Then he smelt the gas and considered it must be coming from the broken gaslight burner above his head.

So... that was the way they intended to dispose of him.

His battered brain tried to do a mental calculation. He'd been in the house about ten minutes before he'd been hit on the head. He had no idea how long he'd been lying there, probably only a few minutes, for the moon, visible through the window, hadn't moved on very much.

He calculated, from the size of the room, that he would be gassed to death in less than twenty minutes. Thirty at most. Long before Angier and Sticks might obey his order to come crashing into the house.

Quest had little fear of death – he'd faced it too often, but this was a singularly stupid way to die. All because he'd let his guard down, fallen into the obvious trap. He really was getting too old and stale to be in this business.

He struggled for a minute or two against the ropes that bound him, but he'd clearly been hog-tied by an expert. Even in his death throes, he felt a kind of frustration that he'd never discover the secrets of the empty house called Tenebrae and his murderous host – the man with no face...

~

Jonas Lyddon sank back into the armchair, looking through the window at the tiny clouds scudding across the moon. A beautiful night in so many ways, one he saw so rarely these days. The foul airs of Manchester and London so often obstructed the night sky. But a fierce wind, blowing down from the Pennines earlier in the day, had cleared the miasma.

One of the curses of old age was that he slept badly. He was more likely to doze in a chair than retire to bed. He tried to read those old familiar books that were a joy to him, but the passion for literature had gone. It was as though he'd exhausted everything in life that had always driven him on. Perhaps that was always the way of it as the years passed by.

Only days before, as the crowds had gathered to remember the Peterloo Massacre, they'd hailed him as one of the survivors of those troublous times. The echoes of their cheers, greeting his speech, had reverberated around the streets of Manchester.

But even then, all these years later, he'd seen the home office spies in the crowd, and the foul looks of the senior police officers who'd come along to the gathering and clapped their hands in a most unenthusiastic way.

The old enemies were still there...

In that odd state, somewhere between consciousness and sleep, his mind journeyed back to the two or three years before Peterloo.

When he'd left this very town as a Blanketeer, trying to take the protest on behalf of the poor to London. A failed attempt to change the world.

Then there was Dartmoor...

He remembered the long walk he'd taken on foot into Devonshire. The walk from Exeter to Moreton, when he'd been near robbed by that rascal Harry Blizzard, and then thrown in his lot with Jasper Feedle and Cock Lorel – rebels, all of them, to their very hearts. Other thoughts too, of Ralph Bonfils and Kitty and Tryphena Jay. Those years when he'd been a revolutionary, before becoming a Parliamentarian.

The swinging, rotting corpses on Gibbet Hill... the Tyburn of Dartmoor...

In his old age, when he thought back to the violent events on Dartmoor, he was quite appalled. Too much killing, too *much* violence. It was one of those reasons he'd had to forsake the wishes of his old friend Josiah Quest, and the secret society known as Monkshood. William Quest had been found destitute and roaming the streets of London. He'd taken up the gauntlet, as the young must do. But Jonas Lyddon feared for him – how long would it be before Quest recognised the results of the horrible path he was journeying along?

A decent young man, Quest. Jonas Lyddon had enjoyed his company on Dartmoor a little time ago. He looked forward to seeing Quest when he returned to London the next day.

He must introduce him to James Brendon, his most invaluable aide, who should be ahead of him in London by now. Brendon had become like a son to him, abhorring violence as much as he did. Someone else there to take up the banner of freedom.

What were those words of Byron?

Freedom, yet, thy banner, torn but flying, Streams like a thunder-storm against the wind.

Good words too. Lyddon had liked Byron and mourned his early death. A lord, an aristocrat – but, for all his wild ways, a man on the side of the people. Most of the good ones were dead, the evil exploiters always seemed to linger on to plague humanity.

The devil always did seem to look after his own...

And in a way, Jonas Lyddon considered, he was no longer really needed either. It was for the Quests and Brendons of the world to carry forward the good fight. Brendon was already doing much of the work that he would have had to attend to himself in days gone by. He'd lost count of the times, in recent weeks, when poor Brendon had journeyed back and forwards by the railway down to London.

If you get too tired to make the journeys then, surely, it's time to stand back? he said aloud to himself. *You're too old to battle on! Put your vanity aside and let the youngsters have their turn.*

Jonas Lyddon laughed, falling into a dozing state that was not far off sleep.

~

Then the hissing of the gas stopped.

William Quest became aware that somebody else had entered the room. Someone quiet of foot, for he hadn't heard anyone come through the door and cross to the gaslight burner. No doubt his would be killers had thought better of this slow death, and returned to expedite matters. It's what Quest would have done himself in his killing times.

A quick end for the enemy, no wish to prolong anyone's suffering.

Ropebound, he twisted across the floor so that he might see the assassin who'd turned off the burner. And there he was... but not the least the kind of figure that Quest had expected to see...

Leaning back against the dusty wall was the pickpocketing youth who'd been following him around for days. The slim lad in the fustian jacket and battered old cap.

'You?'

The youth shrugged and came closer, leaning over him, a knife clutched in hand.

'So... you're working for our faceless friend, are you? Gas not a swift enough death? Ah, well, get on with it then. Or are you expecting me to show fear or beg for mercy?'

'Don't be such a bloody fool, William!'

The youth tossed the cap aside, dark hair tumbling down.

'My God! Rosa!'

'You'll forgive the dirty face, my old love. But you really do have to look the part if you're to get properly into character. And I must say, you've made a bit of a mess of all this, without me at your side. Missed me, my darling? Is that what's got you into such bad, careless habits? I thought you'd spot me out on the streets, the moment I first appeared in your view? But no... I've been trailing you for days and you didn't recognise me. Am I so easy to forget?'

Quest wondered for a moment if this was all some delirious dream, brought on by the gas he'd inhaled. But as she cut the ropes that bound him - not too gently - he caught the scent of her, even above the dispersing gas. Felt her hand against his as she eased his arms from behind his back.

'But why the pretence? Why didn't you just come back to me?'

'Oh yes! You'd have loved that wouldn't you? See me come running back from the stage, cap in hand? You arrogant bastard! I should have left the gas on! Not once... not once... did you come to the theatre and see me. Not once did you come backstage to say how much you missed me... how much I meant to you.'

Rosa stood and turned her back on him.

'But hold on a moment, Rosa. You were the one who walked out on me! Left me alone at one of the darkest moments of my life. You said you wanted to return to the stage? Well, I let you, and...'

'You... *let me*?'

'All right, I put that badly. I'm sorry. I didn't stand in your way, let's put it like that. I was proud to see that you received such good notices. Not your fault that the stench from the river was frightening off the theatre audiences... I think that's what they said, wasn't it? And I did come to see you perform. But why follow me around like this, why the pickpocketing disguise?'

Rosa sank down on to the floor, her back against the wall.

'It seemed a good way to make sure,' she said.

'To make sure of what?'

'To make sure you hadn't lured some other little whore into your bed. I haven't forgotten Angeline Wissilcraft, you know...'

'But you know what happened there? I never took her to my bed...'

'Bet you were bloody tempted!'

'She meant nothing to me. You know what the consequences of my acquaintance with her were? You know exactly what happened?'

Rosa looked down at the floor.

'I was jealous!' she said at last.

'But there was nothing to be jealous about, Rosa. Besides, you once said you could never love me.'

'What I said was, it was a good job we could never love each other. That it was fine when it was all about lust and fun and adventure. That's what I said, William.'

'And it was.'

There was a long silence.

'I was wrong,' said Rosa. 'I've loved you from the day I first tried to pick your pocket, that day in the Strand.'

'You weren't very good at dipping. I felt your hand go in...'

'Yes, because I wanted you to feel it go in, you bastard!'

'I never knew.'

'No... you didn't did you?'

'So what now?'

'Now, William? Well, right now I'd like you to take me out of this dark and miserable place. I'd like you to take me back to a warm room in your house. I'd like you to take me to your bed. And after that, well, I'll make up my mind if I ever want to see you again.'

Twelve

A great crowd had assembled to see Jonas Lyddon off on his journey to London, on the first train. So huge a dawn gathering that there was no room on the platform at Manchester's London Road station. Jonas had thought that his departure was not public knowledge, but here they all were, cheering, and singing the campaigning songs of the olden days.

He turned at the carriage door and waved a gesture of thanks. He found words to express his admiration to them, once more, for remembering the battles of the Blanketeers and the dreadful, though memorable, massacre of Peterloo, all those decades before.

An old man stepped forward, holding a book in his hand.

'For you, sir. A volume of Mr Shelley's political poems. My name is Obadiah Jenks. I was there that day in St Peter's Fields. You shielded me from a soldier's sabre. I've not forgotten it, sir. And I know you're partial to the writings of Mr Shelley. I've inscribed it, Mr Lyddon. *From a friend and ally*. Please do read my inscription as you journey to that big, bad place – London!'

Jonas shook the man's hand, waved once more to the crowd and withdrew into the carriage. He was pleased to see that he had the compartment all to himself. He hung his hat and looked out through the window. A great cloud of steam half-hid the crowds as he waved one more time.

There were many cheers and then the singing of songs as the train left the station. He looked out at the sprawling houses that had been built since he'd first known the place. The manufactories that belched steam and smoke into the atmosphere, a great cloud of which hung over the place like a shroud over a corpse.

How the town had changed in those forty years since he'd first come there. A lad from Devonshire, who'd known nowhere much except the moorland hills.

He reached into a slim leather satchel, designed originally for carrying music, and brought out the account he'd written of his rebellious activities back in 1817 on Dartmoor. Enough in that to get him hanged a dozen times over, he considered! But it was important that the history was written down. History, after all, should be about the common folk of the land – not just about pretentious fat kings and their political hangers-on.

Jonas Lyddon looked out through the window. The train had left the houses behind and was journeying between fields and woodlands. Somewhere there must be the road he'd taken when he walked from Manchester to Dartmoor, in those days when he'd been so full of vigour. Not now, sadly, not now. His breath didn't come the way it once had. All the muscles in his legs ached with a fury he could well do without. Where had the years gone? These disablements had caught up with him so suddenly. A few years before he'd felt as fit as ever – and now?

You're a stupid old fool, Jonas!

He muttered the words out loud and felt very annoyed with himself. He'd never before succumbed to such self-pity.

You're an old man, Jonas!

Once you recognised that fact, it wasn't so bad. Time to hand on the political campaigning to younger men, such as James Brendon and William Quest. So what if you did lack the energy of days of yore? There were still books to read and paintings to view. Old friends whom you could have pleasant conversations with, trusted allies with whom you may reminisce. A garden to stroll around in, even if you couldn't pace vast miles across wild and broken moorland.

A lot to still enjoy!

He put the Dartmoor account back in the satchel, then picked up the little book of Shelley poems he'd placed on the seat next to him. He thumbed through, a nice little collection, he thought. All of the poet's political thoughts in one place, despite the attempts of the establishment and the Shelley family to suppress such radical opinions.

Obadiah Jenks had penned his name on the page next to the preface. *For Jonas Lyddon, who fights for the many and not the few*, said the sentiment. How very kind of him...

Starting to read the preface, he noticed more lines of writing across the foot of the page...

Mr Lyddon, do not stay on the train to London. Your very life is in peril. Make your way to Birmingham where you will find succour and a friend at a tavern called the Cockpit, not far from the new station they've built on what we all once knew as the Froggery.

<u>Do this, I beg you, for your life depends on it.</u>

~

It all came back to Quest as he lay there with Rosa in his arms; the touch of her flesh against his, the scent of her hair, the cries, the sighs and the laughter. Then the peace as they talked of old times and adventures.

The long moments of silence between conversations.

'I don't want you to go away again,' he said.

'Depends on you. I won't be taken for granted.'

'You won't be... I can promise you that.'

'I won't tolerate other women!'

He touched her face.

'There never have been any other women. Not in all the times we were together. How could there be? What other woman could ever compare to you? And not just at pick-pocketing...'

'If I ever find out there is... I'll kill you!'

'A reasonable agreement... I think, Rosa Stanton, that perhaps we'd better make that agreement legal. "Forsaking all others?" What do you think?'

She shot up in the bed.

'Are you proposing to me?'

'I rather think I am.'

'Rosa Quest... it has a sort of ring to it, I suppose. Of course, you'll have to meet my father, the parson, and my young brother. They both think I came to London to be ruined by a rake. Have to put that right.'

'I have to seek their permission?'

Her eyes flashed defiance.

'We don't need anyone's bloody permission!'

'Must ask Sticks... what he thinks...'

She laughed.

'I suppose he is *in loco parentis*, as you've nobody else. Ask him now...'

'Past dawn. He'll be in Hyde Park'.

'What the devil's he doing in Hyde Park?'

'There's some young greenhorn he's taken under his wing. Showing him how to fight. A lad with literary pretensions. Sticks says he's a danger to himself and everyone else, the way he is.'

'And what about you, William. Is it business as usual? You seem so very tired of it all...'

'Oh, sometimes I feel that all the fight's gone out of me. Not long ago I was on Dartmoor, meeting an old friend of my father called Jonas Lyddon. He argued that we should wrestle for a fairer society in Parliament, rather than out on the streets. He's a reformer...'

'A famous reformer, Will. I know of him. A good man.'

'He is... and you'll meet him later today. He's coming down from Manchester on the dawn train. In fact, we must prepare for him. I promised to meet him at the railway station. Will you come?'

'I will indeed. It'll be nice to be in respectable company.'

~

'You're comin' along very well, Daniel lad!'

'Thank you, Sticks. And I do appreciate everything you're teaching me. But I still feel I've a lot to learn.'

Sticks smiled as they sat down with their backs against a tree. Dawn had turned into early morning and the presence of the first pedestrians in Hyde Park meant they'd had to cease their fighting practice.

'Going to be a grand day, I think,' Sticks said. 'You know sometimes, on a pleasant day, I come into these London Parks to read my books in the fresh air. Got me favourites - Daniel Defoe, love him ... one of the first books I ever read proper was *Moll Flanders*. And Mr George Borrow, such a lover of prizefighting and the fancy. You said you'd read *Lavengro*? And Mr Charles Dickens, well, he gave me a sovereign once...'

'You've met Mr Dickens?'

'I have indeed, Daniel. And I've been thinkin' about your own literary ambitions. You know, I'd leave those - unpleasant - books you can buy in Holywell Street well alone. I really would. I can tell from the way you talk that you could be a great writer. Why ruin what could be a great reputation by writing books you wouldn't want your father to see?'

Daniel was silent for a while, then...

'I know you're right Sticks. I came to London for two reasons, and one of them was so that I might try to be a novelist. I've been thinking the same as you about those other books. Not for me... I have no experience of that life. None at all. The problem is that Mr Dugdale - the bookseller and publisher I told you about - has been generous to me. He even owns the lodgings where I live. He might turn me out, if I don't go along with his wishes.'

'And if he does?' Sticks said. 'I'll find you lodgings... aye, and some easy work to go along with 'em. So you have time to write grand books. You have ambition. A fine thing in a young man. So try to write those proper novels. You go and see this Dugdale this very morning. Give notice to quit your lodgings, and then have no more to do with him. I'll be at the walking stick shop in Cheapside for much of the day. Bring your baggage and I'll send you round to some decent diggings.'

'You are very kind, Sticks.'

'Nah, good folk have done the same for me in my time. There was a farmer once... on Dartmoor... gave me work as a lad, when I was near starving. Didn't profit him much, but a kindly act.'

'Then I'll go and see Dugdale this very morn.'

'And there's something else, lad. That other matter... this man you intend to kill. I believe you should forget it...'

'I can't, Sticks... I really can't! If you only knew what he'd done to my family. The ruin and shame he's brought down on us. Everywhere I'd go in my father's parish, I'd hear the villagers mutter...'

Sticks sighed.

'And it's a matter of such shame that you'd take this man's life?'

'I'd call him out... in a fair fight...'

Sticks shook his head.

'Look, lad. You're better than you were, but you'd still be no match for a skilled fighter. And the age of duelling's long past. Gone with the death of the Regent – and a good thing too.'

'I believe there've been more recent duels than that? And I've a pair of fine little pistols in my trunk.'

'Little pistols are not the weapons for duelling. You might well meet an opponent who has a talent for using the real thing. Full-sized duelling weapons. How will it restore your family honour if you end up dead?'

Daniel leaned forward.

'I've *got* to find this man!'

'You've started looking?'

'It's a big city...'

'There are street directories... supposing he's gentry.'

'He is... I'd never thought of that.'

'Look, Daniel, will you do something for me? Give me the name of this rogue and let me seek him out? Then if you must confront him, well, we can do it together. Doing that you might survive the encounter.'

'But it's something *I* have to do!'

'I'm not saying as how you shouldn't, lad. But at least let me watch your back. Come on, Daniel, tell me the name of this villain you intend to kill? Who is he? What's the rascal's name?'

'His name... his name is William Quest!'

Thirteen

'Well, now... *there's* a pretty party, just as expected, Parkin.'

From their place of concealment at Euston railway station, Inspector Honour Bright and Parkin watched the two men and a woman who were walking hurriedly along the far platform. The train from Manchester was already pulling into the station.

'Quest and Angier,' Parkin remarked. 'But who is the woman?'

'At a guess, I'd say that's Rosa Stanton - Quest's mistress. Now there's an interesting thing. I'd been told they'd separated, but from the description I've seen it can only be her. There was a drawing of her in the *Illustrated London News*, when she was working on the stage with Madame Vestris. That's Stanton all right!'

The train was just entering the station. A great cloud of steam emerged from the engine with a sigh, as it came to a halt, hiding their view of the party on the other platform.

'Let's wander across and watch them meeting Lyddon,' said Bright.

~

'Let's get this nonsense over with,' said Anders, as they walked up from the Strand towards Holywell Street. 'Are the men in place?'

Berry smiled.

'We've the street sealed off at both ends and a few men playing the part of pedestrians and gawpers not far from Dugdale's shop. And there's a barrow boy with a nice little battering ram concealed in his barrow. But it won't be easy - every time Dugdale gets raided he barricades the door even more.'

'If only there was a back way in... mind, I'm not averse to breaking the window if we have to... we must get in swiftly. It's well known he keeps a stove at the back so that he might incinerate the worst of his publications.'

'Window is no good - Dugdale's had it barred. If you don't mind me saying, sir, I still think this is a waste of our time, given our other responsibilities.'

Anders tapped his heavy stick on the pavement.

'Ah, but it's our cover, Berry. Our cover.'

~

'That gent seems to be a tad agitated,' said Wren Angier, pointing to a man walking up and down the platform. All of the passengers had alighted and the crowds had dispersed. A porter was opening all the doors, checking that no items of luggage had been left behind.

The agitated gentleman approached them.

'You are Mr Quest?'

'I am.'

'I was told to meet you here, to greet Mr Lyddon as he arrived. And I've a document for you, though I have it concealed elsewhere. My name is James Brendon. I am Mr Lyddon's secretary. But there must be something amiss – Mr Lyddon is not on the train.'

'It was an early train... perhaps he missed it,' said Wren.

'Mr Lyddon *never* misses a train. In any case, I had one of our agents in Manchester send me a message by the electric telegraph confirming his departure. Mr Lyddon definitely left on the dawn train from Manchester. There was apparently quite a crowd to see him off.'

The porter had worked his way down the line of carriages to the engine.

'Has everybody got off the train?' Quest asked him.

'Yes, guvnor... and no luggage left behind, not even a stick or an umbrella – and that makes a change.'

'Well, if he's not on the train then he must have got off somewhere else,' said Rosa.

'But why should he?' said Brendon. 'Normally I travel with him, of course. But he'd made two copies of this important document and was determined that they should come down to London by different routes.'

'What is this document?' Quest asked.

'A full account of Mr Lyddon's adventures on Dartmoor in 1817. A quite damning document with enough in it to get my master hanged a dozen times. I begged him not to pen the work, but he was so determined to leave an historical record of the events. It would be much to his peril if it fell into the wrong hands, Mr Quest. What are we to do?'

Quest thought for a moment.

'Well, there's a possibility he somehow got off this train and caught the next. My friend Jasper Feedle's waiting outside the railway station. He knows Mr Lyddon very well. I'll ask Jasper to stay here and await the next train. Meanwhile, we'll go back to my house in Bloomsbury and I'll send some electric telegraphs to my associates in Manchester. Until we get some further news, well, that's all we can do, I fear.'

'If anything's happened to Mr Lyddon, I'll never forgive myself,' said Brendon.

~

'Something's amiss, inspector,' said Parkin.

Honour Bright rubbed his chin.

'Well, clearly Lyddon wasn't on the train and they all look surprised and agitated. They're leaving and it will be interesting to see where they go. Best you follow them, Parkin. See if you can pick up a constable along the way, who can run messages for you. You'll find me back at Scotland Yard. I must relate this turn of events to the Commissioner. They'll probably go to Quest's house but we can't be sure. Don't lose them, Parkin. Don't lose them...'

~

'You're letting me down very badly, boy,' said Dugdale. 'I've done my very best for you. Encouraged your writing. Given you a roof over your head even. I rarely support young writers of literary promise, like you. Too many come flocking to my door. But I saw real promise in you, real promise.'

The little man paced up and down between the counter and window of his bookshop. After much striding, he paused and picked up a volume from a table in one dark corner.

He lovingly fingered the leather binding.

'Now you see this one, lad? *Venus Revisited*. Written by one of my proteges... a young man with not half your talent, set in the night house run by my old friend Mrs Bendig. Oh, mighty! I should have taken you there for an evening of delights. Would have scattered your inhibitions, Daniel boy. Look, I can see you're not used to the ways of the world. But once you've actually lain with a woman or two, it'll all be different! You'll see. And Daniel, lad... nobody's saying you can't write those great novels you have in mind. Of course you can... but all struggling authors have to keep the wolf from the door in the meantime. I'm sure you can see that? Give it a chance, lad. Give it a...'

'I appreciate your kindness to me, Mr Dugdale, but my mind is set upon a more literary course...'

Dugdale threw up his hands in despair, pacing even faster.

'Then you'll starve, boy! Then you'll starve. The workhouses and rookery slums are full of young men who came to this city hoping to be writers and artists. There isn't any gold in the pavements of London, take my word for it... you'll go down with nary a crust passing your lips and only foul water or small beer to drink, shivering in the dank and cold of some rookery. Just like all the rest. And all because you won't do this other work to support you while you make your name. Why, Mr Dickens... even Mr Dickens did other work while he wrote his grand books.'

'Respectable journalism... not the books you publish, Mr Dugdale.'

Dugdale stopped at the window and faced him.

'Listen lad... I'm proud of every single one of my publications. I fulfil a need in society... and many a fine writer's penned my tomes in the past. Many a man who's now got a great reputation. And you could be like them... you really could. I know talent when I see it. But every writer has to start somewhere, can you see that?'

'Yes, I can see that but... I'm determined upon my course and...'

'You'll realise, Daniel, if you do this, well, I can no longer accommodate you in your present lodgings. I always reserve that room for genuine contributors... so I'd have to ask you to leave the premises by this very night...'

'I'm sorry, Mr Dugdale... but I have been promised other arrangements...'

Dugdale gave a hard stare at the young author.

'Ah, I see it all now, Daniel. You've been poached haven't you? Poached by one of the other publishers in this street. One of those inferior purveyors of interesting volumes... tell me, which one of the thieving villains is it? I'll sort them out and pay you far more than they ever would...'

'I do assure you, Mr Dugdale, I'm working for no other bookseller. The person who's offered me lodgings has nothing at all to do with the book trade. He's in quite a different line of business. Walking sticks and umbrellas...'

'Walking sticks and umbrellas? You expect me to believe that?'

Dugdale's memory ranged across the shops of London that sold such aids. A thought crossed his mind...

'Ah, I think I know the establishment you mean... but no... that company would have nothing to do with the likes of you, though they do work in charity, that's true... but that's purely for the desperate. Not nascent young authors still penning their trumpery first works... no, Daniel. My first guess is the best... it's one of the rogues along this street. Be honest and tell me who it is, eh? Tell me now? And...'

Dugdale stared along the street, as though his malignant look might ferret out a possible literary poacher. Daniel Moonlight watched the little man's expression change from fury to puzzlement and then to alarm. He turned and gazed open-mouthed in Daniel's direction. The young man thought that the bookseller looked positively unwell.

Then Dugdale rushed across to the door, turning the key in the lock and pushing across the three mighty bolts.

'It's the crushers, lad. The crushers. A dozen of them coming on a raid. Help me, boy. Get them books off the table and to the stove in the back room. The Crushers! But they can't convict me without evidence. Quick lad! Quick!'

Even as they both picked up an armful of books, there was a mighty crash against the door of the shop. And then another... and another...

'My God! they're using a battering ram,' Dugdale ejaculated.

The back room was always very hot, for Dugdale always kept the stove blazing away, lest there be exigencies such as this. He thrust his armful of books deep into the flames and glanced as Daniel did the same.

'Grab some more! Over there!'

He pointed to a huge pile on a table.

They loaded them into their arms and began pushing the volumes two or three at a time into the flames. The little shop echoed with the crashes of the battering ram and the cries of the policemen outside.

Daniel looked out and saw that even the reinforced timbers of the doorway were cracking under the assault. The lock came away, tumbling on to the floor and two of the bolts were no longer holding the door in place.

'They're going to get in...'

Even as Daniel said the words the door swung open, coming away at the top hinge. The four men holding the battering ram fell into the shop, followed by two constables dressed as barrow boys and two men in smarter civilian dress.

'All right, Dugdale! We're here to search your shop,' said Sergeant Berry.

The bookseller turned away from the almost overwhelming heat of the stove to face the intruders, a look of triumph on his face.

'What's the meaning of this appalling attack on the rights of a free-born Englishman?' Dugdale demanded. 'How can you justify damaging the property of a legitimate trader in this way?'

'Legitimate?' said Berry. 'You've already served a sentence for purveying your filthy literature and pictures. There are dips in this street more legitimate than you are...'

'Anything left, Sergeant?' asked Anders.

Berry looked again at the stove.

'All gone up, I'm afraid.'

'Just burning some unwanted stock,' Dugdale insisted. 'What's wrong with that?'

'A lot when it's your sort of stock,' said Berry.

He looked at Daniel Moonlight.

'Who are you?'

'A friend of Mr Dugdale's...'

'A customer, more like. Boys of your age shouldn't be reading the sort of thing that gets purveyed here. What's your name?'

'As a law-abiding citizen, I don't believe I'm obliged to give you my name.'

'Really? Well... what do you think, Inspector?'

Anders looked the lad up and down. He liked the look of him, one of those innocents who'd fallen foul of bad company.

He was inclined to see him off with a warning.

'Might be what he says, Sergeant. I'm inclined to send the boy on his way, though I wouldn't want to ever catch him again in such premises. What do you think, Sergeant?'

Berry waved away the heat of the stove.

'To be honest, sir, I'd be inclined to put this youth in a cell for the night. Bow Street's not far away. Bit crowded at the moment, for they've got that pick-pocketing gang slammed up and he'd have to go in a cell with them. Right lot of juicy villains. A night in with them might turn this lad's thoughts well away from unreasonable behaviour in the future.'

'On what charge?' Daniel asked 'You can't just lock people up...'

'But you're *here*. In a shop of dubious reputation,' said Berry. 'For all we know you might be an employee of Dugdale...'

'He's not!' the shopkeeper said.

Dugdale wondered what Daniel might say after a night in Bow Street.

'Just a customer, like I said. And might I point out, Inspector, I object to these slanderous remarks about my reputation being made. You've entered my premises, broken down my door, traduced my reputation. Have you even a warrant?'

Inspector Anders drew out the magistrate's warrant from an inner pocket.

'You still haven't found nothing!' Dugdale exclaimed.

'There's this, inspector,' said one of the constables. 'Must have slipped on to the floor...'

He passed the book to Anders.

'Now what have we here? *Venus Revisited?*'

Anders thumbed through the publication, glancing up and seeing the alarm on Dugdale's face. It was the book that he'd been showing to Daniel during their argument. He'd had it in his hand as he'd paced the shop, dropping it when the policemen launched their attack.

'Hardly nursery rhymes, Dugdale,' said Anders.

'Not mine. Some customer must have dropped it!'

Anders laughed. 'I doubt the stipendiary magistrate at Bow Street will swallow that yarn any more than me.'

'Bet he will! He's a customer of mine!' Dugdale muttered under his breath.

'Cuff him, Sergeant.'

Berry stepped forward, pulling Dugdale's arms behind his back.

'You're hurting me!' the little man groaned.

'This isn't necessary,' said Daniel stepping forward. 'He's a shopkeeper, not a burglar. I'm sure he'll go peacefully, if you'll let him.'

Berry reached out a hand to push Daniel away. The action triggered a memory of a manoeuvre Daniel had practised with Sticks in Hyde Park that very morning. The boy grabbed the sergeant's wrist, twisting it round very suddenly and pushing his knee up into the policeman's chest.

Berry fell backwards on to the floor.

He gazed up at Daniel, then at Anders who gave him a nod.

'Put the darbies on him, constable. One more for Bow Street.'

Fourteen

'I know someone who wants to kill you,' said Sticks.

'I should think you know a great many,' said Quest. 'Who's the latest?'

Sticks had rushed into the sitting room that Quest always used when he was entertaining visitors at his home in Bloomsbury. Rosa Stanton greeted him with a smile, Wren Angier with a quizzical look, and a stranger looked up at him with some interest.

'Sticks, this is James Brendon, secretary to Jonas Lyddon.'

'Is Mr Lyddon not here?' asked the old prizefighter.

'He wasn't on the train. Jasper's waiting for the next one. It's not due in for a couple of hours. Now who's this man who wishes to slay me? You may talk freely in front of our guest.'

'He's the lad I was telling you about. Worse than that... I've spent a number of mornings teaching him the best ways *to* kill you. He calls himself Daniel Moonlight and – apart from killing you – he has ambitions to write novels.'

'I've always said every man of literature should have a sideline,' grinned Wren Angier.

'It might be as well not to give him further instruction,' said Rosa. 'Do you think him capable of killing William?'

'Not face to face, though the last time I talked to the boy, he seemed keen to call you out in a duel. You'd kill him, of course, should that happen. But he's so determined to top you, there's a real danger he might just take a pot-shot at you from some street corner. He says he's got a couple of pistols.'

'Exactly why does he *want* to kill William?' asked Angier.

'Well, he says Will here's brought ruin and disgrace to his family.'

'How?' asked Quest. 'To the best of my knowledge I've never met anyone called Moonlight. Is that his real name? Sounds fanciful to me.'

'I suspect not. One of those writing names more like. Anyways, you're not in immediate danger. The lad's currently occupying a police cell at Bow Street, courtesy of a couple of pals of yours.'

'What pals?'

'Inspector Anders and Sergeant Berry.'

'This is becoming quite fascinating, Sticks. Tell us more,' said Angier.

'Well, after our martial session this morning I thought as how I might tail the young gent to see where he went and who he met. Lest he fall into bad company. And he did.'

'Who?'

'Dugdale – in his shop in Holywell Street.'

'I thought Dugdale had been locked up?' said Rosa.

'Well, he ain't locked up at present. Anyway, the boy hadn't been there many minutes then the police raided the shop, smashing down the door. I was watching all this from the alley across the street. After a while, Anders and Berry came out with both Dugdale and Daniel Moonlight – the darbies on the pair of them. Dragged them down the road to Bow Street. They left a constable behind to guard the shop until the door could be repaired. Chatty bloke. I asked him what was going on? Apparently, Daniel had knocked Berry to the ground. Which means big trouble for the lad. And his father a parson as well...'

'A parson?' asked Rosa. 'What does this Daniel look like?'

'Oh, about twenty at a guess. Dark hair a tad too long, and very dark eyes to go with it. Nose perhaps a bit too big for his face, not that that mars his looks. No, a good-looking lad. But very, very green. Not the sort of lad that'd last very long in a police cell.'

'We've got to get him out of there, Will,' Rosa said.

'I can't see why?' said Angier. 'And if he's determined to kill William, then a police cell's the best place for him surely? Anyway, I can't see how we could. If he's assaulted a police sergeant, they'll have him up before the stipendiary first thing tomorrow.'

'Beaks don't like men who attack a crusher,' said Sticks.

'Anyway, Jonas Lyddon has to be our concern, not this young idiot,' said Quest.

'We have *got* to get him out of there,' Rosa persisted. 'You see, I think this Daniel Moonlight might be my brother!'

~

How it had altered...

Jonas Lyddon had changed trains twice before he arrived at New Street Station in Birmingham. It was early afternoon as he walked out into the street, not really recognising the place.

There seemed little evidence that the Froggery had ever existed. The recently built railway station had swept all the old buildings away. It had been twenty years since he was last here, when the Froggery was a district of tumbling slums, filled with the most wretchedly poor of the city.

You could tell those hovels had been built on marshland by the way water dripped down the inside walls of the poor homes, and how, on wet days, the streets would flood, bringing mud and detritus through doorways where the wooden doors were so rotted that they seldom closed.

Jonas had met an old man who had been born long before even the slums had been built. When this place was a real marsh with a great open pond in its middle. When the few residents huddled in cold shacks by the side of the water, living on fish and eels and the occasional trapped bird.

That old man had detested the slums and Jonas wondered what the long-dead native would have made of the huge railway station that had swept the slums away, much as their building had encroached on the marsh?

Jonas was no lover of slums, but he found the changes of the modern world bewildering. The whole world seemed to be changing. He wondered what had happened to the families who'd lived hereabouts, now that the station and railway had been planted over the places where they had lived?

Out in the street, he felt completely disorientated. These new roads bore little resemblance to the old street pattern and he couldn't quite picture where he was. There was a street trader selling flowers hard by the station entrance, and Jonas felt obliged to ask the way to the Cockpit tavern.

He walked along the new street, as he'd been directed, then turned right into a narrow thoroughfare. And there was the Cockpit – aptly named, for in its day it had been a notorious venue for cock and dog-fighting. To his surprise, the old building had survived the general demolition, though it was now fronted with newer brickwork and a garish painted sign.

The street was busy, but there seemed to be no one who was taking any interest in him, so he went inside. Here too, there was a transformation. In the old days, this had been one long room where the tavern-keeper sold small beer and ale from a table placed by the farthest wall. A flight of steps had led down to a cellar where there had been the cockpit, a venue where both the poorest and the sporting gents of the city had come together to follow their brutal fancy.

But now the Cockpit had been divided into two rooms, with a bar counter placed between them. The landlord had put the cellar to a more innocent use, for he was struggling up the steps with a keg of ale. A great fat man, sweating with the exertion of carrying the load up the steps.

He smiled at Jonas.

'Good day, sir. What would be your pleasure?'

Jonas was served ale in a pewter mug, beginning to wonder if there was a purpose to this journey at all. Perhaps he should have risked staying on the train all the way to London, but no... his instinct for survival, which had served him well for all these years told him that he'd done the right thing...

He put a coin down on the counter in payment, but the landlord pushed it back towards him.

'Are you the gent from Manchester?' said the landlord.

'I have come from Manchester,' Jonas said warily.

'I thought as much.' The landlord gave him a long hard stare, smiling. 'I know you, don't I? Though it must be ten – no twenty years since you were last in these parts. Long before it all changed around here, long before they built that bostin' new station that's improved my trade no end. I know you, sir. For I saw you speechin' at the time of the riots up at the Bull Ring. Ah, brave days, sir! Brave days!' He waved a hand towards the door into the other bar. 'I think you'll find a friend of both of ours in there.'

Jonas nodded and opened the door into a smaller, darker room, with a great coal fire blazing away. At first he thought the place empty, but then noticed an old man sitting at one end of the settle who, having thrown a great lump of coal on to the fire, turned and smiled.

'Jonas Lyddon – in the flesh, I do declare! We always seem to meet in strange places, old pal.'

'I remember the first time we met, Harry Blizzard, when you played footpad and tried to rob me on the high road to Moreton.'

Jonas shook his hand.

'What are you doing here, Harry?'

'As you know, I'm mostly retired from troublemaking, as I was loathe to be pulled away from my wife and our little shop. But I've kept in touch with other renegades. A day or two ago, some lout got drunk in a public house in Manchester. A villain well-known for nefarious doings in those parts. Boasted as how he'd been approached to help kidnap a certain political gent – *you*. He didn't want the work cos he was terribly afeared of trains, but they'd told him too much. Should have silenced him but they didn't...'

'Who are *they*?'

Harry Blizzard shrugged.

'Who's to know? But they were to get on the train at a certain stop down the line. Get into your carriage. A mile or two on, the engine was to be brought to a halt with a cart stranded on the line. A good clear stretch that the driver could see coming. And then the scum in your carriage were going to spirit you away, off the train to a horse conveyance nearby.'

'Why wouldn't they just slit my throat?'

'Oh, no – no – no. They wants you alive, old pal. The drunken lout – a man more used to slinkin' murder – was told that under no circumstances were you to be harmed. And if they want you in captivity that much, there must be a reason for it.'

'They could have just carried me off in Manchester.'

'Oh no, too many people about you, Jonas. They wanted you in some lonely stretch of the country. No witnesses. Nobody to come to your help. Then a closed carriage. All the way to London, our drunken friend had been told.'

'But I was on my way to London anyway. They could have waited until I got there.'

'Ah, but you're a famous man in London. Always people about you. Harder to snatch you there. So your friends in Manchester thought out this plan, that you should break your journey here in Brummagem. And as I'm not that far away, over in the Black Country, they got in touch with me. So here I am...'

'I'm grateful, Harry. How is your wife?'

'Sends her love. Was determined that I should come to you here. Now all we've got to work out is how to get you to your friends in London, without these gentry getting their filthy hands on you.'

'They can't be watching every train...'

'Who's to say? Our friends in Manchester aren't thinking of this as some act of petty villainy. No... mark my words... it's the Class that are behind this. You've made a lot of foes with all those reforms you've fought for... but there's more to it than that... if they want you breathing rather than dead, I'd suggest they see you as someone to bargain with. Got a deeper reason to taking you than just putting you away.'

'I can't think what it could be...'

'They could swing you on the gallows just for what you did on Dartmoor in 'seventeen. They must know of it, even if they can't prove it. You're still a legend in those parts, for the way you took the fight to the enemy. Long memories some people have got in their heads. They might have taken the gibbet pole off Gibbet Hill, but they recall what happened there.'

'You've been back?'

'The wife and I thought we might have one last look at Dartmoor before we croak...'

'Not the same place is it? Not the same place at all...'

'Places never are!'

There was a tap on the door and the landlord signalled to Blizzard.

Jonas warmed his hands by the fire, oblivious to what seemed an agitated conversation. He turned as Harry crossed back to the fireplace.

'We got trouble!'

'What is it, Harry?'

'You don't think you were followed? Well, I think you were. They must have been watching for you at every railway station down the line. The landlord says there's three rascals across the road, seemin' to take a great interest in this place. And as this is now a respectable neighbourhood, it's more than likely it's you they're after.'

'Is there a back way out of here?'

'There's no back way. It went when they built the gun manufactory in the next street. So we can either stay in here, or get out there and face them. If we stay here, there's a chance they'll get others and come in and trigger what the crushers will call a drunken brawl - getting you away in the mayhem. So I'm minded we should get out now and see these scum off, while there's only the three of 'em.'

'But Harry - this isn't Dartmoor forty years ago! We're two crocked-out old men! My fighting days are over. Besides, I've forsworn violence.'

Harry reached into a satchel on the settle by the fireside, producing two stout coshes.

'Mementoes of olden times! Thought as how they might come in useful.'

'Violence Harry!'

'Naw! Breaking heads ain't violence. Rogues like them expect to get their heads bashed from time to time. It goes with their foul employment... And we're two old men, ain't we? So it'll be the last thing those darlings will expect...'

~

'What exactly are you asking me to do, Quest?'

Inspector Anders and Sergeant Berry had installed themselves in a back office in the Bow Street police station, while they dealt with the prosecution of Dugdale and his young helper.

Quest, Rosa Stanton, Wren Angier and Sticks had burst in, brooking no opposition from the policeman guarding the door.

Quest could see the annoyance on Anders's face - the detective had had a busy morning and for some reason was not in the best of moods. During their recent stay in York, they'd been on first name terms.

Now it was back to the more formal "Quest".

'Give me one good reason why I should release the young villain?' said Anders. 'Is that what you want, Quest? A dangerous felon who attacked my sergeant! No, Quest - the boy goes before the stipendiary magistrate here before the day's out. Now go away!'

Quest sat down on a chair facing Anders across the desk.

'Sir Wren Angier here has been in to see this Daniel Moonlight...' he began.

Anders thumped the desk and gave the constable, who was hovering in the doorway, an angry look.

'Constable, I said that nobody was to be allowed to visit either Dugdale or Moonlight, I'll...'

'Oh, don't blame the constable, Anders,' said Wren Angier. 'I threw my weight around and insisted. I am, after all, a member of Parliament. Not the fault of these Bow Street officers. The boy said to me that he acted instinctively when he saw Sergeant Berry assaulting the man Dugdale...'

Berry stepped forward.

'I did not assault...'

Anders held up a hand and silenced him.

'My sergeant was quite legitimately putting the cuffs on a known felon...'

'Behind his back? Was that really necessary?' said Angier.

'Dugdale's a recidivist. Commissioner Mayne's made it quite clear that hardened offenders should be shackled in just such a way.'

'Twisting his arm behind his back in a way that made the man cry out in pain?' Angier continued.

'He was putting it on!' said Berry. 'You've no idea, sir, of the tricks these rogues get up to. They often cry brutality when they're arrested.'

'You weren't in uniform, of course...' Angier pointed out.

'With respect, Sir Wren, we are officers of the detective division. We seldom are in uniform,' said Anders.

'And the constables who assisted you... dressed as barrow boys... costermongers... are they all in the detective division as well?' asked Angier.

'They were constables under my supervision,' Anders replied. 'We made it quite clear, when we entered the premises, that we were policemen.'

'The boy may not have heard you,' said Quest.

'He did!' Anders persisted.

'He might have thought that this man Dugdale was being attacked by business rivals,' Quest went on.

'I'm sure you don't seriously believe that yourself, Quest!' said Anders. 'And if that were the case, why should Dugdale burn his books at all, let alone just the more disgusting publications?'

'It does leave room for doubt though?' said Angier. 'As I understand it, Inspector, no uniformed constables appeared until after Berry here shackled Dugdale. In the heat of the moment, the boy misguidedly struck out. Are you really going to prosecute him for that?'

'Eyes of the law it's not just assault, but battery as well,' said Anders.

'And you intend to bring him before the stipendiary?' asked Rosa.

'I do, Miss Stanton, I will not have my officers attacked.' He looked at her with some suspicion. 'You seem agitated, Miss Stanton? Do you know this boy?'

Rosa leaned forward across the desk.

'Oh, Inspector! He's my brother! My dear sweet brother! A good boy, sir! The son of a parson. Oh my God! The scandal of this will drive my father out of his parish! And our father has a weak heart, Inspector! This will be the finish of him! His only son lagged! Oh, please, Inspector... he's been a foolish boy, but I beg you to spare him... and our family!'

'Save the histrionics for Drury Lane, Miss Stanton! That's by far the worst bit of acting I've seen in all my life. Perhaps you need a playwright to give you adequate lines...'

Rosa retreated and placed her head against the door, seeming to weep.

'Enough, Miss Stanton! Are those fake tears for your brother, or my criticism of your acting? The magistrate will consider your brother's case at four of the clock.'

'Inconvenient for me, for I'm due in the Commons at that time,' said Angier. 'But needs must. I was once called to the bar, Inspector. I shall undertake the lad's defence myself! The stipendiary supports my political party, I believe. It'll be nice to see him again. He's so respectful of members of Parliament.'

'All right! All right! I will get the sergeant at the front desk to admonish the boy... give him an official warning! But listen to me now, all of you. If any single one of you crosses me again, not all the political conniving, not all the doubtful acting, not even the presumption of friendship will save you! I'll have the very last one of you in Newgate Gaol! Now get out of my sight!'

After they had all gone along with the constable, who'd been given orders to release Daniel, Anders looked up at Berry. He said nothing for a while. Then...

'Probably worked out for the best, Sergeant, though I'd have quite liked to have seen your assailant in the dock. But there's no doubt that Quest and his friends would have turned the event into a circus! And that might have foiled our work undercover.'

'Oh, I can take the little that boy dished out. Hardly felt it really, though it was humiliating to be caught out like that! But no doubt about it, we don't really want to draw attention to ourselves - and such publicity might well have annoyed Wissilcraft and the Secret Service, especially if Quest got a mention in the court reporting.'

'Commissioner Mayne's livid enough about the way the Yard's being used by Wissilcraft and his friends as it is. But we can all see the necessity of it. I suppose we'd better have a meeting with Wissilcraft. You see, I think it would help in this dilemma if Quest knew exactly what was going on...'

'Wissilcraft won't like that, Inspector, but forewarned is forearmed.'

~

The two men carefully removed the stained-glass panel from the wall, occasionally glancing up at their master, fear on their faces. When they had done, he stepped forward, running a hand over the roughness of the ancient glass. He had always loved the feel of things... the touch, even the old smell that few others could detect. The men gently wrapped the glass panel in a blanket and lowered it on to a stretcher.

'Be careful with it,' he ordered. 'It is very old! Your lives are at peril if it is at all damaged! Do you understand that?'

Both men nodded as they carried the stretcher towards the staircase.

He waited for several minutes until he heard the back door of *Tenebrae* close behind them. Such a pity! It had been a good house, though only leased, but it had attracted too much attention.

It was time to move the darkness elsewhere.

He heard a step behind him.

'I've set up the candles in the far room, sir. They are all alight.'

Crouch was a small man, scarce half the height of his master.

'I'm leaving now, Crouch. You know what to do?'

'Yessir!'

Crouch turned to look at the gap in the wall, where the glass panel had been.

'They took it away very careful, sir.'

'A good job for them! Do you know, Crouch, that this is the third building it has been set up in since I acquired it? Not counting the medieval place from where it came?'

'I do, sir.'

His master gave a great sigh.

'Such a pity to have to keep moving it! Every move brings a risk of it being damaged. Crouch... I want you to go to the next place and make sure it is safe and secure. If those two dolts have put a single mark upon it, you are to cut their throats! Do you understand that? Now I have business to attend to...'

Crouch ran the back of his hand around the gap where the glass had stood, old mortar coming away at his touch. His master's obsession with the antiquity had always puzzled him. A piece of stained glass – that's all it was, after all? And yet...

He turned to find the room empty, his master gone...

Walking into the far room, he noted that the five candles were all burning quite evenly. He came back through the partition, glancing briefly through the window, looking out at Piccadilly. It seemed quiet enough out there. Anyway, he intended to leave by the rear door...

He walked across to the broken gaslight burner and turned it full on.

~

'I still don't understand why you wouldn't let me see my brother?' Rosa said, as she and Quest walked the streets back to the Bloomsbury house. 'He needs to know I'm here for him.'

They'd left Bow Street police station before the others. Wren Angier and Sticks had remained behind to escort Daniel Moonlight away from custody.

'Your brother will be brought to the house and everything will be explained to him. He'll be there in an hour or two, as soon as Sticks and Wren have taken him to his diggings so that he might fetch his possessions. It'll give the boy time to get over the shock of being arrested.'

'He'll still want to kill you, perhaps?' she glanced sideways at him.

'Well, that's for you to sort out, Rosa. How on earth did he get the idea that I'd ruined you?'

'I can't begin to imagine!'

~

'Definitely on our tail,' said Harry Blizzard, as he and Jonas walked away from the tavern. 'Three that I can see – probably that's the lot of them. Probably think three's enough to deal with two old blokes like us. You know, the trouble with age is you never feel it in your mind. Only dawns on you that you're grave-dodging when you look in a mirror, or try reaching up for summat!'

Jonas looked back at their three followers, who were closer now than they had been.

'This isn't some alley in a rookery, Harry. They'll scarcely try anything here.'

'No, but they'll keep tailing us until they find somewhere more convenient.'

'Perhaps it'd be safer if we went back to the railway station?'

Harry Blizzard looked at him aghast.

'Blimey, you really have lost it, old pal! Just what they want. To get you alone on a train. Every station down the line watched. No doubt you'd be dealt with long afore you got to London.'

'But I must get to London!'

'And you will! Even if we have to pad it every step of the way. But our first task is to get these three louts off our back. And to do that we must take the fight to them, just as we would have done in the old days. That'd be the last thing they expect.'

'It's the last thing *I* expected!'

'Oh, come on! We've faced worse peril than this in our time.'

'Yes, Harry. When we were young! I haven't been in a brawl for twenty years. They'll probably slaughter us!'

Blizzard laughed.

'But what a glorious way to die, eh? No, it seems to me they want you alive, so that puts a handicap on them from the start. They'd probably get in trouble if they break your head. Probably kill me, mind! Now, towards the end of this street there's a blind alley, a relic of the old slums. The sort of deep dark place where the railwaymen take their whores for a tupping. If those lads behind are local, well, they'll know it don't lead nowhere.'

'We'd be trapped...'

'We will indeed. Just like the old days, eh? Oh, who said all the good days were over? Just think of how we'd have dealt with them on Dartmoor in 'seventeen... That's all we got to do.'

'You're mad Harry!'

'Yes... wonderful isn't it? Just when you think you're in some boring old age, an opportunity like this comes along! One last rumble before your gut settles down on the pathway to the graveyard!'

~

The pedestrians in Piccadilly heard a whoosh rather than a bang. Several dived across the road to the far pavement, then watched as the flames engulfed the top storey of Tenebrae. Another explosion took off the roof, throwing the tiles backwards away from the street. There was a great crash as rubble from the roof fell down through the wooden floors, forcing the flames through the lower windows, smashing the glass in each, sending great jets of flame out into the street. A police constable ran along the street, waving his police rattle above his head, crying out for people to take cover. The front door of Tenebrae fell outwards as the gas pipes, on the lower floors of the building, blew open the footings of the building. Chaos reigned as great clouds of black smoke swept over Piccadilly and then across Westminster.

~

There's always a spokesman, Harry Blizzard thought, as the three hulking brutes turned into the alley, blocking out much of the light. This time it was a fat man with a great black beard, who stood on the left side of the trio, rubbing the knuckles on his fist.

Blackbeard looked at Harry.

'Not you we want,' he growled. 'Him...' he gestured towards Lyddon. 'Not goin' to hurt him, just goin' to take him on a little journey. So if he comes quiet, there ain't goin' to be any trouble. See?'

The three men took a pace forward and Harry Blizzard took a step in their direction, before half-turning to face Jonas.

'None of us wants trouble,' said Harry. 'That's certain sure.'

Harry put both his hands away behind his back.

'That's good then,' said Blackbeard.

'Good indeed,' said Harry, 'I'm sorry, mate,' he said to Jonas. 'Best that you go with them. This ain't my fight. I'm too old for fists, I'm sure you can see that, can't you? I'm an old man and I don't want any trouble. These hands ain't up to fighting!'

He took a step closer to the three.

'Very wise,' said Blackbeard. 'Very wise indeed, and...'

Harry Blizzard saw the sudden look of surprise on the villain's face when, as if from nowhere, the cosh came sweeping in towards his nose, smashing it and sending a great geyser of blood down his chest.

The cosh swept hard into his gut before coming away, crashing into his kneecap. Blackbeard fell against the man in the middle, sending him off balance towards Jonas. Lyddon swung his own cosh hard against the side of the man's head, knocking him senseless on to the cobbles. Blackbeard was groaning and trying to scramble to his feet.

'Some bastards just don't know when to lie down!' Harry complained as he brought the cosh down on Blackbeard's head.

Then smashed it down again.

Blackbeard lay stunned and bleeding on the cobbles.

The third man, the youngest and weediest of the bunch, tried to leg it out of the alley, but found Harry Blizzard blocking his path. Harry pushed the end of his cosh hard into the man's stomach, forcing him backwards against the alley wall.

As the man gasped for breath, Harry grasped the cosh with both hands and pressed it hard against the man's throat, giving Jonas a quick smile as he watched his victim struggling for breath.

'Now, old son, I might spare your miserable life rather than choke the life out of you. I've given you a taste of what the gallows has in store – the way it takes your breath away as you go down through the drop – but I'm quite happy to finish the job and force this cosh hard against your throat. Take away every last breath. But in order to do that, you'd better take that breath now – and swiftly. I want to know who put you up to this? Speak or you'll be burning in hell by the time my friend and I leaves this alley.'

Harry eased the cosh away very slightly, watching as the spittle came out of the youth's mouth and a great stream of green snot ran down from his nose. Harry smiled as he saw the terror in the weeping eyes.

'You're a young lad... you don't want to perish in this grubby alley.'

'I dare not!' the youth gasped out the words.

'Oh, I think you do dare... no one else you need to fear, old son. You only need to fear me! Cos if you don't squawk right now you are dead!'

'Tenebrae... Tenebrae...'

'What the hell's Tenebrae?'

'They give the orders... Parkes carried 'em out. Kill Parkes not me. Kill him... not me.'

'Parkes who?'

'Justin... Parkes,' the youth stuttered.

'Justin Parkes? You've got to be joking!'

Jonas saw Harry's puzzled face.

'Him... I tell yer. Justin Parkes.'

Harry took the cosh away and the youth vomited and turned towards the street. As he looked away, Harry brought the cosh down on the back of his head.

'Have a nice nap son!' he said.

'Who's Justin Parkes?' asked Jonas.

'Just a local villain. Not important in himself. A man who fixes things for others, as long as he's paid enough. No doubt he'll get it in the neck for this failure. If not, I'll attend to him much later. Doubt any of his rascals will cross our path again, once we are clear of Brummagem and the Black Country.'

Fifteen

The Newgate Shadow
Daniel picked up the little paper-covered book and examined it with great interest. It was obviously a regular, if occasional, publication, produced by a bookseller in Newgate Street – just a few yards from the great and awful prison that gave it a title. He'd seen such productions before. Indeed, Mr Dugdale sold a variety of them in his bookshop, including the renowned *Newgate Calendar*.

This little book was of that familiar kind; bold and garish headlines: accounts of some of those who had been incarcerated in Newgate and other gaols. A chapter on the highwayman Turpin, the thief and escaper Jack Sheppard – so familiar to Daniel from the pages of Mr Harrison Ainsworth's novel, one of the first books he'd read when he arrived in London.

As he turned the cheap yellowing pages, he found that it contained accounts of more recent trials at the Old Bailey; vivid descriptions of the public hangings outside Newgate Gaol which, though they attracted crowds in the tens of thousands, were not – the anonymous author suggested – quite as merry as those glorious days of the past. When the condemned were taken the length of Oxford Street, stopping at taverns along the way, to dance a jig as they were swung on Tyburn Tree.

The most recent account of a trial at the Bailey was that of Simeon Prowl, a villain who'd survived in the profession of footpad even into old age.

Though he'd been lagged several times for minor offences, spending considerable time in the House of Correction at Clerkenwell, and a spell in Millbank, he had not been deterred from his life of crime. Out of his age, Simeon Prowl was too late and too poor to be a highwayman. He'd never have been wealthy enough to afford a horse...

So he'd spent his criminal career in foot-paddery, haunting the heaths and commons around London with his ancient pistol, robbing the gentry as they made their way home. And as his victims were themselves obliged to walk, not being wealthy enough to afford a horse or carriage, he seldom made much blunt from his dangerous occupation.

So it might have gone on, the writer of the *Newgate Shadow* related, but for one misfortune on a cold autumn night. In all the many times he'd relieved weary travellers of their purses, Simeon Prowl had never had to actually fire his pistol.

He wasn't sure it would even work.

But one evening on Hampstead Heath, his chosen victim, a shop-keeper, travelling a short journey to court a milkmaid who dwelt on the far side of the

Heath, had tried to seize the pistol. It had gone off, putting a ball through the man's throat.

Two constables heard the shot, getting there within a minute, seizing the unfortunate footpad and dragging him away to face the capital charge of murder on the Queen's Highway.

They'd hauled him down to the police office at Bow Street, then sent him across to Newgate to await his trial. And all the time, Simeon Prowl insisted that he'd never intended to actually use the pistol. If the murdered man had not tried to wrest it from his grasp, had simply handed over his purse... well, none of this would ever have happened...

But the killing had come at an unfortunate time for Prowl. Newspaper editors had been railing at the resurgence of crime in the city and how unsafe the place had become. Foot-paddery, they admitted, was now a rare offence, but Simeon Prowl's actions might inspire others to take up robbery on the highway.

And so Simeon Prowl had found himself in the dock at the Old Bailey, watching as the court usher placed the black cap over the judge's wig.

Then he heard the dread words...

You will be taken from here to a place of execution and there you will be hanged by the neck until you be dead. And may God have mercy upon your soul...

But the execution had not yet taken place, the writer said.

First there was talk that the death sentence was to be commuted to Penal Servitude for Life, though the home secretary had denied that, insisting that the gallows were to be put up outside Newgate Gaol in the very near future. As an example to others, Simeon Prowl was definitely to be turned off by the public hangman. And then...

Daniel looked up from his reading as Sticks came into the room at the top of the house, perhaps once a servant's quarter, where he had been deposited with his trunk earlier that afternoon.

'Not the *Newgate Shadow?*' Sticks said. 'Not the best of reading for the likes of you!'

'It is – in its way – interesting.'

'Then you must tell its author when you see him!'

'Its author?'

'You've made his acquaintance already. The little pamphlet was written by a hack who lived above the bookseller's shop in Newgate Street. But he croaked from the pox a while ago. Jasper Feedle has written the past two editions – though why he wants to bother at his age is beyond me? He was ever the scrivener!'

'Jasper whom I met at Rat's Castle?'

'The very same rogue and a great friend of mine. And not just for his penmanship, Daniel. A bonny fighter all those years ago. Fought under Wellington in Portugal and Spain. Lost that leg at the Battle of Waterloo. You should listen to Jasper's yarns, lad. Enough tales there to fill up a dozen novels.'

'Sticks – when am I to meet my host? Or have I? Does this house belong to Sir Wren? You were both so kind to me, freeing me from the police cell at Bow Street, helping me here with my trunk.'

'No, not Sir Wren's house. He has a set of rooms at Albany and another home elsewhere. No... this house belongs to one of the most remarkable men you'll ever meet. He sends his apologies, but he's expecting a friend at the railway station and has been obliged to go there. I'm sure he'll have a long conversation with you on his return. Now I must see to the meal...'

Before Daniel could say anything more, Sticks left the room, shutting the door behind him.

What strange circumstances, he thought.

Who was his mysterious host and how did they persuade that angry police inspector to let him go?

Daniel strode up and down the room for a moment, looking out of the window. The only view was down to a paved yard and a tall house to the rear of it. The room he was in was barely furnished, just a bed and a table, with a ewer of water and a washstand. But anything was better than that stinking cell at Bow Street and the unpleasant characters who'd shared it with him.

He opened his trunk so that he might change his clothes and remove the stink that clung to his apparel from that cell. Having dressed, he opened the secret compartment at the bottom of the trunk.

Ah, there were the gold sovereigns, his only protection from destitution, unless he returned home. And the lovely varnished box containing his pair of percussion-cap pistols. He stroked the fine-grained box, admiring its smoothness. Then he opened the lid...

The percussion caps and the lead balls were there.

But the pistols had gone...

In a panic, Daniel rifled through his clothes, knowing full well that the pistols could never be among them, for he'd always placed them back in the box after holding them.

But where?

Had they been taken from the trunk whilst it was in his lodgings at Holywell Street or here, in this strange house?

He shut the lid of the trunk, deciding to go and report the matter to Sticks. As he crossed to the door he found he was still clutching the pistol box in both hands. He put it down so that he might open the door.

But he couldn't...

At first he thought that the door was just jammed. A shudder ran down his spine as he realised that the door was locked.

He was as much a prisoner here as he'd been at Bow Street.

~

'Wake up, Prowl!'

The darkness of the condemned cell was lit by a dark lantern carried by the turnkey - through the long but narrow barred window, Simeon Prowl could see that it was still dark outside.

He shuddered, thinking that the time had arrived - that they had come for him. That the crowds were already gathered outside Newgate, jostling for the best places to see him go down through the drop.

'Is it my time?'

'No, it ain't, Prowl. The gallows ain't ready and there's some suspicion that you ain't going to be alone on the scaffold when you're turned off. I reckon you got over a week to sweat before you're taken out. And there's a preacher what wants to see you. Waiting outside he is...'

'Don't like God-plaguers!'

'Well, you got to see him. Orders from on high, even over-rode the governor who thinks the prison padre should do the chores. See him you will...'

The turnkey held open the door and the preacher entered.

Apart from his parson's clothes, he had a hat pulled hard down on his head and something like a cowl underneath that, making it hard to see his face in the dimness of the cell. One gloved hand clutched a testament, the other hovered in front of his mouth.

'Don't want no preacher,' Prowl muttered.

'You mind what the judge said, Prowl? May God have mercy upon your soul?'

'There ain't no mercy for the likes of me, and I hates God-plaguers! Just leave me in peace.'

'You've come to such an unpleasant end, Prowl. And how much have you ever made from your villainy? Shillings? You'd have done better pursuing an honest trade...'

'An honest trade? And who'd give me an honest trade? I had to beg and thieve from the day I could stand up. Dippin' pockets and then hauntin' the roads. I had no skill and no letterin'. I was never made for honest trade. And now it's a bit late... and too late for you and your maker as well. You talk about the age of miracles... and yet I'm not seein' the miracle as could get me out of here...'

'And yet miracles do occur, Prowl.'

'Show me! Show me the miracle that ever got a felon clear of the Newgate drop? Show me how your God ever whisked the man or woman away from the scaffold, when the hangman put the hemp rope across their throats?'

'Would you care for me to read from this testament, Prowl?'

'Can't say as I would!'

'Then you're a creature of little faith, I fear.'

'I'm a critter of no faith at all!'

'Yet you should be...'

'Why should I be? I've had the sentence of death hangin' – *hangin!* – over me a good month now. A month sweatin' it out in this condemned cell. Oh, it was better before my trial, when they let me meet up with others in the press room or wander around the yard with the other lags. But just sittin' here, waitin'. Oh, that's the worst part! If they're goin' to top me, why don't they get on with it?'

'Are you so anxious to meet your Maker, Prowl?'

'There ain't no maker! When you're turned off you're turned off. And that's the end of you. No more life than a slug in the gutter you might put your foot down on. Death's the end of everythin'. And all your bible verses and God-plaguin' ain't goin' to change that!'

'Oh, you are a creature of little faith! And yet... well, if you were only to have some faith who knows what might happen...'

'Faith or no faith – I'm for the drop.'

The preacher looked all around the cell.

'Not a pleasant place to spend your last days, Prowl.'

'It's the condemned cell. I expected nothin' less...'

'You see, Prowl, I have it in my power to have you moved somewhere much more pleasant than this damp and stinking hole... to somewhere where you might find a bed that isn't run through with water stains and where you can't hear the shouts of others condemned to die. Where you might get proper food. Money in your purse. Where you might get a life and not a death...'

'You the home secretary then? Or the Queen? They're the only two people that can do that! And with all this talk of the transportation stoppin', it'd still mean being lagged in a convict depot till my last breath.'

The preacher waved his testament-carrying hand towards the door.

'Better than being swung out there, Prowl!'

Simeon Prown looked him in the face for the first time.

For there was a harshness now in that voice.

The gentle, reproving tones of the preacher had gone.

Now it had a menacing pitch. Not unlike that of the judge who'd promised Simeon Prowl his own personal journey into eternity. Or the workhouse master who'd starved and beaten him in those miserable days of his childhood.

'How can you get me moved?' Prowl asked. 'Who are you to have such power as could get me away from the drop?'

The preacher was silent for a long time, still holding the testament in front of his face. The face that Prowl could scarcely make out in the shadows of Newgate's condemned cell.

'Prowl... I am the maker of miracles!'

~

'D'you remember the Hen and Chickens?'

Jonas glanced across at Harry Blizzard and smiled.

'Must be twenty years since I was at the Hen and Chickens. Now *there* was one of the great coaching inns. We must have passed very close on our journey, Harry... The times I caught the London coach from there – in the days I could afford the fare... and they did a tidy good meal for all coach travellers before you set out too. Harry – I do miss those days...'

'Well, even if the stagecoaches still ran regular to London, it'd still be a risk for you, even though a stage might get there in a good long day. If your enemies are watching the railway, they'd be watching the coaches just as much.'

'And there are no coaches left, Harry. Such a pity! For all the convenience and comfort of a railway carriage, they don't match the thrill of a fast coach on the turnpike.'

'Ah, I'll wager you complained as much as me; what with the delays and the bad weather, footpads, and the moaning coachmen who thought they were in the same league as the King of Prussia.'

'I know Harry – I know... but it was more my world you see? I find it hard to relate to this new age. Harder still to get across to young folk the thrill of those days.'

'Romantic hogwash! Have you forgotten the misery? The corpses swinging on the gibbets? The militia blooding their sabres on honest citizens? You fought for all these great reforms and created the land we now live in. Bad as it is, it ain't as bad as those days when we had to fight for freedom with muskets and daggers...'

'I know... I know... but just in a while I yearn for that stagecoach ride... or the days when we had to dodge man-traps in the coverts of the rich. Or battle for our freedom by aiming a Baker rifle at our enemies...'

'Oh, you yearn for somethin' that's best long done with, Jonas. They had their moments those days and I loved them at the time. Sometimes, when I'm sitting by the back fire in my little shop, I hunger for them too. Then I look in the mirror and see an old codger looking back at me... and thank the stars for the quiet old age I never thought I'd live to see.'

'Old codgers... yes, that's what we are. Time for the young to take up the gauntlet, for our fighting days are long past! We're just two old codgers without the energy to struggle on.'

Harry turned and faced him.

'And I would remind you, Jonas. We saw off three villains this very day!'

'Deplorable violence!'

'You did your bit...'

They continued on their long walk through the dark streets.

'Harry... why exactly have we walked to Wolverhampton?'

They'd walked at a good pace, clear across the Black Country.

A dozen or more miles through West Bromwich and Tipton and Bilston – through a dark landscape of manufactories, blazing furnaces and high polluting chimneys, passing huddled houses and slums - where women and children sat on the house steps with despair running through their very souls.

They'd passed little workshops where craftsmen still made goods in a traditional way, strolled in the shadows of the winding gear bringing up men and boys with sweat-blackened faces from a dozen mines. Miners who'd exhausted themselves in long and hard shifts, hewing from the great coal seam known as the Thick.

It was dark now as they took a flight of grimy steps down to the canal basin, where narrow-boats, and the butties they towed, were being loaded with coal by the light of a dozen blazing bonfires.

'This is why we've come.'

Harry pointed down at the foul waters of the cut.

'The canal?'

'What better way to get to London! There's a fly-boat just leaving. Double-crewed, so it won't even pause while two of the boatmen take a nap. A good horse to drag the boat from the tow-path. Men I know, Jonas. Four men who're like brothers to me. Folk I can trust. Might take three days, but they'll get us to London.'

'Us?'

'My good lady would never forgive me if I abandoned you now. Anyroad, she says I'm less likely to get into trouble if I'm by your side...'

Jonas laughed.

'Doesn't she recall what we got up to on Dartmoor?'

'Ah, but we're decrepit old codgers now!'

Sixteen

'I believe I'm owed an explanation, Sir Richard?'

Inspector Honour Bright had demanded an evening meeting with the police Commissioner, insisting that Inspector Abraham Anders and Sergeant Berry were there too.

Police Commissioner Mayne, who was anxious to get off to a dinner party, was not in the best of moods. Word of the meeting had got all round Scotland Yard – and apparently even further into the more secret depths of Westminster, for a fat man had invited himself along, burying the chair he was sitting on.

Honour Bright looked quizzically in the latter's direction.

'I had thought this meeting was to be between ourselves,' he said. 'I do not know this gentleman?'

Mayne waved a hand towards the stranger.

'This is Mr Benjamin Wissilcraft, the head of Her Majesty's Secret Service, Bright. He asked... insisted... that he be present at our conference.' Mayne sighed and looked angry. 'I am obliged to consult him on these matters...'

'I fail to see why?' said Bright. 'This is surely a procedural matter concerning today's behaviour by Anders here. That is what I wish to discuss, nothing more... and certainly I cannot see why it should concern the secret service?'

'Because of Quest!' Mayne groaned.

'Well, yes... that is the root cause of my involvement. But I still cannot see why...'

Wissilcraft shuffled in the chair.

'Perhaps Inspector Bright would care to explain just why he's asked for this meeting?'

Bright thought that the huge man looked very bored.

'Very well...' he began.

'And as briefly as possible, if you please, Inspector?' said Mayne. 'Some of us have other engagements...'

'Very well, sir. I appreciate we are all very busy men. I've asked for this meeting because of a report I received from one of the constables I have placed at Bow Street. He told me that earlier today, Inspector Anders had a meeting with the villain Quest and that renegade member of the Commons, Sir Wren Angier. I believe that Quest's mistress and some other desperate characters were there. As a result of this meeting, Anders released a man who'd been quite properly arrested for aiding and abetting Dugdale, that purveyor of disgusting literature.'

Mayne looked across at Anders.

'What Inspector Bright says is true, as far as it goes,' said Anders. 'But, on reflection, it seemed that the boy we arrested was an innocent bystander who just happened to be in Dugdale's shop at the time. It appears that the youth is the brother of Quest's associate Miss Stanton, hence Quest's involvement. Mr Daniel Stanton had no connection with Dugdale's publishing business, so I could see no reason to hold him.'

'No reason?' Bright spluttered. 'Did he not assault Sergeant Berry? He should be charged and lagged on that count alone! How can our officers consider themselves safe if all and sundry be allowed to use violence against them?'

Berry was aware that they were all looking at him.

'We had no men with us in uniform, Inspector. I feel sure that the boy mistook our intentions. To him we were just men who broke into Dugdale's shop... he probably thought we might be villainous rivals of the bookseller.'

'I'm baffled as to why Sergeant Berry should come out with such rigmarole!' Bright retorted. 'How many villainous rivals put the cuffs on their victims? And I cannot believe that Anders did not identify himself as he entered the premises? Whatever the circumstances, the sergeant was assaulted. Dugdale was held at Bow Street, so why not this young rogue Stanton?'

'Because it was my decision,' said Anders. 'As an inspector, I'm allowed such a discretion.'

Honour Bright looked at them all in turn.

'I'm well aware, Anders, of your friendship with this Quest... a doubtful relationship, surely, for any police officer? I'm mindful of your recent adventures in York, alongside this treacherous rebel. But your task now was to close down sources of vice in this place, no more than that. Dealings with Quest and his renegade activities were placed under my jurisdiction. Any matter relating to Quest and his gang of villains should have been referred to me. Holding this Stanton in custody might have given us some power over Quest himself...'

'If you believe that, you really don't know Quest at all,' said Anders.

Wissilcraft yawned.

'There's much in what you say, Inspector Bright. And to be honest, we have not been altogether fair with you. It might have been better, Sir Richard, if the good inspector here had been taken into our confidence from the start, and...'

'Now look here!' Mayne began...

'Yes, yes, yes...' Wissilcraft continued. 'I know it was my decision to limit the number of individuals who were aware of what this mission was to be about. I was wrong. Given that Bright here was ordered to monitor the activities of Quest, we should have taken him into our confidence from the start...'

'What is this about, Sir Richard? What haven't I been told?' asked Bright. 'Are you telling me that there's some reason why Quest and his associates are untouchable? Oh, I know all about this notebook he's supposed to possess...'

'Does possess,' said Anders.

'Very well, he has possession of a notebook which lists the names and unwise activities of our betters in society. But how damning can it be really? Surely this bluff should have been called long ago?'

'Such a move would be very unwise, Bright,' said Wissilcraft. 'The notebook was compiled by my predecessor at the secret service. If it were to be made public, it could bring down not just the government, but the royal family as well. If the lower orders knew of its content, it might even trigger a revolution in our land. That is why we are wary of annoying William Quest.'

'Forgive me, Mr Wissilcraft. I'm sure I'm being most obtuse, but isn't all that exactly what this Quest wants? Why does he not use the contents of the notebook himself to bring society crashing down in just such a way? As a revolutionary, then surely that would be his aim anyway?'

Sir Richard Mayne glanced across at Wissilcraft.

'Bright has a point there...' he said.

Wissilcraft was silent for a while before replying.

'As I understand it, Inspector, Quest wants a revolution but not with bloodshed. He fears that any uprising of that sort would be crushed and all the reforms that have progressed through Parliament so far might be reversed. At the moment, he believes that using the information in that notebook against certain named individuals can silence their opposition to such reforms. We know that that is his strategy... and it's a strategy that's worked in a surprisingly efficient way. Slowly but surely is the way that Quest works.'

'And in the meantime, Mr Wissilcraft, he's allowed to run riot,' Bright almost yelled. 'To murder people on the streets, dictate to members of the police whom they might not arrest. Subvert the very order of our society...'

Mayne held up a hand, 'Calmly please, Inspector.'

'Then why... why... why did you order me to keep watch on Quest at all?'

'Because we always need to know what the man is doing,' Wissilcraft responded. 'And because it frees up Inspector Anders for a most important mission.'

Bright rubbed his chin.

'I thought Inspector Anders was tasked with putting down the purveyors of vice in this city? Are you telling me that that's not so? If not, why all this pantomime with Dugdale? Why this raid on Holywell Street?' He looked at Mayne. 'Am I being played for a fool, Commissioner? If so, I wish to tender my resignation with immediate effect!'

Then Anders stepped forward, looking Bright in the face.

'Charles, I think we owe you an apology. Your comments are justified. We made a gross error not taking you into our confidence from the beginning. Personally I'm very sorry for that. But our real mission came as a great surprise to me too. There's always a danger when members of the Metropolitan Police are ordered to work in the shadows with the secret service.

We've all overstepped the mark. We *all* owe you an apology. I beg you to reconsider your resignation and work alongside me in our future endeavours.' Anders looked at Wissilcraft. 'I do believe that we should now take Inspector Bright fully into our confidence and tell him the tale from the beginning...'

Seventeen

The Very Reverend Arthur Middleton Stanton, Doctor of Divinity, was waving a warning hand against a sinful world, as he stood in his pulpit.

From time to time his finger would point into the sitting congregation at his only daughter, Rosa. His words became confused as he droned on, sometimes so loud that they were too deafening to hear, then almost inaudible...

Daniel Stanton turned over on the bed, trying to expunge that nightmare from his brain, only to see Rosa looking down at him, an expression of concern on her face. After the trauma of the day, he'd fallen into an exhausted sleep, but a turbulent one – full of dreams.

He woke with a start to find himself quite alone in that empty room. But someone had been there. There was a fresh glass of water on the little table. Sticks perhaps... Sticks the betrayer? His tired mind tried to grasp just why Sticks and Angier had liberated him from Bow Street, only to make him captive in this tiny room?

Daniel crossed to the door and tried the handle. It was still locked. After a moment, he knelt, looking through the keyhole, hoping to get a glimpse of what lay beyond...

But he could see nothing. The key had been left in the other side of the lock. He sighed with frustration and, sitting back down on the bed, resumed his reading of *The Newgate Shadow* and its account of the final judgement passed down on the unfortunate Simeon Prowl.

A few minutes passed before the idea came to him.

Whoever had taken away his pair of pistols had left the accessories in the wooden box – not just the lead balls and percussion caps, but the short length of wire he used to clean the barrels after use. He sought it out and crossing to the door, bent down to look again at the keyhole and then the foot of the door. Yes, there was just enough room under the wood...

Daniel opened out *The Newgate Shadow*, sliding it under the door. It was but a small publication and a falling key might miss it altogether, but he had no alternative. Gently... very gently... he pushed the cleaning wire into the keyhole and against the key itself. The key refused to budge. He was reluctant to push harder, lest the key should shoot out beyond the spead of the pages he'd put under the door.

But if he didn't take the chance, there was no hope of escape...

He held his breath as he rammed the wire against the key... once... then again... and again...

Suddenly there was no obstruction.

He looked through the keyhole... all he could see was a corridor wall not more than a yard away. But had the key fallen clear of those scurrilous pages...

Daniel put the wire down and gradually eased the *Shadow* back under the door, lying down now in the hope of seeing the key... and it was there! right on the far corner of a page. So near the edge that it might yet come away, leaving it beyond reach on the bare boards beyond...

Gently... very gently...

There it was.

He was touching it as it came clear of the door, then holding it...

Daniel felt a satisfaction with himself that he'd seldom experienced before. For the first time in his life he felt triumphant...

He went back to the trunk and, opening the pistol box, took out a handful of shot and several percussion caps. Quite why he wasn't sure, for the confiscated pistols were very probably hidden away somewhere... his instincts seemed to tell him to do it, and Sticks had once told him that such thoughts could well be valuable to a man facing a fight.

Quietly... very quietly, he put the key into the lock and turned... it unlocked the door so silently that he thought for a moment that it hadn't worked. He turned the door knob and breathed a sigh of relief as it opened.

He looked out along the corridor beyond. As he'd surmised, the room in which he'd been held captive was one of four servants' quarters positioned at the top of the house. There were two other doors on the opposite side and another next to his own.

The narrow, bare-boarded passageway led to a steep flight of steps leading down to a wider carpeted corridor, with other doors on both sides. Clearly the bedrooms of the house, Daniel thought. Probably safe enough in this early evening. He was more likely to meet some opposition in the storeys below those.

As he descended to the first storey, he could hear muffled voices behind one of the doors. He crept quietly by, along the corridor, until he reached the final flight of stairs that led to the ground floor of the house.

But just before he reached them, he came upon a door that was open, but fortunately empty of people. He looked in – it was clearly some kind of study. The walls were lined with bookshelves, there was a comfortable chair lined up in front of a blazing fire and a rack of splendid and various walking sticks. An opened swordstick lay across a little table next to an open book and...

Yes, two pocket pistols that Daniel recognised as his own.

He glanced back along the corridor. Voices still came from behind the door of the farthest room. He judged it safe enough to recover his stolen property, and how much better to exit the house armed, he thought.

He took up each pistol in turn and loaded it with a lead ball and a percussion cap. He put one of the guns in his pocket and quietly pulled back the hammer on the other. Now he felt more secure...

It was at that point that he took a close look at the book opened on the table. The third volume of *Lavengro* by Mr George Borrow. As it was one of his personal favourites, he couldn't resist turning a page or two. The reader was clearly near to the beginning. Thumbing back to the cover, Daniel found the library plate that had been pasted in.

Ex Libris - William Quest.

He was stunned! Here he was in the enemy camp. Taken captive by the very man he'd come to London to kill! By one of those appalling coincidences, he'd come across the man Quest and - no doubt - his murderous crew.

He recalled telling Sticks the name of the man he sought, little realising that the old bruiser, he'd thought of as a friend, worked for the opposition. No wonder they'd been so anxious to free him from Bow Street and bring him here for their own ends. Quest! The villain who'd ruined his sister and brought shame upon his family!

Where was Rosa, his beloved sister? No doubt cast aside by this rake! Forced into a life of vice in some London rookery, or even dead! This man Quest had clearly worked out that Daniel was a threat to him. A foe who had to be silenced. And here they were - in the same house together...

Daniel was brought out of his reverie by a door opening and closing along the corridor - a sudden burst of voices that became louder and then quieter again. Then there were footsteps in the corridor...

Hurriedly, Daniel concealed himself behind the open door and waited, pistol in hand...

Then the man was in the room, his back to Daniel. He could see the dark-haired slim figure, dressed not at all fashionably. Watched as the man picked up the book that Daniel had been browsing only a moment before. Noticed the terrible scars on one of his hands...

It was not Angier, or Sticks, or the rogue Jasper that he'd met at Rat's Castle. It could only be William Quest... no other...

Daniel stepped forward, levelling the pistol, bringing it in line with the villain's head.

Felt his finger tightening on the trigger...

'You may believe, Inspector Bright, that our secret service is tasked only with seeking out the revolutionaries in our midst,' Wissilcraft began. 'But there are elements in our society that favour plunging our nation backwards into a most repressive regime, where only a very few triumph at the expense of the many.'

'I can understand that,' Bright replied. 'I think that most reasonable people favour reforms. I myself come from a modest background. I'm aware that much of our crime is generated only by poverty. Remove the poverty and you remove much of the crime.'

'Just so... and to be honest... though perhaps not everyone here would agree,' Wissilcraft looked pointedly at Sir Richard Mayne, 'that not so long ago, in the time of the Regent, we lived under just such repression. Some might argue that we were subject to a dictatorship, not by just the monarchy, but also by those politicians in government, who enriched themselves at the expense of the many. Their actions led to popular revolts and brought us very close to revolution...'

'Perhaps we should get to the point, Wissilcraft,' said Mayne.

'I really do believe we need the background of all this, Sir Richard. Well, there are some elements in our society who yearn for the bad old days. Who have a desperate desire to bring them back. To seize power and wipe out even our Parliament and hopes of future reform. To turn back the tide of improvement in society, if you like.'

'A small minority, I'm sure,' said Bright.

'Minorities can be dangerous,' said Anders. 'Some might argue that this country is run by a minority anyway, and for the sole benefit of that minority.'

Sir Richard Mayne gave Anders a foul look.

'There's a great deal of truth in what you say, Anders, but let's remember that debates are generally conducted at Westminster and not so much now out on the streets,' said Wissilcraft.

'There are still revolutionaries and trouble-makers,' said Mayne. 'And still out on the streets. Look at that man Quest! And radical politicians like Angier, who seek to betray their class.'

'I'm sure nobody would disagree with you,' said Wissilcraft. 'But whatever their failings, neither of those two characters are trying to impose a new dictatorship on our country.'

'Then someone is?' asked Bright.

'Do you recall Samuel Cutler?'

'Yes, I knew Cutler when he was an inspector here at the Yard. He left suddenly under circumstances I never quite understood.'

'He left to join the Secret Service, Inspector,' said Wissilcraft, 'fast becoming one of the very best of my agents. His knowledge of London made him invaluable to me. And, being the younger son of a member of Parliament, he knew the richest in society as well as the less fortunate.'

'I seem to recall he died of a consumption a few months ago,' said Bright.

'That's the tale we put around,' said Wissilcraft. 'The truth is a lighterman pulled him from the Thames one dark night.'

'He drowned? Then why the deception about his death?'

'Sam didn't drown,' said Anders. 'He'd been shot near the heart and was dead when he fell into the river. Our belief is that he was killed while trying to escape from someone. Somewhere near to Limehouse, we think. He fell into the river before his killer could get hold of his body. And that was very unfortunate for Sam's enemies.'

'Why so?'

'Because he carried with him, into the river, a packet of documents of a most damning nature, wrapped in oilskin. But for that, we might never have discovered the truth about a most heinous plot to overthrow what passes as our democracy. But for that – we might never have discovered the existence of Tenebrae...'

~

Daniel had only ever tried firing the pistol outside, and a long way from his father's parsonage. Then it had given out a quiet bark as the percussion cap lit the powder. But here, in this small room, it filled the air with noise. There seemed to have been a considerable blow on his hand as the pistol discharged. His target, the man with the scarred hand, was still clutching the book as he fell to the floor.

~

'And what is Tenebrae? The word means nothing to me,' said Bright.

'The word means darkness, I believe,' said Mayne.

'It does indeed,' said Wissilcraft. 'And the men who own themselves as members of Tenebrae truly intend to bring darkness upon our society. They are the dangerous elements in our country that I mentioned before. They have no regard for democracy. They are opposed to any reform that might benefit the majority of our people. They seek to bring back feudalism, to restore the dictatorship we thought we'd seen the back of...'

'But that is incredible!' said Bright. 'We have our Parliament – our Queen...'

'Not even the Queen is safe,' said Wissilcraft.

'Sam Cutler came across these folk through a club he belonged to,' said Anders. 'Like all societies, Tenebrae has fringe members who are less than discreet. Being an agent, he played along with the individuals he met. Expressed sympathy with their outrageous cause. What he found out horrified him. As you know, Sam was a friend of mine – he confided in me because he believed that these men might have penetrated our secret service, which they assuredly have. But I knew that Wissilcraft was above suspicion. So we took the matter to him.'

Wissilcraft nodded.

'And I suspect that Cutler was correct – these villains have people in place in many of our institutions, including the secret service. That's why I had to call on men I trusted absolutely to investigate them. I knew that Anders and Berry were trustworthy, from my past experience of working with them. But they could not be seen carrying out an investigation openly...'

'And that,' added Sir Richard Mayne, 'is why they were given the cover of suppressing vice in our city. Not that I approve of such tactics...' he looked with some malevolence in the direction of Wissilcraft.

'Then I have been used...' said Bright.

'For which we apologise,' said Anders. 'But you have played a vital part in our mission, Charles. As you will know, I am usually tasked with keeping an eye on William Quest. We needed a most reliable officer of this force to take over that duty. And you, like Wissilcraft here, are above suspicion.'

'But what is the importance of Quest in these matters?'

'The importance lies not so much in Quest, as in the notebook he possesses,' Anders went on. 'The agents of Tenebrae want that notebook very badly. Quest only used it to threaten. Tenebrae want to use its contents to destroy, even though they would like to remove Quest and his fellows along the way. There are others that this society sees as their enemies – Jonas Lyddon for example and Joshua Blount. Men of reason – oh, I do appreciate you might not agree with all that they stand for – but they are the reformist safety valves that stops our society exploding! At the end of the day, they put their country above self-interest – however deplorable their methods.'

'And Samuel Cutler found all this out?'

'Yes, and somehow – we'll never know how – they discovered he was an infiltrator, playing a most dangerous game. They murdered poor old Sam! But one of his last actions, before he died, was to throw himself into the river, probably in the hope that his body, and the revealing documents he had upon his person, might be found by others rather than them.'

'He was the bravest of the brave,' said Wissilcraft. 'Thwarting these scum even as he perished. But for Samuel Cutler, we would know nothing of this plot to bring our society crashing down!'

Bright considered what he'd been told.

'Do we know if this Tenebrae has a leader?' he asked.

'We think they do,' said Anders. 'Well, there were some obscure references in the papers found on Sam's body. He says he caught a glimpse of a man - as a meeting with some inner circle came to a conclusion. There was some gossip among the lower players. "Leader". The word was there in Sam's script. Next to two words: "Apollyon" and "Abaddon". Two titles for the same individual or an indication of the ending of the world perhaps? One in ancient Greek and the other in old Hebrew. You might mind the latter from the Bible...?'

'I'm not sure that I do...'

'Book of Revelations,' said Wissilcraft. 'A wider destruction personalised into an evil angel. "Apollyon - Destroyer of Worlds". More than that - Cutler says that in his glimpse of the man he saw something that gives me nightmares. He describes the leader as a man with no face.'

'But that's absurd...'

'Perhaps... Cutler only saw him at a distance. A mask perhaps? Yes, more than likely a mask. But that in itself suggests something. The leader of such a group must be a well-known individual. Someone recognisable.'

'So what do we do now?' asked Mayne.

Wissilcraft gave a great sigh.

'Oh, Sir Richard - I believe we must do something you will not like. Something that goes against every value you believe in. I really do think we must take William Quest into our confidence. To hunt these villains down, we need a ratcatcher of the first order. A man who knows the underworld of London much better than we do. And, as Quest, himself, is a target for Tenebrae, I'm sure he'll be very keen to give us his assistance.'

'No! Absolutely not!' Mayne spluttered. 'The very idea that my officers should work alongside this murderous criminal? I'd sooner resign as Commissioner than allow such proceedings! This must be undertaken by my officers and your agents, Wissilcraft. No others and certainly not Quest! You'll agree with me, won't you Bright?'

He looked up at Honour Bright, waving a hand in his appeal.

Bright took in a breath and considered for a while before he replied.

'I'm afraid, Sir Richard, that I can't agree with you, If this organisation has infiltrated the secret service, then it will assuredly have its members in the ranks of the Metropolitan Police. The fact that such a group has grown and thrived indicates the truth of that. I deplore this Quest, just as much as you do, Sir Richard – but I'm a pragmatist, a practical man. Although Quest deserves the gallows and I'd love to see him swinging outside Newgate, there's no doubt in my mind that he's just the kind of villain we need to employ. Setting aside his criminal activities, I'm well aware that he's served in such capacities before now. On this occasion, we need to impose a truce with him – and employ William Quest!'

~

'You've ruined my book!' said Quest, holding up the third volume of *Lavengro*. There was a bullet hole clear through the middle of the leather binding. 'Do you not care for the writings of Mr Borrow, or are you just a rotten shot?'

Daniel stood there open-mouthed, his hand still trembling. He couldn't believe that he'd missed his target from just two yards away. Even as he'd spoken, the man Quest had clambered to his feet. In his nervousness, Daniel dropped the pistol to the floor. He hurriedly reached into his pocket, bringing out the other pistol, cocking it even as he levelled it at his enemy.

But something struck his hand with a great blow, sending the other gun flying down towards the carpet. Daniel winced with the pain, noticing, even as he gasped, the heavy knob of the walking stick that had come crashing down on the back of his hand.

He looked up at this new attacker, almost falling to the floor himself.

The blow had been struck by his own sister...

Eighteen

'I'd forgotten quite how beautiful this could be,' said Jonas to Harry Blizzard, as the fly-boat made its paced but gentle way through the Warwickshire countryside.

He stared at the rump of the great shire horse, padding its way with what seemed to be little effort along the towpath. It was a warm autumn afternoon and the leaves on the trees were starting to brown. Now and again, a duck flapped out of the way of the narrowboat and a heron grudgingly removed itself from the canal like some winged prehistoric monster.

As the journey to London was continuous, two of the crew were sleeping in the fore-cabin, while the working crew steered the boat and worked the horse. Fly-boat crews had a reputation for being godless and lawless, but the four men, Harry Blizzard had introduced him to, seemed good souls at heart, lovers of liberty and compassionate. Working the cut all their lives, they took a great interest in the wildlife that abounded close to the water. A knowledge that surpassed, in Jonas's opinion, many of the more book-learned naturalists he'd ever known.

On the lonelier stretches of the cut, he and Harry had stretched their legs, walking the towpath beside the horse. But when they came to a canal-side inn or a farming hamlet, they'd hidden themselves away in the cramped crew quarters at the stern of the narrowboat.

Jonas and Harry had reminisced about old times, particularly looking back to their first meeting when they'd brought rebellion to Dartmoor and managed to avoid being hanged on Gibbet Hill.

'As I get closer to my own end, I often think about the ones we lost there,' Jonas said. 'Those who were dear to us.'

There was a sudden sadness on Harry's face and he was silent for a long while.

'Ah, you've got years to go yet, Jonas. Years! And so have I! Look at this mischief we've got ourselves involved with here! What could be better? I'm not going to drift into the long sleep before I've had lots more fun and adventures! Nor should you!'

He pointed to the document that Jonas had let him read, the account of the Dartmoor uprising. 'That's a good account, though whether it was wise to put pen to paper I'm not sure. Could still get us all swung at Newgate, I reckon. But it'll be nice to think that people unborn will read what really happened, rather than a bland account by someone who wasn't even there!'

Jonas smiled at his friend's considered opinion. Harry's wife had been good for him, ironed out the rough edges, turned the old footpad into a wiser citizen, but somehow left the spirit of adventure in his soul.

'How is he now?' Quest asked, as Rosa came back into the room.

'Tired... bewildered. It's as though he's been having some sort of mental storm! Living a life as though it's in one of the stories he's been trying to write. Having a difficult father was never easy for either of us. You see, all the time he was growing up I was the only real friend he had. The only person he might confide in. When I was snatched away from his life, he needed someone to blame. Some busybody, who'd been in London, told my father and Daniel that I'd been seduced by you and then abandoned to a life on the streets.'

'But that was never true... if anything you seduced me!'

'You see... to Daniel it was so like a story by Ainsworth or Dickens... the ruination of an innocent. I can understand that, can't you? My brother had a very lonely childhood, with little experience of life. He lives in the fictions he reads.'

'You've told him the truth?'

Rosa sighed.

'Yes, I've told him. I don't think he believed me for a while. Not until I told him we intended to marry. He's been mixing in strange company, Will. That old rogue Dugdale's been trying to persuade Daniel to write lurid books for him. And my poor lad couldn't, for he has no experience of life! And all he really wants to do is pen real novels.'

'Do you believe he can?'

'Daniel was always good with words.'

'Surely, if you wish to learn to write, then you need to learn to live first?'

'That is what Daniel thought he'd been doing.'

'If your Daniel had shot me dead, he'd probably have had a very short life. No doubt Jasper would have been scripting his execution in the next edition of *The Newgate Shadow*?'

'More like the home secretary would have given him a free pardon and a reward!'

'Do you think he'll try again... to top me, I mean?'

'I think not. Anyway, not if you make an honest woman of me.'

'Well, I'll certainly wed you, Rosa. Making an honest woman of you might be quite beyond me!'

~

He really was a very easy victim to put the dodge on, Crouch thought, as he followed the man who walked so slowly through the streets of Bloomsbury. Usually in these matters, Crouch always took advantage of his small size, secreting himself behind barrows and street furniture as he closed in on his prey. But this man... this man... so easy to trail.

But where to make the snatch, that was the difficulty? His master had ordered him to be discreet, but taking out a pedestrian in this respectable neighbourhood was just so difficult, with so many very respectable passers-by to give the alarm. Crouch would have given anything to be putting the dodge on this man in St Giles or some other rookery – the kind of place where nobody gave a toss if you grabbed a man, or even put a knife into his ribs...

Crouch glanced back over his shoulder to make sure that the cart was still there – and it was, drawn by an old horse that was somehow still evading the glue factory. Two footpads on the seat and a tarpaulin to conceal the man, as soon as he was took.

Crouch had carried out this task endless times, though he much preferred holding or throwing a dagger to attempting a live capture. Better to kill. Put someone out of their misery with a sudden hurl of a blade. Crouch prided himself on rarely letting his victims suffer. They scarcely knew what had happened to them before they shuffled off the mortal coil.

Shabson Crouch knew a lot about knives. His father, and grandfather before him, had both been arch-stabbers in the rookery of Jacob's Island, mostly demolished now, much to his sadness. That was all that they taught him. His grandfather, another Shabson Crouch, had been turned off by the hangman in front of a great crowd at Tyburn. They still talked about the way that first Shabson had writhed and wriggled, on his way down at the end of the rope.

A kindly man, his grandfather, wise and book read. He'd missed him when he'd gone, for his passing unleashed a vein of cruelty in Crouch's father, another Shabson. Shabson the Second was a nightmare when he got hold of a drink, and Crouch had paid the price with many a beating. Yet his father could be kind when he was broke and sober.

A miserable childhood, though.

Young Shabson Crouch's life had been as up and down as a drunkard's elbow.

At last, Crouch had ended that life of unpredictable violence.

On a dark October night, when his father was sleeping off the gin, he'd come down into the grubby room they shared and slit his father's throat.

Crouch's very first killing...

Crouch was just twelve years old at the time, well – so Old Sally, the decrepit old whore who used to come round to ease his father's lusts, had told him. Old Sally had claimed that she was there at his birth, helped deliver him into his miserable existence even...

So perhaps she was right.

Old Sally had delivered many a brat at Jacob's Island – aye and got rid of many another, before they had a chance to see the light of day. She was dead now, Old Sally. Put down into the ground on top of another dozen bodies in a pauper's grave.

After the killing, Shabson Crouch had gone on the run, fully expecting there to be a great hue and cry as the authorities sought his capture. His grandfather, book-learned as he was, had often told him stories of wanted men in the past – Jack Sheppard and Turpin... Crouch had imagined himself being papered by the beaks, his wanted poster on every tree and alley wall...

But it hadn't happened and it took Crouch a while to realise that nobody cared for a dead drunkard, who'd met a violent end in a rookery. So he'd wandered on away into the unfamiliar countryside of Epping Forest. And it was while he was begging in the fields and lanes that he'd met Benson Spright, coming across his circus as Spright and his troupe struggled to put up the tent on the edge of a small town.

A great gale had been blowing and they were having trouble holding on to the canvas at all – Crouch had watched as they sought to prevent it soaring into the sky. After a moment – and in the hope that they might reward him with a piece of bread – he decided to give them a hand. After ten minutes of struggle, they'd hauled the canvas back on to the ground, securing it with poles and pegs.

Benson Spright had beamed at him, well, Crouch had thought so – for the circus master had so many whiskers concealing his face, it was hard to tell. Well, Spright patted him on the back and then studied the lad for several minutes.

'I thought, at first, as how you was a dwarf,' Spright said, 'you being so tiny. But I can see as you ain't! But you could pass as one and work yourself in as a clown, mebbe! I'll give you food and drink and a share in the takings, for we'm all equal here in our democracy!'

And so Crouch had begun his career with Spright's Circus. First, just helping out with the tent and being the public target of the clown's humour. Then, one day, a rat had dashed across the circus ring, causing the fat lady to scream and flee into the audience. Fast as the rat was, Crouch was swifter. He took out the knife he always carried, threw it twenty feet across the ring, skewering the rodent to the sawdust.

After the show was over, Benson Spright had asked if the throw was just a fluke? So Crouch demonstrated his strange ability time and time again. Had looked up and imagined that – beneath all that hair – Mr Spright was smiling.

And that was how Shabson Crouch became the knife-thrower in Mr Benson Spright's Circus and Menagerie. Helped him improve his killing skills. The best man at chiv-throwing in England. His latest triumph was the killing of Colley Johnson in the Cremorne Gardens. Crouch was proud of that one! So discreetly done – and from the middle of a crowd too!

Crouch watched as the man crossed the road in the middle of another busy crowd, then followed him as he turned down a quieter street. Now this was a better place to make the snatch – a kind of service road running between two prosperous thoroughfares, and nobody about.

He waved the following cart much closer. Signalled one of the men to climb down and join him. Then, cosh in hand, came up behind his victim. Oh, it was easy now, so really easy. Within a moment, the man was wrapped up inside some sacking and bundled under the tarpaulin in the back of the cart.

~

'You are to come with me, Prowl. Now... right now.'

Simeon Prowl had been dozing in the condemned cell. He woke with a start to see the Preacher there, in the shadows by the door, testament in hand. His hat and collar still concealing much of his face.

'I told yer. I don't want no God-botherers!'

'Oh, my dear Prowl! Have you no faith! This is Newgate Gaol and you are in the condemned cell with little time to live. Do you know what a Bridport Dagger is, Prowl?'

Prowl looked across at him, puzzled.

'Not a knife, Prowl. No, not a chiv. A Bridport Dagger's the rope they're going to put around your throat. The rope that's going to choke you to death in front of that great jeering crowd that'll be gathered outside Newgate. Why the dagger? I cannot remember, though Bridport's the place where the rope is made. Just imagine the end of you, Prowl. When the rope tightens. The way your eyes will seem to burst from your head. The way you'll make a mess of yourself, as you spend those last moments swinging in the breeze. Your descent into hell...'

'There ain't no hell,' Prowl growled. 'And if there was, could it be worse than the misery I've had in London?'

The Preacher took a step closer.

'I told you a little while ago that I was a maker of miracles, Prowl. Which all comes from me having faith. Real faith, my friend. And now the time for the miracle has come.'

'What miracle?'

'The miracle that decrees that you won't die by the hangman's rope outside Newgate. The miracle that says you'll feel the fresh air again, well as much as anyone can with the Thames stinking the way it does. The miracle that will let you see the autumn leaves falling from the trees and hear the song of the birds. The miracle that is going to remove you from this foul place for ever, and not the way you imagined. You see, my friend, we are leaving Newgate Gaol right now. You and I together. We are going through this door, then along the grimy passageways that will lead us to the great gate. Then outside, Prowl. Outside.'

'What?'

'It is true, Prowl, it is true.'

'Yer can't get me out of the condemned cell. Nobody can do that.'

'Shall we see, Prowl? Shall we see?'

The Preacher reached backwards and opened the door.

'Time to go, Prowl. Time to go.'

But a moment later he turned.

Ah, this was where the jest ended, Prowl thought. A cruel joke to play on a man destined for death. But then the Preacher reached in to his pack and brought out a long heavy coat.

'What was I thinking of Prowl? We cannot have you seen leaving Newgate in a prisoner's clothes! It might lead to all sorts of speculation. Put on this and we'll be on our way.'

He watched as Prowl wrapped the garment around himself.

'Ah, that's better, Prowl. It was spotting with rain outside and getting dark. But now you are dight for your journey. Dight for your journey.'

Prowl hadn't heard that old word since his childhood. What age was the Preacher living in?

The Preacher swung open the cell door and signalled to Prowl to follow him. Feeling that he was in a dream, the condemned man stepped out through the door. There was a room beyond the death cell, where at least two warders usually sat at a table, playing cards. But now the room was abandoned. His guide led him along the filthy corridor. They passed through four more doors that were kept locked. Each one swung open at the Preacher's touch. All the gates were usually guarded by a warder, but now there were none.

They came, at last, to the entrance hall of the prison, with its great gate at one end. And here, there were two warders who regarded them with some interest as they approached. Prowl watched as the two men glanced at each other, one of them shook his head and the other nodded.

This must be where the jest ends, Prowl thought. A cruel joke to play on a condemned man. What was the point of it? Wasn't being swung from the gallows enough of a revenge for the miserable bastards that took away the lives of the poor?'

But one of the warders crossed to the little access door cut into the great gate, unlocked it with a key and drew the bolt. Then held it open to allow Prowl and the Preacher to step through. Prowl was hardly clear of its wooden step, before the door was pulled shut behind him. He walked out into the rain and looked up at the dripping walls of the old gaol. Along to the place where they mounted the gallows for the public executions – this could not be happening, he thought, but what a cruel dream to come and taunt a man who was about to die...

'Oh, I know what you are thinking. But it's not a dream. The rain really is falling and the hiss of that gaslight is a noise you are really hearing. Now we have a little stroll along Newgate Steet to where some associates of mine are waiting to take you on a journey. Your passage away from the condemned cell and Newgate Gaol. Away from London. Away from everyone who put you here...'

Walking for a couple of hundred yards, they came to where a cart, drawn by an ancient horse, was pulled in to the gutter. Two men stood by, one of them a very small man, scarcely half Prowl's own height.

'Now this is where I must leave you, my dear Prowl, for I have business elsewhere. My associates here will take you on the next stage of your journey. Best, I think, that you climb under the tarpaulin in the back of this cart. Best to be out of the rain and human sight.'

Nineteen

There was an awkward silence in Quest's drawing room.

Rosa sat with her brother, with Sticks nearby, for the old prizefighter was still not convinced that Daniel would not make another murderous assault on the master of the house. Wren Angier stood by the window, looking down into the street, his fingers tapping the sill to break the quiet.

Quest paced up and down, having explained to Daniel his most honourable intentions towards the youth's sister. Daniel Moonlight, as was, appeared to study the patterns on the carpet for a very long time.

He spoke at last...

'You'll forgive me, Mr Quest, but I acted with the best of motives.'

'Bad motives, boy. Bad motives.' Sticks muttered. 'You might have killed William. Indeed, I can only assume there was some fault in your pistol that prevented such a calamity. What we need from you is an assurance that you won't make any further attempts?'

'Daniel has learned the truth,' Rosa said, 'and has given me his word that he will make no further attempts upon Will's life.'

Daniel looked up at Quest.

'You really do intend to wed my sister?'

'Before the month is out,' said Quest.

'So honour is satisfied, m'lad?' asked Angier.

'It is!' Daniel declared. 'Will you shake my hand, Mr Quest.'

He stood and reached out.

'Indeed I'll shake the hand of my brother in the law to be.'

As they shook hands, the door opened and Jasper Feedle entered, followed closely by James Brendon. Quest noted the concern on both their faces. He hardly needed to ask the question.

'No sign of Jonas,' Jasper declared. 'I saw all the trains through, but not a trace. I met Mr Brendon here coming down the street. He's not been lucky either.'

'I've been to all of Mr Lyddon's usual haunts. Called on all the friends he might visit if he is in peril. Even to the Palace of Westminster. But nobody has seen or heard of him,' said Brendon.

'You're both wet from the rain,' said Quest. 'Do dry yourself by the fire. More brandy, Sticks.'

'Where can he be? Where can he be?' Brendon was muttering to himself.

'He definitely got on the train,' said Quest. 'We can be certain of that. But did he leave the train of his own volition, or was he snatched? I've sent an electric telegraph to the agents of Monkshood in Manchester and to several other places along the course of the railway, requiring that they seek out any evidence of what happened to Mr Lyddon. No replies so far, except a further confirmation that he boarded the train. I have to say that I fear for him...'

'He was a game adventurer in his youth,' Jasper remarked. 'He led the rebellion on Dartmoor and we both avoided swinging on Gibbet Hill. But... like me... he's an old man now. We're both lackin' in strength and energy. But he's a cunning character, old Jonas.'

'He's not been well...' Brendon said, almost to himself.

'That's a possibility we haven't considered,' said Quest. 'We assume that his vanishing might have something to do with malevolent forces. But it could be that he became ill on the journey. Felt obliged to seek medical help.'

'Surely we would have heard?' said Wren Angier. 'He would have sent news to us. Still, it would do no harm to send electric telegraphs to all the infirmaries down the length of the railway line – at least any close to a railway station. I'll go now to the telegraph office and send off inquiries.'

Quest nodded assent and, as Angier left the room, turned to Brendon.

'We'll find him, James. Somehow, we'll find him.'

But Angier had been gone for just a few minutes, when he returned in the company of Magnus Blount.

'I met Blount on the doorstep, Will. More worrying news.'

'You'll forgive this intrusion, Mr Quest, but I didn't know who else to turn to. It's my brother, Joshua. He's disappeared. God knows what's happened to him? I saw him set out from the museum on his regular evening walk to our home. Despite being blind, it's a journey he's quite capable of making unaccompanied. I worked late at the museum, before taking the same route. I expected him to be at our home. But he wasn't Mr Quest, he wasn't...'

'Does he never vary the route or call on anyone?' asked Quest.

'He never does. We both go straight home. We had an evening planned where I would read to him. He was looking forward to it. He loves being read to. Despite his blindness, he never minds making his way home alone if I am detained. He values his independence.'

'How long has he been missing?' Angier asked.

'Several hours now. I've called on the police but they've received no word of any accidents, or anyone falling ill. I've even visited the hospitals. I'm at my wits end to know what to do, Mr Quest?'

Quest poured Blount some brandy, deep in thought.

Two of the three people on the list that Colley Johnson had procured from Tenebrae had seemingly vanished from the face of the earth. But for the fact that he'd stayed at home all day, Quest considered that he might have joined them in their vanishing.

~

'Where are we?' Simeon Prowl asked, poking his head over the tarpaulin stretched across the back of the cart. The cart had rumbled through the streets of London for hours, by his estimation. But the noise of people had died away and even the rain had stopped.

'Yer can get out now,' said Crouch.

'Where is this place?' asked Prowl as he climbed down.

He could make out trees and bushes surrounding the dirt track. Two lanterns set at the front of the cart broke the darkness.

'Epping Forest,' said Crouch. 'We've gone as far as we need. Just a walk down the track here's a bit of a cave. You heard of Dick Turpin, the highwayman of the high toby? Well, he used the cave, just as yer going' ter do. A few days, my master says, then yer ter be away.'

Prowl looked all around him.

'I don't like this dark,' he said. 'Where's yer fellow gone?'

Crouch was now alone, standing by the cart.

'I dropped him off a while back,' he said. 'He lives nearby.'

'Who is this preacher yer works for? Is he a preacher at all? Seems a flash gent under the rigging?'

'Ah, yer seen through his 'guise? Nah, he's no preacher. Truth be told, he's more of a devil than a saint. An' that's why yer must obey him to the letter. Even I'm feared of him. Now, take one of these here lanterns and I'll show yer the way to the cave.'

He gestured in the direction of a very narrow path, leading away from the track.

'Off yer go, matey. Ah, you'll sleep snug in this cave. Searched high and low for Turpin, they did. Never caught him till he went away from the locality. Yer cheated the hangman, oh! not many does that!'

Prowl took a lantern, holding it high so he could study Crouch's face.

'How's he do it? Tell me that? Who is he that he can just walk a condemned man away from Newgate? That's what I wants ter know?'

Crouch looked up at him and smiled.

'Best not ter ask questions like that. All I will say, and I'm breakin' my oath by tellin' yer anything, is that my master holds more power than anyone in the land. Those bastards in parlyment, even some judges, and certainly, the warders of

Newgate, has to bow down before him. And why? Cos he has a hold on so many of 'em. No harm in yer knowin' that now. Let's walk on.'

Prowl followed the little man deeper and deeper into the forest, deeper into the darkness, with only the island of light from the lanterns breaking the blackness. Prowl shivered in the cold as they made their way into the gloom.

'How much further? We must have come a mile.'

He heard Crouch give out a great breath.

'I think we're here,' his guide said.

Prowl held up the lantern and looked all around.

'I don't see no cave? And wot's this. The path ends. It stops right here.'

They were in a small clearing, surrounded by thick bushes.

'An' this is as far as we go,' Crouch said. 'There's yer cave. Just by the edge over there. A cave where yer can have a good long rest. D'ye see it now? Over there at the edge of the lantern light?'

And there it was. No cave at all, just a hole in the ground, a several feet long and six feet deep. A darker space in the wildwood, filled with several inches of water from the afternoon rain.

Simeon Prowl felt his stomach heave and a faintness in his head.

He turned to look at Crouch.

The little man had put his lantern on the ground. He was pulling back the hammers on a brace of pistols. Levelled them at Prowl, from just a few yards away. Not all the darkness of the forest could hide the smile on Crouch's face.

'I'm kind of sorry I've got ter do this to yer. Read all about yer in the *Newgate Shadow*. As footpads go, yer a bit of a legend. First, I couldn't understand why me master was so bothered about yer. Yer was goin' ter be topped anyway. But he explained it all to me. Yer sees Mr Prowl, he needs yer space on earth. That's why I got ter kill yer. Must say, I'd prefer ter do this with one of me daggers, but my master insists on these pistols. Still, I'll aim true. Make it as free from pain as I can. Turn round if yer wants to... well, face me then.'

Prowl opened his mouth to speak, but no words came.

From just two yards away, he could see the little man's fingers tighten on the triggers.

~

Somewhere near the river...

That was for sure – even in this sealed room, Joshua Blount could scent the foul stench of the Thames. The pervading odour that swept across London on warmer days. So bad was the smell that Blount surmised that he must be within yards of its malodorous waters.

His blindness had given him incredible powers in his other senses. Not just in his sense of smell, but in other ways.

He had a great gift in sensing the places he was in, that gift that enabled him to wander across familiar parts of London, moving almost as swiftly as any sighted man. And his sense of touch was so remarkable that he could detect what book he was holding in the burgeoning library of the museum.

Joshua knew quite well that he'd been coshed; the lack of consciousness had not lasted long. And from the moment of recovery, he'd felt his way around this room where he was being held captive. He'd soon found the locked door and, feeling his way around the walls he knew that the top three-quarters were wood-panelled. Opposite the door there were no panels, just an arch of stone.

He smiled.

A window once then, but no glass – that suggested the date of the building. Older than the Window Tax, for that was surely why the window had been replaced...

His hearing was also quite remarkable – even through what he suspected were very thick walls, he heard someone blowing what was certainly a coaching horn. Was he near one of the main thoroughfares into the city?

He smiled again.

No!

A wrong first thought. He couldn't hear the babble of any crowds. But the boatmen often gave a blast on such horns, as they navigated their vessels down and up river on foggy days.

His captors had placed him on the floor, left him lying on a clean and very thick carpet; touch and feel suggested a carpet of great quality, suggesting that this room was mostly used for other purposes, transformed into a dungeon solely for his benefit.

His first exploration of its walls had found a hard-backed chair, the one item of furniture that had been left when his prison was created. He took his seat and contemplated his situation, thought back to how he had come to be here. Remembered the known streets he'd been walking down before that sudden blow on the head and the oblivion that followed.

He felt the back of his head. It was still sore but the initial headache had eased.

Who were the men who had brought him here? Well, perhaps Mr William Quest had been right. Mayhap he should have paid more heed to the threatening document that had been read out to him?

Joshua Blount had no doubt but that he was in the hands of very dangerous enemies.

~

It seemed an eternity, watching the little man easing back the triggers on the pair of pistols.

Simeon Prowl wondered just how long his suffering would be? He wondered just what death was like? He was familiar with pain, but even so - perhaps this ending would be swifter than swinging from a rope in the shadow of Newgate Gaol?

Then there was a brief flash of light from both pistols, a hissing sound that echoed across the clearing. But no lead balls heading in his direction. He saw Crouch look down at the guns, saw the look of annoyance on his face. Heard the curses pouring from his mouth.

Both pistols had misfired.

Prowl realised what had happened. It had rained all that afternoon as they'd travelled out of London. Though the rain had stopped, there was still the feeling of wet in the air.

His would-be killer was clearly unfamiliar with barkers. He'd have been wise to keep the powder dry in a powder flask, rather than have the pistols primed all that time. But he hadn't been able to. His victim would hardly have stood still, while he loaded the weapons in front of him.

He heard Crouch swear again, watching as the little man dropped the pistols to the ground. Saw him reaching deep into the pocket of his fustian jacket. Knew that he was searching for some other means of slaying him.

But Simeon Prowl hadn't been a footpad, for much of his life, without learning all there was to know about evading enemies. Many a time he'd had to slink into the undergrowth when a robbery on the high toby had gone wrong. Now he did it again, leaping across the grave that had been dug for him, forcing his way through the thick bushes and into the trees.

Then he ran, fast for a man of his years, down a gentle slope leading even deeper into the forest. He ran perhaps half a mile before he halted behind a rough-barked oak tree.

Then he listened.

Listened most carefully.

He could hear the man running in pursuit of him. Following the line he'd taken down through the trees. But Prowl had been chased many times. He knew the secrets of evasion. The importance of getting off the line of escape he'd been seen to take...

Prowl worked his way, silently, along the slope - away from his initial run. Stepped carefully through the undergrowth, putting each foot down gently lest he crack a twig. After a few hundred yards, he found a particularly thick cluster of bushes. He found his way into their very heart.

Sat down and listened and smiled.

This man, who'd been tasked with his slaughter, obviously had little experience of the countryside. He was crashing through the distant trees, making as much noise as a beater on a pheasant shoot. After a good hour, Prowl heard an end to the crashing – only footsteps as the assassin made his way back up the slope the way he'd come.

Then there was only the noise of the breeze soughing through the high branches, the sounds of little creatures of the night, recovering their courage and emerging from their dens. The distant calling of an owl. All signs that the hunt had been abandoned and that the hunter had left the wood.

It was drier as Prowl emerged from his lair, making his way in the direction of the dawning sun. He knew, from his days of robbery on the highway, that there was a quieter back road into London. A route he'd often taken to the city after a successful hold-up on the busier turnpike.

For all the perils of Newgate, Prowl knew he had to return to London – to a place of familiar streets, and hideouts in the rookeries where even the police were reluctant to go.

And even more than that – he knew of a man of dark reputation who might be able to give him help...

~

'In London by the morning,' said Harry Blizzard.

The fly-boat had made good speed all that day, the gentle but regular plodding of the horse never stopping. It was dark now, and the pair of boatmen who made up the night crew had taken over, one walking alongside the animal and the other steering the long vessel.

Lyddon and Blizzard were sitting on the deck, looking up at the full moon.

'You know I often watch the moon,' said Blizzard, 'when you can see it through the Black Country smog and smoke. Look up at it, I do, and marvel how unchanged it must be. Glaring down at us.' He laughed. 'Sometimes I wonder if there's anyone up there looking back down at me. But no! They say it's a dead place. I read a book all about it. But it's there, that great rock I saw during my adventures in Spain. Watched it all those nights after Waterloo. You remember how clear it was during those nights on Dartmoor?'

Jonas smiled, for he'd already shared that memory in his mind.

'Clear weather we had, much of the time – though I recall a mist that aided my escape from the militia. My God! What adventures we had, Harry! Now we're a pair of codgers, who'd stumble and fall if we had to cross the moorland in a fog!'

'Speak for yourself! I'm not done yet. I'm minded to return there – to Dartmoor. Mrs Blizzard is keen to have a glimpse of it – you know why? Just to say a last farewell to old friends. That moon up there – it shone on them as it shines now on us. And in a few years we'll be gone, and it'll shine on folk yet unborn. But we'll be gone,' he added wistfully.

'Some will remember us...'

'You perhaps, Jonas. Mebbe because of your great works in the Parliament. All those reforms. Oh, but so much left undone! It wouldn't be hard for the gentry – the kings and the dukes and the arrogant Class, to unpick your good work. They still see us as slaves, those bastards.'

'If people want change they'll have to keep fighting for it.'

'Have they our spirit, though?'

'I like to think so, Harry. I really do like to believe they do. You saw the thousands that came out for the Chartist meetings? They haven't gone away. And men like William Quest will carry the fight on...'

'I'm looking forward to meeting him. I recall Josiah Quest.'

'Now he was a good man! A great fighter for reform. He passed on a great legacy to young William. Not an easy task to change the world, but unless men and women stand up to be counted – well, there's no hope. Just a return to degradation and near slavery.'

'And old Jasper Feedle is still working alongside young Quest?'

'That he is, and as much a rascal as ever. Jasper enjoyed seeing Dartmoor again. Met up with that other villain – Weasel. Now there was a ruffian. You recall Captain Tremaine and his band of smuggling cut-throats? I think Weasel's the last one left – he looked about a hundred. Now there's a canny rogue, Harry. You'd have thought Weasel would have swung on the gallows years agone. But still there. Up on that Moor...'

Harry burst out laughing, so hard that the boatmen glanced at him in the moonlight. It took a while before he could speak.

'Oh, my God!'

'What's the jest, Harry.'

'Oh, God! We are old, Jonas!'

'Why so?'

'You just heard us? Thinking back on old times? Reminiscin' like good 'uns. When I was a young villain, I used to hear the old men thinking back to their youth. Going on and on and on about past times. And I used to think – oh, why don't they just shut up... and now here we are doing the same old thing. On and on an on...' He slapped Jonas on the shoulder. 'Come on, Lyddon! Let's shut up and get some sleep, lest we bore that old moon to death!'

Twenty

Shabson Crouch was one of the few who had seen the man's face. Then only by accident, for his employer was careful to shield himself from everyone.

When he was giving orders in dark places, the man was careful to wear a high collar and a hat pulled hard down, so much so that folk who glimpsed him often took him for a hedge-preacher, a man who preached sedition more than religion. It was in that guise that he would go where the questioning public might be...

Then there were the times when he seemed to have no face at all – in the dim light of sinister rooms, in the flickering gaslight, he would wear the mask, giving a presentation of himself that made all those who worked for him shudder.

Once, weeks before, Crouch had found the mask lying on a table. A construction of gauze and muslin. Crouch had held it up to his own face and looked into a broken piece of mirror. As he gazed, he seemed to have no face, no nose or nostrils, no eyes or mouth. No face at all. Yet he could see out perfectly well...

Some of those who worked for the man muttered that he must wear the mask because he had a face that was horribly scarred. Burned in a fire perhaps... or disfigured by the pox or syphilis?

But Crouch knew that it wasn't true – he'd once seen the man roll back his collar, preparing to put on the mask. Beneath the disguise was a very ordinary face. Not handsome, but not hideous either. Not a face that would stand out in a crowd, but much like any other ordinary face in the multitudes of men who thronged the streets of London.

It was not the man's face that Crouch feared, more the man's dreadful temper – and the hard malacca cane he carried. The stick that he would crash down on a chair or table – or across the arms or head of any follower that failed to do his bidding.

Crouch had felt its blow several times. Now he watched the man, expecting to feel its cutting force across his head. For the man was in a ferocious mood. Not even the stench of the river, making it hard to breathe, could take away his fear.

'You blundering fool!'

'Not my fault, sir... the powder was damp. Yer insisted I use pistols. Not used to 'em, sir. Better that I should have used my throwing knives.' He eyed the waving cane. 'Yer see that, sir? Yer do see that?'

Crouch breathed a sigh of relief as the man put the cane down on the table, turning away for a moment and reaching down. His master swung round and Crouch saw that he was wearing that flesh-coloured mask. The shaded face of the preacher had given way to a devil from hell.

'He'll come back to London, sir. He ain't got nowhere else he knows but the city and the roads into it. I got 'em all watched sir. I got a watcher on every turnpike between here and the forest. Men who know him well. We'll get him, sir. No fear... we'll get him.'

'You'd better,' the voice hissed from behind the mask, reminding Crouch of a fangless snake that a fakir had entertained the crowds with between the street stalls in Seven Dials. A creature brought here from India that waved from side to side, hissing hatred at its captor and the passers-by.

'Everything we do depends on Simeon Prowl not being found,' the Preacher said at last. 'If he is taken... if he is taken by the law, then I fear for you, Crouch. I really fear for you.'

Crouch knuckled his forehead, unable to look away from the faceless man, much as the snake in the Dials had held him in just such an hypnotic gaze.

'I would discuss this matter with you further, Crouch. But I have another task in hand.'

Crouch watched as the Preacher took up his malaccan cane once more, waving it through the air. Even now, he expected a blow. But it didn't come. The man turned away, tearing off the mask and putting it down on the table. Crouch saw him put on his preacher's hat and pull up his collar. Then, without a word, the Preacher left the room.

Crouch crossed to the window and looked down into the narrow alley, with its steps leading to the Thames. He waited, for it seemed an age until the man appeared, coming out of the door, walking swiftly away from the river. Not a preacher any more in his new guise, but a flash gent of a kind that was a rarity around the wharves of Limehouse.

So smart, and carrying the lighter cane of a well-heeled man about town.

It was then the thought came into Crouch's mind...

The thought that it might be helpful to know just where this flash gent lived when he wasn't menacing the wharf-rats by this filthy, stinking stretch of the Thames river.

~

'I fear we might not be welcome guests, Anders?'

Honour Bright was walking through Bloomsbury with his fellow inspector, Sergeant Berry and Benjamin Wissilcraft. Anders had never seen Bright so ill at ease.

'I think you'll find Quest amenable, Inspector,' said Wissilcraft. 'I appreciate you'd be happier putting the darbies on him, but practical is what we have to be. I'm sure the day will come when somebody will lay the villain Quest by the heels!'

Anders caught the sly smile on the spy's face.

'He is a criminal as far as I'm concerned,' said Bright. 'But, I do appreciate that desperate times call for desperate measures!'

~

By the time he was halfway along the Ratcliffe Highway, Crouch had begun to wish he'd never started his pursuit of the preacher. The man walked swiftly along the busy road. So fast that even the local pickpockets didn't feel it worth trying to overtake and dip this flash cove with his smart hat and jacket.

Even in the middle of the morning, the Highway was not the safest place to be, for all the thieves of Limehouse were wont to haunt its edge, skulking in the many vile alleys that came up from the wharves. A place of cut-throats, thieving whores, and light-fingered boys.

But the Preacher pushed on regardless of them all, relying on his swiftness to speed past the villains who seldom ventured far from their own criminal parishes. Even the light gentleman's cane could be a source of threat. Many a rogue had encountered thin and deadly blades that might be concealed within that dark bamboo.

Crouch lingered just a few yards behind, using his small height to conceal himself behind the barrows and street stalls. It seemed that the Preacher was easy to put the dodge upon, for he seldom glanced back at the way he'd come. He just strode on, as if all that grim world of the East End belonged to him.

Then, nearly at the end of the Highway, Crouch nearly lost the man he was dodging altogether. He watched as the Preacher signalled with his cane, catching the attention of someone on the far side of the street. Crouch looked across to see who it might be, then he cursed. For a cabriolet came suddenly out of one of the side streets, pulling up right by the man. An arrangement, clearly, for this was no public vehicle. The Preacher exchanged a few words with the driver and got up beside him, then the vehicle sped westwards along the Highway.

Crouch swore, then realised that such a flash gent as the Preacher would be bound to be going up west. Coves such as he seldom lived in the sprawling streets of Limehouse, or Wapping or Whitechapel. No doubt he had some smart gaff way beyond the Aldgate Pump that delineated where the smarter streets of the city began.

Crouch was about to give up, when, by one of those strokes of good fortune, Clarrie Brindley came along in her cart.

Clarrie sold vegetables at a stall in Soho and in her younger days had sometimes sold herself.

She was no more than thirty and had once been so pretty that even Mrs Bendig had considered her employment, as a whore of quality, in her night house for gentlemen in Leicester Square. But Clarrie swore too much and talked in such a deep cockney that no gent would have understood her soothing words. And hard living and the pox soon took away those promising looks.

Now, every day, Clarrie would transport her vegetables from the wharves to hawk on her stall, where the lanes of Soho met the broader reaches of Oxford Street. A profitable enterprise, for her vegetables were always fresh and of good quality, attracting the cooks from many of the big houses. Profitable enough to fund an old horse and a little cart.

'My gawd! Ain't they swung yer yet, Crouch?'

'No they ain't! But if yer goin' up west, it'd be obligin' ter me if yer'd follow that!' He pointed to the cabriolet.

Had they been in a less busy part of town then it would have been likely that Clarrie's old horse wouldn't have kept pace. But these were busy streets and the passage of the cabriolet took nigh an hour to get to Oxford Street, where it halted and its passenger alighted, conveniently close to the road into Soho where Clarrie plied her trade.

She accepted tuppence from Crouch, by way of fare, and promised that she could always be very obligin' to the little man, if he should ever call at her diggings off the Highway. Crouch nodded, and turned away. Clarrie was notoriously pox-ridden and no dodger in his right mind would linger there.

The Preacher was almost out of sight now, striding along towards the junction of the road leading to Tottenham Court. In his rush to catch up, Crouch collided with a pedestrian, and was hastily brushed aside. So violently that he was sore tempted to get out one of his knives and send the gent spinning down to hell. But he remembered his mission and went on, fearing that the Preacher might have got out of sight.

But there he was, still walking fast up the road, never even glancing back the way he'd come. What a fool the man was! Crouch considered. Any rascal from Limehouse, on a sinister mission, would have taken much more care that he wasn't being tailed!

Now they were in the places where the flash gentry lived. Those fine big gaffs with huge windows and attic rooms for their servants. What a life it must be to dwell in such splendour... oh, but not for the likes of me, Crouch muttered aloud, not for the likes of me...

After they'd passed through five more streets, the Preacher halted by a short flight of steps leading up to one of a long line of swell houses. Climbing the steps, he rapped on the door with his cane. After a moment, it was opened – and Crouch gasped in astonishment.

For he recognised the burly figure who greeted the Preacher. Someone well known in all the rookeries of London. Someone well known and feared. A person you never wanted to get on the wrong side of!

Crouch slunk back out of sight, lest this man noticed that he was putting the dodge on his visitor. Not hard to do, for beyond the railings outside these houses were several places that had access to the basement kitchens where the servants worked.

He lurked in one of them for a good hour, but the Preacher didn't come out again, nor anyone else. Crouch felt his guts rumbling for food, and he badly needed a piss. Now he knew the kind of household the Preacher was associating with, he saw little point in lingering. Oh, but how he wished he knew what was going on inside that house?

Seeking an alley where he might relieve himself, he wandered back down the street. After carrying out that necessity, he walked back to the road to Tottenham Court. He turned into that busy thoroughfare.

And then he got a shock that almost made him want to piss again...

Two men were walking towards him, and one was his fugitive victim, Simeon Prowl.

Crouch slapped a hand across his face, trying to hide his features, but knowing it would be no use. For only the night before, he'd spent all those hours in Prowl's company. Faced him with pistols as he tried to kill him. Men seldom forgot the villains they faced in moments of peril. Prowl was a footpad who'd have a good memory for faces. His very survival depended on knowing men he might have robbed.

But then the miracle happened...

Even as Crouch's mind considered why Prowl was better dressed than he'd been just the day before, and why he was in the company of someone who looked like a well-dressed tradesman, he realised the truth.

This man was *not* Simeon Prowl, though he was the very spit and image of him. When he looked closer, he could see very slight differences between this man and Prowl. This man was perhaps a few years older, but then... even then... the likeness was astonishing.

As the two men walked past him, the one looking like Prowl glanced in his direction, but there was not the slightest sign of recognition. Then they were gone, up the road, beyond him...

But the fright of seeing him loosened Crouch's bowels so much that he was obliged to seek a narrow alley leading down towards the rookery of St Giles where, once again, he relieved himself.

~

Joshua Blount heard the door at the far end of the room open and close. Feeling his way along the wall, he reached down and discovered the food and drink. Half a chicken, by his estimation, and a flagon of beer. Whoever his captors were, they intended that he should not starve. Blount was pleased that they were providing beer to drink, rather than water from the river itself, or some cholera-infected local pump.

But how much longer before someone talked to him? How much longer?

~

The latest arrival to the meeting in William Quest's drawing room was Magnus Blount, who looked around in wonder at the number of people crammed into the modest space.

Sticks had had a busy time with visitors that day, for several members of Monkshood, from different levels of society, had tapped on the door; a barrow lad and a bank clerk, a couple of street beggars, the proprietor of a slop shop and a burglar from Seven Dials. All had been admitted to the hall to be given a rewarding coin. All had reported that there was no sign of Joshua Blount – the man they'd been tasked to find.

But there had been earlier visitors too, and Magnus Blount was introduced to the folk sitting in the room.

Wissilcraft, the spymaster, Anders, Bright and Berry from Scotland Yard, Sir Wren Angier and James Brendon secretary to Mr Jonas Lyddon; Miss Rosa Stanton – the actress and adventuress – and her brother Daniel. The one-legged veteran of Waterloo and editor of the *Newgate Shadow*, Mr Jasper Feedle sat on the window seat.

'I apologise for interrupting your gathering, Quest,' said Magnus. 'Had I known you were in such a meeting, I would have postponed my visit. It is just that there has been no word of my brother, Joshua. Such a passage of time since his vanishing has left me deeply alarmed!'

Quest waved a hand.

'To the contrary, I'm glad you are here. We've just been discussing the matter of your brother's disappearance and the similar vanishing of Jonas Lyddon. Undoubtedly the two vanishings are connected – given the document I showed you the other day. I should add that these gentleman from Scotland Yard and Mr

Wissilcraft, from the secret service, are here quite unofficially. They have their own tale to tell about an organisation that puts our society in peril, and which would seem to have some connection with what has happened both to Jonas Lyddon and your brother.'

'And that is why we have come to you, William,' said Wissilcraft. 'To start with we had better tell you what we know...'

He related the story of Tenebrae, of the death of Samuel Cutler and the documents that had been found on his body. He suggested possible reasons why Lyddon and Blount might have been snatched. Very much as it had been explained to Bright at Scotland Yard.

'A dark tale indeed,' said Quest. 'Apollyon and Abaddon. Tenebrae itself, a name that means darkness... a word I'm not unfamiliar with...'

He told them of his adventure in the now-destroyed house in Piccadilly.

'Well, I think that experience proves our belief that you are a target of these villains,' said Anders. 'And you know why, don't you, Will? All because of that wretched notebook that you possess. They want that notebook to add to their power in society and they'll snatch anyone and probably won't hesitate to murder until it is in their hands.'

'I suppose there's a simple solution,' said Wren Angier, looking meaningfully at Wissilcraft.

'You've guessed why we are here, Sir Wren?' said Wissilcraft.

'I have indeed. You want William to either give you the notebook, or assent to its destruction in such a way that its loss will become known to Tenebrae?'

'In a nutshell...'

Quest walked across to the window, sitting on the window seat next to Jasper Feedle. He was silent for a long time before replying.

'If I do that, well, much of the hold I have over society will be gone.'

'Not to mention that these gents from Scotland Yard could collar the lot of us,' said Jasper. 'Without the threat of that notebook, we can all be taken in hand.'

'You could all be taken in hand anyway,' Bright remarked. 'The rule of law must always come before the power held by individuals...'

'Try telling that to the poor...' muttered Jasper.

'I am well aware of the shortcomings of our society, sir, but take away the law and what have you left? The whole world cannot work on your principles of murderous revenge. For what it is worth, I truly believe that you should all be arrested for the murderous criminals that you are. But I am aware that our society has a need for you, and that nobody else can deal with the dangers we face from the present menace.'

Quest gazed out of the window for a long time, watching the pedestrians in the street. Individuals who had no idea of the machinations of the few who determined which way society was run.

He faced them all...

'I will consider the matter of the notebook, but my first consideration must be to find Joshua Blount and Jonas Lyddon. You've approached me to hunt out this Abaddon who rules over a sinister organisation. Well gentleman - I'm prepared to be your ratcatcher. Anything else will depend on what happens with that... the gentry who run this society will not be easy enemies to defeat. Their agents are everywhere apparently - not just in the police and the secret service, but perhaps in the highest levels of government.'

'They've almost topped you once, William,' said Jasper. 'You can stand out on this and not put your head in their noose.'

'Ah, but it already is, Jasper. It already is. Don't forget that it wasn't just Blount and Lyddon on their list. My name is there too. And I've long shared the belief of Napoleon Bonaparte that the best form of defence is attack.'

'I admire your courage,' said Honour Bright. 'Even though I fully intend to bring you to book, once these matters are dealt with. No murderous criminal should escape the gallows.'

Quest nodded.

'I wouldn't yet make an appointment for us outside Newgate, Inspector. There's a very good chance that the villains of Tenebrae will do that task for you. I'm the third on that list and two have already vanished.'

There was a furious tapping on the door of the house.

'I wasn't expecting anyone else,' said Sticks, turning towards the stairs.

'Where will you start, Will?' asked Wren.

Quest shrugged.

'I really don't know. A pity really that we lost them at their house in Piccadilly. To have them pinned down there made it much easier. But one thing is for sure - given their political ambitions, their headquarters has to be in London.'

'A big place,' opined Sergeant Berry.

'Indeed it is...'

'What more can we do?' asked Inspector Anders.

'Very little,' Quest replied. 'Especially if you have informers in your ranks. All that I would ask is that I can leave messages for you. Somewhere discreet, away from Scotland Yard. A place you can check two or three times a day. I might need your support...'

'My set of rooms at Albany is not far away from Westminster,' Wren said. 'The doorman is a good fellow and will act as a courier if we need him. I've known and trusted him for a long while.'

'Ideal,' said Anders.

'And in the meantime...' Quest began.

But the door opened and Sticks entered.

'You won't believe this!' he said, stepping aside to admit two more visitors.

'My God!' said Quest, stepping forward.

Jonas Lyddon and Harry Blizzard entered the room.

James Brendon stood and grasped Lyddon by both hands.

'Oh, Mr Lyddon. This is such a joy to me. I believed that I might never see you again! These gentleman and I have just been discussing your vanishing – and here you are!'

~

Simeon Prowl thought he must be going mad. That or his enemies were cleverer than he'd thought.

Either way he couldn't believe what he saw.

It was the man Crouch, the little villain who'd tried to top him, waiting for him outside the very house he'd crossed London to seek. The flash gaff in Bloomsbury where the man with the dark reputation lived, when he wasn't a footpad or bludger or murdering avenger.

It's not possible...

Prowl had lived up to his name as he'd walked from Epping Forest into the city, taking all the back routes, the deserted alleys, losing himself in the crowds. He'd stolen a jacket that had been hanging up outside a slop shop so that he might change his appearance, relieved a barrow boy of his canvas cap as he brushed through the hordes in a street market.

And yet...

Crouch was there – waiting for him...

Prowl hadn't even come directly to this Bloomsbury gaff. It was well known that the man who haunted the rookeries, under the guise of Bill the Bludger, had a room in Neal's Yard, close to Seven Dials. He'd climbed the steps to it and tapped on the stout wooden door. Though a look at the dust around the locks suggested that nobody had been there for quite a time.

And so, with great care, he'd crossed Oxford Street and made his way up the road to Tottenham Court and into Bloomsbury where – now – all the world knew that this man called Quest lived.

Prowl considered the legend of the man – the man who fought for the poor of the rookeries. He'd encountered Quest a few times in the disgusting lanes of St Giles; only Quest hadn't been a flash cove then – just a begrimed rogue in fustian. But now the secret was out – the man Bill was actually a gent of sorts.

A man who lived a double life.

When the truth had dawned, the rascality of the rookeries had found it hard to believe. That the frightening avenger who knew every turn of the alleys of the Dials and Whitechapel and beyond, the scarred villain with his own brand of murderous justice, might have been reared in the gutter but now was a flash gentleman as well.

Now all the world knew... but Prowl was well aware that, however the man dressed, whatever way he might talk, whether his features might be clean or filthy, whether he be Quest or Bill of Seven Dials, he was still the champion of the poor and the desperate.

And, as he turned into Tavistock Place, Simeon Prowl found that the little killer, Shabson Crouch awaited him. There he was, on a flight of steps leading down to some basement servants' quarter, his ugly little face pressed against the railing, watching and waiting...

It took Prowl a few moments to gather his thoughts, then the realisation came that Crouch might be there for a different purpose. Could he have guessed that Prowl might seek out this man Quest, given that his life was in peril? No! Why should he? There were so many other places an escaping condemned man might seek refuge... no... if Crouch was here, then he'd come for a very different purpose. His interest seemed to be the house. Almost as though he was waiting for someone to emerge.

Then... very suddenly... Crouch came away from the steps, rushing down the road. Prowl only had a second to pull himself in hard against the wall, to watch as the little man sped along the street. At one point, Crouch stopped dead, as he was approached by two men on the pavement on the far side of the road. From his vantage point, Prowl couldn't see who they might be, though their travel-stained clothes suggested they were not quite gentry.

But what to do now?

Prowl half-turned, meaning to go back to the house in Tavistock Place, but then a thought occurred to him. If Crouch was watching the home of this William Quest, then there must be a reason for it. And if he could find just where Crouch hung about, then that information might be a good exchange for any help Quest might give to a fugitive from Newgate Gaol.

Twenty-one

'It is a huge relief that you are with us,' said Quest. 'By all accounts, you were lucky to escape with your life. We owe Mr Blizzard here considerable thanks. A great weight off our minds, though we still have to find Joshua Blount.'

Jonas Lyddon had given them an account of his journey from Manchester, and Quest had told the newcomers about the danger of Tenebrae and the Abaddon with no apparent face.

'But what are we to do now?' asked Anders. 'It's a relief that Mr Lyddon is safe here with us, but both he and you, Will, remain in peril. In normal circumstances I'd offer you police protection, but how can I? We don't know that we can trust anyone beyond the people in this room. Presumably Mr Lyddon will stay here?'

'If I did that, well, I'd remain a prisoner for ever,' said Jonas. 'My work in Parliament might be done, but there are still matters that I have to bring to a conclusion. Besides, our enemies – having failed to capture me – will soon be aware that I am here. They are after William too and are probably keeping a watch on this house. My being here would just be a burden on my friends.'

Honour Bright looked across at Anders.

'I would consider it my duty to offer my services as a guard for Mr Lyddon,' he said. 'I have my pistol with me and we could station my constable, Parkin, here as well. He could guard the door.'

For all their differences, Quest decided that he quite liked Honour Bright.

'Then we are to remain here cooped up like rats in a trap?' said Jonas.

'It might be the safer option,' said James Brendon.

'I would have achieved little in my life if I'd always trod the path of safety,' said Lyddon. 'I do not believe I should remain here. Obviously, I cannot return to my own home, for they'll surely be waiting for me there.'

Quest thought for a moment.

'I think you are correct, sir. I need to be out and about seeking out these villains. Am I not the rat-catcher? And I shall need Jasper and Sticks with me.'

'Not forgetting me,' said Rosa.

'I would be willing to guard Mr Lyddon,' said Daniel. 'I have my pistols.'

'You do indeed, Daniel,' Quest said, 'though I think you need a tad more experience with them. And if we are to be out and about a great deal, I shall need someone to keep guard over this property, remembering how our foes managed to destroy the house in Piccadilly.'

'Then where?' asked Anders.

There was a long silence, then...

'I believe I have the perfect place,' said Wren Angier. 'I've recently purchased a house in Highgate village. Where better to secrete Mr Lyddon? Nobody, apart from Phoebe and the land agent, knows it belongs to me. It's close enough to London to allow Mr Lyddon to attend to matters in hand, but far enough out so that he might avoid casual encounters with people who might gab too much.'

'What would Phoebe say?' said Quest.

'Who is Phoebe?' asked Jonas.

'My... intended,' said Wren. 'she is currently minding the property.'

'I would be reluctant to put a woman in danger,' Jonas said.

'Phoebe has faced many dangers in her young life,' said Wren. 'She would be happy to participate in your protection, Mr Lyddon. I've often told her of your great work for the poor.'

Quest considered just how far Wren Angier had come in such a short time, recalling how this man had himself started out as a money lender and exploiter of the wretched. Angier had been a target for Monkshood and Quest had been sent out to kill him. But - at the assignation - Quest had seen some promise in the man. Watched in later months, as Wren had ditched his bad old ways and overcome real fear to become a most prized associate and good friend. His sparing of Wren Angier had made him feel long and hard about his own path in life.

'That would be ideal,' he said. 'And if Inspector Bright and his constable would offer their services?'

'And me!' said Harry Blizzard.

'Are you not returning to the Black Country and your dear wife, Harry?' Lyddon asked. 'You have already done more for me than friendship demands.'

Blizzard laughed.

'After all those perils you and I faced on Dartmoor? And still managed to avoid getting swung on Gibbet Hill... oh no, Jonas! And remember what we were talking about on the fly-boat? One last adventure, eh? Even for a pair of old codgers like you and me!'

~

This time the man came right into the room with a bowl of food, nudging Joshua Blount on the shoulder and putting the bowl down next to him. The sensitivity nature had given Blount to help cope with his blindness made him feel the very slight heat of the candle the man carried. Of course, Blount thought – had there been a gas lamp he would have heard its hiss.

'More chicken,' the man muttered. 'I shall be back in a moment with beer, safer than the foul water you get round here.'

'Who are you?'

'No talking. I don't hold with keeping a blind man captived, but we all have to do what we are told. But no talking... he was adamant about that. I'll be back soon.'

An educated voice, Blount deduced. Perhaps a clerk who'd fallen on hard times, certainly not one of the denizens of the London waterside. He wondered how this man had come to fall into the clutches of his captors. There'd been an edge of concern in his voice, as though he might be an unwilling participant in these matters. He heard the man step away. A moment later the door closed. But as Blount reached down for the chicken he once more felt the heat of the candle and reasoned that the man - proposing to make an immediate return - had left it nearby.

~

Quest explained that he owned the premises at the rear of his home in Tavistock Place.

'Probably being watched, but they might not have as many watchers round there as here. My idea is that we take Jonas out that way, with his guardians. We'll speed you away in an equipage, Jonas. Furthermore, we'll round up a couple of dozen workers for Monkshood to block the streets nearby, making it harder for these gentry to follow you. I think that's the best we can do. I'll put out a rumour that we've opened up my old room at Neal's Yard. With a bit of luck they might think we are taking you there.'

~

'Limehouse!' Simeon Prowl muttered, watching as Crouch turned off the Ratcliffe Highway into Narrow Street, that most ancient of thoroughfares, lined with so many old buildings between the road and the river.

Prowl had known it well - in a brief period of honesty he'd worked for a few months as a wharfinger in the dockside basins that cut through its farthest end, from the swirling and filthy waters of the Thames. He recalled many a merry time in The Grapes - a tavern that, in his day, was a notorious haunt of ne'er-do-wells. Though it had become all too respectable since that man Dickens had wrote it up, a learned beggar had told Prowl some months before his conviction.

He watched as Crouch walked purposefully along the narrow length of the street. Prowl wondered if this journey was ever going to end? He'd trailed the little man halfway across London and his aged feet were aching with the pounding of the pavements.

He'd had one startling moment right at the start, when Crouch had dived into an alley between two Bloomsbury mews to relieve himself - but after that the man had made considerable speed eastward into and beyond the old city. Now it was Limehouse, that busy part of the port where ships were loaded and uncargoed.

Where warehouses stored tea and tobacco and opium, where the gentry who managed such enterprises lived side by side with the hovels of the wretched and the dens of vice, where opium was taken and whores plied their trade.

Then, close to the end of the street, Crouch suddenly turned into an alley leading steeply down towards the river. Prowl halted at its red-bricked corner. An alley that barely gave room for two men to pass side by side, covered at its lowest end by a building – a warehouse of sorts – forming a dark tunnel, its entrance cluttered with packing cases, old chains and discarded rope.

He watched as Crouch entered the building through a doorway in an otherwise blank brick wall, closing the door behind him. So there you go, Prowl thought. Oh, he'd love to know what went on behind that door. He was sure the man in Bloomsbury would be interested to know that, but Prowl wasn't going to put his head on the chopping block by daring to open the door. And he felt sure that the Bloomsbury gent would be just as fascinated to learn where the little man who was watching his house hung around.

He waited for a moment or two. It was dark now, but – looking through the tunnel – he could see, by the lights coming from the river, that a small rowing boat was moored at the water's edge. There it was, framed like it was in a picture by the walls of the tunnel.

As all was quiet, Prowl took a few steps down the alley, mindful of that door beyond which his would-be killer lurked. He went beyond the door. The alley was steeper now as it dipped down to a short flight of steps leading to the Thames.

He considered whether there was another access to the building from the waterside. He was about to investigate when, to his horror, there was a great cry of anger and the door was flung open. And there was his enemy, Crouch, with another weedy-looking man. They came out and ran up the alley, Crouch yelling obscenities at the other individual.

Had they not been in such a rush... had they glanced *down* the alley towards the river, they would have been sure to see him, even in that poor light. But their interest seemed to be in the busier road above them. Prowl watched as they tore around the corner into Narrow Street. He was about to follow them when the thought occurred to him that they might return just as suddenly. That he might come face to face with the man who'd tried to murder him.

There was a wide platform above the steps leading down to the water – a loading area filled with the detritus of waterside life. He saw that the wall of the building was built sheer out of the Thames, with no access away from the alley.

Then the thought came to Prowl that he might take the rowing boat and find a safer exit from his perilous position. He took one step down...

Then he was grabbed... someone had seized him from behind, pinioning his arms against his body. He felt a face touching the back of his head, breath on his neck, words being muttered right against his ear...

~

The man took just a few minutes to return with the beer, and Joshua Blount noticed that he didn't shut the door behind him.

'Here's the beer!'

The man put the handle of the drinking vessel against Blount's right hand and was obviously bending down towards him. Now was the one opportunity to put his plan of escape into action.

As he felt the vessel against his fingers, Blount shot his hand upwards sending the beer flying into the man's face. At the same time, Blount pinched the wick of the candle, plunging the cell into darkness. He heard the man cry out and swear and he knew that he'd achieved his objective.

The draught from the open door indicated the way he had to go. He brushed against the man as he escaped, heard him stumble. His captor lacked Blount's experience of being in total darkness. Feeling the door as he left the room, Blount pulled it shut. There was the bolt he'd heard sliding back and forth. He pulled it across. He was feeling his way along a brick-lined corridor, by the time the man had found the door and begun hammering upon it with his fists.

But which way out?

Easier than he had envisaged, for a few yards of dank wall led to the wood of a door. It was unlocked and Blount could tell that he was outside.

There were cobbled stones beneath his feet and he could hear the noise of carriages and people talking in the uphill direction, the sounds of the mighty river in the other. He pondered which way to go, first uphill towards the street – but he collided with obstructions – wooden boxes perhaps and something that felt like a stacked anchor chain. This swung him round and forced him downhill towards the water.

He almost panicked. For all his blind experiences of walking through London, he was wary of the river's edge. But he felt tired and sick and just needed to get away from that door. Then he knew he was somewhere right by the Thames. He could hear the water lapping against stones and the cry of a disturbed gull. He dared not move, for just then he heard the door open and shut. A few moments later, the door opened again. He heard men running, at least two of them, their footsteps almost drowned by someone swearing very loudly...

Blount paused, becoming aware that a man was walking nearby. Almost right up to him. He judged that they could not have glimpsed him and surmised that it must be night. He heard the man's heavy breathing and considered that he must have his back to him. Any moment now, this newcomer would turn and see him. In what, he judged, was a futile effort at defence, he flung his arms around the man...

~

'Are you my captor?' the man muttered, his mouth right against Prowl's ear. 'Are you my enemy? For God's sake, if you are, cast me into the river now. I've done you no harm... why do you torment me so?'

Blount released his grip.

'I'm not your enemy,' Prowl replied. 'And if you're fleeing the two men who come out of the building up the alley, well, then we're on the same side, for one of the two has already tried to kill me.'

'Who are you?'

'A friend... and I think it best serves us if we try to get away from here as soon as we can. That pair'll be back as soon as they don't find you in the street. I'll get you away if you'll put your trust in me. But we daren't go back up that alley, lest we runs into them. There's only the river...'

'I cannot swim...'

'You don't need to. There's a rowing boat moored here we might take. I'm no oarsman, but I might get us to the south side of the river. Where might I take you then?'

'I daren't go home... I fear they will be waiting for me there. But there's a friend who might help me in my plight. A man with a reputation for aiding people in trouble. If you could conceal me somewhere and take a message to him... he has a home in Bloomsbury...'

'Bloomsbury? I just come from there. Who is this man?'

'I believe he has several names, but in Bloomsbury he's known as William Quest.'

'Quest! William Quest, the saviour of the poor? Is that the man?'

'He has that reputation.'

'I've just come from his house!'

'Good God! You know Quest?'

'Not as how you'd say know him, though I've seen him in the alehouses of the Dials in another of his guises. The man's a legend to the desperate. And believe me, my friend, I'm a desperate man... both sides of the law are trying to have me topped. I'll go to Bloomsbury to find Quest for you, for he might yet be the saviour of both of us.'

'Then we must trust ourselves to the river...'

'If we can get across, well, I knows of a gaff in The Borough. As safe as anywhere. I'll conceal you there and take any message you like to this Quest. But I beg you, sir... I'll get down on me knees and plead if I have to ... if Quest is a friend of yours, for the love of God get him to help me too.'

~

It was very dark by the time they reached Angier's home in Highgate village. A modest house, Quest thought, set in its own grounds. Phoebe answered the door, seeming surprised at the large party that had descended upon the property.

She gave Quest a hug, remembering how he had once saved her from a vicious pimp. How much better and healthier she looked since Wren had taken her up, he thought. And he could see from the way she and Angier greeted each other, the strength of the love between them.

Jonas Lyddon took her hand.

'My dear, we may be putting your life in peril,' he said, after their mission had been explained to her. 'If you would rather not have us in your home, I would quite understand.'

She smiled. 'Sir, my life has often been in deep peril. But for Mr Quest here, I would have no life at all. The least I can do is give shelter to any friend of his. Now come into the warm, sir. These autumn nights are very cold and I have a fire blazing. I would like to hear more about your adventures.'

Lyddon turned to his secretary.

'James, I've been thinking it might be best if you return to run my affairs from my own home. Someone must be there to guard my papers and to bring any messages that my associates might send. But be wary, lad - for there's a danger to you too. Keep a loaded pistol with you at all times, for these gentry who oppose us are dangerous fellows.'

'I believe I would rather stay here with you, sir,' Brendon replied.

Jonas took him to one side.

'It's like this, lad. I would hate to think of my many papers and records falling into the hands of an enemy. My household staff are elderly and not wary enough to be guardians to my property. You can serve me better there, and convey any messages to me. But as I say - be wary! Make sure you are never followed, for I wouldn't care to put the young lady who lives here in any danger. Do you not agree, Quest?'

William Quest had come over to them and heard the conversation.

'There is some merit in what you suggest,' he answered. 'I can arrange for some members of Monkshood to patrol the street hard by your property. I can make sure that Brendon is never followed if he is coming here. Brendon, you'd better leave with me now and we'll see you safely on your way. Sticks and Jasper and I have arranged to meet Rosa in town and get about our rat-catching business. We'd better leave as soon as I've had a final word with Angier.'

~

'What is this place?' asked Joshua Blount.

'Ah, you're safe enough here,' said Prowl. 'It's a gaff I've used before, though nobody knows that, for I was always knowed under a different name in The Borough. I'm sorry that you had to climb up so many stairs, but we are high in the attic above a builder's workshop. The old Marshalsea Gaol is just across the way. The builder, who owns the gaff, is a cousin of mine and prospers by fencin' stolen goods, when he's not layin' good London bricks. I've had a word with him and he'll keep a watch and bring drink and victuals to you. At first light, I'll go and seek out the man Quest.'

The tide had been sweeping so swiftly up the Thames that it had carried the rowing boat a fair way upstream, though Prowl had had some difficulty in steering it to the south bank of the river. They'd found a jetty at Rotherhithe where they'd made a risky landing, clambering out of the boat up some steps and letting it float away in the direction of London Bridge. A good little vessel, Prowl thought. He was saddened to see it go, though in all probability it belonged to their enemies. Prowl had blown it a kiss, as it bobbed away into the dark night. Then he had led the blind man along countless wharves and a great many dark alleys.

'Tell me more about yourself?' said Blount.

And much to his own surprise, Simeon Prowl did, relating his adventures as a footpad, his conviction for murder – and about the sinister Preacher who had smuggled him out of Newgate Gaol, only to have him nearly put to death in Epping Forest.

'Then we are both in danger from the same enemies,' Blount said. 'But who are they, and why were they so keen – and able – to get you out of Newgate? There is considerable menace in this, my friend. Whatever happens, I will make sure that you are never returned to Newgate, and that you never have to face the gallows. My friend Quest has a reputation for getting men away from such ordeals. But journeying through London in daylight might put you in danger? You could be recognised and taken up by the police?'

'A risk I'm prepared to take, sir! For my life – and yours by the soundin' of it – is even more at peril if we do not seek his help. This man Quest is a legend in the gaffs and kens of the underworld. With his aid, we might both stand a chance of getting away from the law and these men who are threatenin' our very lives.'

~

Crouch looked through the filthy window at the dawn, trying not to glance at his employer, wishing himself back in the dark glades of Epping Forest.

His associate, Ebenezer Booth had been the first to face the Preacher's wrath. Having failed to find the escapee, they had returned to the Limehouse building. Just before the dawn broke, the Preacher had arrived to be given the sorry news of Blount's escape.

'You blundering fools!' the Preacher raged. 'How was it possible to let a blind man get away from you? Did you not scour the streets? Why did you not find and return him for me?'

He waved the heavy blackthorn stick he carried, and both Crouch and Booth eyed it warily. More than once, the Preacher had brought it crashing down on their backs for other incompetences. Time and again, after such beatings, Crouch had promised himself that one day he might well cut his employer's throat if he did it again. Yet the man paid well and Crouch dreaded the thought of struggling to survive in the slums of Whitechapel.

And the man himself looked worried and... frightened?

'You must understand,' the Preacher said, 'that I represent some very powerful and dangerous men. If you fail and I fail... well, who knows what may become of us? There are individuals in this nation who are the power behind everything. Even the politicians and the Queen herself are mindful of that power. And that is why I shall not punish you for letting Blount escape. Because I need you both... do you understand that?'

'It's my belief the blind man tumbled into the river,' Booth began... 'the rowboat has gone. Likely, he felt his way down to the river's edge, touched the painter of the boat and tried to board it. And doing that he drownded himself.'

The Preacher considered the possibility.

'That is possible. A nuisance though, for I had need of Blount for bargaining with. Still, better dead than loose. But as I say, we have another most important matter to contend with. You are handy with a pistol, eh Booth?'

A puzzled look came on Booth's skinny pockmarked face, as he wondered where the conversation was going. He'd served seven years in the army, only being forced out from the debility of the smallpox he'd caught on foreign shores.

'All guns, sir... not just pistols but rifles as well.'

'Good, that's good. Crouch? Do you mind that stinking rogue Jabez Mostin? The one who scarcely washes and has such foul breath?'

Crouch was baffled by the mention of that name.

'He's a fixture at Rat's Castle. But he does little but robbin' on the streets and waylaying gents what goes a-slumming. Not to be trusted, sir, not with the work you have in mind...'

'He has a gang who will do murder if they're paid enough?'

'He does... but you can't think of bringing them in on this... they'd blow us to the law as easy as kiss-my-hand. You can't trust him, sir.'

The Preacher looked out through the window, at the shafts of sunlight that were lighting up a barge on the Thames.

'We don't need to trust him, Crouch. We just need Mostin and his gang to provide a distraction, while we undertake an enterprise I have in mind. If they're all took in the course of that endeavour... well, they won't know anything to talk about to the police. Not about us anyway...'

Crouch shook his head.

'I know Mostin well, but if I approach him he'll split on me... for certain sure.'

The Preacher sat down on a bench by the window, resting his chin on a temple he'd made with his hands.

'That is a risk we'll have to take, Crouch. Fear not, I'll put you way beyond the reach of the law if Mostin blows upon you afterwards.' He saw the look of fear cross the little man's face. 'Oh, not like that, Crouch. Not like that! Despite the fact that you let Blount get away I'm not *that* angry with you.'

'London is getting' dangerous for me, sir? I've a mind to be elsewhere.'

The Preacher studied him for a long moment.

'I know someone up in Manchester who would give you a haven from the storms of this life, and well-paid employment as well. Best that you go there as soon as my next project comes to fruition. But I *shall* need you to journey to Rat's Castle and engage the services of Jabez Mostin. And, to prevent him splitting, you may kill Jabez Mostin as soon as we're done with him. Now let me explain to you both what this project is...'

Twenty-two

Daniel Stanton woke late for the excitements of the previous day had made sleep difficult. As he shaved and dressed, he found it hard to believe that he'd tumbled into such an adventurous world. He wondered what his father would make of the situation? He'd scarcely be pleased that Rosa was living with a man out of wedlock, even if a marriage was planned.

And to find men who were clearly criminals and policemen working together to bring down some great menace to the nation?

He couldn't think it was surpassed in the novels of all his favourite authors. Perhaps, one day, he could pen an account of these doings in some fiction of his own?

Late the previous evening, a message had been delivered from William Quest, explaining that none of them would be returning to the Bloomsbury house that night, and requesting that he make sure that all the doors and windows be secured against intruders.

Daniel checked them all, wondering if there was any danger of the house being besieged and attacked by Quest's enemies. As a final safeguard, he'd found, primed and loaded the two little pistols, hoping that his aim might be better than the last time, should he be called upon to fire them.

Putting the guns on the cabinet beside his bed, he'd turned down the gaslight and endeavoured to sleep. But with his mind filled with strange imaginings, it was gone three before he fell into a restless repose.

After dressing, he picked up the pistols and searched through all the downstairs rooms, once again checking the doors and windows.

He looked out on to Tavistock Place and watched as the pedestrians strolled by and the carriages trundled along the road. It all seemed so normal to him, the world carrying on as usual, oblivious to the perils that haunted the secret and conspiratorial world that was occupying the thoughts of those who had sat in the room upstairs the previous day.

Daniel sat for a while in Quest's study, thumbing through one of the undamaged volumes of *Lavengro*, but he found he couldn't even lose himself in the pages of such an old favourite. He yawned, for the lack of sleep was catching up with him, and he felt himself drifting away...

This would never do! He put the book down and stood, determined to patrol the house, starting with his own bedroom, which was at the back of the house. A much better room than the one he'd been originally confined in, though the view was only into the yard between the two back-to-back properties that Quest owned, with high walls on either side, giving the yard some privacy from the neighbouring houses.

It would have been nice if there had been a little garden there, Daniel considered, though the buildings all around shut out much of the sunlight. No, Quest was wise to keep it as a yard, for few plants would prosper there. And he did have a country home at Hope Down, where he must have a garden?

He was turning away from the window when he saw something atop one of the high walls, something black moving along the sharp edge of the brickwork.

His first thought was that it must be a cat, but as he turned and looked, he could see that it was a dark canvas cap.

He watched, seeing first one hand and then another reach over the top of the wall. Then the head and chest of a man came into view, a man hauling himself over the wall.

For a second, the intruder lay flat along the bricks, and then he swung the other way, holding the top of the wall with both hands, clearly taking a great breath, and then dropping into the yard. The fall was a good ten feet and the man landed badly, sprawled and winded on the cobbles. But after a few moments, he clambered to his feet, looked all round and crossed to where the door and lower windows must be, out of sight from Daniel.

The youth picked up the two pistols that he'd rested on the window ledge and raced downstairs. There were three small rooms at the back of the house and stairs down to the basement kitchen.

There was also the door out into the yard and, even as he came along the narrow corridor, Daniel could hear the sounds of someone trying to open the door. He'd checked the stout lock the previous night and the ease with which it was being opened, suggested that the intruder must have considerable experience as a cracksman.

There he was – the cap pulled hard down on his head and dressed in worn fustian. He held a set of picklocks in one hand and a small jemmy in the other and was breathing as heavily as Daniel himself.

'Stay where you are, or I'll shoot you dead!'

The man cried out, swinging round to face Daniel, the cap flying to the ground.

For a moment, Daniel thought he was going mad! The face that glared at him was familiar from the previous day. He'd sat just by him in Quest's room. For the man was Jonas Lyddon...

Or so he thought at first, for the likeness was astonishing, certainly from a close glimpse or at a distance. But as Daniel looked more carefully, he could see that the likeness was superficial. Near enough, but not quite. For this villain had a slightly wider head and the chin was a tad different. And he was perhaps just a little younger than Lyddon.

But even with those differences, Daniel was astonished at the similarities.

~

Honour Bright took advantage of the daylight to examine the grounds of the house in Highgate, in company with Wren Angier. It was a newly-built property standing some way from its neighbours.

Bright considered the prospects of keeping it secure and shook his head.

'It might have been wiser to get Mr Lyddon well away from London, Sir Wren.'

'In the cold light of day I'm inclined to agree with you, Inspector. Just the first thought to come into my head. Now I think of it, we might have been wiser to remain at Quest's home in Bloomsbury. Only two sides to defend there. Too much open ground around here.'

'My thoughts too. Mind, if there's to be a struggle, we at least won't have innocent pedestrians getting in the way. But had I known that this situation was going to arise, I would at least have brought armaments and more men. But then again, it's likely that Tenebrae has corrupted policemen at the Yard and the secret would soon have been out.'

'I have some guns here, well a few pistols.'

'Then we must equip ourselves with them.'

'What about your constable – Parkin?'

'I doubt the lad has ever used a gun in his life.'

'Well, we'd better teach him the rudiments.'

'I'll see to that, sir. But your – lady...?'

'I've tried to persuade Phoebe to leave. She has a cousin down in Bethnal Green. I suggested that she go to her for a few days, but she refuses to leave. It's a pity we don't have Quest here.'

'Have you known that villain for long?'

'A year or two. He saved my life.'

'Ye-es...'

'Here comes Inspector Anders,' said Wren.

Anders and Berry had escorted Wissilcraft down into Highgate village, so that he might find a carriage to take him into London. The spymaster had agreed to give Commissioner Mayne a briefing on the situation, before going on to his headquarters to read the reports coming in from his own agents.

'Inspector Bright considers this property a hard place to defend,' said Wren.

Anders glanced at the extensive grounds, which set the house some way back from the road.

'So it is,' Anders agreed, 'but it was a good idea, given the little time we had to prepare. It's true that there are too few of us here to defend the grounds, so we must put all of our efforts into the defence of the house. It's a pity that Quest had to leave us. He has more experience than any of us, and Feedle and Sticks are grand fighters. But we have Blizzard with us – and he fought the French under Wellington.'

'A long time ago!' said Bright.

~

'I can't help thinking we're scuppered,' said Sticks.

He, Feedle and Quest were being driven in the closed carriage back to Bloomsbury. Sticks' words broke a long silence and nobody commented on them for several minutes.

'How d'you mean scuppered?' said Jasper Feedle.

'Well, the whole of Monkshood. Everything we set out to do. It's not a secret any more. Half of London has at least heard rumours about William here. Most of the villains in Seven Dials know that Bill the Bludger and Will are one and the same. I think our day is done...'

'I fear you're right,' Quest said quietly.

'If we go on the way we did, Inspector Bright, or some other trap from Scotland Yard will put a rope around our necks. People knowing will mean people getting in our way. Like I say, we're scuppered. And as for finding these gentry – the ones we're hunting – where do we even begin?'

Quest shook his head.

'I really don't know. We had a chance when we found the house in Piccadilly, but now we don't even know where these people are hiding out and not a clue who they are. Their leader could be anyone from the Prime Minister down. The best we can do is to return to Tavistock Place, wash and dress and get food in us, then seek out any gossip in the taverns of London. We know that Tenebrae employ villains from the rookeries – and such men tend to talk too much in their cups.'

'That's a small hope...' said Jasper.

'I know,' Quest said. 'I know. What we need is a bit of luck. And to be honest, I can't see just where that bit of luck can come from.'

~

'Not a game I have a liken' for,' Jabez Mostin muttered, as he sat across the table from Crouch. 'An' why does it have to be today?'

He looked across the dark cellar that was Rat's Castle.

'Look at 'em!'

'I'm a-looking,' Crouch replied. 'A dozen vicious rogues. What more do you want?' There's silver in it for them. And not much danger. You've only got to provide a distraction, no more than that! There'll be a wagonette outside in an hour. My master's keen that we do the job late in the afternoon. So that we got the darkness to flee into.'

'Who is yer master?'

'That ain't any of your business, Mostin. There's a crown in it for every man that comes along and five sovereigns for you. Ain't that enough?'

Jabez Mostin leaned forward.

'I wants the money now.'

'After you've done the job, Mostin. After all, you could take the money and run!'

'What? and get one of yer daggers in me back? Or me throat cut down some dark alley? I ain't as stupid as all that!'

'I hope not, my old friend. I hope not. You shall have the money but these toe-rags, you're bringing along, don't get paid until we're in the wagon on the way back here. And Jabez, if you or anyone else in this rat hole peaches and gives my name to the traps, well... I'll make sure that every single one of you is topped. Every man will have their flesh sliced by a dagger...'

'Nobody'll blow on yer!'

'I hope not. Now have we got a deal?'

Jabez Mostin looked around the candlelit room and nodded, his filthy palm reaching out for his sovereigns.

~

For a moment Quest thought he was going mad...

They had entered the drawing room in Tavistock Place. Daniel was standing by the fireplace, pokering the coals into some sort of life. Quest noticed the pistols on the table nearby. And a man in one of the armchairs who turned to face him, a fellow dressed in shabby and torn fustian. And for a moment, Quest thought that that man was Jonas Lyddon...

'By all that's holy,' said Jasper Feedle. 'Simeon Prowl...'

'Hello, Jasper. Long time since I've clocked you.'

Jasper glanced at Quest.

'I know what you were thinking, Will. And I was nearly took in too. I've known Simeon all these years, and Jonas Lyddon a sight longer, and I've never seen the likeness before. It's the hair, it's all gone. They cut your hair, Simeon?'

'In Newgate, old friend. Prison crop, though I've growed it a tad since then.'

'It's astonishing...' Sticks said. 'Now I look, now I really look, I can see the differences, but at first glance – at a distance I'd have sworn he was the man we've just left up at Highgate village. At first, I thought it was Mr Lyddon.'

'Would that be Jonas Lyddon?' asked Prowl.

'You know of him?' said Quest.

'Everyone knows of Lyddon an' his work for the poor,' Prowl remarked. 'But I heard his name just a few hours ago. From a man I helped get away from some rogues who had him captive. He told me that Lyddon and Quest and himself were in peril. That's why I'm here... I didn't come through your front door neither, lest it's being watched. The lad here caught me climbing over your back wall. And that was a struggle for a man of my years.'

Prowl reached forward for the glass of brandy that Daniel had given him.

'This man you rescued?' said Quest.

'Mr Blount...' Prowl said.

'Joshua Blount...' said Daniel. 'Prowl has told me all about it.'

'Mr Blount, the blind cove,' said Prowl. 'He thought you should know what's happening, and...'

'Hang on a minute,' said Jasper, pointing a finger at Prowl. 'You're in Newgate Gaol! In the condemned hold...'

Prowl laughed. 'Well, clearly I ain't, Jasper. By the way, I did like that account of me you penned in *The Newgate Shadow*. A warder I got acquainted with gave me a copy. Most of what you wrote was true...'

'But you're to hang in three days time,' said Sticks. 'They were putting up the gallows the last time I walked down Newgate Street. By tomorrow, the stalls will be up and the crowds'll be gathering.'

Prowl looked up at him in admiration.

'You're Sticks, ain't you. The prizefighter. Oh, many a bout I saw you in in past days. Gambled and won on you, my friend. And robbed some of the gentry as they wended their way home afterwards. You're a very profitable gent, Mr Sticks – and I'd like to shake you by that hand of yours that felled so many bruisers!'

'That'll come later, Prowl,' said Quest. 'First of all, I want you to tell us exactly *how* you got out of Newgate Gaol, and how you managed to rescue Joshua Blount and just where he is now.'

~

'You have a rough crew,' Shabson Crouch said as he watched the twelve men climbing into the wagonette. 'They all know what they have to do?'

'They knows,' said Mostin. 'And they knows they have ter abandon the wagon and scatter as soon as the job's done. Don't like it though. Don't like it at all. A lot of open ground up where we're goin'. These men are used to the city streets – not bare places.'

'Well, we can hardly bring you all back in the wagonette! It'll be the first thing the traps look out for. It's stolen – it and the horse. We'll just leave it lingering there and hoof it! And best tell your men to keep clear of Rat's Castle for a day or two. Meet here three nights from now and they'll get their rewards.'

'I want mine now!'

'Job first, Mostin. You know the arrangement!'

'I knows the arrangement. But if I'm took I won't be swingin' for yer – or the toffs that employ yer.'

'Oh, you'd better not blow on me, Jabez. Not good for your health.'

'I've never peached in me life, but I don't swing on the gallows fer any man. Nor do a long stretch neither. So yer'd better bear that in mind. And I'd make sure yer got yer little throat cut.'

~

'It's an extraordinary tale,' Quest said. 'You did well in getting Joshua Blount away. We must get word to his brother. But I don't like this course of events. I don't like it at all. This Preacher you talked about... he just walked you out of Newgate? He must have incredible influence to be able to do that. Only the home secretary has that power. Which suggests that they must have been able to put pressure on him.'

'But why?' asked Daniel. 'Why go to all that trouble?'

'Because my old mate here looks like Jonas Lyddon!' said Jasper.

'At first glance,' said Sticks. 'At a distance...'

'Yes, at a distance,' said Quest, deep in thought.

'Well, we know one thing,' said Jasper. 'Simeon's found out where they kept Mr Blount captive. We lost 'em in Piccadilly, but we've found a place that our enemies use. What say we arm ourselves and go and pay them a visit?'

'We could do that,' said Quest. 'But I don't think we should. Not just yet anyway. I fear that we must get back to Highgate as soon as we can. Lyddon's life is, I fear, in very great peril. And in a way I'd never imagined. These rogues... this Preacher... far more cunning and devilish... Prowl here out of Newgate... Blount and Lyddon... and I'm haunted by the thought of a condemned cell that's just waiting for someone to occupy it...'

It was at this moment that Rosa returned from the town.

'You in the drawing room? Been everywhere,' she yelled out as she climbed the stairs. 'Nobody has a hint about anything, though I tried my best. You'll never guess who I bumped into in the Haymarket? Mrs Bendig! Gave me a filthy look. Remembered me from old times. D'you know, she's sold her whore-house and is retiring to Brighton. Honestly, if looks could kill, I'd have been stricken down dead on the pavement! She was just scared enough to talk – and only about herself at that.' She came through the open door of the drawing room. 'My gosh, Mr Lyddon! What are you doing back here? Did you think twice about the Highgate plan, Will?'

Twenty-three

They came out of the last light of the autumn afternoon.

Honour Bright and Parkin were the first to see them, as they were walking back into the house after a patrol of the grounds. A dozen of them at least – all armed with vicious clubs and pouring across the stretch of grass that was too new to be called a lawn. Men used to riot, from the way they were yelling and screaming, Bright thought.

Then he was yelling himself, shouting through the open door that the attack was upon them. He could see Wren Angier and Jonas Lyddon at the far side of the hall, and noted the terrified look on Phoebe's face as she came down the stairs.

'Get to the room at the back, Jonas. Lock the door!'

Harry Blizzard yelled the order as he dashed through the hall on the way to the entrance. He had a pistol in each hand and a look on his face that was both fear and fighting courage. For a moment, Bright caught a glimpse of the old warrior that had so often charged the French in those old battles in Spain and Flanders.

Then Blizzard pushed past him, doing the one thing the tatterdemalion bunch of attackers least expected – not fleeing but attacking. Rushing into the very heart of them, firing the pistols as he went. Bright saw two of the enemy fall and watched as their killer threw the pistols to the ground. He watched as Harry reached inside his coat and brandished two more guns.

The attackers watched as well, all the speed gone out of their charge. They slowed and then they stopped. But Harry Blizzard was not done with them. He discharged another pistol. A man fell screaming, clutching his thigh. And that was enough, for now the attackers turned and fled...

All but one...

Jabez Mostin reached into the long coat he was wearing and pulled out a pistol of his own, shouting a challenge of some sort, though Bright couldn't make out the words. Mostin took a pace forward, levelling the gun, aiming directly at Blizzard. Shouting again and again.

Bright heard Harry cry out. Heard words that were to remain in his head until his last moment on earth...

'You're dead, my beauty! You're bloody well dead!'

Blizzard fired the last pistol. Even through the cloud of smoke, Bright could see Mostin's gun fly up through the air... watched as Mostin cried out and gasped... saw Blizzard's victim throw up his arms and fall backwards on to the ground with a noise that seemed as loud as the pistol shots.

When Bright looked up, the other attackers had vanished as if they had never been there. There were just the three corpses and the wounded man lying on the lawn. The latter crying and groaning, clutching his leg, and pleading for help. Harry Blizzard standing over him.

'Oh, we'll help you my lad! Have no fear of that! But you're goin' to have to sing like a canary before we save either your leg or your life! And if you don't peach to my satisfaction, I'll leave you there to bleed to death!'

Bright and Parkin walked out to him.

'My God! I never thought I'd see such things in London town!' Bright said.

Parkin knelt down by the injured man.

'He will bleed to death unless we stop this wound,' he said.

Bright considered what to do.

'Parkin! That house over yonder - you can just see the roof over the trees. Sir Wren Angier says that it belongs to a surgeon who plies his trade at St Bartholomew's hospital. There's smoke coming from the chimneys, so hopefully the man's at home. Run and fetch him!'

They watched as Parkin sped out of the gate.

'This has been too bloody a field of battle for such young eyes as his to see,' said Bright. 'Too bloody a field of battle for anyone to see!'

'We had lads a lot younger than him at Talevera and Waterloo,' said Harry Blizzard. 'Age has nothing to do with it. Nobody should have to see any sort of battle. Whatever age they are.'

'You killed three... but not this one?'

'I was minded to slay him too. But then... nobody squeals as loudly as a man with a gunshot wound! Do they, my pretty?' he said to the injured villain. 'Who employed you on this?'

'The little man - the little man...'

'What little man?'

'Crouch... Crouch...'

Blizzard looked up at Bright.

'What does he mean, Crouch?'

'There's a rogue we've never managed to arrest for very long... a tiny man, but with a big heart for villainy. His name's Shabson Crouch. But I thought he'd left London.' Bright looked down at the wounded man. 'He employed you? Yet he wasn't with you. Where's Crouch now? Tell me or it's the gallows for you...'

Harry Blizzard put his mouth close to the man's ear.

'You won't even make the Newgate drop, my friend. I'll let you bleed to death here and now. Where is this Crouch?...'

The man turned his head a trifle, gasping with pain as he raised his hand, looking and pointing towards the house. Saliva ran from his mouth as he struggled to speak through his agony.

'Through there... through there... at the back... at the back...'

Then they heard the scream... the despairing and terrified cry of a woman.

~

The carriage sped through the light of the dying afternoon, back the way it had come not so long before. Up the long slope towards Highgate village, Quest glaring through the window almost every minute to see how far they'd gone. He'd sent an urgent message to Anders begging that he join them at their destination.

'We shouldn't have left them alone,' he said.

'Harry's a good warrior!' Jasper Feedle declared.

'Harry Blizzard isn't enough. And Jonas himself is past his best. I'm relying on Wren and his gun collection. We can't expect Inspector Bright to break the rules if they come under attack, though I may have misjudged him! We should have put a palisade of Monkshood men all around the house.'

'We don't know that anything's happening at all,' said Rosa.

'I just have a feeling,' Quest replied. 'An awful feeling...'

~

The door from the back of the house burst open, just as Wren Angier was guiding Lyddon into the room which he'd designed to be the stronghold, if the rest of the property came under attack.

There were four men standing there. One a very little man carrying a club in one hand and a dagger in the other. The second a thin man, his face scarred by smallpox, holding a pistol in each hand. Two street villains, armed with coshes stood behind them.

A fusillade of shots came from somewhere at the front of the house. Wren Angier had watched as Harry Blizzard charged. He hoped the pistols being discharged were Blizzard's and not his opponents. He turned again, facing the immediate threat, reaching behind to push Jonas Lyddon further into the room. He glared at the men who'd broken into his home.

It all seemed terribly unreal.

'Get out of this house, you bastards! I know you! I know you all. I can name every last one of you! I've seen you all in St Giles and Seven Dials. I'll put the mark on every last bastard one of you!'

Wren watched Phoebe in amazement, as she came down the stairs.

He reached out to grab her, but failed, as she stepped between him and the attackers. In recent months the young girl had seemed so different from the streetwalker who'd been forced to work the edges of the vilest rookeries. Acquired the traits of the lady of his house, the real nature that poverty and desperation had robbed from her during her miserable youth.

'Phoebe...' he began.

'I know you Crouch!' she went on... 'and you Booth. And you two scum skulking there behind them. Now get out of this house! Get out now, or I'll scratch your eyes out...'

'Angier's whore!' Crouch yelled. 'All the Dials are laughing at you. You're powerless, you slut...

He reached and grabbed the girl, for she was almost as tiny as he was. He pulled her towards him and held the dagger across her throat. A look of triumph on his face as he glared at the two men in the doorway.

'It's Lyddon we want. Not you or your slut, Angier. You got just a second to come forward, Lyddon – or I'll draw my dagger across her throat.'

Lyddon stepped past Angier.

'I'll come with you, if you let go of the girl now,' said Lyddon.

Crouch beckoned with his finger.

'Come on then...'

He gave Phoebe a vicious punch in the back, sending her sprawling on the floor, and grabbed Lyddon by the arm. He crashed the club down on the side of Lyddon's head. Even before Jonas could fall, the two street villains had grabbed him by the arms and were dragging him backwards out of the house.

Wren knelt down and pulled Phoebe into the doorway, watching Crouch and Booth all of the time. Saw them as they stepped backwards along the hallway. Saw and hated the smirk on Crouch's face.

Then he remembered the pistol inside his jacket.

As he reached for it, Booth fired his weapon.

'One less to peach on us!' he cried out.

Wren Angier stumbled against the door-jamb, with the sensation that a great weight had crashed into his chest. He struggled for breath but it wouldn't seem to come.

He felt someone take him by the hand and then all was darkness.

In his last conscious thought he heard a scream.

He knew it was Phoebe crying out his name...

~

It was like one of those nightmares, Quest thought. The ones where you truly believe you've woken - and then find you haven't. All the way up to Highgate in the carriage, Quest had pictured the scene. And here was something even worse…

As the carriage had pulled up by the house, Constable Parkin had glanced up at him, all the colour gone from his face. He muttered what had happened. Then there were the bodies on the lawn - Quest recognised the corpse of Jabez Mostin among the dead. Saw a street villain he knew by sight, clutching his leg and screaming into the darkness.

Harry Blizzard was sitting propped against the door, head in hands, muttering some words that Quest couldn't make out.

Quest had knelt by his side. 'Harry?'

Blizzard mumbled for a moment before his words became coherent.

'Messed up… messed up, Quest…should have seen it was a diversion… messed up, Quest… messed up…'

He waved a hand into the hall.

Then the nightmare began.

Honour Bright and a stranger were kneeling by a body - it was Wren Angier. Phoebe sat on the bottom step of the stairs, looking wide-eyed at the scene.

Quest looked across to the group assembled by the stairs. Wren Angier lying dead in their midst. He tried to go towards them, but his legs wouldn't move - in a long life of peril, Quest had never experienced this immobility, this absolute, utter shock.

Harry looked up at him.

'My fault, Quest… my fault… should have realised it was a diversion… that they'd come on us from both sides… too old for this, Quest… too bloody old…'

Quest rested a hand on his shoulder.

'No, Harry. You did right.' He looked back towards the lawn. 'I can see what happened. If you hadn't tackled the men out there, well, the house would have been overwhelmed. Everyone here might be dead.'

'Let's go and see,' said Sticks, taking Quest by the arm and guiding him across the hall.

Quest glanced back - Jasper Feedle was in the doorway, helping his old comrade to his feet, taking him outside into the garden, whispering words that Quest couldn't hear.

Honour Bright looked up as he approached, nodding towards the stranger.

'This is Mr Menzies, a surgeon from across the way. Fortunately, he was at home…'

Menzies was a thin man of about fifty with bushy red side-whiskers.

There was just a trace of a Scottish accent...

'The gent is not dead, but I fear for him, for the ball has gone clean into his chest. It might have gone right through him, but it caught the stock of his own pistol. Ah, but it's a bad wound and I must operate at once...'

The surgeon had already taken out a scalpel and a clamp from the bag at his side.

'Will he...?'

'I cannot say... I really cannot... I'm not sanguine... my, it's a bad wound.'

'There's a table in that room,' said Bright. 'Should we get him on to that?'

'If we move him an inch, he'll be dead,' said Menzies. 'I must operate on him here and now. You'll oblige me by taking the lassie here away. These are not sights for a woman to see. I believe there's a man outside shot in the leg. If one of you could go across to my house, and enquire for Mr Westacott – he's my apprentice and can easily deal with him...'

'I'll go,' said Sticks.

'Please take the lassie away...'

Phoebe crouched on the floor.

'No... I'm not leaving Wren.'

'Not the sight for a lassie.'

'I've read that women see just as bad in the Crimea.'

Menzies looked across at her.

'You're a wee girl of courage...'

'I love him,' she said. 'If he's to die, I want to be with him...'

~

Jonas Lyddon had been stunned by the blow, but had feigned a deeper unconsciousness, anxious that his captors should get him out of the house before they could kill anyone else. He was aware of being dragged across the garden being created at the back of the house, then into a narrow lane beyond. They lifted him into a carriage, knotting him by the hands and feet as it sped away.

'You hit him too hard!' a voice said. 'If he's in a bad way or marked, we'll be in a lot of trouble.'

'You think I ain't clubbed anyone before?'

~

Quest stood above the injured man on the lawn.

'I know you, you bloody villain! There's a man coming to tend your leg, but I might just stop him. Let you lose the limb or bleed to death. Nasty wound. Your kneecap will be gone whatever happens. If you've played a part in killing my friend in there... well... he's a baronet and a member of Parliament. So they'll hang you outside the walls of Newgate...'

'Nobody said anythin' about killin',' the man said with a groan.

'Ah, but it happened and you'll swing, being the only one left here alive. I know you don't I? You're more often just drunk in Rat's Castle, since you gave up the house-breaking, Jack Smith? They say you gave up your felonies because you lost your nerve?'

Smith moaned, clutching his leg, 'I know nothin' about what happened inside that house...'

'That won't save you! You are going to swing. Mind, I might just let you bleed to death here and now. Perhaps hanging's best. You'll be a cripple all your life if you live!'

'For God's sake! Help me!'

'Did Jabez Mostin put you up to this?'

Smith gave a slight nod.

'And who employed him?'

'I dunno...'

'You must do, Jack. You must do! And you're going to tell me everything you know, right now. Or I'll spare you the gallows and just let you die with that wound. You're in pain now... imagine how much worse that pain's going to get as the blood drains out of you. Or if I were to put my foot down on your knee...'

'Will!'

Quest turned.

Rosa was beside him.

She put her hand on his arm.

'Leave him, Will.'

'Wren's dying in there. They've taken Jonas. And you want me to leave him alone?'

'He's Jack Smith! Nobody would trust him with a confidence. I doubt Mostin told them anything about who's behind this. This man's just a villain, as we've all been in our time. Just like us!'

'Not like me!'

'No? Had you not been taken in care by Josiah Quest, you might well have been another Jack Smith. A petty criminal getting drunk every night at the Castle, because your nerve had failed you. Look at him, Will. Just look at him! He's pathetic... sad... not worth the bother. Now come away.'

'This is the man Mr Menzies needs you to tend,' said Sticks.

Quest turned, seeing his friend leading a young man, clutching a doctor's bag, across the lawn.

'Now come away, Will.'

~

'I don't like the thought of going so near to that place,' said Booth. 'It makes me shudder every time I pass it.'

Jonas listened with care, feigning unconsciousness, wondering exactly where he was being taken? But despite the thought that it was certainly down the road to death, he did consider that a mystery might be about to be solved. That he might come face to face with the men who ran Tenebrae.

'You thinks as how I do,' said Crouch. 'But orders is orders...'

He looked across at his prisoner. He knew very well the reputation and influence of Jonas Lyddon. Helping his employer to bring this man to his destruction was going to make life in London impossible. Nor did he trust the man with the mask to get him safely away. Crouch had seen too many corpses consigned to the Thames. He was determined not to be one of them.

~

'My God, Quest! What the hell's happened here?'

Inspector Anders and Sergeant Berry had arrived at Highgate after receiving Quest's message. Seen the dead men lying on the lawn and two men being treated in the hall, the groaning Jack Smith and the deathly silent Wren Angier.

Anders took Quest back out on to the doorstep.

'Will Angier live?'

'I fear not, even though he's being tended by a surgeon of such repute. Looking at that wound, it's likely that the ball came very near to a lung, if not through it. Even if he survives the shot, there must be a risk of infection.'

'And the villain Smith?'

'Oh, he'll live.'

'Live to hang,' said Sergeant Berry.

Quest gave the sergeant a grim smile.

'Your Mr Bright seems very keen on that fate for him.'

'If Sir Wren dies, he certainly will,' said Anders.

Quest sighed.

'I was minded to put him down out there on the lawn, but have thought better of it. What's the bloody point in swinging him at Newgate? I believe he knew little of what was to happen here. He certainly never considered that there'd be a shooting. He's a rogue from Rat's Castle, who may well lose a leg – or be on a crutch for the rest of his days.'

'If he doesn't hang, then he'll certainly spend his days at a convict depot,' said Berry.

Quest shook his head.

'If we send him to the gallows, or to Dartmoor, we'll incur the enmity of every person in St Giles and Seven Dials. Jack Smith's a popular villain in those parts. Poverty created Jack Smith. It was poverty that drove him to take part in this enterprise.'

Anders looked at him in silence for a long moment.

'You seem to be advocating letting him go?'

'Why not? Listen, we need the support of the folk who live in the Dials and St Giles. Topping Smith, or gaoling him, will just alienate them more. It would serve nothing but petty revenge.'

'We can't compound a felony!' said Anders.

'Look, Bram. We want the men who paid him to be here. Smith's of no consequence whatsoever. He'll suffer from that wound for the rest of his days. Let that be enough.'

'I don't know...' Anders began.

Harry Blizzard had been listening to the discussion.

'When I was a soldier in Spain, we never hated the enemy foot soldiers for being foot soldiers. Most of them didn't want to be there any more than I did. It was circumstances that drove us all to it. Most of us thought King bloody George and Wellington should fight it out personally with Boney and Marshall Soult and leave the rest of us out of it.'

'Not the same thing,' said Anders.

'Exactly the same thing. I've crippled that man for doing what I once might have been encouraged to do myself. I'll feel guilt about that for the rest of my days. Just let him go. If you like, I'll get a cart and we'll get him to the nearest infirmary. You know, it's what Jonas Lyddon would want.'

'There's a lot of truth in what Harry says,' said Quest.

Mr Westacott, the surgeon's apprentice, came across to them.

'I've stopped the bleeding, but I really can't do more for him here. He really needs to be in a hospital, so that I can treat the leg properly.'

'Will he lose the limb?' asked Harry.

'If there's no infection, it might be saved.'

'I've had a word with Mr Menzies. He says we might use his carriage to convey the man to the nearest infirmary. A good place which has its own surgeon. We need to get him there soon.'

'I'll give you a hand with him,' said Harry Blizzard.

Quest looked at Anders.

The detective nodded assent.

Quest watched as they loaded the injured man into the carriage, deep in thought.

'This is a mess,' he said. 'We'd have been better staying at my house in Bloomsbury. It would have been easier to protect Jonas there than here. I'm a fool, Bram! A bloody fool!'

Anders looked out at the lawn and the corpses of the dead villains.

'No, it should have been safe enough here, Will. But have you thought this through? You were followed here?'

'I don't believe we could have been. We're used to shaking off people tailing us, and I had men blocking the streets as we left Tavistock Place. Unless our enemies had an outer cordon of watchers, they couldn't possibly have known that we were coming up here to Highgate.'

'Unless they already knew...'

'But that's...' Quest took a deep breath. 'I was going to say that's impossible. It could only be possible if there's a traitor amongst us? Let me think...'

He paced up and down the hall.

'Right from the start of this, Bram, our footsteps have been dogged by the opposition. Not just our coming up to Highgate, but way back. With the death of Colley Johnson. And then Jonas Lyddon was nearly taken on his way back from Manchester. And he came to my house quite secretly, yet Tenebrae *knew* he was there...'

'Then there was the snatching of Mr Blount,' said Sticks. 'That was rather conveniently done. Someone who knew his movements very well. I'd have put that down to just being a fluke, but bearing in mind what you've just said...'

'Yes, but who is it? Who is it?'

He looked up as Surgeon Menzies crossed the hall.

'I've removed the bullet. It clipped his left lung and there's been some internal bleeding. But I've done all I can. Sir Wren's in the hands of providence now. He needs to be in bed, but we daren't risk carrying him up the stairs. Better that a bed is brought down and placed in the room next to where he's lying.'

'Is there nothing more we can do?'

Menzies shook his head.

'There's nothing anyone can do. It will all depend on the poor man's constitution and his innate will to live, as I've explained to his young lady. She wishes to nurse him herself, to cater for his basic needs. Good that she does help, for her mind needs occupying. But I intend to send over my housekeeper, Mrs Brackham. Before she came to work for me, she was a professional nurse at St Bartholomew's for some thirty years. She has turned many a doomed patient into a survivor. The girl can help her. And, of course, I'll be on call...'

'Thank you, Mr Menzies,' said Quest. 'But for you he'd be dead already.'

Menzies clasped his hand.

'I do not hold out much hope for your friend, but Mrs Brackham has seen off the shadow of death more times than I can count.'

~

Jonas Lyddon looked at the cold stone walls, though they were hard to see by the light from the tiny window and the feeble gaslight, mostly hidden behind a grille.

He'd been there for a few hours, feigning unconsciousness as his abductors dragged him through a stout wooden door and along a wide corridor. His last view as they brought him out of the sealed coach, was the better lit walls of the Old Bailey. Then he knew where he was being taken...

Newgate Gaol.

A prison warder had opened the door, and they passed two more in the corridor. The uniformed men had looked down at the ground as they went past – as though something was happening that they didn't want to be part of. Just before the door of the cell, some higher official, in civilian clothes, had confronted them. One of his captors had muttered a few words, but then a voice from the darkness had called out to the man. He went away, and Jonas could see that he was talking to some figure hidden in the dank blackness.

The bed in the cell was hard, but Jonas had spent much of his youth sleeping in such uncomfortable places, so he managed some fitful sleep. The two men had left him as soon as they had deposited him there. With the breaking dawn, he had time to sleep.

Why Newgate? He asked himself. It was true that there were a whole raft of felonies he'd committed in his younger days, acts of sedition and rebellion – all for the greater good of the human race. Fights for justice and fairness. But in recent years, he had taken the Parliamentary path of reform. Become a member of the Commons and held a reputation that had won him the respect of the many, if not the enmity of the few.

He thought, for a moment, of the account he'd written of the Dartmoor Rebellion and the events that had culminated on Gibbet Hill. If one of the two copies of that had fallen into the wrong hands, it might be considered to be a criminal confession. But that would surely have warranted an arrest by the police and arraignment before a magistrate – not a violent snatching from a lonely house in Highgate?

Who had the power to take him and secrete him in a cell at Newgate?

He looked around the cell; he'd visited Newgate several times with fellow members of the House, on Parliamentary inspections of the penal system. Seen the interiors of several cells. But this cell, he was in, was older and larger than any of them. Almost a small room, complete with a table and two chairs as well as the harsh bed. This was something different from a holding cell ...

And then the door opened and the man entered. A slim individual, with lank dark hair, and what seemed a permanent smile cutting his face in half. Dressed not in warder's attire but more like a tradesman of the town.

'My dear sir...' the man began.

'By whose authority have I been brought to Newgate Gaol?'

The man rubbed his hands together and took in a deep breath.

'I have no idea, my dear sir. Beyond my remit, for I am not a direct employee of the prison. A casual worker, sir, just that...'

'Then what are you here for?'

'Oh, I always like to meet my gentlemen – oh, and my ladies too.'

'In Newgate Gaol? Do you have a name?'

As it happens, sir, I have two – I was born Billy Jubbins, but – no offence to my father – he was in ironmongery, by the way – or my dear similarly departed mother, it was not a name I have ever favoured. I do think we should all be allowed to change our names, if such be our desire, do you not agree, sir? The name I favour at the moment is Egregious Mountjoy.'

'Egregious? Do you know what it means?'

'I picked the name from the dictionary using a pin, but I did read further, I do assure you, sir.'

'Then you appreciate that it is deprecatory, in the modern sense?'

'Ah, in the modern sense, sir, but according to the dictionary, it was once a title implying distinguishment and notability. Indeed, some of my acquaintances in the tavern across the way tease me that it should be *Sir* Egregious. In view of my twelve years of public service, you see? I'm not like some of the others who've held my distinguished position. Ah, you should see them, sir. A quick glance through the Judas Hole at their clientele. No, being a educated man, though only from

Smithfield, I always care to build up a relationship with the gents and ladies I have to deal with. And I'm sure the gentlemen and ladies appreciate that, don't you see?'

Jonas looked up at the smiling face.

'And what is your distinguished position, *Sir* Egregious?'

Mountjoy held out his arms and gave a slight bow.

'Ah, sir – have you not guessed?'

'I fear so.'

The smile grew even wider.

'Sir – I am the public hangman...'

~

'Anders – we simply cannot cover up what has happened,' said Inspector Honour Bright, as they stood in the doorway of the house, watching the break of the autumn dawn. 'The dead to account for... a member of Parliament perhaps mortally wounded... Mr Lyddon abducted...'

'I would agree with you, in normal circumstances, but we are effectively now under the control of Her Majesty's Secret Service. I've sent a message down to Wissilcraft, requiring his presence here. How much of this is made public must be his decision.'

Quest, with his associates, Sticks, Jasper Feedle and Harry Blizzard, had joined the three policemen on the doorstep.

Bright looked at him. 'I think that this sort of occurrence must be very familiar to such as you, Quest. I have to say, I cannot believe I'm here discussing this matter with you at all, but I recognise that these are extraordinary circumstances. Do you think that Mr Lyddon's abduction should be made public?'

'Shouldn't we leave the decision to Wissilcraft?' said Sergeant Berry. 'If we make this issue public, there's a good chance that the men who took Lyddon away might just kill him. These villains will get rid of him, just as swiftly as if he was any other type of stolen goods.'

'They want Jonas for some purpose,' replied Quest. 'If they wanted his instant death, they could have just come here and shot him. They took him away for a particular reason. They're clearly still bargaining for the notebook, that is probably their first priority, but I fear they have a deeper and more sinister purpose.'

'But what?' asked Sticks.

'I'm not sure – I need time to think...' said Quest, walking out into the garden, followed by Sticks, Blizzard and Feedle.

'I do wonder what is in that man's mind?' said Bright, as they watched Quest stroll away. 'You know him better than I do, Anders?'

Despite everything, Anders laughed, thinking of everything that had happened since he'd first become acquainted with Mr William Quest. Times of peril, certainly, but also a feeling of security that – for now – he and Quest were on the same side.

'All I will say is that Quest has navigated our way out of such dire circumstances before now. He can go anywhere and be anyone, in a way that no policeman can. He has friends that we'd send to the gallows, but they're the kind of friends we badly need in such situations. I obviously don't approve of everything Quest does – and, if I had to do so, I would do my duty and put the darbies on him. Though I hope I never have to do that.'

Quest and his associates had walked across the garden to the gate leading out on to the road. He rested against its wooden bars and looked in the direction of London town.

'Not much more we can do here,' he said. 'Wren is in the best of hands and we have a duty to seek out the men who shot him, and recover our friend Jonas Lyddon.'

'But how hard can it be?' said Sticks. 'We know from Simeon Prowl that they are using a building in Limehouse, probably their headquarters since they were driven out of Piccadilly. Let's just go down there mob-handed and raid the place. As simple as that.'

Quest thought for a moment, watching the dawn.

'But is it as simple as that?'

'They must have took Jonas somewhere,' said Jasper. 'It's a good place as any to start looking.'

'We saw some hard times all those years ago, Jasper,' said Harry Blizzard. 'Us and Jonas. We scraped through the rebellion on Dartmoor and we all come out the other side. It took me a good effort to get Jonas from Manchester to London – and I ain't giving up on him now. When I get my hands on these Tenebrae bastards, I'll send them spinning down to hell!'

'So why not Limehouse?' asked Sticks.

'Because I don't think Jonas will be there,' said Quest.

'Where then?'

'I'll tell you where I think they've got him.'

'Where?' asked Harry.

'I think they've got Jonas in Newgate. That's where I believe they've taken him. Just consider – Simeon Prowl was there in the condemned cell. They just walk him away from the place. Which Tenebrae can do, because they have friends in such high places – perhaps even the home secretary. They remove Prowl because he bears a certain similarity to Jonas Lyddon. They didn't empty that condemned cell for nothing. They wanted the cell for someone else – and that someone else is Lyddon. Ask yourselves this – Simeon Prowl was condemned to hang tomorrow morning. He's no longer there! Has there been a hue and cry, given that he was a condemned killer? No – because Prowl is dispensable to Tenebrae. They have the man they always really wanted in Newgate.'

'Do you mean that?'... said Blizzard.

'I'm not sure what I mean. Not for certain. But I know what I fear. Come on...'

He led them back across the lawn, to where the three policemen were still discussing matters at the door of the house.

'I think, gentlemen, that it might be a good idea if news of what happened here was spread abroad. Mr Lyddon kidnapped and Sir Wren Angier shot down. I do believe that Tenebrae will be expecting us to keep these matters secret. Let's stop playing the game by their rules!'

Rosa came across the hall to join them.

'Wren is breathing a little easier, but he still looks like death!'

'Someone is going to pay a very heavy price for this,' Quest said.

Twenty-Four

'I've gotta get out of London,' said Simeon Prowl. 'Much longer here and I'll get collared. You see that, don't you, Daniel lad?'

They were sitting in Quest's drawing room, Daniel by the window looking out on to Tavistock Place. Before he'd left, Quest had given the youth the duty of guarding both the house and Simeon Prowl. Daniel had his pair of pistols primed and ready on the table in front of him.

'Mr Quest will get you away, I've no fear of that.'

'It's like a nightmare to me, boy! Like a nightmare! The Preacher... well, who's he that took such an interest in getting me out of Newgate and then wanting me dead? And that evil little bastard Crouch - but for fortune I'd be food for worms in Epping Forest. And now the man Lyddon - in peril - him that's such a friend to the poor and desperate - and likely because he favours me in looks. What is it, lad?'

Daniel had leaned forward in the chair.

'Probably nothing - but there's a character across the street who's been lingering there for several minutes. Seems to be taking a great interest in this house. Come and take a look, Simeon.'

Prowl looked out through the lace into the street.

'Nobody I know - and I knows most of the villains in the town.'

'Ah. He's moving on - crossing the road. No wait! I think he's coming here.'

Daniel reached for the pistols and stood looking out the window.

'He's coming to the door - coming a-visiting.'

They both heard a noise downstairs.

'Not the bell - the letterbox,' said Daniel. 'Perhaps a message from Mr Quest. Stay here, Simeon, I'll go and look.'

'He's scooting away,' said Prowl. 'Down the street as if all the devils in hell were after him.'

~

'My friends and I are returning to Tavistock Place,' said Quest. 'It seems that there's little we can do here. Nothing to help Wren Angier, who's in the best of hands. What I would like to ensure is that this house is properly guarded.'

'I'll see to that,' said Wissilcraft, who'd arrived an hour earlier. 'I have a couple of men I trust absolutely. I'll send down a message and have them stationed here, if Anders and Bright are prepared to remain until they arrive.'

'Might I ask you, Quest, just what you intend to do?' said Inspector Bright.

'I really don't know,' he replied.

'Something within the law, I hope Will?' said Anders.

'Depends on your definition of the law, Bram? Whatever, I fully intend to get Jonas Lyddon out of the clutches of these fanatics. Even if it means giving our friend Inspector Bright here, a chance to put a noose around my neck!'

For the first time in all the years he'd known him, Anders saw Bright smile.

'I'm not as inflexible as you think, Quest,' said Bright. 'But the law is the law and I *will* uphold it if I catch you breaking any part of it.'

'Then I'll have to make sure you don't catch me, Inspector,' said Quest.

'I think I should remain here, Will,' said Rosa. 'I believe that Phoebe would appreciate the support of another woman besides our good nurse. Mrs Brackham is most efficient, but I think Phoebe needs a friend who is closer to her in age.'

Quest took her to one side.

'Wren has quite a little armoury here. Prime every gun in the place and keep them close to you at all times. I'll send up a few members of Monkshood to guard the property. I'm sure Wissilcraft won't mind. Anyway, I don't care whether he does.'

'What do you want us to do?' said Anders.

'Just be there for when we need you, Bram. It might be useful if you could round up some constables that you trust absolutely, like Parkin there. Be ready for my message. I might need you with very little notice.'

~

'I get no great pleasure from my work,' said Egregious Mountjoy, 'I do hope that you understand that? Other than a job well done – and I really do like to cause my ladies and gentlemen as little pain and discomfort as possible.' He sighed. 'But the law is the law! If I didn't come to Newgate to turn people off, then someone else would have to do it – and they might not be quite as diligent as I am.'

Jonas Lyddon looked up at him.

'So tell me, Egregious – have you ever before topped someone who has never been found guilty in a court of law, or even faced a trial? Because I presume that's the subject of your visit today? I'm the next man you intend to put on the Newgate gallows, I take it?'

For the first time, the smile on the hangman's face looked pained, forced.

'You must understand, sir, that it is not for me to pass an opinion on judicial matters. I have no great knowledge or concern with jurisprudence. I am – as I've stated – but a public servant. It isn't for me to question the legal process – only to deal with its consequences.'

'So when is my execution to be?'

'Well the gallows are up and ready outside the gaol, so tomorrow – oh, what a pity it is that my gentlemen are no longer taken the length of Oxford Street to Tyburn. The death cart and its content being cheered by the crowds, stopping at the alehouses along the way, with sometimes a pretty woman clambering up to give one of the heroes of the road a farewell kiss. Ah, please forgive my reverie, sir. You see I've only ever turned folk off here at Newgate and at some of the county gaols – Tyburn was before my time you see!'

'How very disappointing for you, Egregious...'

'It is indeed, sir...'

'I understood that the footpad, Simeon Prowl, was on the calendar for execution on the morrow?'

'And he is, sir,' Egregious beamed, 'and that will be the name the crowd will chant, as I place the hood over your head and the noose around your neck.'

'Then you are happy to hang the wrong man?'

'My dear sir, I *never* hang the wrong man – I only ever hang the man that the governor of this place presents to me, do you not see that? Out on the scaffold, the name is irrelevant. At that point, the person to be hanged is no more than an object to me. Some pounds of flesh to be put quickly out of its fear and misery, much as a beast must be swiftly slaughtered by a butcher up in Smithfield.'

'Do you not see a difference?'

'There is *no* difference.'

'I am *not* Simeon Prowl, Egregious.'

'This is not a free country, sir. We are merely the servants of our betters, don't you see? Do you not grasp the points I've tried to make in our most interesting discourse?'

'In a way I fear I do,' said Jonas.

'Never mind, sir. As I've said I'll make the process as painless as is humanly possible. I'm not unmindful of who you really are, and of the great good you have done for so many people in our great nation.' He shrugged. 'Well, I must leave you now, for another gentleman is waiting outside. I'm sure he will deal with all your unanswered questions. But you will note that there is a Bible on the table over there. Perhaps the words of Our Lord will bring you comfort in these final and fleeting hours?'

He gave Jonas Lyddon a last big smile before passing through the door of the cell.

'Until the morning, sir. Until the morning.'

'There's no way it can be done,' said Sticks, as they rode in the carriage taking them back down to Tavistock Place. 'If Jonas is in Newgate Gaol there's no way you can get him out of there, Will.'

'People have broken out of Newgate,' said Quest.

'Jack Sheppard broke out more than once, all those years ago,' Jasper considered. 'Mind, they've changed the whole structure of the place since then. Crocky Campbell got out from the exercise area a pair of years ago, up the wall and over the roofs, but he was twenty and a circus acrobat - they ain't caught him yet!'

'One thing's for sure,' said Quest, 'they won't let Jonas anywhere near the yard. He'll be secured in a cell - almost certainly the condemned cell, given that he's replaced Simeon Prowl.'

'You really think they're goin' to top Jonas?' said Harry Blizzard.

'Yes, I do!'

'But they can't just haul Jonas out and hang him in place of Prowl in front of hundreds of gawpers? Surely someone'd notice,' said Blizzard. 'I'm not goin' to let that happen, even if I have to march in there with guns to spring him. How many men can you raise?'

'Not enough to storm Newgate Gaol,' said Quest. 'We'd never get through the outer gate, let alone into the heart of the building. And even if we should try, they'd have plenty of time to hide Jonas away or even put him to death in some other way. No, we've got to be more subtle.'

'Over the roofs?' Sticks suggested.

'Jonas is an old man,' Quest replied. 'Even if I could get in as far as the condemned cell, through a dozen locked and guarded gates, I'd never be able to get Jonas out the same way.'

'We can't do nothing,' said Harry.

'I don't intend that we should do nothing. And yet...'

Even in the shade of the enclosed carriage, they all noticed the look on Quest's face. Knew that an idea had come to him. It wasn't quite a smile, more a look of sheer devilment.

'What is it, Will?' asked Sticks.

'I think I've just thought of a magnificent way for us all to get ourselves killed. Do or die? We'll either get Jonas away - or be shot down, or find nooses around our own necks. My idea is so mad that I doubt we'll survive it, and they'll probably swing Jonas anyway.'

'You going to tell us what it is?' asked Jasper.

'Oh, yes, but it's just between ourselves – the four of us here in this carriage. First of all though, Sticks, shout up through the window and tell the coachman that we want to go to Newgate Street before we head for Tavistock Place. We'll drop Jasper off there, you can come round to Tavistock Place as soon as you've finished the task I'm going to set you, Jasper.'

'I don't need to see Newgate Gaol nor the scaffold, Will,' said Jasper. 'I've gawped at them many a time.'

'Nor do you need to do either,' said Quest. 'Not if you don't want to. We'll be dropping you at Messrs. Hodgson's, booksellers and printers, number 10 Newgate Street, if memory serves me correct.'

'They publish *The Newgate Shadow*,' said Jasper.

'They do indeed. They do indeed.'

~

There was a long interval after Egregious Mountjoy left the cell, though Jonas could hear him in conversation with someone beyond the locked door. He went nearer, but though he could hear raised voices he couldn't make out what they were saying. After a while he went and sat on the bed.

Five minutes passed... perhaps ten...

Lyddon had no pocket-watch. He'd put it down on a cupboard in his room at Wren Angier's home, not long before he was snatched. His thoughts were now on the poor man who'd been shot down – far better that he'd died himself that cost innocent people their lives...

The door opened, bringing him out of this unpleasant reverie.

A figure stood in the doorway for a little while, regarding him. He recalled the talk of a man who looked like a preacher. The individual who seemed to control Tenebrae. And he knew he was about to face him...

The Preacher crossed the cell, pulling back a kind of hood covering his head. And in the dimness of the cell was a man with no face, just as Colley Johnson had described. Only, even in that light, and with his still perfect eyesight, Lyddon could see that the effect was produced by a very fine mask.

'Well, we are here together at last?' he said.

'We are indeed,' said the Preacher. 'We need pretend no longer, Lyddon. Time to take this mask away.'

But even as the man reached up to remove the mask, Jonas Lyddon knew, from that oh so familiar voice, just who he was facing.

~

'I want everyone here,' said Quest, 'here! you understand? Here in this house. We're under siege for as long as Jonas is in Newgate and Tenebrae exists. I want someone to go over to The Borough and get Joshua Blount from his hiding place. I want his brother Magnus brought here too, for if they can't get Joshua, they might take the brother to exert pressure on us. Better to rope in Jonas's secretary James Brendon as well - he's as vulnerable as the rest, because he knows all the secrets of Jonas's past.'

They had arrived back in Tavistock Place just a few minutes before. Quest was pleased that nobody had bothered Daniel Stanton and Simeon Prowl in his absence.

'Magnus Blount and Brendon are the closest to us,' said Sticks. 'I'll go at once and get them back here.'

'I'll go and get Joshua Blount,' said Quest. 'Daniel - you stay here with Simeon and carry on guarding the house. That way we can...'

'No!' said Daniel. 'I'm not sitting here any longer as a watchdog! Far better that Simeon goes to collect Blount from The Borough. It's his territory, after all. Nobody knows the way in and out as well as Simeon. And I think that I should go with him! I want to play my part in this. I'll take my pistols and if I have to, I'll use them. And far more accurately than I did before.'

'Well, I don't really think...'

'The lad might be right,' said Sticks. 'Remember, Will - you're on the Tenebrae list as well. Far better that you don't wander off on your own. And you're tired, I can see that! Your grand plan to get Jonas away from the gallows depends on you being rested and alert.'

Quest considered for a moment.

'You would be all right, Daniel? Perhaps you'll go with them, Harry?'

Blizzard nodded.

'I'm sure I would be all right,' said Daniel. 'Especially alongside such a skilled footpad as Simeon and Mr Blizzard.'

'I'll look after the boy... and I want to play my part in springing Mr Lyddon from the hangman. I won't stand by and see anyone topped in my place. If you have a plan I'd like to know just what it is. I'd like to know what I can do?'

Quest spent several minutes explaining what he intended to do to save the life of Jonas Lyddon. Even as he did so, he could see their looks of doubt.

'It's incredible!' Daniel declared.

'I doubt it'll work,' said Prowl. 'You're putting a lot of faith in the gallows crowd. I knows them of old. Mr Lyddon's got a great reputation but even so... there must be something else we can do... some more I could do.'

'It's this or nothing!' Quest declared. 'Now let's get on with rounding up our friends.'

Daniel stood.

'Oh my gosh. I forgot! Someone delivered this note just before you got back. A sealed letter, so I didn't open it, delivered by a fly character who belted down the street the moment he pushed it through the letter box.'

He handed the note to Quest, who studied the writing and the seal before opening it. He tore it open and read it before passing it round among the others.

Quest - if you want Lyddon back alive then we want the notebook by tonight. London Bridge Stairs, the fourth step up from the river on the south bank side, at midnight. Please don't try your usual tricks. The hanging morning is very near.

'Are you going to give them the notebook?' asked Daniel.

'Of course not,' Quest replied. 'Even if I wanted to, I'm not in a position to produce it. I keep the notebook far from London. I couldn't get there and back by midnight! But I intend to give these bastards something to occupy their time, you can be assured of that! Now get on your errands, while I consider what else we must do.'

When they had all gone, Quest sat down in his comfortable chair by the fireside. Perhaps it would do no harm to sleep for just an hour? He felt utterly exhausted and sighed aloud that age was catching up with him.

And in that stage that is somewhere between wakefulness and sleep, half-dreamed of and half-remembered the tree, the great oak at Hope Down, where the hedges of the enclosed fields of his land met the great sweep of the downland.

Recalled standing there, all those years ago, with Josiah Quest on one warm summer's afternoon.

'It's a mighty tree!' he'd said.

Josiah had sat down on a great root which emerged from the earth into the field below, looking up into the green leaves and huge branches.

'It must be - what? Eight hundred years old, perhaps even older? Just think, William - as a young tree its leaves sheltered the birds while the Conqueror was fighting King Harold on Senlac Hill. It was already an old tree when Agincourt was fought. I've known it all my life. I come here sometimes - when I wish to have peace to consider matters - and sit on this great root. There's a peace about this place. To me the tree is an old friend.'

'You could imagine Robin Hood hiding up it,' Quest had said.

'Strange you should say that. When I first knew it, the local folk called it Robin Hood's oak. They gathered here whenever they wanted a surreptitious meeting, away from their masters - long before the Quests held this land.'

'It's a long way from Sherwood Forest!'

'Well, lad, my belief is that there wasn't just one Robin Hood, there were many. I think Robin Hood was a common name for any outlaw, wherever he might hail from. Not just common thieves, but all those outside the law who fight for justice - as you will one day.'

'Robin Hood's Oak!'

'That's one name for it - but since the rural war that was fought across this land back in 'thirty, it's acquired another name. Swing's Oak, the hinds call it - after Captain Swing, the supposed leader of those riots, that rebellion.'

Quest stirred in the chair, coming a little more awake.

He smiled, recalling that conversation.

There was a persistent rumour that Josiah Quest had *been* Swing.

'No, not me lad,' Josiah said. 'Not anyone else I know of. If you want my opinion, Swing was a character just like Robin Hood. There wasn't one Captain Swing, but a multitude of them, every rebellious parish in 1830 having a natural leader who acquired the title.'

'What a pity!' William Quest had remarked.

'No, boy! Not a pity at all! Far better that there should be many leading the rebellions against injustice!'

Quest woke up completely, dwelling on what Josiah had said.

Perhaps the time had come to stand back and to just encourage others to campaign for fairness and justice. Had he done the wrong thing by becoming the sole leader of Monkshood?

He reached out to the table and took up the note that had come through his door. Something wrong there, and he couldn't quite decide what it was? But an instinct told him that a game was being played with him. And whenever anyone played such games with him, his nature told him never to participate by the rules of the game laid down by opponents.

A year before, he'd buried a metal chest in the soft downland earth between two mighty roots of Swing's Oak. A metal chest, holding a smaller wooden box containing the notebook that his enemies wished to possess. Enemies. So many enemies, all wanting that notebook - and then Quest smiled, wondering whether what his instinct was telling him now was correct?

This time he would play his own game...

'Why have you done it, James?' asked Lyddon.

James Brendon smiled down at him.

'You know... really... Mr Lyddon, you shouldn't need to ask that. The answer to your question is obvious, right before you. You're a good man in your way, but your objectives are hopeless, can't you see that? England is run on two principles – greed and selfishness. It's all there is at the end of the day, and those of us who practice those principles will never let men like you come along to weaken our position. I learned that lesson as a very small child from my father – before he died.'

'So you are the leader of Tenebrae?'

Brendon leaned against the wall, a hand covering his face as he burst into a high-pitched burst of laughter.

'Tenebrae? Oh, what a fool you are, Lyddon! There *is* no Tenebrae – at least not in the sense you mean. Tenebrae is an invention – a fiction born out of my own mind.' He laughed again. 'And yet you know, Lyddon – so grand was the design of my fiction that Tenebrae has acquired quite the life of its own. The fact that you are here in Newgate quite proves that. That you will hang on the morrow shows what a great artist I am.'

'No Tenebrae?'

'I needed an instrument for my vengeance – Tenebrae is that instrument. And do you know what, Lyddon? There are scores of men in this very city who believe it really exists. Even the home secretary can be persuaded to sign any document at the mere mention of its name.'

'Then why are we here?'

James Brendon took in a great breath.

'We are here because you ruined my life.'

'I thought I'd cared for you – helped a young man get on in society. I recall the day we met in the lobby of the Commons. You were introduced to me as an impoverished scholar who needed a start in life. That is why I took you on as my secretary. You've served the cause well, James...'

'Ah, yes, the cause. As if your feeble reforms and rebellions ever mattered? And it was the huge desire of the Class to frustrate every single one of them that made it so easy to persuade your betters to believe in Tenebrae.'

'Then why do all this now, James? You might have served your cause better if you had carried all this out while I was still a member of Parliament. When I was still in a position of power?'

Brendon sat on the edge of the table.

'You know, I was tempted not to do any of this, Lyddon. Even though I was laughing at the nonsense you spouted in that tired old speech you made in Manchester. But - unfortunately for you - you reminded me of what set me off on my strange journey of revenge. You wrote that account of your rebellion on Dartmoor, way back in 1817 - the bit of history that you refer to as Gibbet Hill. It reminded me of just why I had to see you dead. For those lines you scribbled, brought back all the pain I suffered as a boy. The harshness I experienced as a young man, struggling to make my way in the world. I do confess that there was a more mercenary motive as well - I caught a glimpse of that new will you made, which gives me such a generous bequest.'

'Yes, and I did that not out of duty, James, but from a genuine affection. I'd come to think of you like a son...'

'But I've never thought of you as a father, Lyddon. Only as the man who destroyed my happiness.'

'But why?'

'Because I had a father, though I do confess he scarcely acknowledged my existence. A man you drove out of England, Lyddon. You see, I'm a bastard and I take the name Brendon from my mother. She's dead now, of course - the pox got her as it did my father. She was a bastard too, though a more noble one, for the man who sowed his seed in *her* mother was a peer of the realm. A stupid old fool that you were acquainted with on Dartmoor - Lord Silas? Ah, you recall him, and so you should, for you destroyed him as much as you drove my father to destruction.'

'I see now...' said Jonas, a realisation coming to him...

'My father was...'

'John Haynes...'

'Yes, John Haynes - the man whose reputation you besmirched.'

'Haynes *had* no reputation, James. He was forced into exile by his own greed and dishonesty. He participated in the murder of a man I held dear. I came close to executing John Haynes, but I spared his life.'

Brendon stood, bashing his fist down on the table.

'You ruined him!' he raged. 'Had he been able to remain as a servant of the Prince of Wales, he might have become wealthy and entitled. A knighthood or baronetcy at the least - perhaps even a peerage!'

'He would never have attained such honours,' Jonas replied. 'His dishonesty would have caught him out. And far from ruining him, I gave him the opportunity to flee to the Continent. And years later, I discovered him lying in a gutter in Paris - dying of drink and syphilis. He told me then he had a son with noble blood in his veins – but I assumed the child must be dead, for your father said that both he and the woman he impregnated were syphilitic at the time.'

Brendon nodded.

'Circumstances put that curse upon me.'

'I had your father nursed as he lay dying, James. Buried him at my own expense at Père-Lachaise...'

'But what about me!' Brendon raged.

'I didn't know you lived, James. Had I done so, I would have made sure that you had a good life. Despite the syphilis, you seem healthy at the moment. I can still make your life better for you, if you end this now.'

Brendon leaned towards him.

'Oh you will, Lyddon. You will. I shall get great joy watching you hang. I'll be the preacher at your side as the drop goes down!'

There was silence for a while.

'Why William Quest, James? He was on your list too. He played no part in my deeds on Dartmoor. He wasn't even born in the days of Gibbet Hill.'

'No, he wasn't – but his father Josiah Quest did. The sins of my father have been visited on me. So I thought it only appropriate that the sins of Josiah Quest should descend upon the present leader of Monkshood.'

'And Joshua Blount? He played no part in the Dartmoor rebellion...'

Brendon waved a finger in the air.

'Ah, that's where I've been really clever, Lyddon. You see I considered that if I just put your name and Quest's on the list, it might narrow down my motive far too speedily. I thought it was wise to add another misguided philanthropist – and the fools I encouraged to work for Tenebrae were only too thrilled to see Blount listed. It helped in my deception of them.'

Jonas Lyddon looked up at him, seeing only mania on what had once been a face with gentle expressions. He wondered if Brendon's inherited syphilis had now pushed the man into the dark horrors of insanity?

~

Inspector Honour Bright was used to working long hours without rest, but he recognised that it was an ability that was acquired. So he'd sent Constable Parkin home for the remainder of the day, instructing him to be present at Scotland Yard first thing the next morning.

But to Bright, there was never any such rest when matters were afoot. These were strange times for him. There was a part of him that very much wanted to bring the notorious William Quest to book – and yet... he was beginning to see just why Anders had fallen under the spell of the man.

But one day... one day...

Honour Bright had a feeling that the next progression in these matters might be generated by Quest and his associates. And that was what had brought him close to Quest's home at Tavistock Place. He'd paced up and down for a while, wondering whether to rap the door and see if the master was at home, but could not find an excuse to call which would not look as though he was there as a potential enemy. He considered whether he should return to his own modest home and have a few hours rest, like Parkin. He thought...

But as he looked back along the pavement, from the junction with Marchmont Street, he saw three men come down the steps of Quest's home.

One was the youth, Daniel Stanton, the other the rogue Harry Blizzard – the third he recognised all too well, for it was the footpad Simeon Prowl. Their paths had crossed several times before, though Bright had never quite managed to collar him. A villain who was supposed to be lingering in Newgate on the eve of his execution.

The three were walking with great speed in the opposite direction.

Honour Bright looked round in all directions before he followed them, hiding himself among the pedestrians in Tavistock Place.

~

Sticks returned to the house in the company of Magnus Blount. Two very large men, who worked on the fringes of Monkshood, were stationed in the narrow front hall, being given instructions by Jasper Feedle.

'Where's Brendon?' Feedle asked.

'Well, he wasn't at Mr Lyddon's home. I'll try again later. Where's William?'

'I don't know. He was leaving just as the lads here arrived – driven off in a very fast cabriolet. Didn't say where he was going, neither.'

Sticks looked annoyed.

'I thought the whole idea was that he wouldn't go out alone? He's on their list – the same as Mr Lyddon and Mr Blount. Have the lads no idea where he's gone?'

'None at all. But he's apparently been gone a long while.'

'Do you think Will's gone to get the notebook?'

'Well, apart from him, we are the only two who know where it is – and Rosa of course. It's a long way from London, even with the railway. And William seemed to think he couldn't do it in time.'

'I wish I knew where I could start to look for him, but it's hopeless.'

Twenty-five

'London Bridge,' said Crouch. 'Let's go up to the tavern in The Borough and wet our throats. A long way to go to Limehouse and I'm gaggin."

He and Booth had been on an errand for their master, and were returning to the den in Narrow Street where they were wont to rest.

'Why not?' Booth said. 'Busy tomorrow, with him wanting us there for the hanging. Though I'd rather lay low, mesself.'

As they went up on to the bridge, Crouch halted, looking down at the foul, swirling waters of the Thames.

'I'll be honest with you, Ebenezer, I'm starting to wish we'd never started this. And I'd sooner not go anywhere near Newgate and its scaffold. Just seeing that rope gives me a feeling of hemp a-rubbing my throat. I want out. Out of London, to some quiet gaff where I can keep my head down.'

'You think I don't? I see I've already been papered, though how the news-sheets got the story so quick I'll never know. Special editions too – you see what they're saying? Murderous attack on Angier? The great Jonas Lyddon snatched? If there's police court business with this... no worse... the Old Bailey... you won't see the preacher for dust. It's us that'll swing.'

'I'd go now, Ebenezer. Especially as our descriptions are all over the linen. But we won't get far without the coins we're owed. And more than that, I don't trust the preacher. He knows we could turn Queen's Evidence on him. So who's to say our lives are safe?'

'He keeps a chest full of cottars at Limehouse – and sovereigns are good enough for me. I've seen him adding to them... no doubt he thinks he might have to flee if it all goes wrong. That chest'd do for the both of us.'

'So do we go to the hanging?'

'Aye, for I'd like to see Lyddon turned off! But later – just a moment later, I think we should scoot and make off with his chest, and...'

Crouch pushed him very roughly against the parapet of the bridge, leaning him over so that they were looking down at the Thames.

'What the hell are you...'

'Quiet you fool...' Crouch glanced round.

'What is it?'

'Behind us – just gone past. Three men.'

Booth turned and looked.

'That's Simeon Prowl,' he said.

'It is indeed, and I recognise the young lad there – I've seen him going in and out at that Quest's house. Mind, you'd think Prowl'd be keeping his head down! If he's risking his neck by going in to The Borough, then he's risking it for a purpose.'

'The Preacher wants Prowl. Says he can't afford him on the loose.'

'Then we'll get him! But let's go canny and find out who they're visiting in The Borough.'

~

Honour Bright was nearly across London Bridge, when he saw the two men take off after the very three men he was tailing himself. One of them he recognised, straight away, as the slippery villain Crouch. The taller man with him seemed vaguely familiar, but he couldn't bring a name to mind – not someone he'd ever laid by the heels anyway.

At first, he wondered if the proximity of one set of rogues to the other was deliberate – but judged not by the surreptitious way that Crouch and his comrade were following the others. Pure coincidence then, that they were both coming off London Bridge in the direction of The Borough.

Bright reached inside his jacket, his fingers touching the cosh in his inside pocket. Then he added himself to the little procession making its way up the Borough High Street.

~

They were somewhere near the Marshalsea Prison.

Crouch cursed, for the three men had completely vanished. They'd been easy to follow along the crowded streets, But now they had gone, slipped away in the press of the crowd.

He cursed again, looking along the long line of tall buildings on the opposite side of the street. Nothing, absolutely nothing. He could see the praise of his master slipping away.

'Got to be here,' he muttered. 'Got to be somewhere here...'

'What are we going to do if we find them?' asked Booth. 'There's three of them and just the two of us. We can hardly snatch Prowl away and get him to Limehouse. And we can't kill him. Once the crushers know it's Prowl, the Preacher's plan will be blown.'

'You got your pistols?'

'Got all three – primed and ready. But it don't solve the problem. And it's hardly a quiet bit of street. And the chances of getting all three...'

'Four,' Crouch said.

'What?'

Crouch pointed along the street.

Indeed, a party of four were standing by a doorway, talking to each other.

Crouch gripped his companion's arm so fiercely that Booth almost yelped.

'You see who it is? The blind man that gave us the slip at Limehouse! So that's how he got away. Prowl's in it with them.'

'We can't get them all!'

'How fast can you reload a pistol? The Preacher'll be pleased if we top Prowl and the blind man. Kill the three, reload and kill the blind man! There's rich pickings in this!'

'But if they identify Prowl...' Booth began.

'They won't if you shoot his face off! And what you start I'll finish with my cosh. His own mother won't know him by the time we've finished with him. The crushers won't recognise him – not least this side of tomorrow's execution!'

Booth looked round.

The market was open and the crowds had hurried off in its direction.

'Now!' Booth said. 'We've got to do it now!'

~

'My God!' Bright said under his breath.

He saw the two villains as they walked closer to their prey. More than that, he recognised the four men standing on the pavement beyond them. And particularly noticed the blind philanthropist Joshua Blount, who'd been missing these past few days.

He smiled at the secret that Quest had kept from them all.

Then he saw the taller of the rogues draw out a pair of pistols. Watched, as the two men paced quickly to the little gathering by the doorway. Bright drew out his cosh. He yelled a warning that echoed along the street and chased after them.

~

Daniel Stanton looked up at the warning shout. Two men were closing in fast upon them, one brandishing two pistols and the other a fierce looking neddy of a cudgel. He heard another warning shout and glimpsed the man pursuing them, recognised him as the police detective Honour Bright.

Almost without thinking, he elbowed Joshua Blount back into the doorway, noticing that Prowl had thrown up his arm in a gesture of defence. Heard Harry Blizzard cry out, as the old man grasped his arm. Saw the flash of a discharged pistol and the thud as the lead ball tore into the wall of London Brick, not a foot away from his face.

Daniel hardly realised he'd brought out his own pistols, for he was reacting with instinct rather than conscious thought, levelling them at the attackers. Only when they paused, did he see the fear in their eyes. He watched as the policeman drew level with the two, raising a cosh and bringing it down on the tall man's hand, sending the discharged pistol into the gutter.

But in his rush, Bright caught his foot, sprawling at their feet. In a moment, Crouch had grasped Bright's arm and Booth had levelled a pistol at the policeman's head.

'Back off!' Booth yelled. 'Back off or I'll kill him!'

Daniel was hardly aware of even firing his two pistols, let alone aiming them. He felt the recoil, tasted the stink of the powder, saw the flash of the discharge. Watched, with amazement, as Booth threw his arms into the air, his own pistol flying into the street. Noticed, almost with a split-second fascination, the small hole drilled in the middle of Booth's forehead. Puzzled as to where his other shot might have gone...

As Daniel strode across to his victim, Crouch turned and fled back down the street, jumping over Booth's corpse lying in the gutter...

Daniel's mouth felt so dry... he felt that his tongue was choking him.

He looked down at Honour Bright.

'Oh, my God!' said Daniel. 'I've killed a man! They'll hang me now for sure!'

'Oh no they won't,' Bright said. 'I am a police detective and you just saved my life! But you must understand, lad, I'll have to take Prowl there into custody – he's a convicted murderer and I have no choice.'

'But he's saved my life!' said Joshua Blount. 'That must count for something?'

'It is not my decision,' the policeman replied.

Daniel glanced up the road.

'But – he's...'

There was no sign of Simeon Prowl.

Twenty-six

It was well into the darkness of the autumn evening before Quest returned, exchanging a few words with the guards on the door, then breezing into the drawing room.

'Where have you been, Will?' asked Sticks.

'In a while.'

He looked around the room, giving a welcoming smile to Magnus Blount and a nod to Jasper Feedle.

'Did you get the printing work done, Jasper?'

'All done. All ready for distribution. I've got some of our own lads standing ready, not to mention half the urchins in London. The crowds are already gatherin' for the execution. A thousand or more already, with half the householders in Newgate Street rentin' out their window spaces, and a wooden grandstand erected by the Bailey.'

'A disgusting spectacle!' Magnus Blount declared. 'I share my brother's view that public hangings should be banned - indeed all hangings. Is it true that you fear for the life of Mr Lyddon?'

'That is our belief.'

'But I don't see how it is possible?'

'I fear that it is.'

'Your associates here have intimated that my brother is safe?'

'I trust that he still is,' Quest replied. 'I was hoping that the party we sent out for him would be back by now. Has there been no word, Sticks?'

'Not a sign.'

'And what of James Brendon?'

'I've been twice to Lyddon's house - he's not there.'

'I see...' Quest looked thoughtful.

'Where have you been, Will?' asked Jasper.

'To fetch this...'

He reached inside his jacket and brought out a small package wrapped in canvas.

'Is that what I think it is?' asked Sticks. 'No wonder you were such a while!'

'Sticks. I know you've already made several trips around London, but might I beg that you undertake one more? I would be grateful if you would take this package to London Bridge. Just a few minutes before midnight, I would like you to place it on the fourth step up from the river on the stairs. Then to come away as swiftly as possible. And I mean swiftly - do not linger!'

'I see,' said Sticks. 'But who shall I take with me to watch out for the rascal who comes to pick it up?'

'Nobody, my friend. Just leave the package and come away.'

'You mean you're givin' them this notebook?' said Jasper.

'I certainly am.'

'But we can watch at a distance,' said Sticks. 'Keep both ends of the bridge in sight and there's still time to arrange for a boat to be on the river, for there's a good chance they might come by the water to have the notebook away.'

Quest shook his head.

'No! Under no circumstances are you to keep any watch on it whatsoever. Leave the package and then come away. At five to midnight. It's very important that you do exactly what I've said, Sticks, and...'

They were interrupted by a fierce rapping on the front door, then a loud conversation in the hallway. Quest went to the head of the stairs and looked down at the newcomers. Daniel was guiding Joshua Blount into the house, and Harry Blizzard was looking back through the door in the company of Inspector Anders and Sergeant Berry.

'Can't see anyone on our tail,' said Harry.

'Come on up, gentlemen,' said Quest.

As they passed him, entering the drawing room, Quest noticed the dreadful look on Daniel's face.

'Go easy on the boy, Will,' said Anders. 'He's just killed a man!'

~

Rosa Stanton was standing in the doorway of the Angier house, looking out into the darkness. It was so quiet it was hard to believe what had happened there. The only evidence of the battle being the man who was struggling for his life.

Suddenly it had ceased to be such a great adventure.

Rosa yearned to be away from Highgate, at William's side. She'd seen the look on Quest's face. That revealing expression that came from time to time. The one that told her that he was tired of it all, wanted the world he lived in to go away; the look that said he'd rather be roaming the hills and hangers of Hope Down; yearned to be away from London, with its terrors and menace, its blood and death.

Then, from the room by the stairs, that they'd turned into a sick-room for Wren Angier, came a great cry, a cry from Phoebe...

Rosa felt her heart sink as she rushed back across the hallway.

~

'Where is Bright?' Quest asked, after Anders had given him an account of what had happened in The Borough.

'He is seeing to matters there,' the detective replied. 'Making sure that no blame falls upon the boy. There's no doubt that – but for Stanton – Honour Bright would be dead. And heaven knows what might have happened to Mr Blount here.'

Daniel had only remained with them for a few moments, before retreating to his own room. Quest had seen the look on the youth's face, noted the lack of words. Quest recalled the first time he'd killed a man. He knew all the signs and regretted that Daniel had ever had to know the extent of that horror.

'I'm saddened that anyone has had to die to save my life!' said Joshua Blount. 'All this killing... these deaths... madness... madness.'

Magnus Blount helped him into a chair.

'Thank you for getting my brother back to me,' he said. 'Is there any news of Mr Lyddon and James Brendon?'

Quest had been looking out through the window, noting the three men from Monkshood who were patrolling the street. Considering whether to send someone out to locate Brendon. Trying to banish the dark thought that haunted his mind...

'There's certainly news of Lyddon,' said Anders. 'Sergeant...'

Berry put several newspapers down on the table.

'Special editions,' Berry said. 'The more respectable sheets have a notice on the murderous attack on Sir Wren Angier and the kidnapping of Mr Lyddon. But the others – well, the others...'

Quest picked up the more radical newspapers, which described in detail just what had happened, as Berry went on...

'The more popular newspapers are relating that Mr Lyddon has been taken by the Establishment, to silence his call for reform and his good works for the poor. Interesting to see – as we came here – that the screevers are chalking the same message on the pavements, and there are flysheets already about declaring that the kidnapping is a sign that the Class are declaring war on the desperate and all who fight for better times.'

Quest looked across at Jasper Feedle, noting the proud smile of a successful author.

'The news has led to some disturbances already,' said Anders. 'A great crowd has gathered in Trafalgar Square, not just the poor from the rookeries, but enlightened folk who favour a fairer society. What's more, over a hundred people are maintaining a vigil outside the home of Mr Lyddon. Palmerston and the government have instructed our Commissioner to call in all policemen for urgent duty – the home secretary fears that there could even be a rebellion.'

'What the hell is going on, Wissilcraft?'

The spymaster was in his office, looking down at the crowds marching up Whitehall to Trafalgar Square, when the Home Secretary, Lord Palmerston, burst in to the room. A rare occurrence, and one indicating a sort of panic, for Palmerston rarely visited his minions – usually demanding that they grace the carpet in front of his own desk. He was clutching a document.

'You've seen the newspapers, my lord?'

Even in the gaslight's reflection on the glass, Wissilcraft could see the embarrassment on the face of the politician.

'I have – utter nonsense! The idea that we have somehow removed that meddlesome individual, Lyddon? There's no truth in it!'

Wissilcraft shot round, fixing Palmerston with a look of steel that made even that most powerful of men tremble.

'I hope not, my lord. But I've heard the rumours that the government has been playing fast and loose with men who've campaigned for reform.'

'Nonsense! I have myself championed reform, Wissilcraft. Fought for better hours in the manufactories, opposed the use of small children in hard labour and much more.'

'Indeed you have, my lord – though unkind folk have suggested that these reforms were expedited to stave off open rebellions, that they are just the crumbs from rich men's tables...'

'You sound like a rebel yourself, Wissilcraft?'

'My place here is to prevent civil disruption, nothing more. But a number of awkward documents have crossed this table. I mean, I see you signed a document only the other day, giving someone I've never heard of – a Mr Denwood – complete authority over all the officials of Newgate Gaol. What was that about?'

Palmerston looked flustered.

'Just an administrative matter. Nothing of concern.'

'I would remind you, my lord, that we are not here to deter poachers on your Romsey estate. We are here to safeguard the nation. Your activities regarding Newgate have generated considerable gossip. Would you care to enlighten me?'

'I would not, Wissilcraft. The matter of our prisons comes under my jurisdiction as home secretary and has nothing to do with the Secret Service. You will not refer to it again and that is an order!'

'Very well, my lord. *For now.*'

'These uprisings on the street. Do you think I should call out troops from the barracks?'

'Only if you wish to incite a revolution, my lord. Best leave it to the Metropolitan Police – at least while the protests remain peaceful. I've already made suggestions to the Commissioner. Sir Richard Mayne is quite convinced that he can contain the protests with the men he has at his disposal.' Wissilcraft looked at his watch. 'Now, my lord, if you'll excuse me, there's somewhere I have to be – most urgently.'

Palmerston turned as though to leave, but a moment later turned back.

'My lord?'

'Perhaps, Wissilcraft, I haven't been entirely frank with you. I did give the man Denwood permission to undertake an activity in Newgate – but in turn Denwood produced this...'

Palmerston laid the document down on the desk.

'Believe me, Wissilcraft, there's enough in this document to convict Jonas Lyddon a dozen times over, for sedition, murder and high treason. It is penned by his own hand and gives an account of the man's activities on Dartmoor in 1817. I see Lyddon labels it Gibbet Hill? Appropriate, I think, for it's on a gibbet he belongs.'

Wissilcraft idly turned a few pages.

'Nothing new here, my lord. Here in the service, we've been aware of what happened on Dartmoor for some years.'

'You mean you *knew*? And you've done nothing?'

'What *is* there to do?'

'Treason, Wissilcraft! The killing of members of the militia? Mayhem and murder?'

'All a very long time ago, my lord.'

'There is no limitation on our right to prosecute Lyddon.'

'No, my lord, there isn't. But Jonas Lyddon has – since these days – secured a reputation that's made him immensely popular in the land. Bring him to the Old Bailey and you might just trigger off the revolution you fear. More than that – if you attempt to use this document, it's quite likely that William Quest will publish the notebook kept by my predecessor when he was head of the Secret Service. Which could be quite damning to so many people in public life – members of the royal family, political figures and men of business, even yourself, my lord...'

'You believe we should do nothing?'

'Where Lyddon is concerned, we should let all memory of the Dartmoor events fade away. Far better that way. Why poke a stick into a hornets' nest? As for this document, my lord, I believe it would be wiser to burn it.'

Wissilcraft held out the document.

'Now, if you'll excuse me, my lord, I really must be about my business.'

Lord Palmerston picked up the document and opened the door, halting a moment in the doorway and looking back at the spymaster.

'On your head be it, Wissilcraft. On your head be it!'

~

'You must leave soon,' Quest said to Sticks.

The old prizefighter looked at the clock.

'Only just gone nine, Will. Plenty of time for me to take the notebook to London Bridge. You're certain you don't want me to get someone to put the dodge on whoever picks it up? I could always linger by the bridge myself and tail the man who collects it.'

'Absolutely not, my old friend. We must play this out my way – for the sake of Jonas Lyddon.'

'I don't see how?' said Jasper Feedle, who sat at the table, penning a piece for *The Newgate Shadow*. 'I can't see as how handing it over will make a ha'p'orth of difference, William?'

Quest smiled.

'Oh, you will, Jasper. You will – and probably as soon as tomorrow morning, if my suspicions are correct. But enough of the wretched notebook. I've been giving some thought as to how our enemies discovered that we'd taken Jonas Lyddon to Wren's house. We certainly weren't tailed going there. Which means that there was an informer in our midst.'

'One of the policemen,' suggested Harry Blizzard. 'Never trust a crusher.'

Quest shook his head, 'Normally I'd agree with you, Harry, but I do trust Anders and Berry. And Bright's actions at the house, when it was under attack, put him above suspicion.'

'Then who?' asked Blizzard. 'You tell me and I'll cut the lites out of him!'

'Well, I trust all of you band of villains, and most of those who were in this house when we formulated the plan. Discounting everyone else, there's only one man it could be – James Brendon.'

'Lyddon's secretary! I find it hard to believe!' said Blizzard. 'He's been with him for years, at his side in so many of his struggles.'

'But who else is there, Harry? Who else went off alone after the decision was made? And where is Brendon now? He should be here, anxious that we free Lyddon? But he's nowhere to be found, and...'

The door swung open. Rosa Stanton stood there, wiping away tears.

'Oh, William. It's Wren – it's Wren...'

For that time of night, the old city was quite busy, with crowds streaming across London Bridge, many muttering words against the Class and shouting praises for the good works of Jonas Lyddon.

Sticks had delivered the parcel on to the fourth step up on the bridge stairs, but couldn't resist lingering as he wandered up and down the bridge. He glanced down at the stairs three or four times, but could see little in the darkness – certainly no sign of anyone collecting the package. In the end, he crossed to the far side of the bridge and looked at the dark swollen waters of the Thames.

The tide was sweeping upstream, meeting the flow of the river that had travelled so many miles from the far heights of the Cotswolds. He had vague memories of the place where the river started, for he'd fought many a prizefighting bout in the towns of the west. But as he looked, he was filled with a sudden yearning to walk the entire length of the Thames – all the way from the estuary to where its first drops issued from the ground.

Sticks smiled. His legs were not quite what they were and he knew he'd have to undertake such an expedition soon, while they could still cope with the trudge.

He'd walked much of England in his younger days, seeking casual work – as far as Dartmoor once – and even longer journeys to the prizefighting squares, before fame, reputation, had funded travel by coach. He looked at the river again; yes, one last expedition before he put his feet up for good. Maybe Jasper would come with him. Despite the crutch, the old rifleman was very mobile and still seemed to have boundless energy.

As he regarded the river, he had a feeling that much was coming to an end. That the world of William Quest and Monkshood would soon be no more. London was changing now, too well-policed for those antics to continue. Jonas Lyddon was right – the battle for reform needed to be fought within Parliament.

Over the past couple of years, he'd seen the effect that all the killing and the mayhem had had upon Quest.

Sticks looked up at the stars and remembered how they'd plucked the boy from the streets, saved him from an existence as a pickpocket and beggar, transforming him into a vengeful figure of rebellion. Sticks had always had his doubts about it all, for the boy was already damaged by his childhood. And now, it seemed as if sheer exhaustion and those memories had worn down the lad.

He could see the tiredness every time he studied the face of William Quest.

He'd seen the way Quest had jumped up, pale and shivering, as Rosa had stood in the doorway, her tears falling to the boards.

Like Quest, Sticks had thought she was crying because Wren Angier was dead. Even when she'd explained that they were tears of relief, because Angier had become conscious again, and that the surgeon had given her a smile of relief – even then, Quest's hands were still trembling.

Not Rosa's fault! A while ago – being an actress – she might have used such an entrance for dramatic effect. Not now though, not now. Rosa had changed too – perhaps by seeing how poor little Phoebe had been so shocked by the sight of blood pouring from Wren's chest. Perhaps imagining how easily it might have been her own lover lying there.

Sticks knew that if they went on with this, it could only lead to the death of William Quest, perhaps the ending of all of them.

This was no longer the land of the Regency, when Monkshood had come about, designed in the revolutionary minds of men such as Josiah Quest, Old Marshall and Lyddon himself. Josiah and Marshall were long dead, and even Lyddon had conceded that better ways for a better land needed to be found.

He sighed and looked down again into the tumult of the Thames, swirling around and smashing into the piers of the bridge. Yet, upstream, the flow of its waters could be gentle, peaceful.

And those were the places he wanted to see...

~

'You seem to be keeping remarkably calm, my dear Lyddon,' said James Brendon. 'A pleasant day outside, as you'll see from the sunlight when you are escorted out to the gallows.'

Jonas Lyddon had been studying the Bible, the only book allowed in the condemned cell, musing on the thought that – in previous times – the chaplain who came to console the dead, the Newgate Ordinary, would have written at his dictation a mostly fictional memoir, for sale to the gathering crowds, flocked there to see the subject of the memoir turned-off. A useful way of providing funds, though the corpse never profited.

He'd chuckled at the thought of his old friend and comrade, Jasper Feedle, writing a very special edition of *The Newgate Shadow,* no doubt exaggerating his own contribution to social justice.

But then he considered that if Jasper was writing any obituary in that august publication, it would be for Simeon Prowl. For the chances of anyone knowing that Brendon had put him into Newgate as Prowl's substitute, must be very slim.

'Do you think I might have the company of the Ordinary, James?' he said.

'Ah, I think not, Lyddon.' Brendon held out his arms, showing off his costume. 'My associates call me Preacher behind my back, imagining I never hear them. Part of me always favoured the church as a profession. You'll recall my interest in old ecclesiastical buildings? Yes? Do you know I even own the most wonderful piece of stained-glass from a long destroyed building. Well, today I shall fulfil the function of the Ordinary. I'll escort you out on to the scaffold. See the odious Sir Egregious put the mask over your face and the hempen rope around your throat. Mine will be the last voice you hear before you are dropped into eternity.'

'You think I'm scared, James?'

'Aren't we all scared of death?'

'Not particularly. Besides, I'm an old man with limited time left anyway. I've faced it too often.'

'And always lived. But this time, my dear Lyddon, there will be no escape.'

'Someone may notice that I'm not Simeon Prowl?'

'But it will all happen so swiftly. Down will go the drop and any recognising voice will be lost in the cheering and braying of the crowd. Only later – only later – will it be revealed that it was the notorious Jonas Lyddon that the crowds were braying for. Then it will be revealed just how the swap was engineered. And Lord Palmerston, and his puppets in government, will face the wrath of public opinion.'

'What have you got against Palmerston?'

'Nothing, as such. But it was his sort who cast my father aside. Used him to protect the reputation of the Prince Regent. I shall publish a memoir of my father, to tell the world just how he was abandoned by them. How I was robbed of my inheritance and the title and living I might have had!'

'You've read my own account in Gibbet Hill. You know that isn't true?'

'I know nothing of the sort, Lyddon!'

'You really are deranged, James. I fear that your inherited syphilis has got to your mind. But it's not too late to end this, to get you all the best medical aid.'

'In some asylum?'

'Not in such a place.'

'No!' Brendon screamed the word.

'James...'

'Be silent! You've barely two hours to live, Lyddon. Rest assured, I'll read the burial service loudly as we take you to the gallows, but I do not wish to debate these matters with you any longer!'

Twenty-seven

'A fine day for a hanging!'

Sticks was looking through the window and up at the sky. After a long moment, he turned back into the room to where Quest was sitting.

'That's what they'll be saying, the thousands gathered in the Newgate crowd. A fine day for a hanging. It's what they always say, even if the rain is pelting down or the ice and snow are freezing their hands off. It's always a fine day for a hanging. We'd better start out soon, Will.'

Harry Blizzard, Jasper and Rosa had left the house a little while before, on their way to the gaol, but Quest seemed inclined to linger. Sticks wondered just why?

'D'you think we should go now?'

Quest sighed. 'Oh, I just thought we might have an early visitor - but perhaps not.'

He stood and put on his jacket, with its many pockets. Sticks noticed that some of them held pistols. He watched as Quest reached out and picked up the heavy cane containing a sword stick.

'This is going to be hard work,' said Sticks.

'Nigh impossible unless our plan works. And...'

There was a rapping on the front door of the house. A moment later, one of the Monkshood guards came up to the room.

'A gent to see you, sir.'

'Show him up - hopefully the one I expected, Sticks. Took him longer than I thought, but I had no doubt he'd come. An old friend, I think - of sorts...'

Wissilcraft was ushered into the room, his face as black as thunder.

'You're a cunning bastard, Quest!' he said.

He almost threw the notebook down on to the table.

'How did you know?' Wissilcraft demanded.

'The note you sent. Not in your own handwriting, of course. You're not stupid enough for that! You got your clerk to write it, didn't you? Unfortunately, the same clerk who penned the account for you of events leading up to the fight on Holkham Beach the other year. You'll recall that you kindly sent me a copy. I've a good memory for neat copperplate. A rarity in these rushed times, Wissilcraft.'

'That is not the notebook!' said the spymaster.

'No, but it is the same brand of notebook. I had a screever prepare a duplicate when the original came into my possession, a man who knew the same shorthand as the villain who penned it. I always believed that a copy might come in useful one day. I secreted it at one of my bolt-holes in Berkshire – indeed, I sacrificed much of yesterday fetching it to London.'

'Yes, identical in looks, but *not* in content. Your duplicate might be in shorthand, but that shorthand translates into absolute drivel!'

'Oh, harsh words, Wissilcraft! Extracts from the London chapters of *Oliver Twist*, a touch of Shakespeare and Herrick that I'm fond of, and some verses from King James's Bible. Hardly drivel!'

'You could have just told me that you were wise to my plan?'

There was a touch of anger in Quest's voice when he replied.

'Why the hell should I? You know the situation we are in? Yet you forced me to waste a whole day responding to your little jest! I hold you in some regard, Wissilcraft, but now I'm afraid the gloves are off – I still have the original notebook, and I fully intend to use it, unless you do exactly what I say next.'

'That sounds very much like a threat?'

'Oh, it is. The thing is, old friend, I do wonder if you are complicit in what has happened to Jonas Lyddon?'

'He's vanished and Tenebrae are deemed to be responsible. His disappearance has nothing to do with me, or the secret service.'

'We know where Lyddon is.'

'You *know*?'

Quest studied him, 'And you clearly don't, do you? Hasn't Palmerston told you?'

'What does his vanishing have to do with Lord Palmerston?'

'Palmerston is the home secretary, Wissilcraft. Only he could have agreed that Jonas Lyddon be secured in Newgate Gaol. Where, in a matter of hours, he is to be hanged...'

'Hanged? As I understand it, the only man to be swung today is a villain named Simeon Prowl – a footpad.'

'But Prowl is not in Newgate, Wissilcraft, but we believe that Lyddon is. That he's to be executed in place of Prowl. There's an undoubted resemblance, as I've seen myself. And...'

'It's not possible, besides...' Wissilcraft stopped what he was saying. He recalled his conversation with Palmerston the day before, thought of the permission to undertake some activity in Newgate, granted by the home secretary to a man called Denwood.

'Oh, my God!'

'You genuinely didn't know did you?' said Quest.

Wissilcraft told him what he did know.

'I doubt this man Denwood exists, at least not under that name,' said Quest.'
'Then what are we to do?'
'You will go to Palmerston. You will go to Palmerston right now and get this execution stopped. Tell the home secretary that I will not publish his part in this conspiracy, if Jonas Lyddon is released forthwith.'
'But, Quest – there's only two hours to go. I might not get to Palmerston in time! Besides, he might refuse to oblige you – '
'Oh, I believe he will. You tell Palmerston – from me – that the real notebook contains a great deal of information about his lordship's private activities. That every last portion of his private life will be made public, unless he complies. You'd be surprised just what the notebook does contain regarding the old mongoose! You have two hours, Wissilcraft. Best be on your way!'
He and Sticks watched through the window as Wissilcraft ran out into the street, throwing his great bulk into his private carriage.
'He won't be in time!' said Sticks.
'No, my old friend, he won't. Which means we still have a great deal to do.'
'One thing I don't understand, Will? You read the notebook to us, when it first came into our hands. As I recall, the notebook makes no mention of Lord Palmerston at all? Nothing about these private activities?'
Quest gave a humourless laugh.
'No, Sticks. But Palmerston doesn't know that – and most great men in this land have some guilty secret they don't want the world to know, don't they?'

~

The crowds thronged all along Newgate Street, others fought their way up Old Bailey, determined to get a view of the hanging. Every property-owner, whose upper storeys had a view of the gallows, had rented out space in their rooms and attics – bolder men had even secured perches on the rooftops, some clinging on for dear life, lest they face their own drop down on to the hard roads and pavements beneath.
Pickpockets dipped many a wallet, kerchiefs and watches, from the pockets of men and women who were pressed hard by the multitude gathered there. Purveyors of food and drink charged their way through the great block of individuals, providing sustenance to the waiting crowds. Men pissed on to the streets in their desperation not to lose their places; women crouched down where they were to relieve themselves. In the corners of the walls, and in the dark alleys leading away from Newgate Street, the whores lured gentlemen aside, giving them a distraction from the long wait.

If the public hangings were designed to deter folk from a life of crime, they failed miserably in that intent.

'Must be ten thousand or more,' said Harry Blizzard.

'More than that,' Jasper replied. 'They've all come to see a footpad turned off, or so they think, and that's a rare occurrence these days. But did you hear the chatter? So many people here are discussing Jonas Lyddon, as big a matter to this crowd as the public hanging.'

A high wooden platform had been constructed on the front of the gaol, the sinister gallows tree rising from its centre. A number of policemen in uniform lined the foot of the platform. On its top, not far from the hideous apparatus of death, four prison turnkeys stood. Jasper pointed out the shot-guns leaning against the wall of the gaol.

'This ain't goin' to be easy,' he said. 'Only that rough ladder up the platform from the street, and that designed for the police and not for us.'

'D'ye think we're stuffed?' asked Harry.

Jasper gave him a sly smile.

'Might not just be Jonas knockin' on the gates today,' he said. 'It all depends on the crowd - it all depends on the crowd. I'm sure they all loved Simeon Prowl in their way, but they wouldn't hesitate to see a footpad topped. A great death for a villainous hero of the people. But Jonas Lyddon - their own champion - well, that's a different matter. And here comes our boys and girls...'

Rosa was forcing her way through the crowds, a procession of children and Monkshood volunteers in her wake, all of them carrying pamphlets headed by the name of Jasper's publication. The author smiled in greeting, taking one of the publications, admiring his own handiwork.

'Not bad - even if I says it as shouldn't.'

'Shall we start?' Rosa asked.

'Why not!'

Rosa waved a hand and her distributors struggled their way into the heart of the crowd, handing this special copy of *The Newgate Shadow* to any onlookers who looked as though they might be able to read. Harry looked over Jasper's shoulder at the copy he held.

'You've done very well with that, Jasper,' said Blizzard.

'I am rather proud of my penmanship - and I had the etching showing Jonas's face done special by my associate Paddy Kelly - oh, a grand Irish lad and a wizard hand in the picture trade. You can see the likeness, Harry? Ain't it a stunner? And Paddy only ever set eyes on Jonas just the once, such is his skill.'

THE NEWGATE SHADOW
Special Edition

*In the interests of Truth and Justice, we wish to reveal to the People of London that Simeon Prowl is NOT being hanged this day. The **Class** are using this execution to MURDER that Great Champion of the Poor, Master JONAS LYDDON.*
They have confined Master Lyddon in Newgate Gaol these past days and now intend to hang him in front of you all.
For the sake of the Life of Jonas Lyddon and the Ancient Liberties of This Land, we CALL Upon All True-Born Englishmen to RISE UP and SET Master
JONAS LYDDON
FREE!
If you are reading this then please read it aloud, so that folk around you who might not be lettered can hear this VITAL message.
FREE JONAS LYDDON!

Already, they could see the people in the crowd reading the pamphlet, at first silently to themselves, and then nudging the person next to them, pointing fingers at the words on the yellow paper. Some had turned to smaller knots of folk in the crowd, reading aloud the contents. Soon, there was muttering everywhere.

Like a breeze finding its way through dense undergrowth, Jasper and Harry could hear the name Jonas Lyddon coming from all corners of the crowd, at first with the rows of people near to them, then further and further back.

Then, as a wave might crash on the seashore, the two words – *Jonas Lyddon*. Again and again, that name rose from the crowd, taken up as soon as the handbill had been read.

Jonas Lyddon? Jonas Lyddon? Jonas Lyddon?

Suddenly, there was a great shout as a shackled man, accompanied by a preacher, was brought out on to the platform, accompanied by two more turnkeys and the hangman himself.

There was a great silence, as the condemned man was led towards the hanging rope. All they could hear was the preacher extolling the first words of the burial service.

Jasper looked out across the crowd, the people were motionless, silent...

'It hasn't worked!' he said to Harry.

'There's Quest and Sticks,' Blizzard replied, pointing to where the ladder was propped up against the platform. Two of the policemen had stepped forward, blocking their access to the ladder, long truncheons at the ready.

Then...

Then came a great roar from the crowd.

Over and over again...

Jonas Lyddon!

Jonas Lyddon!

Jonas Lyddon!

The crowd went mad, chanting Lyddon's name as they swept forward, forcing the policemen, standing on the street, back against the wood of the hanging platform. Jasper and Harry forced their way through, Jasper using his crutch to push people aside, until they stood behind Quest and Sticks at the foot of the ladder.

One of the policemen blocked the ladder, noticing that Quest wore the attire of a gentleman.

'Get back, sir, or I'll be obliged to put you under arrest!'

Harry Blizzard pulled out a pistol.

'No, you get back, lad – or I'll be obliged to blow your brains out!'

'I will not move, sir. You must use your pistol if you want to remove me! Please consider yourselves under arrest!'

Quest could see the terror in the young man's eyes, admiring his courage. He wondered just what to do to counter such bravery? Held out a hand to lower the pistol that Blizzard had raised.

'It's all right, constable!' said a voice behind them. 'You can let these gents go up the ladder. You know me, for we worked together on that murder in Walthamstow last year?'

'Yes, Inspector Anders!'

Quest looked over his shoulder, to where Anders was standing, a pamphlet in his hand.

'Is this really true, Will?'

'Yes it is, Bram.'

'I had a message from Wissilcraft, but found it hard to give it credence. I've sent Sergeant Berry down to his office to seek a confirmation. You had best get up the ladder, for I see the hangman's about to put the noose about that poor man's neck!'

Quest climbed the ladder to the cheers of the crowd, producing a pair of pistols as he gained the top. Harry Blizzard followed him at a speed which was amazing for a man of his age, his own pistols covering the surprised turnkeys before they could seize their shot-guns. The four men raised their arms as Harry levelled his pistols in their direction, to another great cheer from the crowd.

Quest walked across the platform.

'Sir Egregious is it not? You'll oblige me by removing the noose from that gent's throat.'

Egregious Mountjoy looked shocked.

'I cannot do that, sir! In all my born days as a hanging man, I ain't never took the hempen rope away once it's been placed. It would go against every standard of my profession!'

Quest leaned forward, whispering in his ear.

'This man isn't Simeon Prowl, Mountjoy. This man, the one you've hooded and are about to hang, is Mr Jonas Lyddon. Top him, Egregious, and you will be guilty of murder. They'll hang you with your own rope!'

The hangman glanced round at the preacher, then back at Quest, finally at the crowd. Shaking his head, he reached forward and eased the noose back over Lyddon's head.

There was a great roar of approval from the crowd.

Then the row died down as Quest walked forward.

'This man is Mr Jonas Lyddon - the pamphlet tells the truth! He was to be murdered here today in front of you all. Killed because he's spent his life fighting for the likes of us. The Class hate men like him - for they are desperate to keep you in your place. In poverty and despair, so that they might enjoy all the best things in life while you suffer!'

His audience clapped and cheered.

There were cries of "Down with the Class!".

At the back of the crowd some men took up a chorus, singing in English, the words of *la Marseillaise*.

Some of the Class, up in the garrets, men and women who'd come to see a hanging, shuddered at this revival of the rebel hymn - not heard much since the troubles of the 'forties, reviving memories of the revolution in France, the century before - recalled how their parents spoke in fear, of how just such a revolution might come to the shores of England...

A song that had been adopted by the protesting poor all across Europe.

But then the singing stopped and there was a silence.

Quest wondered why, then he noticed that the preacher had stepped forward.

James Brendon was holding up his arms for their attention.

'People of London! Be not deceived! This is a revolutionary plot – for this man is *not* Jonas Lyddon! He is Simeon Prowl, the footpad and murderer. Condemned to death in a fair trial.'

There was complete silence for a good minute.

Then a voice rang over the canyon of the street.

'No he ain't!'

The crowd turned, looking up at the rooftop of a tavern opposite the hanging tree. A solitary man stood atop one of the gables. An old man, the seeming double of the man who remained shackled on the platform.

'He ain't! The man over there's Jonas Lyddon. Look closely at me, those of you who've crossed my path – know me for who I am.'

There was a gasp from the crowd, like an autumn breeze.

'I can see the faces of men and women I know, down there among you! Know me for who I am, all of you! I'm Simeon Prowl, who should be facin' the drop today. They tried to kill me quietly and put that gent in my place. That man across there – the one posing as a preacher. He's not the Newgate Ordinary, but the man who tried to have me done away with!'

'A lie! All a lie!' Brendon shouted back.

'No it ain't,' Prowl cried back. 'I've come here to give myself in charge. Even though they'll hang me. Would I do that if I wasn't Simeon Prowl? That preacher is a liar and a murderer. I don't mind them hanging me, if only I can see that bastard swinging at my side!'

Anders came up the ladder on to the platform, followed by Sergeant Berry.

He passed Quest a piece of paper.

'Berry has just brought this from Wissilcraft,' he said.

Quest read it through and then addressed the crowd.

'This notice is from the home secretary, Lord Palmerston. It acknowledges that a terrible mistake has been made and that the man beside me is indeed Mr Jonas Lyddon!'

The mob pressed forward, yelling and cheering.

Anders ordered a turnkey to remove the shackles and hood from Jonas Lyddon. As this was being done Quest looked around for Brendon, but the Preacher had vanished back into the gaol.

'He's mine, Quest,' said Harry Blizzard, taking up the pursuit.

'You must calm this mob down, Quest,' said Anders. 'Or God knows what might happen. There'll be trouble if you don't. Wissilcraft fears that Lord Palmerston might yet call out the cavalry to ride these poor devils down.'

Quest stepped forward and held up a hand.

The people were silent once more.

'My fellow Londoners! Go back to your homes,' Quest said. 'Don't rise to the bait of the Class who want to use this abuse of justice to suppress your liberty and take your lives. But remember this day, and what they tried to do in your name!'

As they dispersed, he noticed that some of them were saying his name.

It's Quest! It's William Quest! Quest!

That was too much recognition. Quest knew his life was to be changed for ever.

'After today, I think I have no career,' said Anders.

'You are the hero of the hour, Bram!'

'No, Will. Someone will have to pay for this exhibition and – rest assured – it won't be Lord Palmerston and his like.'

Harry Blizzard came back out on to the platform.

'The bastard got away, Quest. He'll be down in the crowd now, looking like someone else!'

'Never mind, Harry. We know where he's likely to go.'

'Limehouse!' said Sticks.

'Get back down that ladder. Get Jasper. See if you can get Simeon Prowl away from here. He's more than paid for his crime and I'd be sorry to see him swing.'

~

Shabson Crouch had watched the proceedings from the corner of Newgate Street and Old Bailey.

Watched as James Brendon fled from the platform.

Said to himself, as he took off in the direction of Limehouse, 'I ain't swingin' for you, matey. Time as how I got my payment in full!'

~

Inspector Honour Bright made his way along Tavistock Place and saw the youth sitting on the steps of Quest's house, his head in his hands. Ah, the Stanton boy, he said to himself.

'All right, lad?' he asked, sitting on the step next to him.

Daniel Stanton looked up.

'Inspector...'

'You didn't go to see the hanging then?'

'No... I never want to see anyone else die.'

Bright put a hand on his shoulder.

'I do understand, you know...'

'Have you ever killed anyone, Inspector?'

225

'Never in the way you were forced to do. And, by the way, I came here today to stress that no action will be taken against you for the death of Booth. Indeed, there has been some suggestion that you be presented with a scroll – a commendation from the Commissioner, for saving the life of a policeman.'

Daniel sighed.

'I don't want any sort of commendation.'

'I told them that you wouldn't, Daniel. In answer to your question, I've never had to kill a man in the way you did. But there are six men and one woman dead because of my actions. Six men and one woman hanged by the neck. Oh, society will say they deserved it, and society decreed the death penalty, not me. But each time... on execution day... I have taken myself off to find some quiet place where I might be alone with my thoughts.'

'You have a reputation, Inspector, for harshness...'

'We all have a reputation, lad. Coming here, I was thinking of William Quest. Now there's a man who's killed far more men than I have, every one of them a murder, for all his killings were done outside the law. And if I could, I'd arrest him and send him to the gallows. But it's evidence, you see lad.'

'But do you believe in execution in any form?'

'Ah, well, the Commandment says "Thou Shalt Not Kill!" doesn't it? It gives no definition beyond that. I do not believe it right to kill anyone in any circumstances, for I can never shake off my Christian upbringing.'

Daniel dwelt on his words for a while.

'Yet you still help to send people to the gallows?'

'I do, Daniel. Because I am a serving policemen, and that is what the law decrees – however wretched it might make me feel! Inspector Anders... now there's a good man and a fine detective. But like Quest, he has an ambivalent attitude towards the law. You see, for me, there is no ambivalence. The law is the law, however much I might care to alter it.'

'But you go on?'

'This is a dangerous city. It needs proper policing. For myself, I consider public executions an abomination. The crowds gathered there are not deterred at the sight of someone being turned off – indeed they revel in it. Whatever crime it was that put the noose around the victim's neck. If society decided to hang Queen Victoria in public, they'd be there in just such numbers. And such villainy goes on at these toppings!'

'I believe that there's a call to end public hangings?'

'And so there should be,' said Bright. 'But I favour an end to all hangings. They do not deter criminals – indeed, most of the murders I've investigated, were done on the spur of the moment, lad. By men – and a woman – who would never have had a thought in their heads about the consequences... of the noose. So if it is not a deterrent, then why hang anyone, in public or in private? Revenge? Yes, there's an element of that.' He smiled. 'One of the favourite texts thundered by the parson when I was a boy was "Vengeance is Mine, Saith the Lord. I Will Repay" – and those are words which still haunt my thoughts.'

'It's all such a mess.'

'It is, lad. It is. But what are you going to do? I trust you will not use the activities of William Quest as an example?'

'No, I shall never kill again!'

'They tell me you wish to write books?'

'I do – I did! But it seems so pointless, when our society is in such a mess. Last night... last night... I even thought of joining the police...'

Bright laughed. 'A writer's fantasy, I think?'

'Perhaps so...'

'I believe you have too sensitive a nature, Daniel. You might do more good with your writing. Proper books, mind! Not the scurrilous sort of pamphlets that that rogue Feedle produces! Expose the horrors of society if you must, like Mr Dickens. But try and give people hope as well. And should you need the views of a tired old policeman, you can always find me at Scotland Yard.'

He took Daniel's hand and gave it a firm shake.

Twenty-eight

It didn't take Shabson Crouch very long to get to Limehouse, for he hitched a ride in a cart which was going way past Whitechapel. Then, knowing the streets and the alleys so very well, he made his way down to the river, following the swift, gurgling waters of the Thames - through the wharves and then up to the Ratcliffe Highway.

The Highway was busy with folk and Crouch looked up and down the street, mindful that he'd seen the Preacher coming away from Newgate. He could only be coming to the old building in Narrow Street, for where else could this man on the run go?

Crouch had watched the proceedings at Newgate with great interest, heard the speeches of Simeon Prowl and the notorious William Quest. Listened to his master's protestations. And knew that it was all up for the Preacher.

Once, a month ago or more, he'd noticed the Preacher heading off to the wharves in a most furtive manner, and decided to put the dodge on him.

He'd followed him and secreted himself between a pile of tea-chests, as his master held a discussion with a wharfinger called Holroyd, a villain of the docklands well known to have connections with the captains of a dozen ships that plied the route between the Thames and France. Heard the Preacher making a provision to have himself and his luggage shipped to the Continent, if necessity demanded it.

As now it does! Crouch said to himself.

Not that he'd ever seen the Preacher with much in the way of luggage. But there was the chest full of cottars - and who needs luggage when you have so many sovereigns?

There was, of course, the little stone-set window of stained-glass that the Preacher seemed so obsessed with.

But that was heavy, and his master would need at least two men to carry that to any departing vessel. Would he take it at all? Crouch considered that he would, for it seemed to be the object he loved best in all the world.

He'd often seen the Preacher pressing his face against it; watched as he ran his fingers over the glass; heard him babble away to the glass window as though it might be a brother or a lover.

Who would take the window to a vessel for him? The Preacher had never mentioned such a task to Crouch or Booth in all the time they had served him. No doubt the Preacher had a coterie - ah, there was a word he'd once heard the Preacher say, asking for its meaning? - a coterie of hidden servants, all there to do his bidding.

He wondered if these anonymous folk had also received the hard beatings from the Preacher's blackthorn stick that he and Booth had put up with, only because of the generous pay? That blackthorn stick, the very sight of which had made Crouch tremble, though the beatings were sparing, just now and again when the Preacher's underlings had made some mistake.

As he walked down Narrow Street, Crouch could almost feel that heavy, thorny stick crashing down on his back and shoulders, or sometimes against his legs. Heard the maniacal cries of rage, mixed with laughter, as the Preacher used that foul instrument of punishment...

The Preacher should be in the booby hatch, he'd told Booth, more than once...

And so he should, for anyone who screamed and laughed like that, while inflicting pain, belonged in an asylum for lunatics.

Well, thought Crouch, let the bastard laugh and scream all he liked now, when he came to Limehouse and found his chest of cottars gone for good.

We'll see how you like it, my bucko, when you find yourself and your cottars stolen? Let's see how you'll flee the country without any sovs to help you on your way?

Crouch looked up and down the street, but there was no sign of anybody, let alone the Preacher. Crouch chortled, for it might take the man longer to get here, not having a friend with a cart or knowing the short-cuts to the Highway. And getting a cabriolet might be difficult with so many gentry coming away from the failed execution.

As Crouch turned down the alley, towards where the steps went down to the Thames, he had another, deliciously malevolent thought.

He'd smash that window of old glass in to so many pieces...

~

'So this is the place?'

Unlike the crowds that had sought a cabriolet at Newgate, Quest had made provision to have his closed carriage ready and just a street away. Even then, it had taken them an hour to press through the dispersing crowds, and there had been more delays with a crashed coach at the start of the Ratcliffe Highway, which had forced them to get out and walk.

'Yes, Narrow Street,' said Sticks in reply to Harry Blizzard. 'And that alley at the end is the one we want.'

Quest had expected to be doing the journey on his own, for he'd sent the others in search of Simeon Prowl. But they'd caught up with him in the carriage, reporting that Prowl was nowhere to be found. Sticks had seen policemen out on the rooftop but, once again, the old footpad had dodged his way out of trouble.

'Old Sim's as slippery as an eel!' Jasper had remarked. 'But every beat peeler in London'll be looking for him now. And for all he did for Jonas, they won't hesitate to swing him. Is Jonas all right, Will?'

'I told Anders and Berry to escort him to Tavistock Place. He'll be safe enough there with our boys guarding the place. Jonas was shaken up – who wouldn't be? – but he's still the old rebel at heart from those Dartmoor and Manchester days. He'll probably outlive us all!'

'D'you really think that bastard Brendon will come here?' asked Harry.

Quest shrugged.

'I don't know, Harry. If not here, then where? For all we know, he has a dozen bolt-holes that we don't know about. But we have to start somewhere.' He looked down the alley to where the filthy waters of the Thames lapped the ancient stone steps. 'Well, there's a rowing boat down there. Didn't Prowl take one to get Joshua Blount across the river?'

'Doubt that's anything to do with Brendon,' said Jasper. 'Perhaps the owner recovered it from the far bank where Prowl left it. Or it could be just any old boat that someone's moored there.'

'Something in it, though,' said Quest, as they walked down the grimy alley to the slippery steps. 'Some sort of chest...'

There was indeed a small wooden chest pressed hard against one of the thwarts of the rowing boat, partly concealed by a torn piece of canvas and the oars.

'Someone wanted to hide it,' said Sticks, 'though it wouldn't have stayed hid long in a neighbourhood like this.' He pushed the oars out of the way and pulled aside the canvas. 'Well, there's a lock on it, Will, but some fool's left the key in it. Might as well have a look...'

The lid creaked as he opened the chest and Quest noticed the old prizefighter's mouth gape as he looked inside. After a moment, Sticks heaved the chest round to face them.

'Well, what d'ye think?' he said.

The little chest was crammed to the very top with gold sovereigns.

'I do believe we are on the right track,' said Quest.

'Could belong to anyone,' said Jasper. 'Doesn't necessarily mean this is Brendon's hoard...'

Quest smiled, 'Jasper! I'm sure you don't believe that any more than I do! There's many a hard-working wharfinger and sailor dwelling in these parts, but I doubt they get paid in cottars! No, this is Brendon's hoard and it's been put in this boat either by him, or one of his villains. Careless though, for anyone might have come down here from the street and robbed him of his funds. The fact that it's in the boat at all suggests that it wasn't intended to be left here for more than a few minutes.'

'Then he's inside that building?' said Jasper.

'I suspect so,' said Quest. 'Or someone is. They've stashed the coins and gone back for something else. Time we found out whether Brendon's here or not? Jasper – you've handled boats? Might be a good idea if you deprive our enemy of this one – and its cargo. You might row it across the river and then take this chest back to Tavistock Place. Those sovereigns will make a generous donation to our charity for the poor. Harry, perhaps you'll go with him…'

'Oh, no, Quest. That bastard's mine, for what he tried to do to my old comrade! I'm going in that building with or without you!'

Quest could see the lust for revenge in the old man's eyes, and knew that he wouldn't be able to change his mind. Harry Blizzard was old, but Quest had been amazed at his energy over the past few days. A long time since Blizzard had been a rebel and a slayer of enemies, but Quest accepted the offer. He'd rather have had Sticks or Jasper at his side, but knew that this was Harry Blizzard's mission, as much as his own.

'Very well. Sticks, you go with Jasper across the river.'

Sticks looked reluctant to go, but just nodded – he knew very well that once William Quest had made up his mind, he was not to be gainsaid.

Quest and Harry watched the two men row away.

'Come on, Harry! Let's put an end to this business!'

~

Crouch was sweating as he returned to the building, for the chest was heavy with sovereigns, and the cobblestones of the alley green with slime. Thrice he'd nearly slipped as he'd made his way down to the boat.

Finding the vessel there was a stroke of good fortune, he considered, for the Preacher's own rowing boat had been stolen at the time of Joshua Blount's escape. This one could only have been left temporarily by some river boatman. Crouch hoped he wouldn't come back for a while.

He'd loaded the chest down into the boat and actually unshipped the oars, preparing to row away, when a malicious thought came into his mind. As he'd struggled out with the chest, he'd glanced across at the stained glass set in its stone tracery. Remembered his promise to himself to destroy the Preacher's most precious relic.

Sitting there, with the oars dipping into the water, he'd considered whether to just abandon that vengeful idea. After all, he'd got enough money to set himself up for many years, a long way from London. But then the memories came back – the times when the Preacher had cuffed him across the face; the disparaging comments when he'd done his best to carry out the faceless man's wishes; the feel of the blackthorn stick crashing against his back.

He'd watched the Preacher, covertly, so many times. Saw his head pressed against the glass, heard those whispered words of love to what was just a physical object. Crouch had never been able to understand it, considering it part of his employer's madness. Many a time he'd come away to tell the late and unlamented Booth what he'd seen, tapping the side of his head with his fingers, and muttering the words "booby hatch, that one – for sure!"

No, destroying the glass would be the ultimate revenge.

He'd shipped the oars and put them, with a piece of old canvas, across the chest, hoping again that the owner of the boat wouldn't come back for a while. He'd walked up the alley, picking up a detached cobble on the way, grinning maliciously at the thought of how the Preacher would react when he saw his smashed treasure.

'Let's see how you like bein' on the receiving end, my beauty!'

~

'Quite a lock on that door,' said Harry Blizzard. 'Certainly want to keep nosey folk out. Shame that someone forgot to turn the key. And very silly to leave the key in place.'

'Let's go canny,' said Quest. 'I'm always suspicious when doors are too easy to pass through. Might be a trap.' He took out the little percussion pistol he always carried. 'Where these gentry are concerned, we must expect anything, and be ready to fire.'

He noticed that Harry was carrying one of the smart pistols that belonged to Wren Angier. Saw the determined look on the old man's face. Caught a glimpse of the formidable warrior that Blizzard must have been, when he was engaged in battle with the French all those years before.

They were scarce a yard through the door when they heard a scream.

~

Crouch climbed the steps to the top of the building, to where the Preacher had made his headquarters. Nasty wooden steps, rotting away like much of the interior of the old warehouse. He'd almost fallen, coming down them with the chest, when one of the treads – dry and holed with woodworm – had cracked and broken down to dust. As rotten as my whole miserable life, Crouch considered.

His breath was coming in short stabs as he reached the top storey of the building, a dark place lit only by a narrow window overlooking the river.

A grim place which should have been pulled down years before, he'd always thought – much as they were pulling down the decayed buildings of Jacob's Island, that foul rookery on the other bank of the Thames, where he'd been hatched, and spent a miserable childhood of abuse and thievery.

It took him a while for his eyes to get used to the dimness of the room, which was stacked at one end with some long-forgotten cotton bales, shipped in from the Yankee shores and, never taken away when the building was abandoned to the worms and the rats.

'Need a bit more light for this work,' he muttered aloud, lighting the oil lamp which was the usual source of illumination for this top room of the old warehouse. He hung it on the hook by the door, and crossed to the table on which stood the stained glass window in its stone tracery frame.

He pulled back his arm, preparing to cast the stone, when another idea came to him.

To smash the glass would be so easy! Perhaps, in time, the Preacher would get over his grief? Far better to torment the faceless man for much, much longer. Let him puzzle and grieve over its vanishing... make him search for it for years, never knowing what had befallen his great treasure?

Now that would be much better...

Crouch glanced at the window looking out over the Thames. It was just wide enough to throw the glass through – and the river ran deep and fierce, hard against the building, which had been built out into the flow. There was no fall in the tide as its dirty water swirled below the walls of the warehouse, no strand on which the window might ever be found – and the drop from that height would almost certainly smash the glass anyway.

He crossed to the open window and looked down at the river, smiling at the very thought of such sweet revenge. He tossed the cobblestone out and watched as it splashed into the water. Worth all the beatings in the world to have such a vengeance!

A moment later he had his arms around the stone frame of the window itself, starting to lift its heavy weight...

'I think not, Crouch!'

The little man put down the window, looking into the dark shadows beyond the light of the lamp. He could not see anyone in the far gloom. His hand shot up to his head, tapping in disbelief.

'Come away from my stained glass, Crouch!'

And there was the Preacher, striding round from beyond the cotton bales, holding that familiar and stout blackthorn staff in both hands. Crouch shuddered, for even without the mask that the man delighted to wear, he looked menacing.

'What have you done with my sovereigns, Crouch? Thought you'd rob me? Oh, Crouch, you don't have the intelligence to take me on. Where are they, Crouch? If you don't tell me, oh, I will have to punish you.'

Crouch shuddered as Brendon's voice became that so familiar high-pitched shout. He looked at the blackthorn stick and trembled, already feeling the weight of it, the mounds that had been thorns, sweeping hard against his back. In his heart, he knew there was no escape.

'The sovereigns, Crouch?'

'In the boat, the rowing boat down by the steps,' Crouch replied, like a child reciting a catechism, as though his voice and the confession had nothing to do with his conscious mind.

'And my window, Crouch? What were you going to do with that? Ah, perhaps you were rescuing it for me? Going to take it away in the boat with my money. Somewhere safe, that you might take me to later?'

Crouch nodded furiously.

'Yessir! Just that, sir!'

The Preacher stepped forward.

'You're a liar, Crouch! And all liars must be punished!'

The words were whispered. Crouch could only just hear them. He couldn't look away from the grinning face, those dark eyes that burned into his own.

'You are a liar, Crouch! And I am done with you!'

Caught in the man's gaze, he hardly saw the blackthorn as it was swung in a great circle, smashing against his head. As he fell to the floor, he heard the crazed laughter of the Preacher.

Crouch was stunned – for how long he couldn't guess – but never found the comfort of unconsciousness. He felt his hands being tied with rope, but could do nothing to resist. Felt and smelt the hempen noose being placed around his throat. As he came to, he could not fight back as he was lifted on to the old wooden chair, left behind by some manager of the warehouse.

He looked up at the rafter above his head, seeing the rope that had been swung over it. Watched as the Preacher secured the other end to a hook on the wall. Saw the laughing man come back across the floor.

Shabson Crouch screamed in the moment that the chair was kicked away.

~

'What the hell was that?' asked Harry Blizzard, as the scream echoed around the building and then came to a sudden stop. 'It sounded like a man seeing all the devils of hell!'

'Let's find out,' said Quest, leading the way up the stairs.

The first storeys of the warehouse were completely empty, as they looked into each one, ascending the narrow steps. But halfway up, they heard a sound below them.

'Sounded like the door opening again,' Quest remarked.

'We couldn't have shut it properly,' said Harry. 'Probably flapping in the breeze from the river.'

'Let's hope so. But keep an eye back on those steps, Harry.'

Then they came to the long room at the top of the building, where an oil lamp burned on a hook near to the door. A room empty, apart from a stack of cotton bales across the far end. Empty apart from the bales – and a corpse swinging from one of the rafters.

'Shabson Crouch!' said Quest.

Crouch was swinging in the wind that came from the window, his eyes bulging and most of his tongue sticking out of his mouth, twisting round to lap at one cheek. A dark stain ran down his legs, where the hanging man had pissed himself in his death throes.

'There's your scream!' said Harry Blizzard.

'He died quickly without a drop,' said Quest. 'I've seen men swing for an age before they were finally turned off. Death came quickly for this poor devil – I know him of old. He'd have come to the gallows sooner or later.'

'Oh, I hastened poor Crouch on his way,' said a voice from the shadows. 'Hung on to his legs and pulled him down to stop that infernal noise he was making. Please don't turn suddenly, my dear Quest. And drop those pistols to the ground. My two guns are levelled and I shan't hesitate to fire. I mean it! Put those weapons down! That applies to you as well, Blizzard.'

Quest and Blizzard reached out and put their pistols on to the table.

'I've seen that piece of stained glass before,' said Quest.

'Ah, my pride and joy,' said Brendon. 'Hundreds of years since that stained glass was made by a real craftsman. I acquired it from one of those religious houses destroyed by mad King Henry. Somehow it had survived his vandalism. Now there was a villain for you, Quest! A destroyer of all that was rare and beautiful.'

'And are you going to destroy us, Brendon?'

The Preacher sighed.

'In many ways, my dear Quest, I admire you. We're very alike you and I, Quest, indeed! For I've heard what set you off on your path of vengeance. Very similar circumstances, you and I. The death of a father, eh? Your friend Jonas Lyddon implied that I am insane, Can you believe that, William? But if I am, then so must you be, for I have a suspicion that you've killed far more men than I have, Quest...'

Brendon walked round them, the pair of pistols held high. He sat down on one of the bales of cotton.

'Oh, Quest, I can see from your face that you recognise the truth in my words? We are not so very different!'

'Oh, I still believe we are, Brendon.'

'As I said, I have a kind of respect for you, Quest – and you too, Blizzard. I'm a fair shot with these pistols. I'll aim for your hearts, so that you both might have a quick death. And this is where it ends...'

Brendon raised the pistols an inch higher.

And then there was a great flash of light.

The cotton bale, that Brendon rested upon, exploded in flames, consuming the man in a sheet of fire. Just for a second, Quest could see the puzzled look on Brendon's face. Heard the pistols discharge, their lead balls going up into the ceiling. Saw the fire run, a wave of orange, across the other stacked bales, rushing upwards to the rafters and into the dry and rotten wooden ceiling of the room.

It seemed to Quest and Blizzard as though the whole world was on fire.

There was no scream from the burning man. In that moment, Quest saw Brendon take in a great gasp of breath, which dragged the fire down into his throat and lungs.

Then he was hidden by a fierce explosion as all the bales ignited, its force throwing Quest and Blizzard backwards towards the door. As Quest was pulling it shut to give them some time to escape, he found Simeon Prowl standing there.

'Didn't know what else to do,' Prowl was muttering. 'Had no gun... threw the oil lamp. Didn't know what else to do. Didn't know what else to do...'

'Like Hell's furnace!' said Blizzard.

'Let's get out of here!' said Quest.

As they came away from the door, there was another roar of fire from within the room and a great cracking sound.

When they were fleeing down the steps, it occurred to Quest that it must be the noise of the stained glass window breaking in the heat.

L'ENVOI

In the papers of the notorious Victorian adventurer William Quest, I found this journal entry, placed and dated Hope Down, Christmas 1854.

This has been the most splendid Christmas I can quite remember, not least because of the great gathering at Hope Down. So many old friends. So many memories recounted.

I was saddened that Anders and Berry could not join us for the Christmas celebrations – but my two detective friends have now taken up their new posts with the constabulary in Norwich.

As Anders predicted, somebody had to appease the anger of Commissioner Mayne, who felt so used during the Tenebrae affair. Anders will love Norfolk, but I am not so sure about Berry, who has no great liking for rural places. Anders has kindly invited me to Norwich in the New Year, and I have consented to go – though I fear it might bring back unpleasant memories of my childhood.

Both men did come down here at the tail end of November, to the little church at Stoke, to be present at the double wedding of Rosa and myself, and Wren and Phoebe. Poor Wren suffered the most from our recent adventure, though his strength improves day by day. Three days before the snow began, Wren and I walked twenty miles over the Downs, and he was scarcely more out of breath at the end than I was!

We are both trying to get in much more walking, for we all get little enough exercise when we are in London. The Downs are perfect for such fitness endeavours.

Sticks has become our trainer – for he is determined that, come the spring, we are all to walk from London to the source of the Thames. At first, this was to be an adventure for just Sticks and Jasper. But now both Wren and myself have been included in the number. More than that, Harry Blizzard and Jonas Lyddon – both of whom are staying with us for Christmas – have included themselves in our grand walk.

I have leased the London house for a year, determined that time and memory should expunge my name from the lips of the many who have become aware of my identity and reputation. I have promised Rosa that the old life is over, and that we will play little part in society, except for my role as a country landowner. My dear Rosa seems to have abandoned all her theatrical ambitions for the time being, seemingly content to help my housekeeper, Mrs Vellaby, to run our little estate.

Only the Critzman brothers are to remain in London, to run their walking stick shop and administer the charity for the poor. Though they favour an eventual retirement to one of our smaller cathedral cities.

And we are to have new neighbours!

Sir Wren and Lady Angier have purchased an old farmhouse just two miles away from here, having decided that the Highgate property held too many bad memories. Wren will stay in his set in Albany when Parliament is sitting, but hopefully will be here a great deal so that we might explore the Downs together. I think there are grand times ahead!

And Simeon Prowl?

Simeon was the real hero of the hour, putting his life in jeopardy so many times. I very much wanted to give the old footpad a quiet retirement in a cottage close to Hope Down. But Jonas Lyddon suggested that Simeon was so closely linked with our enterprise that it would only be a matter of time before this neighbourhood was searched, or some local uttered an indiscreet word. So Jonas arranged for Simeon to find a funded rest in a town in the distant north. I hope that one day I might meet him again.

Daniel Stanton, sometime Daniel Moonlight, has set himself down in a cottage in our village where he is penning a novel based on our recent adventures.

I sometimes think I have lived much of my life as though it was some adventurous fiction. Sometimes, in our candlelit evenings, I catch Rosa looking across at me. I see the question on her lovely face: are the secret and violent days really over for good?

Who knows for sure? though I think of nothing more wild now than long tramps across the Downs and dawn dips in cold and lonely dewponds. After all, how could Monkshood function when half of London knows of its existence? With the secrecy gone, then surely our nefarious society must be gone as well?

And we had one more surprise the morning before the snows began...

I decided that we should move the notebook from its buried location below Swing's Oak. Sticks and I walked there just after the late dawn, spade in hand. To my horror, there was a hollow dug next to the position of the box, the teak wood exposed to the weather and cracked open...

'God, Will! Some villain's been at it!' Sticks exclaimed. 'They got the notebook!'

But as it happens, nobody had. The rain-soaked box fell apart in my hand, exposing the canvas wrapping which had been pulled apart. The waterlogged notebook came apart in my hands.

'Must have been lying there in the wet for weeks,' I remarked. 'Good fortune that nobody came across it! Ah, well – no use to us any more, old friend!'

'But somebody must have dug it up! And if I could get my fist around their head, I'd...'

He broke off, no doubt thinking I had gone mad with my hysterical burst of laughter.

'Will?...'

'You'll have to climb the oak to do it,' I laughed, pointing up to the top branches, to where a chuntering squirrel was looking down at us. 'There's your villain, Sticks! No doubt he disturbed the box while he was looking for his buried acorns! My fault. I should have buried it deeper!'

'You villain!' he shouted up at the squirrel. 'But Will, you know what this means? We can never use the notebook, either to expose a member of society or as a protection for ourselves? We're sunk!'

'Not altogether,' I remarked. 'We did have that copy made, listing all the wrong-doings of the Class. As for our protection? well, as long as they believe that we have the notebook - that's all we need.'

And perhaps it is, for the old days are over.

Both Jonas and Wren have suggested that I stand for Parliament, assuring me that my reputation would easily get me elected in some Radical seat, but I have politely declined - at least for the present. I am content to live a quiet life here at Hope Down, seeing to village affairs and enjoying my rural rambles.

Christmas night is here, and I must finish penning these words and go down to join my friends.

I brought here for a little stay, that Dartmoor rogue Weasel, who played such a distinguished part in the rebellion of 'seventeen. I thought he might be good company for those veterans of those stirring times - Jasper Feedle, Harry Blizzard and his dear wife, and Jonas Lyddon. I can hear those grand old men singing one of their raucous songs.

I think, sometimes, of my childhood escape from Norfolk, my boyhood as a dip and beggar in the rookeries of London, my dangerous existence as William Quest and Bill the Bludger, haunting the alleys of Seven Dials, St Giles and Whitechapel...

Is it really all over?

THE END

THE QUEST SAGA

What readers are saying about William Quest...

"A page turner of a mystery from the start... I couldn't put this one down for long as I was caught up in the twists and turns of this richly constructed tale... Great author, fantastic book... Such a unique story and very well told... A new hero for these times has entered literature and is destined to capture the attention of all those yearning for a better chapter within the human saga - it is William Quest... Great read! Couldn't put it down... Superb plotting, believable characters, and a very effective writing style....a real feel for history and storytelling"

The Shadow of William Quest
A mysterious stranger carrying a swordstick walks the gaslit alleys and night houses of Victorian London. What is he seeking? London in 1853 - a mist-shrouded city where the grand houses of the wealthy lie a stone's throw from the vilest slums and rookeries of the poor. Who is this man so determined to fight for justice against all the wrongs of Victorian society? What are the origins of the mysterious William Quest? In a pursuit from the teeming streets of London to the lonely coast of Norfolk, Inspector Anders of Scotland Yard is determined to uncover the truth. To an explosive climax where only one man can walk away....

Deadly Quest
A reign of terror sweeps through the Victorian underworld as a menacing figure seeks to impose his will on the criminals of London. On the abandoned wharves of the docklands and in the dangerous gaslit alleys of Whitechapel, hardened villains are being murdered, dealers in stolen goods and brothel keepers threatened. The cobbles of the old city running with blood, as pistol shots bark out death to any who resist. Who can fight back to protect the poor and the oppressed? The detectives of Scotland Yard are baffled as the death toll mounts. There is, of course, William Quest - Victorian avenger. A man brought up to know both sides of the law. But Quest faces dangers of his own. Sinister watchers are dogging his footsteps through the fog, as Quest becomes the prey in a deadly manhunt, threatened by a vicious enemy, fighting for his life in a thrilling climax in the most dangerous rookery in Victorian London. Dead Quest or Deadly Quest?

Dark Shadow
John Lardiner runs down a street in the ancient city of York and vanishes off the face of the earth. In a dangerous race against time, Victorian adventurer William Quest is summoned to York to solve the mystery - what has happened to John Lardiner? Forced into an uneasy alliance with the city police, William Quest finds his own life in peril. Men who pry into the disappearance of John Lardiner end up dead. In York's jumble of alleys and narrow medieval streets, William Quest finds himself pursued by a sinister organisation. Can he solve the

mystery of John Lardiner's vanishing before his enemies bring his adventurous career to an end?

Gibbet Hill

1817: Jonas Lyddon, rebel and revolutionary, returns home to Dartmoor, finding a land beset by trouble. Poverty in the villages and lonely farmsteads. Landowners enclosing the wild stretches of moorland where the poor grazed their animals. A perilous countryside where soldiers - unwanted after the defeat of Napoleon - haunt the woodlands, preying on unwary travellers. But Jonas Lyddon also encounters the beautiful Kitty Jay and her sister, Tryphena, victims of a cruel society that has cast them aside. Both of them seeking love and belonging. Two women who hold out hope for better and kinder times. Can Jonas Lyddon lead the struggle for justice in this wild place? Fail and you end your days... hanging on the sinister and windswept Gibbet Hill. *A prequel - complete in itself - to the William Quest Novels.*

The Sean Miller Adventures

Balmoral Kill

Sean Miller - a rogue of the first water; a former Army sniper, he seems unable to stay out of a fight." Sean Miller's fighting a guerrilla war in Spain when he's called back to Britain. His task? To seek out an assassin as dangerous as himself. A sniper whose deadly aim could plunge the world into war. As the shadow of the Nazis falls across Europe, a sinister conspiracy plots a secret war closer to home. Miller's pursuit leads from the menacing alleys of London's East End to the lonely mountains of Scotland. A duel to the death where there can be only one victor in the Balmoral Kill. A fast-paced action thriller by the author of Dangerous Game and the William Quest adventures.

Dangerous Game

Sean Miller's on his way back to fight in Spain when he's diverted to Devon. To undertake a mission for renegade members of the German Secret Service, trying to stop the Nazis plunging the world into war. A secret agent lies dead in a moorland river and the one man who can keep the peace is an assassin's target. As the hunter becomes the hunted in an epic chase, Miller encounters his greatest enemy in a dangerous game of death across the lonely hills of Dartmoor.

Printed in Great Britain
by Amazon